Robert Ludlum is the author of 34 novels, published in 32 languages and 40 countries, and at one time was the world's bestselling author with his blend of sophisticated plotting and extreme pace. There are more than 210 million copies of his books in print. He is best known for *The Scarlatti Inheritance*, *The Chancellor Manuscript* and the Jason Bourne series – *The Bourne Legacy*, *The Bourne Identity*, *The Bourne Supremacy* and *The Bourne Ultimatum* – among others. Visit his website at www.CovertOne.com.

By Robert Ludlum

The Bancroft Strategy
The Ambler Warning
The Bourne Legacy (*with Eric Van Lustbader*)
The Tristan Betrayal
The Janson Directive
The Sigma Protocol
The Prometheus Deception
The Matarese Countdown
The Cry of the Halidon
The Apocalypse Watch
The Road to Omaha
The Scorpio Illusion
The Bourne Ultimatum
The Icarus Agenda
The Bourne Supremacy
The Aquitaine Progression
The Parsifal Mosaic
The Bourne Identity
The Matarese Circle
The Gemini Contenders
The Holcroft Covenant
The Chancellor Manuscript
The Road to Gandolfo
The Rhinemann Exchange
Trevayne
The Matlock Paper
The Osterman Weekend
The Scarlatti Inheritance

THE COVERT-ONE NOVELS

The Altman Code (*with Gayle Lynds*)
The Paris Option (*with Gayle Lynds*)
The Cassandra Compact (*with Philip Shelby*)
The Hades Factor (*with Gayle Lynds*)
The Lazarus Vendetta (*with Patrick Larkin*)
The Moscow Vector (*with Patrick Larkin*)

THE
BANCROFT
STRATEGY

ROBERT LUDLUM

An Orion paperback

First published in Great Britain in 2006
by Orion
This paperback edition published in 2007
by Orion Books Ltd,
Orion House, 5 Upper St Martin's Lane,
London WC2H 9EA

3 5 7 9 10 8 6 4 2

A CIP catalogue record for this book
is available from the British Library.

ISBN 978-0-7528-8172-0

Printed and bound in Great Britain by
Mackays of Chatham plc, Chatham, Kent

The Orion Publishing Group's policy is to use papers
that are natural, renewable and recyclable products and
made from wood grown in sustainable forests. The
logging and manufacturing processes are expected to
conform to the environmental regulations
of the country of origin.

www.orionbooks.co.uk

JAFFEIRA: . . . I've engag'd
With men of souls, fit to reform the ills
Of all mankind.

—Thomas Otway, *A Plot Discovered* (1682)

PROLOGUE

East Berlin, 1987

It was not yet raining, but the leaden skies would open before long. The air itself seemed expectant, apprehensive. The young man crossed from Unter den Linden to Marx-Engels-Forum, where giant bronze statues of socialism's Teutonic fathers stared toward the city center, sightless eyes fixed and intent. Behind them, stone friezes depicted the joyful life of man under communism. Still not a drop of rain. But soon. Before long, the clouds would burst, the heavens would open. *It was a historical inevitability*, the man thought, mordantly recalling the socialist jargon. He was a hunter, tracking his prey, and he was closer than he had ever been. It was all the more important, therefore, to conceal the tension that welled inside him.

He looked like a million others in this self-proclaimed worker's paradise. His clothes had been acquired at the Centrum Warenhaus, the vast department store at Alexanderplatz, for clothing of such visibly shoddy manufacture was not sold just anywhere. But more than his garb lent him the appearance of an East Berlin menial. It was the way he walked, the stolid, dutiful, draggy gait. Nothing about him suggested that he had arrived from the West just twenty-four hours earlier, and, until a few moments ago, he had been sure that he had attracted no notice.

A pang of adrenaline tightened his skin. He thought that he recognized the footsteps behind him from his traipse through Karl-Liebknecht-Strasse. The pattern seemed familiar.

All footsteps were the same, yet all were different: there were variations in weight and gait, variations in the composition of soles. Footsteps were the solfège of the city, one of

Belknap's instructors had told him: so commonplace as to pass beyond notice, and yet, to the trained ear, capable of being distinguished like different voices. Had Belknap done so correctly?

The possibility that he was being followed was one he could not afford. He *had* to be wrong.

Or he had to make it right.

A junior member of the ultra-clandestine branch of the U.S. State Department known as Consular Operations, Todd Belknap had already gained a reputation for finding men who sought not to be found. Like most trackers, he worked best on his own. If the task was to place a man under surveillance, a team – the larger the better – was optimal. But a man who had vanished could not be placed under conventional surveillance. In those cases, the full resources of the organization would be enlisted in the service of the hunt: That was a matter of course. Yet the spymasters at Cons Ops had long since, learned that there could be advantages, too, in letting loose a single, gifted field agent. Allowing him to move about the world solo, unencumbered by an expensive entourage. Free to pursue insubstantial hunches. Free to follow his nose.

A nose that, if all went well, might lead him to his quarry, a renegade American operative named Richard Lugner. Having chased after dozens of false leads, Belknap was now certain he had the scent.

But had someone picked up on *his* scent? Was the tracker being tracked?

To turn around suddenly would be suspicious. Instead, he stopped and feigned a yawn, looking about as if taking in the giant statues, but ready to make a swift evaluation of whoever was in the immediate vicinity.

He saw nobody at all. A seated bronze Marx, a standing Engels: massive, glowering over verdigrised beards and mustaches. Two rows of linden trees. An expanse of poorly maintained turf. Across the way, the hulking, long, coppery glass box known as the Palast der Republik. It was a coffin-like building, as if built to entomb the human spirit itself. But the forum seemed vacant.

There was scant reassurance in that – yet was he really certain of what he had heard? Tension, he knew, made the mind play tricks on itself, see goblins in shadows. He had to quell his anxiety: An agent who was excessively keyed up could make errors of judgment, missing real threats while preoccupied by imagined ones.

Belknap impulsively walked toward the malignant shimmer of the Palast der Republik, the regime's flagship building. It housed not only the GDR parliament, but performance spaces, restaurants, and endless bureaucratic offices that processed countless bureaucratic applications. It was the last place anybody would dare follow him, the last place a foreigner would dare show himself – and the first place Belknap thought of to make sure he was as solitary as he had hoped. It was either an inspired decision or a beginner's error. He would know which soon enough. He willed himself into a state of bored complacency as he made his way past the granite-faced guards at the door, who glanced impassively at his worn-looking identification card. He continued through the balky turnstile, the long wraparound entrance hall smelling of disinfectant, the endless directory of offices and rooms, mounted overhead like the flight times at an airport. *You don't pause, you don't look around; act as if you know what you're doing and others will assume that you do.* Belknap might have been taken for – what? A low-level office worker back from a late lunch? A citizen in need of documents for a new car? He rounded the corner, and then another corner, until he arrived at the doors on the Alexanderplatz side of the building.

As he walked away from the Palast, he studied the images reflected on the building's mirrored glass. A lanky fellow in workman's shoes and a lunch pail. A big-breasted frau with puffy, hungover eyes. A pair of gray-suited bureaucrats with complexions to match. Nobody he recognized; nobody who triggered any sense of alarm.

Belknap proceeded to the grand promenade of Stalinist neoclassicism known as Karl-Marx-Allee. The extra-wide streets were fronted with eight-story buildings – an endless stretch of cream-colored ceramic tiles, tall casements, rows of Roman-style balusters above the shop level. At intervals, decorative tiles showed contented laborers, such as the ones who had built the promenade three and a half decades earlier. If Belknap recalled his history correctly, it had been those very laborers who led a rebellion against the socialist order in June 1953 – an uprising ruthlessly crushed by Soviet tanks. Stalin's favored 'confectioner's' style of architecture was bitter indeed to those who were compelled to bake it. The promenade was a beautiful lie.

Richard Lugner, however, was an ugly one. Lugner had sold out his country, but he hadn't sold cheap. The fading tyrants of Eastern Europe, Lugner had grasped, had never been more desperate than they were now, and their desperation matched his avarice. The American secrets he had been purveying, including the names of deep-cover American assets in their own Soviet-style security bureaus, could not be passed up; his treachery presented a rare opportunity. He made separate deals with each member of the Eastern bloc. Once the 'goods' had been sampled and proven authentic – the identity of perhaps one American asset, who would be carefully monitored before being arrested, tortured, and executed – Lugner was able to name his price.

Not every merchant stays on good terms with his customers, but Lugner had obviously taken precautions: He must have led his clients to suspect that he had kept a few cards to himself, that his stores of American secrets were not wholly depleted. As long as that possibility remained, such a man would have to be protected. It was appropriate that he should have found quarters among the Stasi officials and GDR nomenklatura who had settled in what had once been proclaimed 'workers' housing,' even as the true workers found themselves forced into featureless boxes made of concrete slabs. To be sure, Lugner was not a man to stay in one place for long. A month and a half before, in Bucharest, Belknap had missed him by a matter of hours. He could take no chances of that happening again.

Belknap waited for a few battered-looking Skoda cars to

4

pass, and crossed the boulevard just before the intersection, where a decrepit-looking hardware store advertised its wares. Would anybody follow him in? Had he only imagined that tail in the first place? A cheap door of Plexiglas and enameled aluminum banged behind him as he entered – a screen door that had no screens – and a dour gray-haired woman with a slight mustache peered at him bleakly from behind a counter, making him feel as if he had interrupted something, committed an act of trespass. The cramped space was suffused with the smell of machine oil; the shelves were filled with items that – it was clear at a glance – nobody had much use for. The dour woman, the shop's *Eigentümer*, continued to scowl as he found items that suggested someone doing maintenance in the apartment blocks: a pail, a container of ready-mixed plaster, a tube of grout, a wide-bladed spackling knife. Within a city in constant need of repair, the tools would immediately explain his presence almost anywhere he appeared. The counter woman gave him another grudging, the-customer-is-always-wrong glare, but sulkily took his money, as if accepting compensation for an injury.

Gaining entrance to the apartment block turned out to be child's play – an ironic advantage of life within a high-security state. Belknap waited as a couple of pungently perfumed hausfraus with canvas bags of groceries entered the doorway marked Haus 435, and followed them in, his tools earning him not merely instant legitimacy but unspoken approval. He got off at 7 Stock, the floor above theirs. If he was right – if his scrawny, greasy-haired informant was playing it on the level – he was only yards away from his quarry.

His heart started to thud, a tom-tom of anticipation that he could not dampen. This was no ordinary quarry. Richard Lugner had eluded every conceivable snare, having designed more than a few when he was still in the service of the United States. American intelligence officers had accumulated a vast compendium of reported sightings in the past eighteen months, and gave credence to few. Belknap himself had drilled dozens of dry holes during the past three months, and at this point, his superiors were only interested in a bona fide DPS, a 'direct and positive sighting' of his quarry. This time, though, he wasn't merely staking out a bar or café or airport lounge; this time he had an address. A real one? There were no guarantees. Yet his instincts – his nose – told him that his luck had turned. He had taken a stab in the dark and had struck something.

The next moments would be crucial. Lugner's quarters – evidently a substantial suite, with windows facing both the main street and the narrow side street, Koppenstrasse – were down one long hallway, and then a short one. Belknap approached the door to the suite and set down his pail; from a distance, he would look like a workman repairing one of the missing floor tiles in the corridor. Then, checking that the hallways were clear, Belknap knelt down before the lever handle – round doorknobs were almost never seen in this country – and inserted a small optical scope through the keyhole. If he could establish a DPS, he could effectively keep a watch while a proper exfiltration team was mobilized.

A big if – yet this time the trail was short enough that Belknap felt hopeful. It had begun with a late-night visit to the pissoir of the Friedrichstrasse train station, where he had eventually accosted one of the so-called Bahnhof Boys, the male prostitutes who frequented such sites. They shared information with far greater reluctance than they did their bodies, as soon became clear, and for a much steeper price. The very predilections that had led Lugner to cross over, he had always been convinced, would betray the betrayer. An appetite for underaged flesh: Lugner's indulgences would have caught up with him had he stayed in Washington, and it was not an appetite easily or long slaked. As a privileged guest of the Eastern bloc countries, Lugner could count on the fact that his appetites would be overlooked, if not abetted. Then, too, operating in a police state, the Bahnhof Boys were, of necessity, a close-knit group. If any of their number had been 'entertained' by a generous American with a pitted face and a taste for thirteen-year-olds, Belknap figured it wasn't improbable that the news had spread among his brethren.

It had taken a good deal of cajoling and reassurances, not to mention a sheaf of Marks, but the hustler finally went off to ask around, returning two hours later with a scrap of paper and a triumphant look on his lightly pimpled face. Belknap remembered his informant's sour-milk breath, his clammy hands. But that scrap of paper! Belknap dared to take it as vindication.

Belknap twisted the fiber-optic scope, moving it slowly into position. His were not the most practiced fingers. And he could afford no slips.

He heard a noise behind him, the scrape of boots on tile, and whirled around to see the business end of a short-barreled SKS carbine. Then the man holding it: He wore a dark blue-gray uniform with steel buttons, and a beige plastic communicator strapped beneath his right shoulder.

Stasi. The East German secret police.

He was an official sentry, no doubt, assigned to guard the eminent Herr Lugner. He must have been seated within a dimly lit, recessed corner, hidden from view.

Belknap rose slowly to his feet, his hands raised, affecting bewilderment while calculating his counterstrike.

The Stasi sentry barked into his beige walkie-talkie with the distinctively hard consonants of a true Berliner, his other hand loosely gripping a handgun. The distraction of the communicator meant that the sentry would be ill-prepared for a suddenly aggressive move. Belknap's own gun was holstered at his ankle. He would pretend to be showing the sentry the contents of his spackling kit while retrieving a tool far more lethal.

Suddenly he heard the door to the apartment open behind, felt the warm air inside – and felt a forceful blow to the side of his neck. Powerful arms wrestled him to the ground, hurled him facedown onto the wooden parquet of the foyer. Immediately someone had a boot on the back of his head. Unseen hands patted him down, extracted the small handgun secreted in its ankle holster. Then he was hustled into an adjoining room. A door closed behind him with a heavy *thunk*. The room was darkened, the main blinds closed; the only light came from a narrow bay window that faced the side street, and the gloom outside hardly penetrated the gloom within. It took him a few moments before his eyes adjusted.

Goddammit! Had they been on to him all along?

Now he made out his surroundings clearly. He was in something like a home office, with a costly-looking Turkish flatweave on the floor, an ebony-framed mirror on the wall, and a large Biedermeier-style desk.

Behind it stood Richard Lugner.

A man he had never met, but a face he would know anywhere. The slitlike mouth, the deeply pitted cheeks, the two-inch-long scar that curved across his forehead like a second left eyebrow: The photographs did him full justice. Belknap took in the man's small, malevolent, anthracite eyes. And, in Lugner's hands, a powerful shotgun, its twin boreholes bearing down on him like a second pair of eyes.

Two other gunmen – well-trained professionals, it was obvious from their bearing, their firing stance, their watchful gaze – stood to either side of Lugner's desk, their weapons trained on Belknap. Members of his private guard, Belknap immediately guessed – men whose loyalty and competence he could trust, men on his own payroll, men whose fortune depended upon his. For a man in Lugner's position, the investment in such a retinue would have been well worth it. The two gunmen now crossed over to Belknap, holding their weapons level as they flanked him.

'Persistent little bugger, aren't you?' Lugner said at last. His voice was a nasal rasp. 'You're like a human *tick*.'

Belknap said nothing. The configuration of gunfire was all too clear, and professionally arranged; there was no sudden move he could make that would change the geometry of death.

'My mother used to remove ticks from us kids with a hot match head. Hurt like hell. Hurt the critter more.'

One of his private bodyguards emitted a soft, throaty laugh.

'Oh, don't act like such an innocent,' the traitor went on. 'My procurer in Bucharest told me about your conversation with him. It left his arm in a sling. He didn't sound happy about it. You've been *bad*.' A moue of ironic disapproval. 'Fighting never solves anything – weren't you paying attention in seventh grade?' A grotesque wink. 'Pity I didn't know you when you were in seventh grade. *I* could have taught you a few things.'

'Screw you.' The words flared from Belknap in a low growl.

'Temper, temper. You have to master your emotions, or your emotions will master you. So tell me, greenhorn, how'd you find me?' Lugner's gaze hardened. 'Am I going to have to garrote little Ingo?' He shrugged. 'Well, the child did claim he liked it rough. I told him I'd take him to a place he'd never been before. Next time we'll just take it to the next level. The final level. I don't guess anybody will mind all that much.'

Belknap shuddered involuntarily. Lugner's two hirelings just smirked.

'Don't worry,' the traitor said in a voice of pretend reassurance. 'I'll be taking *you* to a place you've never been before, too. Have you ever discharged a point-fourteen Mossberg tactical shotgun at close range? At a man, I mean. *I* have. There's nothing like it.'

Belknap's gaze moved from the fathomless black of the shotgun muzzle to the fathomless black of Lugner's eyes.

Lugner's own gaze drifted to the wall just behind his captive. 'Our privacy won't be disturbed, I can promise you. Wonderful thick masonry in these apartment blocks – the soft lead pellets will hardly blister the skim coat. Then there's the soundproofing I had installed. I figured it wouldn't do to disturb the neighbors if some Bahnhof Boy turned out to be a *groaner*.' Flesh retracted from porcelain teeth in a hideous simulacrum of a smile. 'But you'll be taking a different kind of load today. You see, this Mossberg will actually blast away a large portion of your midriff. It will, mark my words, leave a hole you can reach your arm through.'

Belknap tried to move but felt himself clamped in place by hands like steel.

Lugner glanced at his two henchmen; he had the air of a

television chef about to demonstrate a surprising culinary technique. 'You think I'm exaggerating? Let me show you. You'll never experience anything like it.' There was a quiet *snick-click* as he released the safety of the shotgun. 'Not ever again.'

Belknap was able to make sense of the ensuing seconds only in retrospect. A loud crash of window glass; Lugner, startled by the sound, turning to the bay window to his left; muzzle flash from a handgun, a split-second later, sparking into the darkened apartment like a lightning bolt, glaring off mirrors and metal surfaces; and –

A plume of blood at Richard Lugner's right temple.

The traitor's expression suddenly went slack as he collapsed on the floor motionless, the shotgun falling with him like a stroke victim's cane. Someone with perfect aim had put a bullet through Lugner's head.

The guards spread out in either direction and aimed their weapons toward the broken window. The work of a sniper?

'Catch!' a voice called out – that of an American – and a handgun came sailing through the air toward Belknap. Belknap snatched it by sheer reflex, alert to the half-second of indecision between the two gunmen, who now had to decide whether to shoot first either at the prisoner or . . . the lanky stranger who had just swung through the four-paned casement. Belknap dropped to the floor – felt a bullet zing just above his shoulder – and fired twice at the gunman closest to him, striking him in the chest. Center mass: standard procedure for shooting on the fly. But it wasn't adequate for a close-range standoff like this one. Only a central-nervous-system shot would instantly neutralize the threat. Mortally wounded, scarlet blood gouting from his sternum, the first gunman began discharging the rounds in his magazine wildly. The sturdily constructed suite amplified the *boom* of the large-caliber shells, and, in the gloom, the repeated white muzzle flare was painfully bright.

Belknap fired a second time, shooting the man in the face. The gun, an old-style semiautomatic Walther, favored by certain ex–military types because it reputedly never jammed, fell heavily to the floor, followed by its owner moments later.

The stranger – he was tall, agile, clad in tan workman's coveralls, glittering with shards of broken glass – leaped to one side to avoid the other hireling's fire even as he returned fire with a single perfect head shot, another instant drop.

The stillness was eerie, long seconds of the profoundest quiet that Belknap had ever known. The stranger had looked almost bored as he dispatched Lugner and his crew, nothing indicating that his pulse had risen in the slightest.

Finally, the stranger spoke to him in a languid tone. 'I assume they had a Stasi lookout stationed in one of the alcoves outside.'

Which was precisely what Belknap should have assumed. Not for the first time, he silently cursed his stupidity. 'I don't think he'll be coming in, though,' Belknap said. His mouth was dry, his voice scratchy. He could feel a muscle in his leg trembling, vibrating like a cello string. Outside of training exercises, he had never stared down the wrong end of a shotgun before. 'I think the play was to leave their special guest to his own devices in . . . disposing of unwanted visitors.'

'I do hope he has a good housekeeper,' the man said, flicking shards of glass from his tan coveralls. They were standing among three bleeding corpses, in the middle of a police state, and he seemed in no hurry at all. He extended a hand. 'My name's Jared Rinehart, by the way.' His handclasp was firm and dry. Standing close to him, Belknap noticed that Rinehart was free of sweat; not a hair was out of place. He was a model of sangfroid. Belknap himself, as a glance in the mirror confirmed, was a mess.

'You made a frontal approach. Ballsy, but a little headstrong. Especially when there's a vacant apartment one floor up.'

'I see,' Belknap grunted, and he did, immediately working out Rinehart's movements, the nimble sense of situational strategy behind them. 'Point taken.'

Rinehart was slightly elongated, like a Christ in a mannerist painting, with long, elegant limbs, and oddly soulful

11

gray-green eyes; he moved with a feline grace as he took a few steps toward Belknap. 'Don't beat yourself up for missing the Stasi man. I'm frankly in awe of what you've accomplished. I've been trying to track down Mr. Lugner for quite some months, and without any luck at all.'

'You caught up with him this time,' Belknap said. *Who the hell are you?* he wanted to ask, but he decided to bide his time.

'Not really,' said his rescuer. 'I caught up with *you*.'

'With me.' The footsteps in Marx-Engels-Forum. The disappearing act of a true pro. The reflection of the lanky workman ghosted in the amber-tinted glass of the Palast der Republik.

'The only reason I got here was by following you. You were something, let me tell you. A hound on the trail of a fox. And me, breathlessly following like some country gent in jodhpurs.' He paused, looked around with a stock-taking air. 'Goodness gracious. You'd think some hotel-room-trashing rock star had paid a visit. But I think the point's been made, don't you? My employers, anyway, won't be at all displeased. Mr. Lugner had been such a bad example to the working spy, living high and letting die. Now he's a very *good* example.' He glanced at Lugner's body and then caught Belknap's eye. 'The wages of sin and all.'

Belknap looked around him, saw the blood of three slain men seeping into the red carpet, oxidizing to a rust hue like the one it had been dyed. A wave of nausea passed over him. 'How'd you know to follow me?'

'I was reconnoitering – or, to be honest, *loitering* – around the souks of Alexanderplatz when I thought I recognized the cut of your jib from Bucharest. I don't believe in coincidence, do you? For all I knew, you were a courier of his. But connected in one way or another. The gamble seemed worthwhile.'

Belknap just stared at him.

'Now then,' Jared Rinehart went on briskly. 'The only question is: Are you a friend or a foe?'

'Excuse me?'

'It's rude, I know.' A mock wince of self-reproach. 'Like talking shop at dinner, or asking what people *do* for a living at cocktail parties. But I have practical interest in the issue. I'd rather know now if you're, oh, in the employ of the Albanians. There was a rumor that they thought Mr. Lugner had kept the really good stuff for their Eastern bloc rivals, and you know what those Albanians are like when they feel stiffed. And as for those Bulgarians – well, don't get me started.' As he spoke, he took out a handkerchief and daubed at Belknap's chin. 'You don't encounter that combination of lethality and stupidity just every day. So that's why I've got to ask – are you a good witch or a bad witch?' He presented the handkerchief to Belknap with a flourish. 'You had a little splash of blood there,' he explained. 'Keep it.'

'I don't understand,' Belknap said, a mixture of incredulity and awe in his voice. 'You just risked your life to save mine . . . without even knowing whether I was an ally or an enemy?'

Rinehart shrugged. 'I had a good feeling, let's say. And it had to be one or the other. A chancy business, I grant, but if you're not rolling the dice, you're not in the game. Oh, before you answer the question, you'll need to know that I'm here as an unofficial representative of the U.S. Department of State.'

'Christ on a raft.' Belknap tried to bring his thoughts into focus. 'Consular Operations? The Pentheus team?'

Rinehart just smiled. 'You're Cons Ops, too? We ought to have a secret handshake, don't you think? Or a club tie, though they'd have to let me choose the design.'

'The bastards,' Belknap said, whipsawed by the revelation. 'Why didn't anybody tell me?'

'Always keep 'em guessing – that's the philosophy. If you ask the op boys at 2201 C Street, they'll explain that it's a procedure they occasionally use, especially when there are solo operatives involved. Separate and de-linked clandestine units. They'll say something fancy about operational partition. The potential downside is you trip over your tail. The upside is you avoid groupthink, lockstep, get a wider variety of approaches. That's what they'll tell you. But the truth, I bet, is that it was an ordinary screwup. Common as crabgrass.' While he spoke, he turned his attention to a mahogany-and-brass liquor stand in one corner of the study. He lifted up a bottle and beamed. 'A twenty-year-old slivovitz from Suvoborska. Not too shabby. I think we could both stand a wee dram. We've earned it.' He splashed a little in two shot glasses, pressed one on Belknap. 'Bottoms up!' he called out.

Belknap hesitated, and then swallowed the contents of the shot glass, his mind still whirling. Any other operative in Rinehart's position would have maintained an observation post. If a direct intervention had to be staged, it would have been timed to a moment when Lugner and his henchmen had put their weapons away. Some moment *after* they had been used. Belknap would have been given a posthumous ribbon to be placed on his casket; Lugner would have been killed or apprehended. The second operative would have been praised and promoted. Organizations valued prudence over valor. Nobody could be expected to enter, alone, a room that contained three gunmen with weapons drawn. To do so defied logic, not to mention all standard operational procedures.

Who *was* this man?

Rinehart rummaged through the jacket of one of the slain guards, retrieved a compact American pistol, a short-barreled Colt, released the magazine, and peered inside. 'This yours?'

Belknap grunted assent, and Rinehart tossed him the weapon. 'You're a man of taste. Half-jacketed nine-millimeter hollowpoints, scalloped copper on lead. An excellent balance between stopping power and penetration, and definitely not standard-issue. The Brits say you can always judge a man by his shoes. I say his choice of ammunition tells you what you need to know.'

'Here's what *I'd* like to know,' Belknap said, still piecing together his fragmented memories of the past few minutes. 'What if I *weren't* a friend?'

'Then there'd be a fourth corpse here for the cleanup crew.' Rinehart put a hand on Belknap's shoulder, gave a squeeze of reassurance. 'But you'll learn something about me. I take pride in being a good friend to my good friends.'

'And a dangerous enemy to your dangerous enemies?'

'We understand each other,' his voluble interlocutor replied. 'So: Shall we leave this party at the worker's palace? We've met the host, paid our proper respects, had a drink – I think we can go now without giving offense. You never want to be the last to leave.' He glanced at three slack-faced corpses. 'If you'll step over to the window, you'll notice a bosun's chair and scaffolding, which is just the thing for an afternoon of window-washing, though I think we'll skip that part.' He led Belknap through the smashed casement and onto the platform, which was secured to cables anchored to the balcony of the apartment above. Given all the maintenance work done on these apartment buildings, it was unlikely to attract notice on the side street, seven floors below, even if there had been anyone around.

Rinehart brushed a remaining fragment of glass from his tan coveralls. 'Here's the thing, Mr. . . . .'

'Belknap,' he said as he steadied himself onto the platform.

'Here's the thing, Belknap. You're how old? Twenty-five, twenty-six?'

'Twenty-six. And call me Todd.'

Rinehart fiddled with the cable lanyard. With a jerk, the platform started a slow, erratic descent, as if lowered by a series of tugs. 'Then you've been with the outfit for just a couple of years, I guess. Me, I'll be thirty next year. Have a few more years of seasoning on me. So let me tell you what you're going to find. You're going to find that most of your colleagues are mediocre. It's just the nature of any organization. So if you come across someone who has genuine gifts, you watch out for that person. Because in the intelligence community, most of the real progress is made by a handful of people. Those are the gemstones. You don't let them get lost, or scratched, or crushed, not if you give a damn about this enterprise of ours. Taking care of business means taking care of your friends.' His gray-green eyes intent, he added,

'There's a famous line from the British writer E. M. Forster. Maybe you know it. He said that if he ever had to choose between betraying his friend and betraying his country, he hoped he'd have the guts to betray his country.'

'Rings a bell.' Belknap's eyes were glued to the street, which thankfully remained vacant. 'Is that your philosophy?' He felt a drop of rain, solitary but heavy, and then another one.

Rinehart shook his head. 'On the contrary. The lesson here is that you need to be careful about picking your friends.' Another intent look. 'Because you should never have to make that choice.'

Now the two stepped onto the narrow street, leaving the platform behind.

'Take the pail,' Rinehart instructed. Belknap did so, recognizing the wisdom of it at once. Rinehart's coveralls and cap were a formidable disguise in a city of laborers; carrying the pail and spackling kit, Belknap would look like a natural companion.

Another heavy drop of rain splashed on Belknap's forehead. 'It's gonna start coming down,' he said, wiping it away.

'It's *all* going to come down,' the lanky operative replied cryptically. 'And everyone here, in his heart of hearts, realizes it.'

Rinehart knew the city topography well – he knew which stores connected two streets, which alleys backed onto others that led to yet other streets. 'So what did you think of Richard Lugner after your brief encounter?'

The traitor's pitted face of malign impassivity returned to him like a ghostly afterimage. 'Evil,' Belknap said shortly, surprising himself. It was a word he seldom used. But no other would do. The twin boreholes of the shotgun were etched in his mind, as were the malevolent eyes of Lugner himself.

'What a concept,' the taller man said with a nod. 'Unfashionable these days, but indispensable all the same. We somehow think that we're too sophisticated to talk about evil. Everything is supposed to be analyzed as a product of social

16

or psychological or historical forces. And once you do that, well, evil drops out of the picture, doesn't it?' Rinehart led the younger man into an underground plaza that connected a square that had been split by a motorway. 'We like to pretend that we don't speak of evil because we've outgrown the concept. I wonder. I suspect the motivation is itself deeply primitive. Like some tribal fetish worshippers of ancient times, we imagine that by not speaking the name, the thing to which it refers will vanish.'

'It's that face,' Belknap grunted.

'A face only Helen Keller could love.' Rinehart mimed the motion of Braille-reading fingertips.

'The way he looks at you, I mean.'

'*Looked*, anyway,' Rinehart replied, stressing the past tense. 'I've had my own encounters with the man. He was pretty formidable. And as you say – evil. Yet not all evil has a face. The Ministry of State Security in this country feeds off people like Lugner. That's a form of evil, too. Monumental and faceless.' Rinehart maintained a level tone, but he did not hide the passion in his voice. The man was cool – maybe the coolest Belknap had ever known – but he was not a cynic. After a while, Belknap realized something else, too: The other man's conversational flow wasn't simply a matter of self-expression; it was an attempt to distract and calm a young operative whose nerves had just been severely jarred. His very chatter was a kindness.

Twenty minutes later, the two of them – workmen from all appearances – were approaching the embassy building, a Schinkel-style marble building now sooted by pollution. Large raindrops were falling intermittently. A familiar loamy smell arose from the pavement. Belknap envied Rinehart his cap. Three GDR policemen eyed the embassy from their post across the street, adjusting their nylon parkas, trying to keep their cigarettes dry.

As the two Americans approached the embassy, Rinehart pulled up a Velcro tab on his coveralls and revealed a small blue coded nameplate to one of the American guards standing at a side entrance. A quick nod, and the two found themselves on the inner side of the consulate fence. Belknap felt a few more drops of rain, landing heavily, darkening the tarmac with black splotches. The heavy steel gate clanged shut. A short while before, death had seemed certain. Now safety was assured. 'I just realized that I never answered the first question you asked me,' he said to his lanky companion.

'Whether you were friend or foe?'

Belknap nodded. 'Well, let's agree we're friends,' he said in a sudden rush of gratitude and warmth. 'Because I could use more friends like you.'

The tall operative gave him a look that was both affectionate and appraising. 'One might be enough,' he replied, smiling.

Later – years later – Belknap would have reason to reflect on how a brief encounter could set the course of a man's life. A watershed moment splits life into a before and an after. Yet it was impossible, except in retrospect, to recognize the moment for what it was. At the time, Belknap's mind was filled with the ardent yet banal thought *Someone saved my life today* – as if the act had merely restored normality, as if there could now be a going back, a return to the way things were. He did not know – he could not know – that his life had changed irreversibly. Its trajectory, in ways both imperceptible and dramatic, had shifted.

By the time the two men stepped under the olive-drab awning that extended from the side of the consulate, its plasticized fabric was thrumming with rain, water sliding off it in sheets. The downpour had begun.

PART ONE

CHAPTER ONE

Rome

Tradition holds that Rome was built on seven hills. The Janiculum, higher than any of them, is the eighth. In ancient times, it was given over to the cult of Janus – the god of exits and entrances; the god of two faces. Todd Belknap would need them both. On the third floor of the villa on the via Angelo Masina, a looming neoclassical structure with facades of yellow ochre stucco and white pilasters, the operative checked his watch for the fifth time in ten minutes.

This is what you do, he silently assured himself.

But this was not the way he had planned it. It was not the way anybody had planned it. He moved quietly through the hallway – a surface, blessedly, of solidly mortared tile: no squeaking floorboards. The renovation had removed the rotting woodwork of a previous renovation . . . and how many such renovations had there been since the original construction in the eighteenth century? The villa, built upon an aqueduct of Trajan, had an illustrious past. In 1848, in the great days of the Risorgimento, Garibaldi used it as his headquarters; the basement, supposedly, had been enlarged to serve as a backup armory. These days, the villa once again had a military purpose, if more nefarious in nature. It belonged to Khalil Ansari, a Yemeni arms dealer. Not just any arms dealer, either. As shadowy as his operations were, Cons Ops analysts had established that he was a significant supplier not only in South Asia but also in Africa. What set him apart was how elusive he was: how carefully he had concealed his movements, his location, his identity. Until now.

Belknap's timing could not have been better – or worse. In the two decades he had spent as a field agent, he had come to dread the stroke of luck that arrives almost too late. It had happened near the beginning of his career, in East Berlin. It had happened seven years ago, in Bogotá. It was happening again here in Rome. Good things come in threes, as his good friend Jared Rinehart wryly insisted.

Ansari, it was known, was on the verge of a major arms deal, one that would involve a series of simultaneous exchanges among several parties. It was, from all indications, a deal of enormous complexity and enormous magnitude – something that perhaps only Khalil Ansari would be capable of orchestrating. According to HUMINT sources, the final settlement would be arranged this very evening, via an intercontinental conference call of some sort. Yet the use of sterile lines and sophisticated encryption ruled out the standard SIGINT solutions. Belknap's discovery had changed all that. If Belknap was able to plant a bug in the right place, Consular Operations would gain invaluable information about how the Ansari network functioned. With any luck, the rogue network could be exposed – and a multibillion-dollar merchant of death brought to justice.

That was the good news. The bad news was that Belknap had identified Ansari only hours before. No time for a co-ordinated operation. No time for backup, for HQ-approved plans. He had no other choice but to go in alone. The opportunity could not be allowed to pass.

The photo ID clipped to his knitted cotton shirt read 'Sam Norton,' and identified him as one of the site architects involved in the latest round of renovations, an employee of the British architectural firm in charge of the project. It got him in the house, but it could not explain what he was doing on the third floor. In particular, it could not justify his presence in Ansari's personal study. If he were found here, it was over. Likewise if anyone were to discover the guard he had knocked out with a tiny Carfentanil dart and stowed in a cleaning closet down the hall. The operation would be terminated. *He* would be terminated.

Belknap recognized these facts dully, dispassionately, like the rules of the road. Inspecting the arms dealer's study, he felt a kind of operational numbness; he saw himself from the perspective of a disembodied observer far above him. The ceramic element of the contact microphone could be hidden – where? A vase on the desk, containing an orchid. The vase would serve as a natural amplifier. It would also be routinely inspected by the Yemeni's debugging team, but that would not be until the morning. A keystroke logger – he had a recent model – would record messages typed on Ansari's desktop computer. A faint chirp sounded in Belknap's earpiece, a response to radio pulse emitted by a tiny motion detector that Belknap had secreted in the hallway outside.

Was someone about to enter the room? Not good. Not good at all. It was an appalling irony. He had spent the better part of a year trying to locate Khalil Ansari. Now the danger was that Khalil Ansari would locate him.

Dammit! Ansari was not supposed to be back so soon. Belknap looked helplessly around the Moroccan-tiled room. There were few places for concealment, aside from a closet with a slatted door, at the corner near the desk. Far from ideal. Belknap stepped quickly inside and hunched down, squatting on the floor. The closet was unpleasantly warm, filled with racks of humming computer routers. He counted the seconds. The miniaturized motion detector he had placed in the hall outside could have been set off by a roach or rodent. Surely it was a false alarm.

It was not. Someone was entering the room. Belknap peered through the slats until he could make out the figure. Khalil Ansari: a man tending everywhere toward roundness. A body made of ovals, like an art-class exercise. Even his close-trimmed beard was a thing of round edges. His lips, his ears, his chin, his cheeks, were full, soft, round, cushioned. He wore a white silk caftan, Belknap saw, which draped loosely around his bulk as the man padded toward his desk with a distracted air. Only the Yemeni's eyes were sharp, scanning the room like a samurai's rotating sword. Had Belknap been seen? He had counted on the darkness of the closet to provide concealment. He had counted on many things. Another miscalculation, and he would be counted *out*.

The Yemeni eased his avoirdupois upon the leather chair at his desk, cracked his knuckles, and typed in a rapid sequence – a password, no doubt. As Belknap continued to squat uncomfortably in the recessed bay, his knees started to protest. Now in his mid-forties, he had lost the limberness of his youth. But he could not afford to move; the sound of a cracking joint would instantly betray his presence. If only he had arrived a few minutes earlier, or Ansari a few minutes later: Then he would have had the keystroke logger in place, electronically capturing the pulses emitted by the keyboard. His first priority was just to stay alive, to endure the debacle. There would be time for postmortems and after-action reports later.

The arms dealer shifted in his seat and intently keyed in another sequence of instructions. Messages were being e-mailed. Ansari drummed his fingers and pressed a button inset in a rosewood-veneered box. Perhaps he was setting up the conference call via Internet telephony. Perhaps the entire conference would be conducted in encrypted text, chatroom style. There was so much that could have been learned, if only . . . It was too late for regrets, but they churned through Belknap all the same.

He remembered his exhilaration, not long before, when he had at last tracked his quarry to earth. It was Jared Rinehart who had first dubbed him 'the Hound,' and the well-earned honorific had stuck. Though Belknap did have a peculiar gift for finding people who wished to stay lost, much of his success – he could never persuade people of it, but he knew it to be true – was a matter of sheer perseverance.

Certainly that was how he had finally tracked down Khalil Ansari after entire task forces had returned empty-handed. The bureaucrats would dig, their shovels would bang against bedrock, and they would give it up as futile. That was not Belknap's way. Each search was different; each involved a mixture of logic and caprice, because human beings were a mixture of logic and caprice. Neither ever sufficed by itself. The computers at headquarters were capable of scanning vast databases, inspecting records from border control authorities, Interpol, and other such agencies, but they needed to be told what to look for. Machines could be programmed with pattern-recognition software – but first they had to be told what pattern to recognize. And they could never get into the mind of the target. A hound could scent out a fox, in part, because it could think like a fox.

A knock at the door, and a young woman – dark hair, olive skin, but Italian rather than Levantine, Belknap judged – let herself in. The severity of her black-and-white uniform did not disguise the young woman's beauty: the budding sensuality of someone who had only recently come into her full physical endowments. She was carrying a silver tray with a pot and a small cup. Mint tea, Belknap knew at once from the aroma. The merchant of death had sent for it. Yemenis seldom did business without a carafe of mint tea, or *shay*, as they called it, and Khalil, on the verge of a concluding a vast chain of trades, proved true to form. Belknap almost smiled.

It was always details like those that helped Belknap track down his most elusive subjects. A recent one was Garson Williams, the rogue scientist at Los Alamos who sold nuclear secrets to the North Koreans and then disappeared. The FBI spent four years searching for him. Belknap, when he was finally assigned to the task, found him in two months. Williams, he learned from a domestic inventory, had a pronounced weakness for Marmite, the salty, yeast-based spread popular among Britons of a certain age as well as former subjects of the British Empire. Williams had developed a taste for it during a graduate fellowship at Oxford. In a list of the contents of the physicist's house, Belknap noticed that he had three jars of it in the pantry. The FBI demonstrated its thoroughness by X-raying all the objects in the household and determining that no microfiche had been hidden anywhere. But its agents didn't think the way Belknap did. The physicist would have retreated to a less-developed part of the world, where record-keeping was slipshod: It was the logical thing to do, since the North Koreans would have lacked the resources to provide him with identity papers of a quality that would pass in the information-age West. So

Belknap scrutinized the places where the man went on vacation, looking for a pattern, a semi-submerged preference. His own tripwires were of a peculiar sort, triggered by the conjuncture of certain locations and certain distinctive consumer preferences. A shipment of a specialty foodstuff was made to an out-of-the-way hotel; a phone call – ostensibly from a chatty 'customer satisfaction' representative – revealed that the request had originated not with a guest but with a local. The evidence, if one could even call it that, was absurdly weak; Belknap's hunch was not. When Belknap finally caught up with him, at a seaside fishing town in eastern Arugam Bay, Sri Lanka, he came alone. He was taking a flyer – he couldn't justify dispatching a team based on the fact that an American had special-ordered Marmite from a small hotel in the neighborhood. It was too insubstantial for official action. But it was substantial enough for him. When he finally confronted Williams, the physicist seemed almost grateful to have been found. His dearly bought tropical paradise had turned out the way they usually did: a fugue of tedium, of stultifying ennui.

More clicking from the Yemeni's keyboard. Ansari picked up a cellular telephone – undoubtedly a model with chip-enabled auto-encryption – and spoke in Arabic. His voice was at once unhurried and unmistakably urgent. A long pause, and then Ansari switched into German.

Now Ansari looked up briefly as the servant girl set down his cup of tea and she smiled, displaying perfectly even white teeth. As Ansari turned back to his work, her smile disappeared like a pebble dropped into a pond. She made her exit noiselessly, the perfectly unobtrusive servitor.

How much longer?

Ansari raised the small teacup to his mouth and took a savoring sip. He spoke again into the phone, this time in French. *Yes, yes, all was on schedule.* Words of reassurance, but lacking all specificity. They knew what they were talking about; they did not have to spell it out. The black marketeer clicked off the telephone and typed another message. He took another sip of the tea, placed the cup down, and – it

26

happened suddenly, like a small seizure – he shivered briefly. Moments later, he sprawled forward, his head falling on his keyboard, motionless, evidently insensate. Dead?

It couldn't be.

It was.

The door to the study opened again; the servant girl. Would she panic, raise the alarm, when she made the shocking discovery?

In fact, she showed no surprise of any sort. She moved briskly, furtively, stepping over to the man and placing her fingers at his throat, feeling for a pulse, obviously detecting none. Then she pulled on a pair of white cotton gloves and repositioned him in his chair so that he seemed to be leaning back, at rest. Next she moved to the keyboard, typed a hurried message of her own. Finally, she removed the teacup and carafe, placing them on her tray, and left the study. Removing, thus, the instruments of his death.

Khalil Ansari, one of the most powerful arms dealers in the world, had just been murdered – in front of his eyes. Poisoned, in fact. By . . . a young Italian servant girl.

With no little discomfort, Belknap rose from his squatting position, his mind buzzing like a radio tuned midway between two stations. It wasn't supposed to go down this way.

Then he heard a quiet electronic hooting sound. It came from an intercom on Ansari's desk.

And when Ansari did not respond?

Dammit to hell! Soon the alarm really would be raised. Once that happened, there would be no way out.

Beirut, Lebanon

'The Paris of the Middle East,' the city had once been called, as Saigon was once heralded as the Paris of Indochina and conflict-roiled Abidjan the Paris of Africa: the designation more of a curse than an honor. Those who remained there had proven themselves survivors of one sort or another.

The bulletproof Daimler limousine smoothly negotiated the mid-evening traffic on rue Maarad in the troubled city's downtown, known as Beirut Central District. Streetlights cast a hard glow on the dusty streets, as if laying down a glaze. The Daimler navigated through the Place de l'Etoile – once hopefully modeled on the Parisian center, now merely a traffic-snarled roundabout – and glided along streets where restored buildings from the Ottoman and French Mandate eras stood alongside modern office blocks. The building before which the limousine finally stopped was perfectly unremarkable: a dun-colored seven-story structure, like half a dozen in the neighborhood. To an experienced eye, the wide external frames around the limousine's windows gave away the fact that it was armored, but there was nothing remarkable about that, either. This was, after all, Beirut. Nor was there anything unusual about the sight of the two heavyset bodyguards – both wearing taupe poplin suits, in the loose fit preferred by those whose usual getup required a holster as well as a tie – who piled out of the car as soon as it came to a stop. Again, this was Beirut.

And what of the passenger they were guarding? An observer would have known at once that the passenger – tall, corn-fed, attired in an expensive but boxy gray suit – was not Lebanese. His national origin was unmistakable; the man could just as well have been waving the Stars and Stripes.

As the driver held the door open for him, the American looked around uneasily. Fiftyish and straight-backed, he exuded the bred-in-the-bone privilege of an interloper from the planet's most powerful nation – and, at the same time, the unease of a stranger in a strange city. The hard-sided briefcase he held might have provided a further clue, or merely raised further questions. One of the bodyguards, the smaller of the two, preceded him into the building. The other guard, his eyes darting around him tirelessly, stayed with the tall American. Protection and captivity so often looked the same.

In the lobby, the American was accosted by a Lebanese man with a wincelike smile and black hair that appeared slicked back with unrefined petroleum. 'Mr. McKibbin?' he said, extending a hand. 'Ross McKibbin?'

The American nodded.

'I'm Muhammad,' the Lebanese man said in a whispery voice.

'In this country,' the American returned, 'who isn't?'

His contact smiled uncertainly and led his guest through a cortege of armed guards. These were strapping, hirsute men with small arms in polished hip holsters, men with wary eyes and weathered faces, men who knew how easily civilization could be destroyed, for they had watched it happen, and resolved to side with something of greater durability: commerce.

The American was ushered into a long room on the second floor with white stuccoed walls. It was arranged like a lounge, with upholstered chairs and a low table with urns of coffee and tea, but its ostensible informality did not disguise the fact that it was a place for work, not for play. The guards remained outside, in a sort of antechamber; inside were a handful of local businessmen.

The man they called Ross McKibbin was greeted with anxious grins and quick hand pumps. There was business to be conducted, and they knew that Americans had little patience for the Arabic traditions of courtesy and indirection.

'We are most grateful that you could meet with us,' said one of the men, who had been introduced as the owner of two cinemas and a chain of grocery stories in the Beirut area.

'You honor us with your presence,' said another chamber-of-commerce type.

'I am just a representative, an emissary,' the American replied airily. 'Think of me as a placement officer. There are people who have money, and people who need money. My job is to place one with the other.' His smile snapped shut like a cell phone.

'Foreign investment has been quite hard to come by,' another of the locals ventured. 'But we are not the sort to look a gift horse in the mouth.'

'I'm not a gift horse,' McKibbin shot back.

In the antechamber, the smaller of the American's bodyguards stepped closer to the room. Now he could see as well as hear.

Few observers, in any case, would have had any trouble discerning the various power inequities within. The American was plainly one of those intermediaries who made a living by contravening international law on behalf of parties who had to operate in secrecy. He represented foreign capital to a group of local businessmen whose need for such funding was far greater than any scruples they could afford about its provenance.

'Mr. Yorum,' McKibbin said briskly, turning to a man who had not yet spoken, 'you're a banker, are you not? What would you say are my best opportunities here?'

'I think you will find everyone here to be an eager partner,' replied a man whose squat face and tiny nostrils suggested the countenance of a frog.

'I hope you will consider Mansur Enterprises favorably,' one of the men interjected. 'We've had a very robust return on capital.' He paused, mistaking the disapproving looks around him for skepticism. 'Truly. Our books have been carefully audited.'

McKibbin turned a chilly gaze to the man of Mansur Enterprises. 'Audited? The parties I represent prefer a less formal system of bookkeeping.' Floating up from outside was the sound of squealing tires. Few paid it any mind.

The other man flushed. 'But of course. We are, at the same time, quite versatile, I assure you.'

Nobody uttered the phrase 'money laundering'; nobody had to. There was no need to spell out the purpose of the meeting. Foreign dealers with unaccountable reserves of cash sought businesses in poorly regulated markets like Lebanon to serve as fronts, as entities through which illicit cash could be sluiced, emerging as legitimate business earnings. Most would be returned to the silent partners; some could be retained. Both greed and apprehension were palpable in the room.

'I do wonder whether I'm wasting my time here,' McKibbin went on in a bored tone. 'We're talking about an arrangement that depends on trust. And there can be no trust without candor.'

The banker ventured an amphibious half-smile, blinking slowly.

The fraught silence was broken by the sound of a group of men rushing up the wide terrazzo stairs: late arrivals to a meeting elsewhere? Or – something else?

The harsh, concussive noise of automatic gunfire stilled idle speculation. At first, it sounded like a burst of firecrackers, but the burst went on too long, and was too fast, for that. There were shrieks – men forcing air through constricted throats, emitting a keening chorus of terror. And then the terror spilled into the meeting room, like a rampaging fury. Men clad in keffiyehs charged in, aiming their Kalashnikovs at the Lebanese businessmen.

Within moments, the room had turned into a tableau of carnage. It looked as if a disgruntled painter had splashed a can of crimson paint against the stuccoed walls; men sprawled everywhere like red-drenched mannequins.

The meeting was over.

Rome

Todd Belknap raced to the study door and, clipboard in hand, made his way down the long hallway. He would have to brazen it out. His planned means of escape – descending to the inner courtyard and exiting through a delivery chute – was no longer possible: It would require time he could no longer afford. He had no choice but to take a more direct route.

When he reached the end of the hallway, he paused; at the landing below, he could see a pair of sentries making their rounds. Flattening himself in the crook of an open guestroom door, he waited several minutes for the guards to move on. Fading footsteps, the jingle of keys on a chain, the closing of a door: the ebbing sounds of movement in retreat.

Now he stepped lightly down the stairs and, casting his mind back to the blueprints he had studied, he opened a narrow door just to the right of the landing. It would take him to a back staircase that would avoid the main floor of the villa and lessen the risk of exposure. Even as he stepped through the threshold, though, he could sense that something was not right. A small twinge of anxiety arrived before he was conscious of the explanation for it: raised voices and the sound of rubber soles slapping against hard flooring. Men running, not walking. The disruption of routine. Meaning: Khalil Ansari's death had been discovered. Meaning: Security at the compound was now at high alert.

Meaning: Belknap's chances of survival were dwindling with every minute he remained inside.

Or was it too late already? As he raced down a flight of stairs, he heard a buzzing sound, and the swinging grate at the bottom of the landing clanged shut electronically. Someone had activated a high-security state for all points of egress and ingress, overriding the ordinary fire-safety presets. Was he trapped on this flight of stairs? Belknap raced back up and tried the lever knob to the floor above. The door opened and he pushed through it.

Straight into an ambush.

He felt an iron grip around his left upper arm, a gun pressed painfully against his spine. A heat-and-movement sensor must have revealed his position. He whipped his head around and his eyes met the granite stare of the man gripping his arm. It was another, unseen guard, then, who had the gun to Belknap's back. It was the less challenging position, and therefore occupied by someone who was surely junior to the man to his side.

Belknap took another look at him. Swarthy, black-haired, clean-shaven, he was in his early forties, at a stage of life where the seasoning of experience conferred an advantage that was not yet offset by any loss of physical vigor. A young man with muscles but limited experience could be overcome, as could the superannuated veteran. But everything about the way this man moved told Belknap that he knew precisely what he was doing. His face betrayed neither overconfidence nor fear. Such an opponent was formidable indeed: steel that had been hardened by duress but not yet fatigued.

The man was powerfully built, yet moved with agility. He

had a face of planes and angles, a nose with a thickened bridge that had obviously been broken in his youth, and a heavy brow that jutted out slightly over reptilian eyes – those of a predator examining his fallen prey.

'Hey, listen, I don't know what's going on,' Belknap began, trying to sound like a bewildered factotum. 'I'm just one of the site architects. I'm checking on our contractors. That's my job, okay? Look, just call the office, get this thing straightened out.'

The man who had shoved a gun in his back now walked alongside him to his right: mid-twenties, lithe, brown hair cut *en brosse*, sunken cheeks. He exchanged glances with the senior guard. Neither dignified Belknap's chatter with a response.

'Maybe you don't speak English,' Belknap said. 'I guess that's the problem. *Dovrei parlare in italiano . . .*'

'Your problem isn't that I don't understand,' said the senior guard in lightly accented English, tightening his iron grip. 'Your problem is that I do understand.'

His captor was a Tunisian, Belknap guessed from his accent. 'But then – '

'You wish to speak? Excellent. I wish to listen. But not here.' The guard stopped walking for a moment, jerking his captive to an abrupt stop. 'In our lovely *stanza per gli interrogatori*. The interview chamber. In the basement. We go there now.'

Belknap's blood ran cold. He knew all about the room in question – had studied it on the blueprints, had researched its construction and equipment even before he had confirmed that Ansari was the villa's true owner. It was, in plain English, a torture chamber, and of truly cutting-edge design. *'Totalmente insonorizzato,'* the architectural specifications had stipulated: completely soundproof. The soundproofing materials had, in fact, been special-ordered from a company in the Netherlands. Acoustic isolation was achieved by density and disconnection: The chamber was floated and lined with a dense polymer made of sand and PVC; sturdy rubber seals lined the door frame. A man could scream at the top of his lungs and be entirely inaudible to someone standing outside, just a few feet away. The elaborate soundproofing guaranteed that.

The equipment contained in the basement chamber would guarantee the screams.

Evildoers always sought to sequester the sight and sound of their deeds; Belknap had known this since East Berlin, a couple of decades earlier. Among connoisseurs of cruelty, *privacy* was the invariable watchword; it sheltered barbarism in the very midst of society. Belknap knew something else, as well. If he were taken to the *stanza per gli interrogatori* it was all over. All over for the operation; all over for him. There was no possible escape from it. Any form of resistance, no matter how hazardous, would be preferable to allowing himself to be taken there. Belknap had only one advantage: the fact that he *knew* this, and that the others did not know he knew this. To be more desperate than your captors realized – a slender reed. But Belknap would work with what he had.

He allowed a dull look of gratitude to settle on his face. 'Good,' he said. 'Fine. I understand this is a high-sec facility. Do what you need to do. I'm happy to talk, wherever you like. But – Sorry, what's your name?'

'Call me Yusef,' the senior guard said. There was something implacable even in the pleasantry.

'But, Yusef, you're making a mistake. You got no beef with me.' He slackened his body slightly, rounding his shoulders, subtly making himself physically less intimidating. They did not believe his protestations, of course. His awareness of that fact was all he needed to keep from them.

Opportunity came when they decided to save time by frog-marching him down the main staircase – a grand, curving structure of travertine adorned with a Persian runner – instead of the concrete rear stairs. When he saw a glimpse of the streetlights through the frosted window bays to either side of the massive front door, he made a quick, silent decision. One step, a second step, a third step – he jerked his arm from the guard's grip in a feeble gesture of wounded dignity, and the guard did not bother to respond. It was the hopeless fluttering of a caged bird.

He turned to face the guards, as if trying to make conversation again, seemingly careless of his footing. The runner was well cushioned with an underlay that snaked along the treads and risers; that would be helpful. A fourth step, fifth step, sixth step: Belknap stumbled, as convincingly as he could, pretending he had missed his footing. Now he pitched forward, gently, falling on his slack left shoulder, while secretly breaking his fall with his right hand. 'Shit!' Belknap yelped, feigning dismay as he rolled down another couple of steps.

'*Vigilanza fuori!*' the seasoned guard, the man who called himself Yusef, muttered to his partner. The guards would have only seconds to decide how to respond: A captive had value – the value of the information he could provide. Killing him at an inopportune moment could, in the fullness of time, lead to recriminations. Yet a non-lethal shot had to be aimed with great care, all the more so when the target was in motion.

And Belknap *was* in motion, righting himself from a sprawl and now springing off a step as if it were a starting block, bounding down the rest of the staircase, his ankles like tightly coiled springs, and then surging toward the Palladian-style door. Yet the door itself was not his target; it, too, would have been magneto-locked shut.

Abruptly, Belknap veered off to one side of it – to a two-foot-wide ornamental segment of leaded glass, an echoing, though narrower, Palladian shape. The city of Rome forbade any visible change to the villa's facade, and that included the ornamental panel. The blueprints ultimately called for it to be replaced with an identical-looking panel that would be rendered of a bulletproof and unbreakable methacrylate resin, but it would be months before the replica, which required the collaboration of artisans and engineers, would be ready. Now he threw his body at the panel, leading with his hips and averting his face to avoid laceration and –

It gave way, noisily popping out of its frame and shattering upon the stone outside. Elementary physics: The energy of motion was proportional to mass times the square of velocity.

Belknap righted himself swiftly and took off down the stone path in front of the villa. Yet his pursuers were merely seconds behind him. He heard their footfalls – and then their gunfire. He darted erratically, trying to make himself a difficult target, as muzzle flashes punctuated the darkness outside like starbursts. Belknap could hear bullets ricochet off the statuary that decorated the villa's front grounds. Even as he tried to dodge the handgun fire that was aimed at him, he prayed that no unaimed ricochet found him. Gulping for breath, too frenzied to inventory his injuries, he veered to his left, sprinting to the brick wall that marked the end of the property, and vaulted over it. Razor-edged concertina wire slashed and sliced at his clothing, and he left half his shirt on its barbs. As he dived through the gardens of neighboring consulates and small museums on the via Angelo Masina, he knew that his left ankle would soon start sending shooting pains, that muscles and joints would eventually protest their abuse. For the moment, though, adrenaline had taken his body's pain circuitry offline. He was grateful for that. And grateful for something else, too.

He was alive.

Beirut

The conference room was rank with the foulness of perforated bodies betraying their contents: the old-penny stench of blood, mingled with odors alimentary and fecal. It was the fetor of the slaughterhouse, an olfactory assault. Stuccoed walls, pampered skin, costly fabrics: All were drenched in a syrup of exsanguination.

The smaller of the American's bodyguards felt a searing pain spread across his upper chest – a bullet had hit his shoulder and possibly pierced his lung. But consciousness remained. Through slightly parted eyelids, he took in the carnage in the room, the awful swagger of the keffiyeh-clad assailants. The man who called himself Ross McKibbin alone had not been shot, and, as he stared, evidently paralyzed by horror and disbelief, the gunmen roughly slammed a mud-colored canvas hood over his head. Then they hustled the startled American away, swarming back down the stairs.

The bodyguard, gasping for breath, as his poplin jacket slowly reddened with his blood, heard the low growl of the van's engine. Out the window he was able to catch a final glimpse of the American, his arms now bound together, roughly thrown into the back of the van – a van that now roared off into the dusty night.

The poplin-clad guard withdrew a small cellular phone from a concealed interior pocket. It was an instrument to be used only for emergencies: His controller at Consular Operations had been emphatic about it. His thick fingers slick with arterial blood, the man pressed a sequence of eleven digits.

'Harrison's Dry Cleaning,' a bored-seeming voice prompted on the other end.

The man gulped for air, trying to fill his injured lungs before he spoke. 'Pollux has been captured.'

'Come again?' the voice said. American intelligence needed him to repeat the message, perhaps for voiceprint authentication, and the asset in the poplin suit did so. There was no need to specify time and location; the phone itself contained a military-grade GPS device, providing not merely an electronic date-any-time stamp but a geolocation stamp as well, accurate to within nine feet in the horizontal plane. They knew where Pollux had been, therefore.

But where was he being taken?

Washington, D.C.

'Goddammit to hell!' the director of operations roared, his neck muscles bunching visibly.

The message had been received by a special branch of the INR, the U.S. State Department's Bureau of Intelligence and Research, and was relayed to the top of the operations org chart within sixty seconds. Consular Operations took pride in its organizational fluidity, a far cry from the sluggish and lumbering pace of the larger spy agencies. And the top managers at Cons Ops had made it clear that Pollux's work was a high priority.

Standing at the threshold of the D.O.'s office, a junior operations officer – café-au-lait skin; black, wavy hair that grew tight, dense, and low – flinched as if he himself had been berated.

'Shit!' the director of operations shouted, slamming his desk with a fist. Then he slid back his chair and stood up. A vein in his temple pulsed. His name was Gareth Drucker, and although he was staring at the junior ops man in the doorway, he was not actually seeing him. Not yet. Finally, his eyes did focus on the swarthy young staffer. 'What are the parameters here?' he asked, like an EMT verifying pulse-rate and blood-pressure stats.

'We just got the call in now.'

'"Now" meaning – ?'

'Maybe a minute and a half ago. By a recruit of ours who's in pretty bad shape himself. We thought you'd want to know ASAP.'

Drucker pressed an intercom button. 'Get Garrison,' he ordered an unseen assistant. Drucker was a lean five foot eight, and had been likened by one colleague to a sailboat: Through slight of build, he bulged when he got the wind in him. He had the wind in him now, and he was bulging – his chest, his neck, even his eyes, which seemed to loom behind his rectangular rimless glasses. His lips were pursed, growing short and thick like a prodded earthworm.

The junior ops officer stood aside as a burly man in his sixties strode into Drucker's office. Light from the early afternoon sun filtered through Venetian blinds, bathing the cheap government-issue furniture – a composite-topped desk, a badly veneered credenza, battered enameled-steel file cabinets, the faded velvet-covered chairs that had once been green and were still not quite any other hue. The nylon industrial carpeting, always having been the approximate color and texture of dirt, was a triumph of camouflage if not of style. A decade of foot traffic could scarcely detract from its appearance.

The burly man craned his neck around and squinted at the junior operations officer. 'Gomez, right?'

'Gomes,' the junior officer corrected. 'One syllable.'

'That'll fool 'em,' the older man said heavily, as if indulging a lapse of taste. He was Will Garrison, the Beirut operation's officer-in-charge.

The junior man's swarthy cheeks reddened slightly. 'I'll let you two talk.'

Garrison sought and obtained a glance of approval from Drucker. 'Stay here. We're both going to have questions.'

Gomes stepped into the office with a chastened, summoned-to-the-principal's expression. It took another impatient gesture from Drucker before he sat down on one of the green – somewhat green, *had* been green, more green than anything else – chairs.

'What's our move here?' Drucker asked Garrison.

'You get kicked in the balls, you double over. That's the move.'

'So we're screwed.' Drucker, the winds of outrage having gusted out, now looked as worn and battered as everything else in his office, and he was by far the newest thing in it, having held the position of D.O. for just four years.

'Royally screwed.' Will Garrison was perfectly cordial around Drucker, but he could not be called deferential. He had more years on him than any other senior Cons Ops manager, with an accumulated store of experience and connections that, just often enough, proved invaluable. The years had not mellowed him, Gomes knew. Garrison had always been a hard-ass by reputation, and if anything, he was only more so now. Around the shop, people liked to say that if there were a Mohs scale of hard-assedness, he'd pretty much top it out. He had a long memory, a short temper, a jut-jaw that jutted more when he was irate, and a temperament that started out at the setting 'Vaguely Pissed' and got worse from there.

When Gomes was in college, at Richmond, he once bought a used car that had a broken radio: The frequency dial was stuck on a heavy-metal station and the volume dial was stuck at the halfway point, so that it could only be turned louder. Aside from the heavy-metal part, Garrison reminded him of that car radio.

It was just as well that Drucker had little interest in any org-chart rituals of subservience. The bureaucratic nightmare, Gomes's colleagues all agreed, was the classic 'kiss-up, kick-down' kind of guy. Garrison might kick down, but he didn't kiss up, and Drucker might kiss up, but he didn't kick down. Somehow it worked.

'They took his shoes off, too,' Drucker said. 'Dumped on the side of the road. So long, GPS transponder. They're no fools.'

'Mother of Christ,' Garrison rumbled, and then, shooting a glance at Gomes, he charged, 'Who?'

'We don't know. Our man at the scene said – '

'What?' Garrison jumped.

Gomes felt like a suspect under interrogation. 'The asset said the captors barged in on a meeting that had been set up between – '

'I know all about the goddamn meeting,' Garrison snapped.

'Anyway, it was a hood-and-hustle job. The bad guys threw him into a van and disappeared.'

'The bad guys,' Garrison repeated, dyspeptic.

'We don't have much on the captors,' said Gomes. 'They were fast and they were brutal. Shot up everybody else in sight. Headdresses, automatic weapons.' Gomes shrugged. 'Arab militants. That's my opinion.'

Garrison stared at the young man the way a butterfly collector with a long needle stares at a specimen. 'Your opinion, huh?'

Drucker turned to the OIC. 'Let's get Oakeshott in here.' He barked the order over the intercom.

'I'm just saying,' Gomes continued, trying to keep the tremor out of his voice.

Garrison folded his arms on his chest. 'Our boy got snatched in Beirut. You venture Arab militants were involved.' He spoke with exaggerated precision. 'I bet you were Phi Beta Kappa in college.'

'I didn't do the Greeks,' Gomes muttered.

Garrison made a sibilant *pfut*. 'Goddamned greenhorn. Somebody gets snatched in Beijing, you'd announce you think a Chinaman did it. Some things go without saying. If I ask you what kind of van, don't tell me 'the kind with wheels.' *Com*-fucking-*prende?*'

'Dark green, dusty. Curtained windows. A Ford, our guy thought.'

A tall, reedy man with a thin face and a nimbus of graying hair stepped into the office. A herringbone tweed blazer draped loosely around his narrow torso. 'So whose operation was this?' asked Mike Oakeshott, the deputy director for analysis. He dropped himself on another of the more-green-than-not chairs, folding up his long, attenuated arms and spindle shanks like a Swiss Army knife.

'You know damn well whose,' Garrison growled. 'Mine.'

'You're the officer-in-charge,' Oakeshott said, with a knowing stare. 'Who designed it?'

The burly man shrugged. 'Me.'

The senior analyst just looked at him.

'Me and Pollux,' Garrison amended, with a concessive shrug. 'Pollux, mainly.'

'Another Tour de France of backpedaling, Will,' said Oakeshott. 'Pollux is a brilliant guy when it comes to operations. Not a guy for needless risk. So factor that in.' A glance at Drucker. 'What was the game plan?'

'He was undercover for four months,' Drucker said.

'Five months,' Garrison corrected. 'Legend was 'Ross McKibbin.' An American businessman who walked on the shady side of the street. Supposedly a go-between, scouting out laundering opportunities for narco-moohla.'

'That's the right kind of bait if you're after minnows. He wasn't.'

'Damn right,' Drucker said. 'Pollux had a slow-infiltration

strategy. He wasn't after the fish. He was looking for the other fisherman. The bait just got him a place on the wharf.'

'I get the picture,' Oakeshott said. 'It's George Habash revisited.'

The senior analyst did not need to elaborate. In the early 1970s, the Palestinian resistance leader George Habash, known as the Doctor, hosted a secret summit in Lebanon for terror organizations around the world, including ETA in Spain, the Japanese Red Army, the Baader-Meinhof gang, and the Iranian Liberation Front. In the years that followed, Habash's organization, and Lebanon generally, became a place where terrorists from all over came in search of armaments. The Czech-model Skorpion machine gun that was used to murder Aldo Moro had been acquired in the Lebanon arms mart. When the leader of Autonomia, the Italian revolutionary group, was arrested with two Strela missiles, the Popular Front for the Liberation of Palestine actually claimed the missiles as their property and requested their return. By the fall of the Berlin Wall, though, the Lebanon arms markets, the relay systems through which extremist organizations from around the world could buy and sell the tools of their deadly campaigns, had settled into a long decline.

No longer. As Jared Rinehart and his team had confirmed, the nexus was being revived: The circuits were buzzing again. The world had changed – only to change back. A ballyhooed new world order had grown old fast. The intel analysts recognized something else as well. Armed insurrection did not come cheap; the State Department's Bureau of Intelligence and Research estimated that the Red Brigade spent the equivalent of a hundred million dollars a year maintaining its five hundred members. Extremist groups today had extreme needs: plane travel, special weaponry, marine vessels for transport of munitions, the bribery of officialdom. It added up. Plenty of legitimate businessmen were desperate for a quick cash infusion. So were a small but significant number of organizations devoted to organized mayhem and destruction. Jared Rinehart –

Pollux – had devised a strategy to get into the buy-side of the equation.

'Espionage ain't bean bag,' Drucker mused softly.

Oakeshott nodded. 'Like I said, Pollux is as smart as they come. Just hope he didn't outsmart himself this time.'

'He was getting close, making good progress,' Garrison said. 'Want to get in tight with the banking community? Start making loans and they'll come around soon enough, just to take a look at you. Pollux knew that one of the guys at the meet was a banker, with fingers in a lot of pies. A rival, not a supplicant.'

'Sounds pretty elaborate, and pretty expensive,' Oakeshott said.

Garrison scowled. 'You don't get into the Ansari network by filling out an application.'

'The penny drops,' said Oakeshott. 'Let me see if I've got this right. The same night that Ansari's supposed to be in his citadel of evil, finalizing a three-hundred-million-dollar chain deal for midsized armaments – the same night that he's dotting t's, authorizing digital signatures, and stowing a shitload of cash in one of his numbered accounts – we've got Jared Rinehart, a.k.a. Ross McKibbin, sitting down with a roomful of greedy shopkeepers in Beirut. Then he's snatched by a band of towel-heads with Kalashnikovs and attitude. Same night. Anybody think that's just an accident?'

'We don't know what went down,' Drucker said, gripping the back of his chair as if to keep his balance. 'My gut says that he played the part of the rich American businessman too well for his own good. The guys who bundled him off probably figured he was worth a lot as a hostage.'

'As a U.S. intelligence agent?' Oakeshott sat up very straight.

'As a rich American businessman,' Drucker persisted. 'That's what I'm saying. Kidnapping is pretty common in Beirut, even now. These militant bands need cash. They're not getting it from the Sovs anymore. The Saudi royals have pulled back. The Syrians are turning into skinflints. My guess is that they took him for the guy he claimed to be.'

Oakeshott nodded slowly. 'Puts you all in a pretty pickle. Especially with what's happening on the Hill.'

'Christ,' Drucker muttered. 'And tomorrow I've got another meeting with that goddamn Senate oversight committee.'

'They know about the op?' Garrison asked.

'In general terms, yeah. Given the size of the budget item, there was no way around it. They're probably going to have questions. I sure as shit don't have any answers.'

'What kind of a budget item are we looking at?' Oakeshott asked.

A bead of sweat on Drucker's forehead pulsed along with the vein beneath it, glinting in the sun. 'Half a year means major sunk costs. Not to mention the manpower involved. We've got considerable exposure here.'

'Pollux's chances are going to be better the sooner we do something,' Gomes said earnestly, breaking in. 'In my opinion.'

'Listen to me, kid,' Garrison said with a baleful stare. 'Opinions are like assholes. Everybody's got one.'

'The Kirk Commission finds out what's gone down,' Drucker put in quietly, 'I'm going to have two. And I don't mean opinions.'

Despite the shafts of midday sun, the room had come to seem shadowed, gloomy.

'I don't mean to be out of line, but I'm confused,' Gomes said. 'They took one of our guys. A key player, too. I mean, Jesus, we're talking about Jared Rinehart. What are we going to do?'

For a long moment nobody spoke as Drucker turned toward his two senior colleagues and silently canvassed their opinions. Then he gave the junior officer a styptic look. 'We're going to do the hardest thing of all,' the director of operations said. 'Absolutely nothing.'

CHAPTER TWO

Andrea Bancroft took a hurried sip of bottled water. She felt self-conscious, as if everyone were staring at her. As a glance around the room confirmed, everyone *was* staring at her. She was in the middle of her presentation on the proposed deal with MagnoCom, widely seen as an up-and-coming player in the cable and telecom industry. The report was the biggest responsibility the twenty-nine-year-old securities analyst had been given so far, and she had put a great deal of time into the research. This wasn't just another backgrounder, after all; it was a deal in motion, with a tight deadline. She had dressed for the presentation, too, in her best Ann Taylor suit, with a blue-and-black plaid pattern that was bold without being forward.

So far, so good. Pete Brook, the chairman of Coventry Equity Group and her boss, was sending her approving nods from his seat in the back. People were interested in whether she had done good work, not in whether she was having a good-hair day. It was a thorough report she was delivering. A *very* thorough report, she had to admit. Her first few slides summarized the cash-flow situation, the various revenue streams and cost centers, the write-offs and capital expenditures, the fixed and variable expenses that the firm had incurred over the past five years.

Andrea Bancroft had been a junior analyst at Coventry Equity for two and a half years, a fugitive from grad school; to judge from Pete Brook's expression, she was in for a promotion. The qualifier 'junior' would be replaced with 'senior,' and her salary could very well hit six figures before the year was over. That was a lot more than her fellow grad students were going to see in academe any time soon.

'It's clear at a glance,' Andrea said, 'that you're looking an impressive ramp-up in revenue and in customer base.' A slide with the upward-sloped curve was projected onto a screen behind her.

Coventry Equity Group was, as Brook liked to put it, a matchmaker. Its investors had money; the markets had people who could put that money to good use. Undervalued opportunities were what they looked for, with a particular interest in PIPE opportunities – private investment in public equity, or situations where a hedge fund like theirs could acquire a bunch of common stock or equity-linked securities at a discount. Those typically involved distressed firms with a serious need for a fast cash infusion. MagnoCom had approached Coventry, and Coventry's investment-relations manager was excited by the prospect. It seemed in surprisingly good shape: MagnoCom, as its CEO explained, needed the cash not to weather a bad patch but to take advantage of an acquisition opportunity.

'Up, up, up,' Andrea said. 'You see that at a glance.'

Herbert Bradley, the plump-faced manager for new business, nodded with a look of pleasure. 'Like I said, this ain't no mail-order bride,' he said, looking around at his colleagues. 'It's a marriage made in heaven.'

Andrea clicked to the next side. 'Except what you can see at a glance isn't all there is to see. Start with this write-off list of so-called onetime expenses.' These were numbers that had been buried in a dozen different filings – but, when gathered together, the pattern was unmistakable and alarming. 'Once you drill down, you find that this firm has a history of disguising equity-for-debt swaps.'

A voice from the rear of the conference room. 'But why? Why would they need to?' asked Pete Brook, rubbing his nape with his left hand, as he did when he was agitated.

'That's the one-point-four-billion-dollar question, isn't it?' Andrea said. She hoped she was not coming across as cheeky. 'Let me show you something.' She projected a slide showing revenue intake, then superimposed another slide showing the number of customers acquired over the same period. 'These figures ought to be in a tandem harness. But they're not. They're both rising, yes. Only, they're not rising *together*. When one zags down in a quarter, the other might zag up. They're independent variables.'

'Jesus,' Brook said. She could tell from his crestfallen expression that he got it. 'They're shamming, aren't they?'

'Pretty much. The acquisition cost per household is killing them, because the service is so deeply discounted for new customers and nobody wants to renew at the higher rate. So what they've done is run two flattering figures up the flagpole: customer growth rates and revenue growth rate. Assumption is, we're going to look at the big picture and see cause and effect. But the revenue is smoke and mirrors, ginned up by equity swaps, and by hiding the money they're losing on growing the customer base through all these supposed onetime charges.'

'I can't believe it,' Brook said, slapping his forehead.

'Believe it. That debt is a big bad wolf. They just put it in a dress and a bonnet.'

Pete Brook turned to Bradley. 'And they had you saying, 'What lovely big teeth you have, Grandma.''

Bradley fixed Andrea Bancroft with a stern gaze. 'You sure about this, Miss Bancroft?'

'Afraid so,' she said. 'You know, I used to do history, right? So I figured the history of the company might shed some light on things. I looked way back, back before the DyneCom merger. Even then, the CEO had a habit of robbing Peter to pay Paul. New bottle, old wine. MagnoCom has a business plan from hell, but the financial engineers they hired are pretty brilliant, in a twisted way.'

'Well, let me tell you something,' Bradley said in a level voice. 'Those pissers met their match. You just saved my goddamn ass, not to mention the firm's bottom line.' He grinned and started applauding, having calculated that a quick surrender to the winning argument was the better part of valor.

'It would have all come out on the Form Eight-K,' Andrea said as she gathered her papers and started to walk back to her seat.

'Yeah, after the deal was inked,' Brook interjected. 'Okay, ladies and germs, what have we learned today?' He looked around at the others in the room.

'Get Andrea to perform your due diligence,' one of the traders said with a snort.

'It's easy to lose money in cable,' another one cracked.

'Give it up to Bangin' Bancroft,' called out another would-be wit, this one a more senior analyst who hadn't caught the flimflam in his first pass through the PIPE proposal.

As the meeting started to break up, Brook came over to her. 'Solid work, Andrea,' he said. 'More than solid. You've got a rare talent. You look at a stack of documents that looks completely in order, and you know when something's off.'

'I didn't *know* – '

'You sensed it. Then, even better, you worked your ass off to *prove* it. There was a lot of ditch-digging behind that presentation. I bet your spade banged against bedrock more than once. But you kept digging, because you knew you'd find something.' The tone was of assessment as much as commendation.

'Something like that,' Andrea admitted, tingling slightly.

'You're the real deal, Andrea. I can always tell.'

As he turned to speak to one of the portfolio managers, one of the secretaries approached her, clearing her throat. 'Miss Bancroft,' she said. 'A call you might want to take.'

Andrea floated back to her desk, hydroplaning on relief and pride. She *had* kicked ass, just as Pete Brook said. His look of gratitude was genuine, and so was his praise afterward; there was no doubt about that.

'Andrea Bancroft,' she said into the handset.

'My name is Horace Linville,' said the man who called, needlessly. That much was on the call slip. 'I'm an attorney with the Bancroft Foundation.'

All at once Andrea felt herself wilting. 'And what can I do for you, Mr. Linville?' she said without warmth.

'Well . . .' The lawyer paused. 'Mostly it's about what we can do for you.'

'I'm afraid I'm not interested,' Andrea replied, almost testily.

'I don't know if you're aware that a cousin of yours, Ralph Bancroft, recently passed away,' Linville persisted.

'I wasn't,' Andrea replied, her voice softening. 'I'm sorry to hear that.' Ralph Bancroft? The name was only vaguely familiar.

'There's a bequest,' he said. 'Of a sort. Triggered by his death. You'd be the recipient.'

'He left me money?' The lawyer's elliptical formulations were beginning to irritate her.

Linville paused. 'The family trusts are quite intricate, as I'm sure you appreciate.' He paused again, and then lurched into an elaboration, as if aware that what he said might have been taken the wrong way. 'Ralph Bancroft had been a member of the foundation trustees, and his passing leaves a vacancy. The charter specifies eligibility, and the percentage of members that must belong to the Bancroft family.'

'I don't consider myself a Bancroft, really.'

'You're a trained historian, no? You'll want to be fully informed of the antecedent circumstances before you make any final decisions. But I'm afraid we're on a very tight schedule here. I'd like to drop by and present these details to you formally and in person. Apologies for the short notice, but it's an unusual situation, as you'll see. I can come to your house at half-past six.'

'Fine,' Andrea said, her voice hollow. 'That's fine.'

Horace Linville turned out to be a wren-drab man with a pear-shaped head, sharp features, and an unfortunate ratio of scalp to hair. A driver had taken him to Andrea Bancroft's modest Cape Cod–style house in the Connecticut town of Carlyle, and waited outside as he entered. Linville brought with him a metal-sided briefcase with a combination lock. Andrea led him into the living room and noticed that he glanced at the seat of the armchair before sitting on it, as if examining it for cat hairs.

His presence made her feel oddly self-conscious about her home, a place she had on a twelve-month rental, in a not-so-expensive neighborhood of a generally somewhat pricey town. Carlyle was one or two train stops too far from Manhattan on Metro North to make it a proper bedroom community, but some of its inhabitants did the commute. She had always taken some measure of pride in her Carlyle address. Now she thought about what her place must seem like to someone from the Bancroft Foundation. It must seem . . . small.

'Like I said, Mr. Linville, I don't really consider myself a Bancroft.' She had seated herself on the sofa, at the other side of the coffee table.

'That's not quite to the point. By the foundation's guidelines and charter, a Bancroft is exactly what you are. And with Ralph Bancroft's passing – with the departure of any member of the board – a series of eventualities are triggered. There's a . . . disbursement that accompanies this responsibility. A bequest, if you like. That's how it's always been done at the foundation.'

'Let's put history aside. I work in finance, as you know. We like things to be clear and specific. What's the specific nature of the bequest?'

A slow blink. 'Twelve million dollars. Is that specific enough?'

The words vanished like smoke rings in the wind. *What* had he said? 'I'm not following.'

'With your authorization, I can wire those twelve million dollars into your account by the end of the banking day tomorrow.' He paused. 'Does that make things clearer?' He removed a set of documents from his briefcase, arrayed them on the table.

Andrea Bancroft was dizzy, almost queasy. 'What do I have to do?' she choked out.

'Serve as a trustee of one of the most admired charitable and philanthropic organizations in the world. The Bancroft Foundation.' Horace Linville let a moment of silence elapse yet again. 'Not everyone would find this terribly onerous.

Some might even regard it as an honor and a privilege.'

'I'm stunned,' she said finally. 'I don't know what to say.'

'I hope it's not inappropriate for me to make a suggestion,' the lawyer replied. 'Say yes.'

Washington, D.C.

Will Garrison ran a hand through his steel-gray hair; in repose, his basset eyes and jowly face might have seemed kindly. Belknap knew better. Anyone who had encountered the man did. There was an earth-science logic to it: The hardest rock was born of pressure over time.

'What the hell happened in Rome, Castor?'

'You got my report,' Belknap said.

'Don't bullshit me,' the older man warned. He stood up and twisted closed the blinds that hung over the interior glass wall of his office. The room had the bolted-down look of a ship captain's office: no loose articles in sight, everything squared away, secured. A tidal wave could have rocked the office and shifted nothing. 'We've sunk God knows how much in resources and personnel into three separate Ansari ops. The directive was clear. We get inside, we see how it works, we follow the tentacles where they go.' A display of tea-colored teeth. 'Except that wasn't good enough for you, was it? Instant gratification takes too long, huh?'

'I don't know what the hell you're talking about,' Belknap replied, wincing involuntarily. It hurt when he breathed: He had cracked a rib when he vaulted over the brick wall outside the villa. His left ankle had been strained and sent up shooting pains when it had to bear any weight. But there had been no time even for a visit to a medic. Hours after his escape from Ansari's men, he was in the Rome airport, boarding the first commercial flight to Dulles that was available. It would have taken longer to secure transport from one of the U.S. military bases in Livorno or Vicenza. Belknap barely gave himself time to brush his teeth and finger-comb his hair before he raced to Cons Ops headquarters on C Street.

'You've got brass ones, I'll give you that.' Garrison returned to his chair. 'Showing up here like this with that concerned expression on your face.'

'I'm not here for tea and cookies, okay?' Belknap replied testily. 'Start talking sense.' Though he and Garrison had a reasonably functional working relationship, they had never clicked personally.

Garrison's chair squeaked as he leaned back. 'The regs – they must annoy the hell out of you. You're like Gulliver and the little people are tying you down with dental floss, right?'

'Goddammit, Will –'

'From your perspective, the shop must be getting more tight-assed every year,' the aging intelligence officer went on. 'The way you figured it, you were just serving justice, right? Instant, the way you take your coffee.'

Belknap learned forward. He could smell the Barbasol shaving cream Garrison used, a sharp menthol fragrance. 'I hustled my ass over here because I thought I'd get some answers. What happened yesterday wasn't in anybody's goddamn playbook that I know of. Suggests another factor's at work. Maybe you know something I haven't been privy to.'

'You're good,' Garrison said. 'We could have you fluttered and see just how good.' *Fluttered*: subjected to a polygraph examination – to a lie detector.

'What the hell, Garrison?' Belknap felt his guts beginning to curdle.

Pretend solicitude barely masked a smirk as Garrison pressed on. 'You've got to remember who you really are. The rest of us sure do. Times change. It can be a bitch to keep up. Think I don't know that? These days, James Bond himself would find himself remanded to Alcoholics Anonymous, probably forced to join some program for sexual addiction, too. I've been around the block longer than you, so I remember. The spy game used to be the Wild West. Now it's the Mild West. Used to be a sport for the jungle cats. Now Puss-in-Boots is running the goddamn show, am I right?'

'What are you talking about?' The turn in the conversation was making Belknap's skin crawl.

'I'm just saying I can see where you're coming from. After what happened, a lot of people would have lost it. Even someone without your history.'

'My history is just that. History.'

'Like the man says, there are no second acts in American life. No second acts, and no intermissions, either.' Garrison held a thick file a few feet above his desk and with a dramatic flourish let it drop. It made a smacking sound as it landed. 'Do I need to cite chapter and verse? A temper is what they used to call what you've got. Now they call it a rage-management issue.'

'You're talking about just a few episodes.'

'Yeah, and John Wilkes Booth only shot a man once. But it was a doozy.' Another tea-colored smile. 'Remember a Bulgarian pisser named Drakulic? He still can't sit right.'

'Eight girls under the age of twelve suffocated to death in his trailer because their families were a little short on the money he was demanding to smuggle them into the West. I saw those corpses. I saw the bloody scratches on the inside of the trailer from when those girls ran out of air. The fact that Drakulic is still sitting at all is a tribute to some goddamn *supreme* self-control.'

'You *lost* it. You were supposed to be collecting information on the trafficking techniques, not playing avenging angel. Remember a Colombian gentleman named Juan Calderone? We do.'

'He had tortured five of our informants to death, Garrison. Melted their faces with a goddamn acetylene torch. Did it personally.'

'We could have put pressure on him. He might have made a deal. He could have had usable intelligence.'

'Trust me.' A quick, wintry grin. 'He didn't.'

'That wasn't your call to make.'

The field agent shrugged stonily. 'You don't actually know what happened to Calderone. All you have is your conjecture.'

'We could have done an inquest. Conducted an investigation. It was my decision to let sleeping dogs . . . die.'

Another shrug. 'I made my decision. You made yours. What's there to talk about?'

'What I'm saying is that there's a pattern. I've let you off the hook several times. We all have. We've let things slide because you've got gifts we value. Like your buddy Jared always said, you're the Hound. But now I'm thinking that we've made a mistake letting you out of the kennel. What happened in Rome might have felt right to you, but it was wrong. Very wrong.'

Belknap just stared at the seamed face of his superior officer. In the harsh light of the halogen desk lamp, Garrison's cheeks looked quilted. 'Start making sense, Will. What the hell are you trying to say?'

'You colored outside the lines for the last time,' said the aging manager, rumbling like a distant thunderstorm, 'when you killed Khalil Ansari.'

Horace Linville watched Andrea closely as she read through the documents; whenever she lifted her eyes from the page they seemed to catch his. Paragraphs were given over to the definition of terms, the detailing of contingencies. But the upshot was that the foundation's charter mandated that a specified percentage of the board had to be members of the family, and so the sudden vacancy was to be filled by Andrea. The bequest was contingent upon her acceptance. An additional honorarium would come with her service as a trustee of the family-run foundation, a sum that would escalate with each year she served.

'The foundation has an extremely impressive record,' Linville said after a while. 'As a trustee you'll share a responsibility to make sure it continues to in the future. If you think you're prepared for it.'

'How does anybody prepare for something like this?'

'Being a Bancroft is a good start.' Linville looked at her over half-moon glasses and gave her a lipless smile.

'A Bancroft,' she echoed.

He held out the pen. He had not just come to explain; he had come for her signature. In triplicate. *Say yes.*

After he left, the signed document neatly tucked into his briefcase, Andrea found herself pacing, giddy yet apprehensive. She had gained an unimaginable prize, and yet felt weirdly bereft. There was logic to the illogic: Her life – the life that she had known, had struggled to shape – would change beyond recognition, and there was loss in that.

Her eyes darted around the living room again. She had gussied up the Ikea lounger by putting a nice Berber weave on it. It looked posh, even though she had picked it up for a song at a flea market. The coffee table from Pier 1 looked like it cost at least twice what she paid for it. The wicker furniture – well, you could find that sort of thing in expensive houses in Nantucket, no?

Never mind how Horace Linville saw it. How did *she* now see it? She'd told herself she was going for shabby chic. But, regarded without sentiment, maybe it really looked just shabby. *Twelve million dollars.* This morning, she had three thousand dollars in her savings account. From the perspective of a financial professional – as a trade executed by a fund, as the valuation of a proposed deal, as a tranche of convertible debentures – twelve million wasn't much. But as an actual chunk of cash in her actual bank account? It almost didn't compute. She couldn't even say the amount out loud. When she tried, speaking to Horace Linville, Esq., she started giggling, and had to choke it off with a pretend attack of coughing. *Twelve million dollars.* The sum now ran through her mind, like one of those catchy jingles one couldn't drive from one's head.

A few hours ago, it was a source of satisfaction that she earned a salary of eighty thousand dollars – and had hopes to hit six figures before long. And now? She couldn't fathom the sum. Not in the small private world of Andrea Bancroft. A stray fact drifted into her mind: The entire population of Scotland was about five million. She could – one of the silly thoughts that flitted through her consciousness like flies –

give a couple of boxes of raisins to every single inhabitant of Scotland.

She remembered freezing up when Linville placed the fountain pen in her hand. The long moments that elapsed before she inked her name to the documents. Why had it been so hard?

She continued to pace, numb, exhilarated, and strangely agitated. Why had she found it so hard to say yes? Linville's words returned to her: *A Bancroft* . . .

Precisely what she had spent her life trying not to be. Which wasn't to say the renunciation required great effort. When her mother severed ties with Reynolds Bancroft after seven years of marriage, she found herself not only a single mother of a young girl but a sudden outsider. She had been warned, hadn't she? The prenuptial agreement – something the family attorneys had insisted upon and drafted – meant that, as the instigator of divorce proceedings, she would be left with nothing at all. The agreement would be enforced as a matter of principle and, perhaps, her mother once darkly surmised, as a warning to others. The welfare of mother and daughter received not a moment's consideration from the clan. Yet the divorcée had no regrets.

The marriage to Reynolds Bancroft wasn't just unhappy, it was something worse: It was embittering. Laura Parry was a small-town girl with big-town looks, but those looks never brought the happiness they promised. The young swell who had romanced her soured after their marriage, feeling obscurely trapped, even gulled, as if her pregnancy had been some sort of snare. He became petulant, cold, and then emotionally abusive. Their infant daughter he regarded as little more than a noisy inconvenience. He drank heavily, and Laura began to drink, too, at first in a futile effort to join with him, and then in an equally futile attempt to defend herself. *Some fruit ripens on the vine, honey*, she used to tell Andrea. *Some fruit just shrivels up.*

As a rule, though, she simply preferred not to discuss the subject. Before long, Andrea's memories of her father became shrouded in fog. Reynolds, a first cousin of the family patriarch, might have been a bad seed, but when his kin closed ranks, Laura came to loathe the Bancroft clan as a whole.

It had always been a matter of loyalty to her mother to be a Bancroft who was not a Bancroft. Once in a while, in the public high school outside Hartford she attended, and, with greater frequency, in college, somebody would raise an eyebrow at Andrea's surname and ask her whether she was 'one of *those* Bancrofts.' She would always deny it. 'Different,' she would say. 'Completely different.' It felt like the truth, anyway, and it felt like betrayal to embrace the wealth that her mother had spurned. 'Precious bane' was what her mother always called it, meaning the birthright of the Bancrofts. Meaning, well, the money. When she walked away from Reynolds, she walked away from a whole way of life, from a world of luxury and indulgence. What would she think of Andrea's decision? Those triplicate signatures? That *yes*?

Andrea shook her head, scolding herself. It wasn't the same decision. Her mother had to escape a bad marriage, or lose her soul. Maybe the fates were somehow making it up to her, giving back to one generation what was taken from another. Maybe it would help her *find* her soul.

Besides, though Reynolds Bancroft might have been a son of a bitch, the Bancroft Foundation itself was undoubtedly a very, very good thing. And what of the paterfamilias behind it, its strategist and chief: Wasn't he a Bancroft, too? However much he fought the limelight, the facts were the facts. Paul Bancroft wasn't just a great philanthropist; he was one of the great minds of postwar America – a onetime academic prodigy, a major moral theorist, a man who had truly turned principles into practices. A clan that had a Paul Bancroft among its number had ample reason for pride. If *that* was a way to be a Bancroft, well, she could only aspire to be worthy of it.

Andrea's mind, and mood, cycled up and down. She caught a glimpse of herself in a mirror and her mind suddenly filled with the image of her mother's wan, drawn face. Andrea's last glimpse of her before the car accident.

Maybe this wasn't a good time to be alone. She still felt raw from her recent breakup with Brent Farley. She ought to be celebrating, not dwelling on painful memories. Friends for dinner – that's what the occasion required. She and her friends always talked about doing things spontaneously; for once, why not try it? She made a couple of phone calls, made a quick shopping trip, set the table for four. *Très intime*. The ghosts would be dispelled soon enough. It was only natural that she was having a hard time adjusting to the news. But – *Christ* – if this wasn't a cause for celebration, what was?

Todd Belknap leaped from his seat. 'Are you shitting me?'

'Please,' Garrison drawled. 'How convenient that the mark dies just before you managed to get the surveillance devices online. So there's no record of what really went down.'

'Why the hell would I have killed him?' Belknap stiffened with outrage. 'I'm in the asswipe's private office, I'm about to wire up the cockpit for the whole goddamn network. You're not thinking.'

'No, *you* weren't thinking. You were blinded by rage.'

'Yeah? And why's that?'

'Our vices are always the flip sides of our virtues. At the butt-end of love and loyalty you find blind, destructive rage.' Garrison's cold gray eyes probed Belknap like a speculum moving through his innards. 'I don't know how you heard or who leaked it to you, but you found out what happened to Jared. You figured Ansari was behind it. And you lost it.'

Belknap reacted as if he had been slapped. 'What happened to Jared?'

'Like you don't know?' Garrison's voice dripped with scorn. 'Your asshole buddy had just been kidnapped in Beirut. So you snuffed out the guy you took to be responsible. A rage reaction. Blew the whole operation as a result. Just your speed, too.'

'Jared was . . . ?'

Pouchy gray eyes high-beamed Belknap. 'You're going to pretend you hadn't known? You two were always connected like you had some invisible hookup between you. Two tin cans on a taut string, no matter where on the planet you were. Pollux and Castor – there's a reason the ops boys always called you that. Twin heroes of ancient Rome.'

Belknap found himself speechless, paralyzed, encased in ice. He had to remind himself to breathe.

'Except, as I recall, only Pollux was immortal,' the burly manager went on. 'Best you keep that in mind.' Now he tilted his head back. 'And here's something else to keep in mind. We don't know that Jared's abduction had anything to do with Ansari. Could have been any one of a dozen militant orgs operating in the Bekaa Valley region. Any of them could have mistaken him for the man he was playing. But rage doesn't reflect, does it? You acted on impulse, and as a result you've put thousands of operational man-hours into jeopardy.'

Belknap struggled to contain himself. 'Jared was closing in on the financiers of terror. He was working the buy-side.'

'And you were working the sell-side. Until you trashed the operation.' The veteran's quilted cheeks formed a sneer.

'Are you deaf as well as dumb?' Belknap snapped. 'I'm saying he was closing in when they did the smash-and-grab. That means something. You're telling me you believe in coincidences? I never knew a spy who did.' He broke off. 'Forget about me. We need to talk about Jared. About how to get him back. You can run all the inquests and assessments you want. All I'm saying is, hold off for another week.'

'So we can find out what else you can wreck? You don't get it. You're exactly what this organization can't afford anymore. It needs to be about the work, not about you, but you're always making it about your own dramas, aren't you?'

A surge of disgust. '*Listen* to yourself, for Chrissakes – '

'No, you listen to me. Like I say, it's a whole new era. We got the goddamn Kirk Commission shoving a gloved finger up our ass. The cost-benefit equation doesn't run in your favor any longer. I can't even begin to tot up the damage you did with your half-cocked Roman revenge drama. So here's the deal. You're on immediate administrative suspension.

We're going to start an inquest, following all the rules and regs. I suggest you give the internal assessors your complete cooperation. You play nice and we work out a severance. Mess with us and I'll see you get what's coming to you. That could mean charges, penalties, even jail. Everything's going to be by the book.'

'What book? Kafka's *The Trial*?'

'You're out, Geronimo. For good, this time. Improvisation, instinct, that legendary nose of yours, all that good shit – you made a career of it. But the world has changed and you forgot to change with it. We're looking for a silver bullet, not a goddamn wrecking ball. Nobody here can trust your judgment. Which means we can't trust *you*.'

'You've got to let me do what I do. Send me out, goddammit. I'm needed here.'

'Like fur on flounder, pal.'

'Right now you need to flood the zone. Send out anybody who's not nailed down. You ferret things out quicker when you've got more ferrets.' He stopped. 'You said Bekaa Valley. You think it was one of Faraad's paramilitary groups?'

'Possibly,' the officer-in-charge said, almost sullenly. 'Nothing's been ruled out.'

A shiver ran down Belknap's spine. The members of the Faraad al-Hasani group had a reputation for extraordinary viciousness. He recalled the photographs of the last American they kidnapped, an executive from an international hotel chain. The images were etched in acid.

'You remember what happened to Waldo Ellison?' Belknap prompted in a low voice. 'You saw the pictures, same as me. There were soldering-iron burns over fifty percent of his body. His testicles were found in his stomach, partly digested – they forced him to swallow them. They'd even whittled off most of his nose with a box cutter. They took their time, Will. Slow and steady. That's what it was like for Waldo Ellison. That's what it's going to be like for Jared Rinehart. There's no time to waste. Don't you realize that? Don't you realize what's in store for him?'

Garrison paled, but his resolve was unshaken. 'Of course

I do.' A long moment passed before he added, freezingly, 'I'm just sorry it wasn't you instead.'

'Listen, damn you, you've got a problem.'

'I know. I'm looking at it.' Garrison shook his head slowly. 'Put your shit in boxes or I'll put *you* in a box. Cartons or curtains – your choice. But you're out of here.'

'*Focus*, Will! What we need to be talking about is how we're going to exfiltrate Jared. The odds are good that a ransom demand is going to arrive, maybe sometime today.'

'I'm sorry, but we're not playing it that way,' the manager said tonelessly. 'Decision is, we stand pat.'

Belknap leaned in close. He could smell Garrison's shaving cream again. 'You've got to be joking.'

Garrison jutted his jaw like a weapon. 'Listen up, you asshole. Jared spent the better part of a year creating the character of Ross McKibbin. Some of his best handiwork went into this. And thousands of man-hours went into supporting the op. Reality check: It would be totally out of character for Ross McKibbin's employers to take any of the measures you've suggested. Drug merchants don't pay ransom. That's for starters. And they don't mobilize a hundred operatives to sweep Bekaa Valley for a misplaced emissary. We do anything like that, we've just announced that Ross McKibbin is a U.S. cat's-paw. Which not only endangers Jared Rinehart, but all the assets we had to use in order to backstop the legend. Drucker and I looked at the same facts, came to the same conclusion. If Ross McKibbin is burned, dozens of other assets and operatives are going to be jeopardized. Not to mention an operational budget upwards of three million dollars. A wise man once said, 'Don't just do something, stand there.' You need to size up the situation before you blunder in. That's something you've never really understood. In this case, the right thing to do isn't whatever guns-blazing bullshit you're imagining.'

Belknap fought to dampen the rage that began to roil within him. 'So your plan of action is . . . no plan of action?'

Garrison met his gaze. 'Maybe you've been on active deployment too long. Tell you one thing. I lived through the old Church Committee hearings from the early seventies. Word on the street is, this new Kirk investigation is going to make those hearings look like a tongue bath. Everybody in the intel community is walking on eggshells right now.'

'I can't believe you're talking about Washington bullshit at a time like this.'

'Field agents never get it. The office is just another field. Capitol Hill is just another field. Battles are won and lost here, too. If a budget requisition gets crossed out, an operation gets crossed out. The last thing we need is news of any operational irregularities to make the rounds. The last thing we need is you.'

Belknap listened to the parade of rationalizations with a visceral sense of revulsion. Operational man-hours, budgetary allocations – that was what was behind the 'prudence' that the O.I.C. was urging. The vaunted concern with security and safety was a smokescreen, nothing more. Garrison had been a manager so long that he could no longer distinguish between lives and budget lines. 'You make me ashamed to be in the same profession as you,' Belknap said, numbly.

'There's nothing we can do that wouldn't make things worse, goddammit!' Garrison's eyes sparked and glinted. 'Can you get past yourself for a single goddamn moment? You think Drucker likes the idea of standing back? You think *I* want to be sitting here with my thumb up my ass? None of the folks here do. Not an easy decision to make, for any of us. All the same, there's unity of command on this one.' He let his gaze drift off to the middle distance. 'I don't expect you to see the bigger picture, but we can't afford to act. Not just now.'

A fury whipped through Todd Belknap's very being like a cyclone scouring across a blighted plain. *You mess with Pollux, you'll have Castor on your ass.*

With a sudden movement of his arm, Belknap swept the lamp and telephone console off Garrison's desk. 'Do you even *believe* your goddamn excuses? Because Jared deserves better from us. And he's going to get it.'

'It's over,' Garrison said quietly.

Rage gave Belknap strength, the way it always did, and he would need all the strength he could get. Jared Rinehart was the finest man he had ever known, a man who had saved his life more than once. The time had come to return the favor. Belknap knew that Jared was probably being tortured even now, that his odds of survival were dwindling with every passing day, every passing hour. His very musculature stiffened, a resistance of the soul that had become a resistance of the body, as he stormed out of the federal building. A swirl of emotion filled the empty core of his being – fury, determination, and something uncomfortably close to bloodlust. *It's over*, Garrison had declared. *It's over*, Drucker had declared. Belknap knew how wrong his superior officers were.

It had only just begun.

CHAPTER THREE

Rome

There were procedures to be followed, and Yusef Ali – still charged with the security of the establishment on via Angelo Masina – followed them, reporting in regularly to the cramped communications room situated at a rear corner of the villa's second floor. A series of messages were relayed to him, in various idioms, and with various degrees of urgency. Yet the gist was plain: The late master himself had masters, masters until now unseen. The establishment was now theirs. The security breach had to be repaired, the weak links replaced. Failure – and there *had* been failure – was to be punished.

The administration of it would be Yusef Ali's task. Their expectations of him were high; he would need to take care that he did not disappoint them. He assured them that he would not. His life had not been that of someone averse to risk, but neither was he one for taking foolish chances.

Yusef Ali had been reared in a Tunisian village that was only a hundred miles from the coastline of Sicily. Fishing vessels could make the passage across the Cap Bon from Tunisia to Agrigento or Trapani in a morning, depending on the currents. Italian lire were as common as dinars in the coastal settlements near Tunis. From an early age, Yusef spoke Italian as well as Arabic, negotiating prices for his father's catch with the Sicilian fishmongers. He was in his mid-teens when he learned that there were even more lucrative forms of import and export for someone whose discretion could be counted upon. Italy had a small-arms industry, was one of the largest exporters of pistols, rifles, and ammunition in the world; in Tunisia, there were eager and adept middlemen who transshipped such weaponry to areas where the demand was surging – perhaps Sierra Leone one year, Congo or Mauritania another. The smuggling obviated end-use certificates and the other feckless bureaucratic attempts to limit the arms trade. The movement of arms could no more be halted by such regulations than the ocean's currents could be arrested by drawing lines on a map. It was a matter of linking supply and demand – and North African merchants had for centuries taken advantage of Tunisia's ports to make a specialty of it, whether the valuable in question was salt, silk, or gunpowder.

Yusef Ali himself was something of an exported valuable. He had first distinguished himself when he repelled a half-dozen brigands who had sought to hijack a shipment of Beretta handguns he was helping shepherd to an inland depot near Béja. Yusef was part of a team of four young men entrusted with the cargo, and he swiftly realized that at least two of his fellows were complicit in the attack – had provided information to the brigands, doubtless for cash, and were only pantomiming resistance when they arrived with guns drawn. Yusef, for his part, pantomimed acquiescence, opening the trailer for the brigands, opening a crate as if to demonstrate that the goods were what they had come for, before abruptly turning his own automatic pistol on them. They fell like those small brown birds, the pipits and shrikes, on which Yusef had practiced his marksmanship during long afternoons in the dusty countryside.

After Yusef gunned down the brigands, he leveled his pistol at the turncoats, and could read their treachery on their panicked faces. Then he gunned each of them down as well.

The delivery was made without further incident. And Yusef Ali found that he had made a name for himself. When he was in his early twenties, he found himself with new employers: Like so many small-scale arms merchants around the world, they were incorporated into a larger and well-organized network. To join the network was to prosper; to resist it was to be destroyed. Pragmatists to the core, these merchants found the choice was not a difficult one to make.

Their higher-ups would exert their privileged status by commandeering from them persons whose particular talents they required. Yusef Ali came from a tribal community in which such feudal devotion was commonplace; he accepted the training he received with gratitude; he accepted the greater responsibilities with which he was entrusted with grave sobriety. Besides, his employer's sense of discipline came ridged with an outsized degree of cruelty. Having taken a position in Ansari's own household, Yusef had seen what punishments had befallen others who stumbled in the course of their responsibilities. At times he had helped carry them out.

Indeed, he was doing so again. The young guard who had been drugged and stowed in a cupboard – his own demonstrable lack of vigilance could be described as nothing other than failure. Yusef had asked him to recount precisely how he had been overpowered, again and again. The guard, though humbled, had denied that he had done wrong. He had to be made an example of.

Now Yusef watched as the young man dangled with his feet just a few feet from the ground, the hawser around his neck securely attached to a beam in the interrogation chamber, his hands corded tightly together. *Better you than me*, the Tunisian thought mordantly. The young guard was strangling very slowly, his face a deep scarlet, a faint burble coming from his mouth, a feeble flow of air forced through compressed flesh and accumulating drool. With distaste, Yusef noticed the dark patch of wetness at the man's groin. Though the man's neck was broken, death would not come soon. He had at least another two hours of conscious life remaining to him. Time to contemplate his deeds and misdeeds. Time to contemplate his dereliction of duty.

Others would come for the body in the morning, Yusef knew. And they would see. They would see that Yusef did not countenance failure. They would see that Yusef would maintain the highest standards. Examples would be made. Weak links would be replaced.

Yusef Ali would make sure of it.

Andrea poured herself a glass of wine and went upstairs to change. She just wanted to feel normal. But 'normal' was proving elusive. She felt . . . like Alice in Wonderland, having swallowed a potion and grown enormous, because the Cape Cod now seemed like a dollhouse, the rooms shrinking around her. In the hall outside her bedroom she stumbled on a sneaker, one of a pair of unlaced men's running shoes. *Goddamn Brent Farley*, she thought, seething for a few seconds. *Well, good goddamn riddance.* The thought would have been more satisfying if she had been the one to call it quits, but that was not how the relationship played out.

Brent was a few years older than she was, another finance guy out of Greenwich, a vice president for sales development at a specialty reinsurance firm. He was silver-tongued, deep-voiced, ambitious – a man who dressed well, played squash as if his life depended on the outcome, checked his personal portfolios several times a day, and would browse his BlackBerry during what was meant to be a romantic date. They had a blow-out fight about that about a week before. 'I think I'd have a better chance of getting your attention if I were texting you right now,' she'd complained at a restaurant. All she wanted was an apology. She never got it. Instead, the argument escalated, with Brent making references to her 'small-time' mentality; she was, he said, a 'downer.' Methodically, he gathered up his things from her house, loaded them into his black Audi sports car, and drove off. No door slamming, nothing flung, no squealing tires in the driveway. He wasn't even angry, not really – that was the hardest thing to take. He was dismissive and contemptuous, yes, but he wasn't really angry. She wasn't worthy of anger, it seemed. Too *small-time*, obviously.

She opened her closet. Had Brent left anything here? Not that she could see. Her gaze settled on her own clothes, and she felt something small and wistful well up. Hanging neatly from padded hangers were her business suits, evening dresses, weekend wear, every hue of blue and peach and beige.

Her wardrobe – not extensive but well-chosen – was always a point of pride with her. She was an aficionado of discount outlets like Filenes Basement, could spot under-priced item of upscale apparel like a heron spotting a fish. And there were often bargains to be had, as she'd counseled friends, if you weren't a snob about labels. A lot of those bridge-collection brands, like Evan Picone and Bandolino, could bring out something truly handsome, almost indistinguishable from the outfits they were copying. *Guess what I paid for this* – it was a game she and her girlfriends used to play when they weren't complaining about work or men, and Andrea was a champ of it. The cream silk blouse that she got for thirty bucks? Suzanne Muldower had yelped; she'd seen something identical at Talbot's for a hundred and ten. Andrea now fingered the fabrics wistfully, the way she used to page through her high-school yearbook, amused and embarrassed by who she used to be: the pretension, the innocence, the freckles.

Suzanne Muldower – a friend since the age of eleven, the one who had known her longest – was the first to arrive. The invitation was last-minute, but Muldower didn't have much to cancel: just a double date with her microwave and DVD player, she admitted. Melissa Pratt – a willowy blonde with what Andrea privately thought of as a downtown attitude, and slowly ebbing hopes for an acting career – arrived a few minutes later, with her boyfriend of the past eight months, Jeremy Lemuelson, a chunky little guy who worked as a civil engineer in Hartford, owned two vintage Stratocasters, and, because he painted in his spare time, considered himself something of an artist.

Dinner was nothing fancy, as she warned: a pot of fettuccine with some store-bought pesto, a few side dishes she got at the prepared foods counter at the Carlyle Market – and a big bottle of Vouvray.

'So what's the four-one-one?' Suzanne asked, after tasting the pasta and making the obligatory noises of admiration. 'You said we were celebrating tonight.' She turned to Melissa. 'And I told her, 'Let me be the judge of that.''

'Brent bought you a ring, didn't he?' Melissa put in. She

shot Suzanne an I-told-you-so look, premature in victory.

'Brent? *Please.*' Andrea clucked, smiling beneath slitted eyes. Melissa and she had shared an apartment when Andrea was in grad school, and even then she took a sisterly interest in Andrea's romantic successes and failures.

'You got a promotion?' Suzanne's turn.

'A bun in the oven?' Melissa looked concerned.

'Garlic bread, actually,' Andrea said. 'Smells good, doesn't it?' She trotted out to the kitchen and brought it to the table, a little crisper than ideal.

'I already know. You won the lottery.' Jeremy's sardonic contribution. His cheek was swollen with half-chewed food, like a squirrel's.

'Close,' Andrea told him.

'Okay, girlfriend, out with it!' Suzanne reached across the table and gave her hand a squeeze. 'Don't make us suffer.'

'I'm dying here,' Melissa chimed in. 'Now *give!*'

'Well, the thing is . . .' Andrea looked at the three expectant faces around her and suddenly the lines she'd rehearsed in her head seemed awkward and boastful. 'The thing is that the Bancroft Foundation has decided to . . . reach out to me. They want me to be on the board. A trustee.'

'That's amazing,' Suzanne shrilled.

'Any money in it for you?' Jeremy asked, massaging a callus on his right forefinger.

'Actually, there is,' Andrea said. *Twelve million dollars.*

'Yeah?' A gentle prod.

'It's really generous. An honorarium just for serving and . . .' She faltered, berating herself silently: What a phony she was becoming! 'Oh, shit, listen to me. They're giving me . . .'

The words would not come out. *She could not say them.* Nothing would be the same among them once she did. She hadn't thought this through. And yet *not* saying it – especially if and when they found out later – would be the corrosive thing. Not for the first time that evening, she found herself choking on the number. 'Look, let's just say it's *crazy* money, okay?'

'Crazy money,' Suzanne repeated acidly. 'Would that be bigger than a breadbox?'

'Is this one of those I-could-tell-you-but-then-I'd-have-to-kill-you situations?' Melissa put in. She once had a guest, i.e., nonrecurring, role in a soap opera episode with a plot element like that.

'You know, I'm hazy on my arithmetic. Is 'crazy' greater or less than 'mad phat'?' Jeremy asked, exasperated.

'Hey, you're a *private person*,' Suzanne said, in a voice that could curdle milk. 'We need to respect that.'

'Twelve,' Andrea said quietly. 'Million.'

The others looked on in stunned silence until Jeremy half-choked on a nastily swallowed mouthful of pasta. He knocked back a glass of the Vouvray. 'You're shitting me,' he said at last.

'This is a joke, right?' Melissa asked. 'Or, like, an improv thing?' Melissa turned to Suzanne. 'When I was taking acting classes, at the studio? Andrea used to help me with my improv exercises, and I always thought she was better at them than I was.'

Andrea shook her head. 'I can hardly believe it myself,' she said.

'And so the caterpillar turns into the butterfly,' Suzanne said, a spot of red appearing on each cheek.

'Twelve million dollars,' Melissa said softly, almost singing the syllables the way she did when she was trying to memorize a part. 'Congratulations! I couldn't be happier for you! This is un-buh-lievable.' The last word turned into three.

'A toast!' Jeremy called out, refilling his wineglass.

The mood was jubilant and joshing, but by the time the meal turned into coffee and cordials, their excitement for her had – or was she imagining it? – somehow edged into envy. Her friends were spending her money for her in their imaginations, coming up with *Lifestyles of the Rich and Famous* scenarios that were both outlandish and banal. Jeremy talked, with a faint air of defiance, about a rich man he knew – he did yardwork for him when was a teenager – who 'was just like the guy next door, never put on any airs'; and there was a hint of reproach in his story, as if Andrea wasn't going to measure up to the Pepsi bottling-plant mogul of Doylestown, Pennsylvania.

Finally, after the tenth reference to Donald Trump and eighty-foot yachts, Andrea said, 'Can we talk about something else?'

Suzanne gave her a who-are-you-trying-to-kid look. 'What else is there to talk about?' she asked.

'I'm serious,' Andrea said. 'How are *you* doing?'

'Don't patronize me, sweetheart,' Suzanne returned, pretending to be insulted. Except that wasn't quite it, Andrea realized. Her friend was pretending to be pretending to be insulted.

So this is what it was going to be like.

'Anyone for some herbal tea?' Andrea asked, brightly. She could feel a headache coming on.

Suzanne stared at her, unblinking. 'You know how you always said you weren't one of those Bancrofts?' she asked, not unkindly. 'Well, guess what. You just became one.'

In a darkened room illuminated only by the bluish glow of a flat-panel monitor, agile fingers caressed gently concave keycaps; the LCD screen filled and emptied. Words, numerals. Requests for information. Requests for action. Payments assured. Payments revoked. Reward conferred and reward withheld; sanctions and incentives systematically applied. Information came in. Information went out. It was a computer networked to countless others around the world, receiving and generating a pulse of binary digits, a cascade of ones and zeros, of logic gates in closed or open position, each as insubstantial as the atoms from which mighty edifices are built. Instructions were digitally issued, modified. Data was collected, collated, and assessed. Sizable sums flashed around the world, digitally transferred from one financial institution to another, and another, ending up in numbered accounts nested within other numbered accounts. More instructions were issued; more agents were enlisted through a multiplex of cutaways.

Within the room, a face was illuminated only by the moon-glow of the screen. Yet the recipients of the communications were denied even that glimpse. The guiding intelligence remained hidden to them, as vaporous as the morning mist, as distant as the sun that burns it away. A snatch of an old spiritual drifted into the person's mind. *He's got the whole world in his hands.*

The tapping of the keys was almost lost among the ambient noises, but these were the sounds of knowledge and action, of the resources to translate the first into the second. These were the sounds of power. In the lower left corner of the keyboard were the key caps marked command and control. It was not an irony so much as an aptness, and not one lost upon the person seated before the computer. That soft crackling was, indeed, the sound of command and control.

A final, encoded transmission was made. It concluded with one sentence: *Time is of the essence.*

Time, the one entity that could be neither commanded nor controlled, would have to be honored and respected.

Agile fingers, a soft crackling of keys, and the sign-off was typed.

GENESIS.

For hundreds of people around the planet, it was a name to conjure with. For many, it meant opportunity and quickened their sense of avarice. For others, it meant something very different, and made their blood run cold, haunted their nightmares. *Genesis.* The beginning. But of what?

CHAPTER FOUR

Belknap slept during the flight to Rome – he had always taken pride in his ability to store up sleep, given the opportunity – but his sleep was troubled, memory-haunted, even tormented. And when he pulled himself from his slumbers, the memories crowded his mind like flies on a carcass. He had lost so much in his life, and he refused to let Rinehart confirm a hateful pattern: the destruction of those he cared most about. Sometimes it felt like a curse, the sort found in Greek tragedy.

Once, his life was going to be different. Once, Belknap – having been deprived, in his early adulthood, of his own family – was himself going to be a family man. The memories swam into view, darted into darkness, eluded his grasp, then, in a gyre of pain, circled back to bruise him.

The wedding itself had been a quiet affair. A few friends and colleagues of Yvette's at the State Department's Bureau of Intelligence and Research, where she worked as a translator; a few colleagues of Belknap's, whose parents had died long before and who had no close family. Jared, of course, was his best man, and his hovering, friendly presence was a kind of benediction in itself. The first night of their honeymoon at a resort near Punta Gorda, Belize. It had been the end of an enchanted day. They had seen parrots and toucans perched in palm trees, dolphins and manatees sporting in the azure waters, and had been astounded by the call of the howler monkey – it was almost like the roar of the ocean – before they learned the source. Before lunch, they had taken a boat out to the small reef, visible as a line of white surf about half a mile offshore, and there, as they went diving, another magical realm revealed itself to them. There were the vibrant colors of the coral itself, but also of the swarms of iridescent fish, boundlessly various. Yvette knew their names, and in several languages, too – one legacy of having a diplomat father who had been posted at all the major European capitals. She delighted in pointing out the purple vase sponges, the fairy basslet fish, the squirrelfish, the parrot fish – unlikely names for unlikely creatures. When he approached a fish that looked like a Japanese fan, with delicate white and orange stripes, Yvette touched his hand and they surfaced. 'That's a lionfish, my love,' she told him, her brown eyes glittering like the water. 'Best admired from a distance.' She explained that its spines could deliver a potent toxin. 'It's like an underwater flower, isn't it? But as Baudelaire said, *'Là où il y a la beauté, on trouve la mort.'* Where there is beauty, one finds death.'

Belize was not paradise; they both knew there was poverty and violence around, none of it very far away. Yet there *was* beauty here, and that beauty contained a kind of truth. It was a truth, at the least, about themselves: their ability to perceive and be transported by the sublime. At that reef, he experienced something that he wanted to hold on to. He knew that, just as those luminous dazzling, vibrant fish looked dull and gray when brought to the surface, his own inner truth was unlikely to survive his workaday existence. *Then know it now*, he urged himself.

That evening, the moonlit beach: The memory was fractured, a heap of lacerating splinters. He could not retrieve them without bleeding. Fragments. Yvette and he had been capering on the sand. Had he ever felt so carefree? Never before, and surely never again. He remembered Yvette, running toward him on the private beach. She was naked, and her hair – somehow golden even in the silvery light of the moon – was flowing over her shoulders, and her blissful expression was itself a source of radiance. He had not noticed, just at that moment, what looked like a small fishing schooner anchored offshore. The two pinpoint pulses of light from the schooner. Had he seen the muzzle flashes, or imagined them later, when trying to make sense of what he did see: the bullet that pierced her throat, her soft, lovely throat; the bullet that pierced her torso? Both projectiles large-caliber, and, in combination, instantly lethal. Except that he hadn't seen the bullets, either, only their consequences. He remembered that she fell toward him, as if to embrace him, and that it took his stunned mind long seconds to comprehend what had happened. He heard a roar – like the distant guttural clamor of the howling monkey, like the pounding of the surf, but so much louder – and he did not immediately recognize that he was its source.

Where there is beauty, one finds death.

What he remembered about the funeral, back in Washington, was mostly that it rained. A pastor spoke, but it was as if the sound was turned off in Belknap's head: A dark-clad stranger with a professionally somber expression, a stranger whose mouth was moving, no doubt reciting prayers and uttering ritual solace – what had this man to do with Yvette? He was seized by the unreality of all before him. Again and again he plunged into the depths of his mind, trying to bring back that incandescent truth he had experienced at the coral reef that day. Nothing remained. He had the memory of a memory; but the memory that mattered had vanished, or else secreted itself within a hard shell, rendering itself forever inaccessible.

There was no Belize, no beach, no Yvette, no beauty, no timeless truth; there was only the cemetery, a swath of some thirty aggressively green acres overlooking the Anacostia River. If it had not been for Jared Rinehart's steadfast presence, he doubted that he could have held it together.

Rinehart was a rock. The one stable point in his life. He had grieved for Yvette alongside Belknap, but he had grieved for his friend even more. Belknap would not countenance being pitied, however, and Rinehart had sensed this as well, tempering his compassion with mordancy. 'If I didn't know better, Castor,' Rinehart said at one point, putting an arm around his friend's shoulder and gripping him with a warmth that belied his words, 'I'd say you were bad luck.'

For all the raging anguish Belknap felt, he managed to smile, and, briefly, to laugh.

Then Rinehart met his eyes. 'You know I'll always be here for you,' his friend said quietly. He spoke simply, directly; a blood oath made by one warrior to another.

'I know,' Belknap replied, the words half-trapped in his throat. 'I know.' And he did.

An inviolate bond of loyalty and honor: This was a deep truth as well. In Rome, it was the truth that would have to sustain him. Those who harmed Pollux would never be safe from Castor. They had surrendered their right to safety.

They had surrendered their right to *live*.

The Town Car that arrived at Andrea's house was absurdly incongruous: a Mercedes-Benz 560 SEL – long, sleek, black. On her modest street of small houses with small yards it was as out of place as a Lipizzaner stallion. But the board meeting was set for this afternoon, and, Horace Linville had explained, getting to the foundation headquarters involved a number of unmarked turns in Westchester County. So the car had been sent for her. It wouldn't do for her to get lost.

Toward the end of the two-hour trip, the driver went from one narrow road to another one, evidently old cow paths that had only recently been paved. Few of the lanes had signs. She tried to remember the sequence of turns, but wasn't sure she would be able to repeat the trip on her own.

Katonah, forty miles north of Manhattan, was a peculiar combination of rusticity and wealth. The actual village, part of Bedford Township, was a veritable stage set of Victorian charm, but the real action was found in its sylvan outskirts. That was where the Rockefeller family maintained a sizable compound, as did the international financier George Soros and scores of billionaires who had no public profile at all. For some reason, people who lived lives of wealth beyond all imagining often imagined themselves living in Katonah. The hamlet was named after the Indian chief from whom it was purchased in the nineteenth century, and, for all its rural appeal, its spirit of commerce – the buying and selling of

76

property, knowledge, souls – had scarcely diminished in the years since.

The bumpy road began to test even the cushioned suspension of the Mercedes SEL. 'Sorry it's a little rocky,' said the blandly equable driver. The area they were driving through was lightly timbered, disused farmland that had been reclaimed by the woods sometime in the past several decades. Finally, a handsome brick house came into view – a Georgian redbrick quoined and corniced with Portland limestone. Three stories with a slate mansard roof, it was imposing without being pretentious.

'It's gorgeous,' Andrea said softly.

'That?' The driver coughed, trying to conceal a chuckle. 'That's the gatehouse. The foundation's about a half-mile down the drive.' At the car's approach, a section of the black sword-topped wrought-iron fence swung open, and they made their way down an allée of lindens.

'My God,' Andrea said a few minutes later. What looked, from a distance, like a hillock, a swelling of the earth, stood revealed as a vast, curving structure of shingle and stone, something old but unusual. It had nothing of the usual English-country-house kind of grandeur – there was no Gothic masonry; there were no leaded windows, no wings or courtyards. Instead, it was composed of simple shapes – cones, columns, rectangles – and built of wood and locally quarried sandstone. Its palette of earth tones – rich hues of rusty red, sepia, umber – was why it so readily blended into its surroundings. Which made it all the more startling when Andrea came close enough to take it in – its size, the elegance of every detail: the wide oval porches, the sawtooth shingled walls, the gently asymmetric forms. It was immense, and yet it was so lacking in ostentation that its immensity seemed on the scale of nature, not artifice.

Andrea felt breathless.

'It's a beaut,' the driver agreed. 'Not that Dr. Bancroft has a lot of use for it. Up to him, he'd have sold it off and moved into a bed-and-breakfast. But they say the charter won't have it.'

'Good thing.'

'I guess it's part yours now.' The car pulled up to a graveled parking area to one side of the vast building. Andrea felt weak-kneed as she made her way up a low porch and into a light-flooded foyer. Smells of old wood and furniture polish were just detectable. A starched woman greeted her at once, with a wide smile and a thick three-ring binder.

'The agenda,' the woman – stiff coppery hair, upturned nose – explained to Andrea. 'We're *delighted* to have you on board.'

'This place is amazing,' Andrea said, gesturing around her.

The woman's lacquered hair barely moved as she nodded vigorously. 'It was built in 1915, from a design of H. H. Richardson's, we're told – a design he'd never been able to get built during his lifetime. Thirty years after his death, the world was at war, and this country was preparing to jump into the fight. A dark time. But not for the Bancrofts.'

That was right, Andrea mused – wasn't there some story about a Bancroft who had made a fortune in munitions during the First World War? Her historical interest had never extended to her father's family, but she had picked up the basic lineaments.

The trustees' room was on the second floor, multipaned windows facing onto a terraced garden, which was profusion of vibrant colors. Andrea was escorted to a seat on one side of a long table, a sort of Georgian banquet table, where at least a dozen others, some combination of trustees and foundation staff members, were already gathered. An elegant tea-and-coffee service had been set up in one corner of the room. The men and women around the table were bantering quietly, and as Andrea made a show of paging through the binder, she heard countless references that were just above her head: clubs she hadn't quite heard of, brand names that might have been a kind of yacht but might have been a kind of cigar, admission directors of grand-sounding boarding schools she had never heard of. From a door at the opposite end of the room, a couple of suited men emerged, accompanied by a much younger assistant. The conversational murmur began to die down.

'Those are program officers from the foundation,' the man seated to Andrea's right explained. 'Means it's show-and-tell time.' Andrea turned to her neighbor: slightly pudgy, salt-and-pepper hair, an overgenerous application of gel preserving visible comb tracks. His tanned face did not match his white and hairless hands, and the fringes of hair around his forehead had acquired a faint orange tint.

'I'm Andrea,' she said.

'Simon Bancroft,' he said, something wet and buzzy in his voice. His eyes were gunmetal gray, and inexpressive. His forehead was oddly immobile, she decided; his eyebrows scarcely moved as he spoke. 'You're Reynolds's girl, right?'

'He was my father,' she responded, insisting on a shade of meaning doubtless lost on him. She wasn't Reynolds's girl; she was, if anything, Laura's girl.

Scion of the outcast.

She felt a surge of hostility toward the man beside her, like the molecular call of some ancient blood feud, and then, oddly, it passed. What really disturbed her, she realized, wasn't a sense of being out of place; it was her sense of *belonging*. An outsider, an insider: Which was she now?

What if it were up to her to decide?

Loose the hound, Todd Belknap thought mordantly. *Loose the hound of hell.*

Every manhole cover in Rome was emblazoned with the initials 'SPQR.' *Senatus Populusque Romanus*: The Senate and the People of Rome. Once a grand political gesture, he reflected; now, like so many grand political gestures, little more than a logo. With a small crowbar, the operative prized up the cover and descended a scuttle ladder until he found himself on a rickety-seeming wooden catwalk in a fetid space about twenty feet high and five feet wide. He flicked his flashlight to its medium setting, moving the beam around to inspect his surroundings. The sides of the concrete cavern shimmered with water bugs. Cables, most the thickness of a cigarillo, lined the sides like swagged drapery – black, orange, red, yellow, blue. Fifty-year-old telephone cables hung alongside coaxial from the seventies and eighties, and modern fiber-optic cable freshly installed by municipal utilities like Enel and acea. The sheathing colors would have meant something to most people who drove an Enel van and wore an Enel uniform, Belknap supposed. He'd just have to be an exception.

Beads of water formed at the ceiling, gathered strength, and dripped down at irregular intervals. Belknap consulted a small luminescent compass. The villa was an eighth of a mile ahead, and he easily traversed most of the distance, the main utilities tunnel running parallel to the street.

Can't keep a good man down, he mused. *Or a bad one.*

Will Garrison's threats and protests had passed through Belknap like a bad plate of clams. Had he sometimes gone too far in the past? No doubt. Belknap wasn't one to wait for a walk sign before crossing at an intersection. He wasn't good with paperwork. The arc of the universe is long, but it bends toward justice, a prophet had said, and Belknap hoped that was true. If it took too long, though, Belknap was happy to do the bending himself.

He was not an introspective sort, but he had no illusions about himself, either. He could be irascible, hotheaded, even brutal, no doubt. There were moments – rare ones – when fury overrode his conscious will, and in those moments he knew what it must be like to be possessed. He valued, above all, loyalty: It was a motive force in his life. He could think of nothing more despicable than disloyalty – except it wasn't a matter of thinking. The conviction was visceral, part of the fiber of his very being.

There was a three-foot gap in the catwalk where the tunnel, following the street above, made a bend. Belknap noticed it just in time and jumped across it. His tools – the crowbar, the grapnel launcher – banged uncomfortably against his thigh. Though the grapnel launcher was a compact model, its housing made of a lightweight polymer, it was still bulky, and the three-pronged grappling hook kept slipping out of the Velcro straps.

Despite Garrison's squid-ink cloud of rationalizations, Belknap's every instinct told him that there was a connection between Ansari's murder and Jared Rinehart's disappearance. Yet there was more than instinct to consider. Belknap's friends at Consular Operations – his real friends – weren't going to cut him off because of Garrison's shit storm, and when he pressed one of them, he learned about a few highly suggestive intel reports. These were sourced to so-called 'unspecified channels' – highly confidential assets – and, as his analyst friend warned, the picture was still murky. But the early indications were that Rinehart's kidnappers had been either enlisted or co-opted by another, far more formidable organization. The puppet masters had puppet masters. The murder of Khalil Ansari was consistent with this pattern – a stealthy takeover of one network by another, more powerful one.

He had to be close to the villa now. Yet the pathway he had been walking along would not lead him to the villa itself; the cable entered the house through hardened PVC pipes only a few inches in diameter. The conduits for water and sewage were less than a foot across. Having cross-checked the architectural blueprints with a geological survey, however, Belknap realized that there was another way in. The two hundred and sixty miles of the Roman aqueduct systems – all but thirty miles of which were subterranean – had required a legion of laborers to maintain, working under the direction of the Curator Aquarum, the keeper of the waters. And the Curator Aquarum had always insisted that the waterways be constructed with an eye toward their upkeep and repair: The ancient equivalent of access panels – sheathed openings – were installed at regular intervals so that blockages could be swiftly cleared. In the honeycombed earth beneath the streets of Rome, modern utilities tunnels regularly intersected with the chutes and dropshafts of the ancient aqueducts, including the aqueducts of Trajan. Belknap again checked his compass, along with a pedometer-like device that measured horizontal displacement. Between the two instruments, he would be able to gauge his position.

Now he stopped in front of a hinged metal gate and made his way into an adjoining tunnel, where the gas and water mains ran. The air was as stagnant as ditchwater, thick with mold and mildew and centuries of slow fungal growth. Whereas the utilities tunnel ran approximately parallel with the street above, the cavernous space he had entered soon began to slope downward, every step taking him deeper and deeper into the earth. The air, too, seemed to grow denser and more sulfurous as he descended.

The tunnel – only it was truly more like a cavern at this point, after so many centuries, with a crumbling roof and a debris-cluttered floor, closer to a natural geological formation than a man-made conduit – alternately narrowed and flared, and reaching his destination required much doubling back, many circuitous turns in the subterranean maze. Some of the passageways had probably not been traversed by a human being in centuries.

The unwelcome thought came to him that if he should drop either his flashlight or his compass he could easily be lost forever, a moldering skeleton to be encountered by the next foolhardy explorer however many years in the future.

Beneath his hardhat, his hair was soaked in sweat; he had to stop and tie a handkerchief around his forehead, bandana-style, to keep it from dripping into his eyes. At last, he was, by his calculations, almost directly beneath the villa – but fifty feet beneath it, the depth of a prairie well.

The basement storm grate indicated on the architectural schematics was what had first given him the idea. These were not an uncommon feature among villas built over the ancient and now-empty waterways, it seemed. It was, indeed, the easiest way to alleviate basement flooding during heavy rains. To prevent clogging, a shaft would be dug straight down until it met with one of the disused Roman tunnels.

Now he pushed the slide on his flashlight all the way forward, shifting its beam to its brightest mode. A few minutes of searching revealed a lichen-covered mound of earth on the rocky tunnel floor, and above it, far above it – he held a small pair of digital binoculars to his eyes and peered – was a grate. He folded down the prongs of the pneumatic grapnel gun, aimed it vertically, and squeezed on the triggering device. With a soft popping noise, the nozzle discharged the folded hook and an attached pair of linked polypropylene lines. A *clank* told him that the grappling hook had caught. He gave the trailing line a tug, and it held firm. With another tug, the polypropylene skein unfolded into a sort of ladder. It seemed flimsy, insubstantial, but appearances were deceptive. The braided microfilament structure would hold many times his body weight.

He began to climb. The transverse lines were spaced two feet apart between the two main filament braids, and by the time he was a third of the way up, a slip of the foot would be fatal. All would be for naught, of course, if someone was already in the basement, had seen the grappling hook. But the odds were very much against it. A security guard would make a pro forma inspection – indeed, he was counting on the fact – but only once or twice a night.

The grate, when he finally reached it, was heavy – perhaps two hundred pounds of steel, secured in place by its own massive weight – and the filament ladder would not provide him sufficient purchase to lift it. Belknap's stomach clenched. To have come so far . . . to be *inches* away . . .

Desperately, he looked around at the lining of the shaft where it met the basement storm drain. A collar of steel, like the mouth of a funnel, had been installed there – it looked like seven-gauge sheet metal – and, with his small crowbar, he bent the material in two places so that it flared out and provided a makeshift ledge. Positioning his feet on opposite sides of the shaft, he pushed up at the grate. It was an unnatural angle of exertion; his elbows were higher than his shoulders as he started to push. The massive grate did not budge.

Belknap's heart began to hammer, not from the exertion so much as from frustration, a sense of frustration he would not permit to edge into despair. He thought of Jared Rinehart, held somewhere by hirelings of the Ansari network and utterly subject to their will. *You choose a friend with care,* Jared had once said. *And then you never let him down.* Jared had kept his word. Would Belknap?

Belknap knew so many who had lost their lives for no good reason, whether at home or in the field. Mac 'the Mountain' Marin had survived dozens of high-risk ops only to succumb at home to a burst aneurysm in some tiny vessel in the brain. Mickey Dummett – a man whose torso was stippled with four bullet entry-wound scars – gave up the ghost at a country intersection where a station-wagon driver failed to notice a stop sign. Alice Zahavi was shot dead in the course of an operation, but an operation so badly conceived from the get-go that it would have had no tactical or intelligence justification even if everything had gone right. These were good men and women to whom the fates assigned senseless, contemptible deaths. Just the hands they were dealt. Belknap took a deep breath. To give up his life in order to save a man like Jared Rinehart – there would be nobility in that. In an age where heroism was an endangered attribute, he could imagine worse deaths than this, and few better.

Now Belknap surged upward with every fiber of his body, possessed of a strength that somehow came to him as much as from him.

The grate moved.

Up, and over. He slid the massive disk off to one side, just enough to squeeze a hand through, and then used his other hand to push it further away. Hard metal on smooth concrete: quieter than he might have supposed.

And so, forty minutes after parking the utilities van, he made his way into the very place he had sought so desperately to avoid: one that had been designed to the exquisite – and profoundly twisted – specifications of the late Khalil Ansari.

Now came what Belknap always found the hardest part of all.

Waiting.

As the program officers launched into their overviews, Andrea concentrated, at first, on appearing composed and self-assured. Before long, however, she found herself riveted by the presentations. They should, by all rights, have been tedious. Yet she couldn't get over how *extensive* the foundation's activities were. Clean-water and vaccination projects in the Third World, literacy programs in Appalachia, programs to eradicate polio in Africa and Asia, programs to provide micronutrient supplementation throughout the world's less-developed regions. Each foundation officer talked about the projects he or she oversaw in precise terms: costs, prospects, plans for the future, assessments of efficacy. The language was flat, pedestrian, uninflected. Yet what they were talking about was quite remarkable – one project after another that would transform the lives of thousands. In one instance, it involved the construction of waterways in impoverished regions, allowing irrigation and proper agriculture where only a subsistence living had been possible. A few photographs, displayed on a wall-mounted monitor, made the results vividly clear: The desert truly was being coaxed into bloom.

Like the Rockefeller Foundation, Bancroft had branch offices all over the planet, but it was careful to keep its overhead costs under strict control. Again and again, the presenters conveyed a businesslike ethic of 'value for money,' a refreshing clarity of vision for a nonprofit charitable organization, she thought – especially because 'value,' in this context, referred to lives saved, suffering averted.

Perhaps that should not have been surprising, she reflected, given the man behind the foundation.

Paul Bancroft. It was a name that elicited trepidation and awe. Dr. Bancroft had always maintained a low profile: not for him the black-tie galas, the bold-type mentions in the society pages. What could never be kept entirely quiet was his multifaceted genius. Andrea recalled when, taking a junior-level seminar in the foundations of economics, she was obliged to master a set of multivariate functions known as

Bancroft's Theorem – and, delving into it, discovered that its inventor was actually a cousin of hers. Dr. Bancroft had been still in his twenties when he made major contributions to game theory and its applications to moral philosophy. But it was a more practical kind of wisdom that had created the foundation: a series of brilliant investments and speculations that had turned a handsome family fortune into an immense endowment, and transformed what had been a small-to-midsized foundation into one that encircled the globe.

The three o'clock presentation was given by a program officer named Randall Heywood: a red, leathery face that suggested too many years under a tropical sun, a bullet head with a close-cropped fringe of dark hair. His field was tropical medicine, and he was in charge of a program that directed funds toward research and development of malaria treatments. Ninety million dollars would be given as seed money to a group at the Howell Medical Institute, another ninety to a group at Johns Hopkins. Heywood spoke briefly about 'molecular targets,' about vaccine protocols, about the special challenges presented by the pathogen, about the inadequacy of vaccines currently in development. About the million lives that were claimed each year by the most aggressive malaria parasite, *Plasmodium falciparum*.

A million lives. A statistic? An abstraction? Or a tragedy.

Heywood spoke in a low rumble. There was something overcast about him. *A storm cloud at dawn*, Andrea thought. 'The results so far, well, we're not seeing any breakthroughs on the horizon. Nobody wants to over-promise. The whole field has been a series of high hopes and dashed hopes. But there we are.' His eyes roamed around the long table, inviting questions.

Andrea set down her teacup with an audible clink – Spode on Spode, politer than clearing her throat, she thought. 'Forgive me – I'm new to all this – but we'd been told earlier that the foundation looks for areas that are underserved by the marketplace.' She paused meaningfully.

'And vaccines are a good example,' Heywood said, nodding sagely. 'The value of an inoculation is greater than its value to any one individual, because if I'm inoculated, it helps you, too. I can't spread a pathogen to other people, and, of course, society doesn't have to pay the cost of my sick days, absences from school, hospitalization. Any health economist would say that its value to the community could be twenty times greater than what an individual would pay for it. That's why governments have always directly invested in vaccination. It's ultimately a public good, same as public sanitation, clean water, or what have you. In this case, though, the disease is worst in the most impoverished places in the world, where there simply aren't the resources necessary. Places like Uganda, Botswana, or Zambia have an annual health-care budget that comes to maybe fifteen dollars per capita. Here, it's closer to five thousand dollars.'

Andrea's eyes focused on Heywood as he spoke. His ruddy complexion made the paleness of his eyes all the more striking. He was powerfully built, had large hands, nails bitten to the quick. A type, then, with whom she had some experience: a man's man . . . with a nervous stomach. A bruiser with a glass jaw.

'That puts things into perspective,' Andrea said.

'It's a dollars-and-cents calculation. Drug companies are terrific at drug development when there's a real market for it. But they don't have a financial incentive to spend huge sums to develop treatments for people who can't afford to pay for them.'

'Which is where the Bancroft Foundation comes in.'

'Which is where we come in,' Heywood said, nodding somberly. The neophyte was up to speed. 'Basically, what we're trying to do is prime the pump.'

He started to shuffle his papers, but Andrea was not finished yet. 'Forgive me,' she said. 'I've been in commercial finance, so maybe I'm looking at this cockeyed. But instead of trying to pick the winning team ahead of time, why not provide an incentive for any research team that licks the problem?'

'I'm sorry?' Heywood massaged the bridge of his nose.

'Put a pot of gold at the end of the rainbow.' A quiet titter went around the table, and Andrea could feel herself blushing. She regretted having spoken up. *But I'm right,* she thought fiercely. *Aren't I?* 'It's hard to *direct* innovation. But I'm guessing there are hundreds of laboratories and research groups – in universities, in nonprofit research institutes, at biotech firms, too – that could hit on something real if they tried to. You make it worthwhile for *all* of them to compete, and you can harness all that creativity. You said the drug companies and biotech firms are great at drug development. Why not give them an incentive to get there first, too? Promise to buy a million or so doses of an effective vaccine at a fair price. Which means giving every potential investor that incentive as well – effectively *magnifying* the sums you put in.'

The program officer's ruddy face bore a look of suppressed exasperation. 'What we're trying to do,' he explained, 'is get people off the starting block.'

'And you're choosing the candidates you think have the best chance of winning.'

'Exactly.'

'You're placing a bet.'

The program officer fell silent for a moment.

From across the table, a distinguished-looking man with a full head of wavy gray hair caught Andrea's eye. 'And *your* model is – what?' he asked her. 'A sort of Publishers Clearinghouse Sweepstakes for medical researchers? 'You may already be a winner' – that sort of thing?' His voice was smooth, almost honeyed. The challenge was in his words, not his tone.

Andrea Bancroft's face went hot. But the objection was off-base. Something she'd read in one of her history books came to her. She met her challenger's gaze. 'Is the idea so new? In the eighteenth century, the British government offered a prize for anyone who could figure out how to measure longitude at sea. If you look into it, I think you'll find that the problem was solved and the prize money collected,' She forced herself to take another sip of tea, hoped nobody noticed the tremble in her hand.

The gray-haired man gave her a long, appraising look. His features were sharp and symmetrical, given warmth by his brown eyes; his attire – a charcoal tweed jacket, a buttoned sweater-vest with a houndstooth pattern – distinctly professorial. One of the program consultants?

Now she lowered her gaze to the tea in her cup, suddenly abashed. *Way to go, Andrea*, she thought. *Making enemies on your first day here.*

But her larger sense was one of excitement: These were people who didn't just talk about changing the world, the stuff of a million freshman dorm conversations – these were people who were actually doing it. And they were smart about it. Very smart. If she ever had a chance to meet Dr. Bancroft herself, she would have to stop herself from gushing.

The program officer gathered his papers. 'We'll certainly take your remarks under consideration,' he said, in a matter-of-fact tone. It was neither dismissal nor acquiescence.

'My, my,' said the bronzed man to Andrea's left. Simon Bancroft, she remembered. He gave her a quick smile: mock congratulations, perhaps, though ambiguous enough to be represented, later, as the real thing.

A half-hour recess was called. The other trustees drifted off in clusters, some to a room downstairs where coffee and pastries were served; others walked around the gallery or sat outside, settling on parasol-sheltered chairs, straining to read the little displays of their BlackBerrys and wireless PDAs. Andrea herself wandered aimlessly, feeling suddenly alone: the transfer student freshly arrived at school. *Wouldn't want to sit down with the wrong crowd at the cafeteria*, she thought sardonically. She was pulled out of her reveries by a smooth baritone.

'Miss Bancroft?'

She looked up. The professor guy in the tweed and vest. Something unclouded about his gaze. He had to be around seventy, but his face, in repose, was scarcely lined, and the way he moved conveyed a certain vitality. 'Would you join me for a stroll?'

They ended up walking together down a slate path behind the house, descending down several terraced gardens and across a small wooden bridge over a stream, and then through a maze of privet hedges.

'It's like another world here,' Andrea said. 'Plunked down in the middle of another one. Like a restaurant on the moon.'

'Oh, that place. Great food, but no atmosphere.'

Andrea giggled. 'So how long have you been with the Bancroft Foundation?'

'Long time,' the man said. He stepped lightly over small branches. Corduroy trousers and sturdy brogues, Andrea noticed. Professorial but elegant.

'You must like it.'

'Keeps me out of trouble,' the man said.

He seemed in no hurry to bring up their disagreement, but she still felt awkward about it. 'So,' she said after a pause, 'did I make a fool of myself?'

'I'd say you made a fool of Randall Heywood.'

'But I thought – '

'You thought what? You were absolutely right, Miss Bancroft. *Pull*, not *push* – that's going to be the most efficient use of foundation resources when it comes to medical research. Your analysis was completely on the money. So to speak.'

Andrea smiled. 'I wish you'd tell the big guy that.'

A questioning look from the older man.

'I mean, when do I get to meet Dr. Bancroft anyway?' As she spoke the words, she had an inkling that she had already made a misstep. 'Okay, let me back up for a sec – who did you say you were?'

'I'm Paul.'

'Paul Bancroft.' Comprehension arrived like heartburn.

'Afraid so. Bound to be a disappointment, I know. Apologies, Miss Bancroft.' A smile played around his mouth.

'Andrea,' she corrected. 'I feel like such a idiot, is all.'

'If you're an idiot, Andrea, we need more idiots. I found your remarks to be exceptionally astute. You immediately set yourself apart from the fine ruminants around you, distinguished cud-chewers all. I daresay some were impressed.

You even held your ground against me.'

'You were playing devil's advocate, then.'

'Wouldn't put it that way.' He arched an eyebrow. 'The devil doesn't need an advocate. Not in this world, Miss Bancroft.'

The senior guard Yusef Ali rounded the corner of the darkened hallway, the powerful beam of his flashlight sweeping through every corner of the villa on via Angelo Masina. There could be no lapse of thoroughness, even now. Especially now. There had been so much uncertainty since the demise of their master. But the new master, he knew, was no less demanding. The physical security of any facility was no greater than the vigilance with which it was inspected.

Now, in a small room in the rear of the ground floor, the Tunisian checked a screen that displayed the status of the perimeter sensors. The electronic sensors reported themselves to be in a 'normal' state, but Yusef Ali knew that human observation could only be supplemented, never supplanted, by the methods of electronic detection. His evening walkthrough was not complete.

It was in the basement that he finally noticed something distinctly awry. The door to the *stanza per gli interrogatori* was ajar. Light spilled out of it, piercing the gloom.

It was not supposed to have been left like that. A pistol in one hand, Yusef Ali strode over to the chamber, opened the heavy door – it glided slowly on powerful, soundless hinges – and stepped inside.

At once, the lights went out. A powerful blow knocked the weapon from his right hand, while another blow swept his legs from under him. How many assailants were there? Disoriented by the sudden darkness, he could not tell, and when he tried to lash out, he found that his hands had been manacled. Another forceful blow, at the square of his back, sent the guard staggering to the floor.

Then the door to the interrogation chamber sucked shut behind him.

*

'Okay, now I'm really confused,' said Andrea Bancroft.

An elegant shrug. 'I was merely curious to see whether you'd hold your ground when you were in the right.' The man's gray hair turned silver in the midafternoon sun.

'I can't believe it – I can't believe I'm here, walking along a path with *the* Paul Bancroft. The guy who invented Bayesian networks. The Bancroft's Theorem Bancroft. The guy who – oh, God, I'm having flashbacks to graduate school. Forgive me. I'm embarrassing myself again. I'm a bobby-soxer meeting Elvis.' She could feel herself blushing.

'Elvis has left the building, I'm afraid.' Paul Bancroft laughed, a low musical laugh, and they turned right on the flagstone path.

The sylvan grounds gave way to meadow – ryegrass and yarrow and nameless wildflowers of all varieties, yet no thistles or burrs, no poison oak or ragweed. A meadow without noxious weeds: Like so much at the Katonah estate, it looked natural, effortless, and yet it had to be the result of a great deal of unseen attention. Nature perfected.

'Those things you mentioned – I feel like someone who penned a few catchy pop songs in the early sixties,' Paul Bancroft said after a while. 'As an older man, I find that the real challenge is to put precepts into practice. Enlist the mind to serve the heart – get those theories into the harness.'

'They've taken you a long way. Starting with the basic notion of utilitarian ethics. Let's see if I've got it right: Act so as to produce the greatest good for the greatest number.'

A low chuckle. 'That's how Jeremy Bentham put it in the eighteenth century. The phrase, I believe, originated in the writings of the scientist Joseph Priestley, and of the moral philosopher Francis Hutcheson. Everyone forgets that modern economics is, technically speaking, concerned precisely with the maximization of utility, which is to say happiness. Applying the welfare functions of Marshall and Pigou to the axioms of neoutilitarianism should have been an obvious exercise.'

Andrea fought to dredge up the classroom memories – knowledge and skills quickly mastered for exams and papers, just as quickly forgotten. 'The urban legend, as I remember, was that you formulated the Bancroft Theorem as a homework assignment in an undergraduate course. A term paper for a sophomore seminar, something like that. Is that really true?'

'Well, yes,' the hearty gray-haired man replied, his unlined face now lightly gleaming with perspiration. 'As a stripling lad, I was clever enough to have worked it out, not clever enough to have realized that it hadn't been worked out a thousand times before. The problems were easier back then. They had solutions.'

'And now?'

'They seem only to lead to more problems. Like Russian nesting dolls. I'm seventy, and looking back I find it hard to value that sort of technical cleverness as much as others do.'

'That's quite a recantation, coming from you. Didn't you get a Fields Medal?' The Fields Medal was the most prestigious award in mathematics, the discipline's equivalent of the Nobel. 'For some early work in number theory, if I'm remembering right. Back when you were at the Institute for Advanced Study.'

'Now you've really got me feeling my age,' her companion said with a grin. 'I've still got the actual medal in a shoebox somewhere. It bears a quote from the Roman poet Manilius: "To pass beyond your understanding and make yourself master of the universe." Haunting.'

'And humbling,' she added.

A wind rustled the tall meadow grasses and Andrea shivered briefly. They were walking toward a stone wall. It was ancient-looking, like the sort of pastureland divisions that crisscrossed the English Cotswolds.

'But now you're able to put all that greatest-good-for-the-greatest-number stuff into practice,' she went on. 'Having a foundation at your disposal must make it easy.'

'Do you really think so?' A hint of a smile. Another test.

Andrea paused, and gave a serious answer. 'Not easy, no. Because there's the issue of opportunity costs – of what else you could have done with any grant. And there's the question of downstream consequences.'

'I knew I saw something in you, Andrea. A quality of mind. A genuine measure of independence. An ability to think through problems by yourself. But as for what you were saying – you know, you put your finger on it exactly. Downstream consequences. Perverse effects. It's the snare of all ambitious attempts at philanthropy. Our greatest battle, really.'

Andrea nodded vigorously. 'Nobody wants to be the pediatrician who saved the life of little Adolf Hitler.'

'Precisely,' Paul Bancroft answered. 'And sometimes an effort to ameliorate poverty results only in more poverty. You dump free grain on an area – and put the farmers out of business. Next year, the Western aid agency isn't around, and neither are the local farmers, who were forced to eat their seed grain. We've seen this sort of thing happen again and again over the past decades.' Bancroft's gaze was alert and focused on her.

'And with disease?'

'Sometimes you have treatments that, by addressing the symptoms of an infectious disease, end up by increasing the transmission rate.'

'You don't want to be the doc who gives Typhoid Mary an aspirin so she can go back to work in the kitchen,' Andrea said.

'My God, Andrea, you were *born* to this.' The laugh lines around his eyes gathered into a smile.

Once more she found herself blushing. A reclaimed birthright – was that what it was? 'Oh, come on,' she said quickly.

'I just mean you have a knack for thinking about these things. Perverse consequences come in all shapes and sizes. That's why the Bancroft Foundation always has to think five steps ahead. Because every action has an effect, yes – but those effects, too, have effects. Which have yet further effects.' She felt the force of a powerful intellect directed toward a deep problem, and determined not to be defeated by it.

'It must be enough to induce paralysis. You start thinking about these knock-on effects, and you wonder about doing anything at all.'

'Except' – there was an intellectual fluidity and grace to the way Paul Bancroft spoke now, gliding in and out of her sentences – 'that there's no exit from the conundrum.'

'Because there are consequences to *in*action, too,' Andrea put in. 'Doing nothing has knock-on effects as well.'

'Which means you can never decide not to decide.'

It wasn't sparring; it was more like dancing, the back and forth, the to and fro. She was exhilarated. She was talking with one of the great minds of the postwar era about the greatest issues of the day and she was holding her own. Or was she flattering herself? A tabby dancing with a lion?

They moved along a gentle incline, a knoll flecked with bluebells and buttercups, and did not speak for a bit. She found herself in a sort of fugue. Had she ever met anyone so extraordinary? Paul Bancroft had all the money in the world; he didn't care about money. He only cared about what money could do, if targeted with extraordinary care. In college and in grad school, Andrea had spent time with academics who were desperate to get their papers published in the right journal, to get included on the right academic panels at the right conferences – needily, hungrily pursuing the most withered laurel. Yet here was Paul Bancroft, who had published enduring work before he was old enough to purchase alcohol, who, in his mid-twenties, received an appointment to the Institute for Advanced Study, once the lair of Einstein, Gödel, and von Neumann, and the country's most illustrious research center – and who, a few years later, gave it up in order to devote his energies to the foundation and its expansion. The man was hardheaded and big-hearted: a truly rare combination, and a thrilling one.

Being in his presence made all her past ambitions seem so *shrunken*.

'So the first task of doing good is to avoid doing bad,' she said, finally, musingly. They were walking downhill now. She heard a soft fluttering and looked up to see a brace of wood ducks lift up into the air before her eyes, in a cloud of vibrant plumage. Tucked behind the knoll, it turned out, was a small, clear pond, perhaps half an acre in size. Water lilies clustered around its banks. The ducks had obviously decided to wait among the trees until the human visitors had moved on.

'God, they're lovely,' Andrea said.

'That they are. And there are men of a certain stripe who can't see them without itching for a shotgun.' Paul Bancroft approached the pond, picked up a pebble from near its edge, and with boyish skill skipped it across the water's surface. The stone bounced twice, landing on the opposite bank. 'I'll tell you a story.' He turned to face her. 'Have you ever heard of Inver Brass?'

'Inver Brass? Sounds like a lake in Scotland.'

'And so it is, though you won't find it on any map. But it's also the name of a group of men – and originally it *was* all men – who came from around the world and met up there back in 1929. The organizer was a Scotsman of great means and ambition, and the people he gathered together were men of the same stamp. It was a small group, too. Six people: all influential, all rich, all idealistic, all determined to make the world a better place.'

'Oh, *that's* all.'

'Does it seem so very modest?' he asked jestingly. 'But yes, that was why Inver Brass was founded. And, from time to time, they would send vast sums of money to distressed regions, the idea being to diminish the suffering and, in particular, the violence that arose from deprivation.'

'A long time ago. A different world.' There was a distant chittering of a squirrel somewhere in the canopied woods across the glen.

'As it happens, though, the founder of Inver Brass had ambitions beyond his own life. The group was regularly re-constituted in ensuing decades. One thing remained the same: The leader, whomever it might be, was always code-named 'Genesis.' As the founder had been.'

'An interesting role model,' Andrea ventured. She found

another small pebble, made an effort to skip it along the water, but the angle was wrong. It plunked down and disappeared.

'Maybe more of a cautionary tale,' Bancroft countered. 'They weren't infallible. Far from it. The fact is, one of their feats of economic engineering inadvertently led to the rise of Nazi Germany.'

Andrea faced him. 'You can't be serious,' she said in a quiet voice.

'Which pretty much canceled out all the good they did. They thought about causes and effects – and forgot that effects, too, are causes.'

Through scudding clouds, the sun dimmed and brightened. Andrea fell silent.

'You look . . .'

'Stunned,' Andrea said. And so she was: a trained historian, stunned by the history of Inver Brass, stunned by the casualness with which Dr. Bancroft had related it. 'The notion that a cabal like that could have shifted the course of human history . . .' She trailed off.

'There's a great deal that never appears in the history books, Andrea.'

'I'm sorry,' she said. 'Inver Brass. From a lake in Scotland to the ascent of the Third Reich. This takes a little getting used to.'

'I've never met a faster study,' the aging savant murmured in an almost intimate tone. 'You see it before most people do: Doing the right thing isn't always easy.' He looked off to the acreage on the other side of the long, low stone wall, a stretch of artfully piled shale.

'You must be haunted by the story of Inver Brass.'

'And humbled,' he put in with a significant glance. 'As I say, the imperative is always to think forward. I'd like to believe that the Bancroft Foundation has some grasp of the elementals of historical causation. We've learned that the straight shot is often less effective than the carom shot.' He skipped another pebble across the pond. This one touched down three times. 'It's all in the wrist,' he told her with a wink. He was seventy, and he was seven. He had taken the heaviest burdens in the world upon his shoulders, and yet there was something about him that was lighter than air. 'You remember Voltaire's rallying cry: *Ecrasez l'infame!* – Crush the horror! It's mine, too. But the hard question has always been: How? As I say, doing the right thing isn't always easy.'

Andrea took a deep breath. Clouds were beginning to gather overhead, not just to scud. 'It's a lot to take in,' she said at last.

'That's why I want you to dine at my place tonight – *en famille*.' He gestured toward a house a few hundred yards on the other side of the stone wall, mostly concealed by foliage. So Bancroft resided in an adjoining parcel of land, his house a mere twenty-minute walk from the foundation.

'Seems you live over the shop,' Andrea said, with a careless giggle. 'Or next to it.'

'Beats commuting,' he said. 'And if I'm in a hurry, there's always a bridle path. Is that a yes?'

'A long-winded one. Thank you. I'd love to.'

'I have an idea my son would enjoy meeting you. Brandon's his name. He's thirteen. A wretched age, everyone says, but he wears it rather well. Anyway, I'll let Nuala know you'll be coming. She's – well, she looks after us. Among other things, I'd guess you'd call her the governess. But that sounds so Victorian.'

'And you're more of an Age of Enlightenment guy.'

Laughter rippled through him.

Having made the great man laugh, Andrea suddenly felt buoyed by a wave of unreasonable happiness. She was over her head, out of place – and somehow she had never felt more at home.

You were born *to this*, her cousin had said, and, thinking of her mother, Andrea felt a moment of coldness. Yet what if he was right?

Todd Belknap manacled the guard's wrists and ankles, stripped him naked with a few strokes of a knife, and then chained the manacles to the heavy cast-iron chair. Only then did he switch the lights back on. To overpower such a man required speed and stealth, and those advantages were temporary. The steel fetters were needed to make it permanent.

Now, in the harsh fluorescent light, the seated man's olive complexion appeared sallow. Belknap stepped in front of him and watched his eyes widen and then narrow with recognition and realization. The one who had called himself Yusef was both startled and dismayed. The very intruder he had meant to torture had taken over the torture chamber.

Belknap, for his part, surveyed the gear crowding the dungeon's walls. Some of the devices were unfathomable; his imagination wasn't sick enough to conceive how they could be put to use. Others he recognized from a visit he had made once to the Museum of the Pusterla, in Milan, a horrifying collection of medieval torture implements.

'Your master was quite a collector,' Belknap said.

In the chair, the Tunisian drew his angular face into a scowl of defiance. Belknap would have to be very clear about how far he was prepared to go. The captive's nakedness, he knew, would help bring home the vulnerability of the flesh, all flesh.

'I see you've got an actual iron maiden here,' the operative went on. 'Impressive.' He walked over to the tomblike container, which was lined with metal talons. Its victim, when forced inside, would be slowly pinioned, his own shrieks magnified by the enclosure. 'The Inquisition lives. Thing is, it wasn't just a fascination with antiques that led your late master to go medieval. Think about it. The Inquisition went on for centuries. Torture, too. That means decade after decade after decade of trial and error. Learning from experience. Learning how to play a man's pain fibers like a goddamn fiddle. The expertise they accumulated was incredible. Nothing we could hope to rival. Some of the art was lost, I'm sure. But not all.'

The seated man just spat at him. 'I tell you nothing,' he said in his lightly accented English.

'But you don't even know what I'm going to ask,' Belknap returned. 'I'm just going to ask you to make a decision, that's all. A choice. Do I ask too much?'

The guard glowered but was silent.

Now Belknap opened the drawer of a mahogany cabinet and removed an implement he recognized as a *turcas*, designed to rip out fingernails. He placed it on a large, leather-lined tray in sight of the prisoner. Next to it he placed a steel pincer, a thumbscrew – a vice with protruding studs designed to compress and then crush the joints of a person's fingers and toes – and a metal wedge designed to dig out, very slowly, someone's fingernails by the root. During the Inquisition, a common method of torture involved extracting the nails from fingers and toes as slowly as possible.

He presented the gleaming array of implements to his prisoner and spoke a single word. 'Choose.'

A bead of perspiration slowly ran down the man's forehead.

'Then I'll choose for you. I think we should start small.' He spoke in a coaxing voice as he glanced around the shelves again. 'Yes, I know just the thing – how about the pear?' Belknap asked, his eye falling upon a smooth ovoid object with a long screw projecting from the end, like a stem. He brandished it in front of his captive, who remained silent. *La pera*, one of the most notorious implements of medieval torture, was designed to be inserted into the rectum or vagina. Once inside, the projecting screw would be rotated and the iron pear would expand while spikes began to protrude from small holes, mutilating the victim's internal cavity in a slow and excruciating manner.

'Feel like a bite of pear? I think this one would like a bite of you.' Belknap pressed a lever recessed in the frame of the heavy iron chair and a hinged panel swung down from the center of the seat. 'You'll see. I'm full-service. Not a clockwatcher. Whatever it takes, for as long as it takes, that's what I'll do. And when they find you in the morning – '

'No!' the guard yelped, his sweat-slick flesh beginning to emit the acrid stench of fear. Belknap's calculation appeared to have been correct; his captive was evidently shaken as much by the humiliation of the prospect – the forcible penetration itself – as the bloody agony that would ensue.

'Don't worry about embarrassing yourself,' Belknap went on, relentlessly. 'The wonderful thing about this chamber is that you can scream as loud as you like, as long as you like. Nobody will be able to hear a thing. And, like I say, when you're found in the morning – '

'I tell you what you want to know,' the guard blurted, a whimper in his voice. 'I tell you.'

'The servant girl,' Belknap barked. 'Who is she? Where is she?'

The guard blinked. 'But she vanished. We thought – we thought *you* had killed her.'

Belknap lifted an eyebrow. 'When was she hired? Who is she?'

'Maybe eight months ago. She was checked out thoroughly. I made sure of it. Eighteen years old. Lucia Zingaretti. Lives with her family in the Trastevere. An old family. Modest. But respectable. Devout, in fact.'

'The kind who understand about unthinking obedience to ultimate authority,' Belknap said. 'Where?'

'A ground-floor apartment on via Clarice Marescotti. Khalil Ansari was very particular in who he would permit in his establishments. He had to be.'

'She disappeared the night Ansari was killed?'

Yusef Ali nodded. 'We never saw her again.'

'And you – how long were you with Ansari?'

'Nine years.'

'You must have learned a lot about him.'

'A lot and a little. I knew what I needed to know in order to serve. But not more.'

'There was an American. Kidnapped in Beirut. Same night as Ansari was killed.' Belknap studied the Tunisian's expression as he spoke. 'Did Ansari arrange this?'

'I do not know.' The response was uninflected, expressionless. Not careful, not crafted. 'We were not told about it.'

Again, Belknap studied the Tunisian closely and decided he was telling the truth. There would be no shortcuts here, but then he hardly expected that there would be. For the next twenty minutes, he continued to burrow in, gradually eliciting a vague picture of Ansari's establishment on via Angelo Masina. It was a coarse mosaic pieced together from large tiles. Yusef Ali had received instructions that his master's business concerns were, in effect, under new management. The basic elements of the management team would remain in place. The security breach had been identified and remedied. The security staff was to maintain vigilance until further instructions arrived. As for events in Beirut or the Bekaa, Ali had no direct knowledge. Ansari had dealings there, yes; everyone knew that. But it had never been a posting of Yusef Ali's. One did not ask needless questions, not if you wished to remain in Khalil Ansari's employ.

But Yusef Ali *had* been in charge of security at via Angelo Masina. Which left the servant girl. Belknap's one lead. The Tunisian did not have to be pressed further to provide the exact address where her family lived.

The chamber was growing muggy, close. At last, Belknap glanced at his watch once more. He had, if not what he needed, than all he was likely to get. He noticed that he still held *la pera* in his left hand, had been gripping it throughout the interrogation. Now he set it down and moved toward the door to the soundproofed dungeon. 'They'll find you in the morning,' he told Yusef Ali.

'Wait,' the guard said in a hushed, urgent voice. 'I have done what you ask of me. You must not leave me here.'

'You'll be found soon.'

'You will not release me?'

'I can't take that risk. Not while I'm making my exit. You know that.'

Yusef Ali's eyes widened. 'But you must.'

'But I won't.'

After a few long seconds, the man's eyes clouded over with resignation, even despair. 'Then you must do me one service.' The manacled guard jerked his head toward his pistol, still lying on the floor. 'Shoot me.'

'I said I was full-service. But not *that* full-service.'

'You must understand. I have been a loyal servant of

102

Khalil Ansari, a good soldier and a true one.' The Tunisian's gaze was downcast. 'If they find me here,' he went on, in a strangled voice, 'I will be disgraced and . . . made an example of.'

'Tortured to death, you mean. As you have tortured others to death.' *Where are you now, Jared? What are they doing to you?* The urgency of Belknap's mission seemed to push against his chest cage.

Yusef Ali made no demurral. He must have known precisely how agonizing and humiliating such a death could be, having helped inflict it upon others. A slow and excrutiating death that would strip every atom of dignity and pride from someone who valued dignity and pride above all.

'I do not deserve it,' he declared, his voice harsh and defiant. 'I deserve better!'

Belknap turned a vault-style wheel and retracted a series of dead bolts. The door glided open and a coolness drifted inside.

'Please,' the man husked. 'Shoot me now. It would be a *kindness*.'

'Yes,' Belknap agreed levelly. 'That's why I won't.'

CHAPTER FIVE

As Andrea Bancroft made her way along the bosky path to Paul Bancroft's house, her mind filled with drifting skeins of half-formed thoughts. The air was fragrant from the mounded borders of lavender, wild thyme, and vetiver grass fringing the gentle berm that subtly screened one property from another. Bancroft's house seemed to be of similar vintage as the foundation's, and in a harmonious style. Like the foundation's headquarters, the facades of aged brick and red sandstone melted into the landscape in a way that made it all the more impressive when at last its outlines could be clearly made out, and one realized how much of it had been in plain sight all along.

At the door Andrea was met by a uniformed woman of around fifty; her hair was a mixture of red and gray, and her broad cheeks were freckled. 'You'll be Miss Bancroft?' she asked, with the faint brogue of an Irishwoman who had spent most of her adult life in America. Nuala, wasn't it? 'The gentleman will be down presently.' She gave Andrea a look that segued swiftly from appraisal to approval. 'Now, what can I get you to drink? A taste of something nourishing?'

'I'm fine, I think,' Andrea replied hesitantly.

'You're telling me. How about a light sherry, then? The gentleman likes it quite dry, if that agrees with you. Not like the sticky stuff I grew up on, I can tell you that.'

'Sounds perfect,' Andrea said. The servants of a billionaire were bound to be stiff and starched to the nth degree, weren't they? But the Irishwoman was practically loosey-goosey, and that had to be a tribute to her employer. Paul Bancroft was obviously not a stickler for ceremony. This wasn't someone who wanted members of his staff to walk on eggshells, terrified of a trespass.

'One fino coming up,' the Irishwoman said. 'I'm Nuala, by the way.'

Andrea shook her hand and smiled, already beginning to feel welcomed.

Nursing her glass of fino sherry, Andrea began to take in the prints and paintings that hung in the dark wood-paneled foyer and adjoining parlor. She recognized some of the images, some of the artists; others, no less captivating, were unknown to her. She found herself drawn to a black-and-white drawing of a gargantuan fish on a shore somewhere, a fish so vast that it dwarfed the fishermen who surrounded it with ladders and knives. A dozen or more smaller fish spilled from its mouth. Where a fisherman had sliced open the leviathan's belly, another bevy of smaller fish had tumbled out.

'Arresting, isn't it?' Paul Bancroft's voice. Andrea had been studying the picture so intently that she had not heard him arrive.

'Who's it by?' Andrea asked, turning around.

'It's an ink drawing by Pieter Bruegel the elder, from 1556. He called it *Big Fish Eat Little Fish*. He wasn't one for decorous indirection. It used to hang in the Graphische Sammlung Albertina, in Vienna. But, like you, I found myself drawn to it.'

'And you swallowed it whole.'

Paul Bancroft laughed again, heartily, with his whole body. 'I hope you don't mind dining on the early side,' he said, 'The boy's still at the age where he has a bedtime.'

Andrea sensed that her host was eager to have her meet his son but anxious as well. She was reminded of a friend who had a child with Down Syndrome – a gentle, sunny, smiling child, whom the mother loved and felt pride in and, on some dark unacknowledged plane, some tincture of shame about, too . . . a shame that itself inspired shame.

'Brandon, was it?'

'Brandon, yes. Apple of his father's eye. He's . . . well,

special, I guess you might say. A little unusual. In a *good* way, I like to think. Probably upstairs on the computer, IM-ing someone unsuitable.'

Paul Bancroft, too, had a small glass of sherry in his hands, and had taken off his jacket, though the houndstooth sweater vest made him look as professorial as ever. 'Welcome,' he said, raising his glass in a toast, and the two settled down in tufted leather chairs in front of an unlighted hearth. The walnut paneling, the old, worn Persian carpets, the simple hardwood floors, darkened with age: It all seemed ageless, tranquil, a kind of luxury that scorned luxury.

'Andrea Bancroft,' he said, as if savoring the syllables. 'I have learned a thing or two about you. Graduate study in economic history, am I right?'

'For two years, at Yale. Two and half. Never finished the dissertation.' The fino was pale straw in color. She took a sip of it and the flavors blossomed in her mouth, her nose. It had a light toffee-like scent, tasted deliciously of nuts and melon.

'No wonder, given your independence of mind. It isn't an attribute that's valued there. Too much independence breeds discomfort, especially among would-be gurus who don't quite believe what they're saying.'

'I guess I could claim I wanted to be more grounded in the real world. Except the humiliating truth is, I dropped out of grad school because I wanted to make more money.' She stopped, appalled that she had actually said it out loud. *Great going, Andrea. Be sure to tell him about the factory outlet sale you drove two hours to get to last weekend.*

'Ah, but our means contour our preferences,' her cousin replied lightly. 'You're not just clear-eyed, you're honest, too. Two things that don't always come in one package.' He looked off. 'I suppose it would be disloyal of me to express ferocious disapproval of my late cousin Reynolds, but then, as the utilitarian William Godwin wrote near the end of the eighteenth century, "What magic is there in the pronoun 'my,' to overturn the decisions of everlasting truth?" The circumstances in which your mother was left are something else I recently learned about, to my dismay. But . . .' He shook his head. 'A subject for another occasion.'

'Thank you,' Andrea said, suddenly embarrassed and eager to change the subject. She couldn't help but think back to her closets filled with knockoffs of costly designs, her aspirations, the pride with which she paid off her charge-card balances in full every month. It seemed so absurd now. Would she have left the sheltering groves of academe if she hadn't been concerned about money? Her academic advisers had been encouraging; they'd assumed that she would soon be wheeling along on the tenure track, making the sort of decisions and compromises that they had made. Meanwhile, her student loans grew more onerous; she felt suffocated by the bills she couldn't quite pay, the credit-card debt she serviced with the minimum payment due as she watched it grow from one month to the next. Perhaps, too, on some scarcely conscious level, she yearned for a life where she wouldn't have to study the numbers on the right-hand column of the menu – for the life that had almost been hers.

She felt a strange moment of upheaval as she reflected back on all those 'practical' choices and worldly accommodations she had made – and for what? Her salary as a securities analyst was considerably more than what she could have expected as a junior faculty member; but it was, she now saw, a trivial sum. With her grubby fixation on discounts, she had discounted herself.

When she looked up, she realized that Paul Bancroft had been speaking.

'So I know what it's like to lose someone. My wife's death was shattering both for me and my son. A difficult time.'

'It must have been,' Andrea murmured.

'Alice was twenty years younger than me, for one thing. She was supposed to have been the one to carry on. To wear black at my funeral. But somehow she got a short straw in some infernal genetic lottery. It makes you realize how fragile life is. Unbelievably resilient. Unbelievably fragile.'

''Work for the night cometh,' right?'

'Sooner than we know,' he said softly. 'And the work is

never done, is it?' He took another sip of the pale-straw fino. 'You'll have to forgive me for dragging down the mood. It's the fifth anniversary of her death this week. There's the consolation that what she left behind is as precious to me as anything.'

The scrambling sound of coltish footsteps – someone taking the stairs two at a time, then jumping down to the landing.

'Speaking of whom . . .' Paul Bancroft said. He turned to the new arrival, who was standing in the arched doorway to the parlor. 'Brandon, I'd like you to meet Andrea Bancroft.'

The mop of curly blond hair was what she noticed first, and then the boy's apple cheeks. His eyes were an unclouded blue, and he had his father's fine symmetrical features. He was, she decided, an exceptionally handsome boy, even beautiful.

Then he turned to her and his face broke in a smile. 'Brandon,' he said, extending a hand. 'Nice to meet you.' His voice had not yet acquired the husk of adolescence, but it was deeper than a child's. A beardless youth, as the ancients would have said, but with a perceptible darkening of the down on his upper lip. Not yet a man, no longer a child.

His handshake was firm and dry; he was a little shy but not awkward. He sprawled on a nearby chair and maintained eye contact with her. There was none of that 'command performance' resentment that children his age have around guests. He seemed genuinely curious.

She was curious herself. Brandon wore a blue plaid shirt, untucked, and gray trousers with lots of zippers and pockets, pretty much standard garb for his cohort.

'Your father guessed that you were instant-messaging unsuitable people,' Andrea said lightly.

'Solomon Agronski was whuppin' my behind,' Brandon said merrily. 'We were doing DAGs, and I was way off-base. Got my ass handed to me.'

'This some kind of game?'

'I wish,' Brandon said. 'DAGs – it's, like, a directed acyclic graph. I know – snooze city, right?'

'And this Solomon Agronski . . .' Andrea prompted, still at a loss.

'Handed me my ass,' Brandon repeated.

Paul Bancroft crossed his legs, looking amused. 'He's one of the country's foremost mathematical logicians. Runs the Center for Logic and Computation at Stanford. They've developed quite a correspondence, if that's the word for it.'

Andrea tried to hide her astonishment. This was a far cry from Down Syndrome.

The boy sniffed her glass of sherry and made a face. 'Yuck,' he said. 'Wouldn't you like some Sprite instead? I'm gonna have some.'

'Actually, I'm okay,' Andrea said, laughing.

'Suit yourself.' Then he snapped his fingers. 'I know what we could do. Let's shoot some hoops.'

Paul Bancroft traded glances with Andrea. 'I'm afraid he thinks you're here as a playmate for him.'

'Naw, seriously,' Brandon persisted. 'Want to show me your moves? While it's still light?'

Paul cocked a brow. 'Brandon,' he told his son, 'she's just arrived and she's not exactly dressed for the playground, is she?'

'If I had the right shoes,' Andrea said, apologetically.

The boy was all business. 'Size?'

'Seven and a half.'

'Which is seven in a man's size. Each size represents an increment of a third of an inch, starting at three and eleven-twelfths inches. Did you know that?'

'Brandon's filled with fun facts,' his father jested. But there was no mistaking his doting gaze.

'Some of them are even correct,' the boy chirruped. 'Brainstorm!' he announced, leaping up from the chair. 'Nuala's an eight! Close enough, right?' He scampered down the hallway, and from a distance they could hear him call out: 'Nuala, can Andrea borrow a pair of your sneakers? Pretty please? Pretty pretty pretty please.'

Paul Bancroft crooked a smile at her. 'Resourceful, no?'

'He's . . . remarkable,' Andrea said, risking polite under-statement.

'He's already certified as an international chess master. When I achieved the rank, I was twenty-two. People said I was precocious, but there's no comparison.'

'An international chess master? Most kids his age spend their time doing Grand Theft Auto on their PlayStations.'

'Guess what. Brandon does, too. He's always playing Sim City. The thing to remember is, he's just a kid. He's got the intellectual firepower to make significant contributions to a dozen fields, but – well, you'll see. He's also a kid. Loves video games and hates to clean his room. He's an American thirteen-year-old. Thank goodness.'

'You ever have to tell him where babies come from?'

'No, but he's asked some pretty pointed questions about the molecular basis of embryology.' A contented look settled on the savant's face. 'He's what they call a sport of nature.'

'Sounds like a good sport, anyway.'

'With a good nature.'

Brandon galumphed back into the parlor triumphantly holding a pair of canvas sneakers in one hand, green track pants in another.

His father rolled his eyes. 'You can say no, you realize,' he told her.

Andrea changed in a bathroom off the foyer. 'You've got five minutes,' she told Brandon when she emerged. 'Time enough to show me your stuff.'

'Fine. You want to see my moves?'

'*Bring* it, on kid,' she deadpanned, spoof streetwise. 'You gotta represent.'

The court – basic concrete with chalked lines – was tucked behind a tall privet hedge to one side of the house.

'You gonna show me your old-school moves?' He tossed the basketball from behind the three-point line. It glanced off the rim but didn't go through. Andrea stepped in and scooped up the ball, doing a fast dunk. She'd played varsity basketball in high school, still remembered the basic plays.

'Just keepin' it real,' Andrea returned. Brandon drove to the hoop and picked up the rebound; he was unpracticed and inexperienced, but surprisingly coordinated for a boy of his age. He seemed to study her stance when she put the ball through the net, and copied her moves. Each time he shot, he came a little closer. By the time they returned to the house – she insisting on keeping to the five minutes they had agreed on – they both had color in their cheeks. She changed out of the athletic shoes and track pants in a small powder room off a side parlor – how many did this house have, anyway? – and returned to the sitting room with the leather furniture.

The dinner was simple but delicious – a sorrel soup, grilled poussin, savory wild rice, a salad of lamb's lettuce – and Paul Bancroft steered the conversation back to the issues they had discussed earlier, without appearing to hold forth.

'You're a woman of many talents,' he said, with a twinkle. 'What do they call it? 'Ball control.' I'd say that's what you have. A skill that applies to argumentation as well as to competitive sport.'

'It's just a matter of keeping your eye on the ball,' Andrea said. 'See what's in front of your eyes.'

Paul Bancroft tilted his head. 'Was it Huxley who said that common sense was just a matter of seeing what's in front of your eyes? That's not quite right, is it? Lunatics see what they take to be in front of their eyes. Common sense is the gift of seeing what's in front of the other person's eyes. That's what makes it something we have in *common*. And what makes the skill itself, in turn, so *un*common.' His expression grew serious. 'You think about the history of our species, and it's striking the way that evil – institutions and practices that we all recognize to be insupportable – had been countenanced for centuries. Slavery. The subjugation of women. The extravagant punishment of consensual, victimless activities. All in all, hardly an edifying spectacle. But Jeremy Bentham, two hundred years ago, called everything right. He was one of the few men of his generation who truly belong to our moral modernity. Indeed, he was father to it. And it all began with the simple utilitarian insight: Minimize human suffering – and never forget that each person counts for one.'

'Dad's idea of the eleemosynary,' said Brandon, stumbling over the last word. 'However you say it.'

'Try el-ee-uh-mosynary,' Bancroft said, correcting his son's pronunciation. 'From the Latin *eleemosyna*, alms.'

'Got it,' the boy said, a new datum stored away. 'But what about the idea that you should treat others as *ends*, never as *means*?'

Paul caught Andrea's eye. 'He's been reading Kant. German mysticism, when you come down to it. Rots the brain, I tell you. Worse than Grand Theft Auto. We've had to agree to disagree.'

'So you have a problem with adolescent rebellion, too, huh?' Andrea smiled.

Brandon looked up from his plate and returned her smile. 'What makes you think it's a 'problem'?'

Suddenly the hooting of a distant owl could be heard. Paul Bancroft looked out the window, where tall trees were silhouetted in the dusk. 'The owl of Minerva, Hegel said, flies only at dusk.'

'Then wisdom comes too late,' Brandon said. 'Thing I don't get is how the owl got a reputation for wisdom, anyway. What an owl is, actually, is just an efficient killing machine. That's the one thing it's good at. Flight's nearly silent. Their powers of hearing are almost like radar. Ever see one fly? You see these big wings flapping, and it's like someone turned the sound off. That's 'cause they've got tattered fringe feathers that break up the sound of rushing air.'

Andrea tilted her head. 'So you never hear it coming until it's too late.'

'Pretty much. Then there's four hundred pounds of pressure at the tips of each talon, so by that point you're history.'

Andrea took a sip of the simple and refreshing Riesling that Nuala had poured. 'Not wise, then. Just deadly.'

'Efficient when it comes to means-end rationality,' Paul Bancroft put in. 'Some would say there's a kind of wisdom in that.'

'Are you one of them?'

'No, but efficiency has its place. Too often, though, talk of such things is taken to be heartless, even when it's in the service of kindness. You were talking about perverse consequences earlier, Andrea. That can be an intricate subject indeed. Because, once you accept the logic of consequentialism – the notion that acts must be judged by their consequences – then you realize that the puzzles go beyond the matter of good deeds that have bad effects. We must also grapple with the conundrum posed by bad deeds that have good effects.'

'Maybe so,' Andrea reflected. 'But there are some acts that are simply heinous in themselves. I mean, it's impossible to imagine anything good coming out of, oh, the assassination of Martin Luther King, Jr., let's say.'

Paul Bancroft lifted an eyebrow. 'Is that a challenge?'

'I'm just saying.'

The savant took a small sip of wine. 'You know, I met Dr. King on one or two occasions. The foundation helped him with financing at a couple of critical junctures. He was truly a remarkable man. A great man, I'd even say. But not without certain personal flaws. Small ones, lowly ones, but ones that could have been amplified by his foes. The FBI was always ready to leak sullying reports about personal indiscretions. In his final years, he was preaching to dwindling crowds, on a downward spiral. In death, he became a potent symbol. Had he lived, he would have been a far diminished one. His assassination was a galvanizing event. It actually catalyzed the legal fulfillment of the civil-rights revolution. Crucial legislation barring discrimination in housing was passed only in the wake of that tragic event. Americans were shaken to the core of their being, and the country became a kinder place as a consequence. If you want to say that the man's death was a tragedy, I won't argue. But that one death accomplished vastly more than many lives.' The aging philosopher spoke with mesmerizing intensity. 'Was it not more than redeemed by its positive consequences?'

Andrea put her fork down. 'Maybe as a matter of cold calculation . . .'

'Why cold? I never understand why people think that the calculus of consequences is cold. The betterment of humanity sounds abstract, yet it entails the betterment of individual men and women and children – each with a story that could tug at your heart and ravage your soul.' The tremor in his voice bespoke conviction and resolve, not diffidence or doubt. 'Remember, there are seven billion people living on this small planet. And two-point-eight billion of them are under twenty-four years of age. It's *their* world we need to maintain and improve.' The savant's eyes drifted toward his son, who, with the appetite of a growing boy, had already cleaned his plate. 'And that's a moral responsibility as grave as any.'

Andrea could not tear her eyes away from the man. He spoke with penetrating logic and a gaze as clear as his argument. There was something magical about the force of his conviction, the sinuous power of his mind. Merlin, of Arthurian legend, must have been inspired by someone like him.

'Dad's a big one for running the numbers,' Brandon said, perhaps embarrassed by his father's intensity.

'The harsh light of reason tells us that a prophet's death can be a boon to humanity. On the other hand, eradicate sand fleas in Mauritius, say, and you may discover that the knock-on consequences are dire indeed. In either scenario, the line we draw between killing and letting die is something of a superstition, don't you think?' Paul Bancroft pressed on. 'It makes no difference to the one who dies because of our action or failure to act. Imagine that a runaway trolley is hurtling down the tracks. If it continues on its course, it will kill five people. If you throw a switch, it will kill only one person. What do you do?'

'Throw the switch,' Andrea said.

'And save five lives. Yet you have thus sent a trolley toward an individual with foresight and deliberation, knowing that it will kill him. You have, in a sense, committed homicide. Had you done nothing, you would have no direct complicity or involvement in the deaths. Your hands would be clean.' He looked up. 'Nuala, once again you have outdone yourself,' he said as the red-cheeked Irishwoman brought more wild rice to the table.

'You're saying it's a kind of narcissism,' Andrea said slowly. 'Clean hands, four lives needlessly lost – a bad deal. I get it.'

'How we feel must be disciplined with what we think. Passion must be within reason, so to speak. Sometimes the noblest act of all is also the one that most appalls.'

'I feel like I'm back in a college seminar again.'

'Do these issues strike you as academic? Merely theoretical? Then let's make them real to you.' Paul Bancroft looked gnomic, a man with a surprise in his pocket. 'What if you had twenty million dollars to spend on the uplift of your species?'

'Another what-if?' Andrea allowed herself a small smile.

'Not exactly. I'm not speaking hypothetically any longer. Before our next board meeting, Andrea, I'd like you to identify a particular project or cause that you'd like to spend twenty million dollars on. Work out exactly which, and exactly how, and we'll do it. Straight from my discretionary funds. No deliberation or conferral. It will be done on your say-so.'

'You're joking.'

Brandon gave her a sideways look. 'Dad's not a big prankster,' the boy told her. 'He's not Mister Leg-pull, believe me.'

'Twenty million dollars,' Paul Bancroft repeated.

'On my say-so?' Andrea was incredulous.

'On your say-so.' The maven's age-etched countenance was grave now. 'Choose wisely,' he counseled. 'Every hour of the day there's a trolley car hurtling out of control. But the choice isn't between one of two tracks. It's between one of a thousand tracks, or ten thousand tracks, and what lies ahead on each course is far from clear. We must make our very best guesses, with all the intelligence and discernment at our disposal. And hope for the best.'

'You're dealing with so many unknowns.'

'Unknowns? Or partially knowns? Incomplete knowledge is not the same as ignorance. Informed judgments can still be made. Indeed, they must be made.' His gaze did not waver. 'So choose wisely. You'll find that doing the right thing isn't always easy.'

Andrea Bancroft felt dizzy, intoxicated, and it was not because of the wine. How many people had a chance to make a difference like that, she wondered. She had been given the ability to snap a finger – and transform the lives of thousands. It felt . . . almost godlike.

Brandon interrupted her reveries. 'Yo, Andrea, you gonna be up for another quick game of hoops after dinner?'

Rome

Trastevere – the neighborhoods to the west of the Tiber River – was, for many residents, the real Rome, its medieval warren of streets having largely escaped the nineteenth-century rebuilding that transformed the city center. Squalor plus age equals cachet: Was that how the formula worked? Yet there remained corners that time had forgotten, or, more accurately, remembered – corners where the rising tide of new money had left only driftwood and detritus. Such was the ground-floor apartment of a dark side street where the Italian girl had lived with her parents. The Zingarettis were an old family, in that they knew the names of their forebears from hundreds of years ago. But those forebears had invariably been servitors and subalterns. It was tradition without grandeur, lineage without history.

The Todd Belknap who arrived at via Clarice Marescotti 14 was scarcely recognizable as the person who had infil-trated Ansari's dungeon hours before. He was immaculately attired, shaved, bathed, lightly scented: an Italian's idea of officialdom. It would help. Even Belknap's American accent might help rather than hinder; Italians were reflexively sus-picious of their own countrymen, and usually with good reason.

The conversation did not go smoothly.

Ma non capisco! – But I don't understand, the girl's mother, a black-garbed crone, kept repeating. She looked older than most women her age, but also stronger. A vocational trait: She was, in the British idiom, 'a woman who does.'

Non c'è problema, insisted the father, a potbellied man with rough, callused hands and thickened nails. *There's no problem.*

But there *was* a problem, and she did understand – understand more than she pretended, anyway. They sat together in their gloomy sitting room, which smelled of burned soup and mildew. The cold floor, doubtless once tiled, was a rough, unvarying gray, as if slathered with a layer of grout in preparation for tiles that never arrived. The lamps were of low wattage, their shades frayed by heat and age. None of the chairs matched. They were a proud family, but not a house-proud one. Lucia's parents were clearly aware of her beauty, which they seem to have regarded as a potential vulnerability – indeed, a likely source of heartbreak, to her and to them. It meant early pregnancy, the flattery and then the predations of unscrupulous men. Lucia had assured them that the Arab – they referred to her employer only as *l'Arabo* – was religiously devout, disciplined by zealous obedience to the Prophet's word.

And where was she now?

When it came to the crucial question, the girl's parents feigned obtuseness, incomprehension, ignorance. They were protecting her – because they knew what she had done? Or for another reason? Belknap would get through to them only if he persuaded them that the girl was in danger, and that candor, not evasion, would best protect her.

It was hard work. To gain information, he had to pretend to have information that he lacked. Again and again, he told them: Your daughter is in danger. *La vostra figlia è in pericolo.* He was not believed – which meant that they were in touch with her, that she had given them reassurances. If she had truly disappeared unexpectedly, they would be unable to conceal their anxiety. Instead, they feigned confusion as to her whereabouts, retreating into vagueness: She said she had gone on a trip, she had not elaborated further, but perhaps it was for her employer. No, they did not know when she would return.

Lies. Tales proven false by the ease with which they were related. Amateurs believed that liars gave themselves away by their anxiety, their nervousness; just as often, Belknap knew, they betrayed themselves by their lack of nervousness. That was the case with Signor and Signora Zingaretti.

Belknap let a long moment of silence elapse before he started on them again. 'She has been in touch with you,' he said. 'We know this. She has assured you that everything is fine. She believes that everything is fine. But she does not know. *She does not know that she is in imminent danger.*' He made a quick throat-cut gesture. 'Her enemies are resourceful, and they are everywhere.'

The Zingarettis' wary gaze told him that they regarded the American interloper as a potential enemy. He had induced a flicker of hesitation, a glimmer of concern where there had been none before; but he had not won them over. Still, a small fissure had appeared in the stone wall, their front of obliviousness.

'She has told you not to worry,' he began again, calibrating his words to their expression, 'because she does not know that she has cause to worry.'

'And you do?' the crone in black asked, her mouth a little tent of disapproval and suspicion. Belknap's story had not been the truth, exactly, but he hewed to the truth as closely as he could. He told them that he was from an American agency, part of a high-level international investigation. The investigation had uncovered special knowledge of *l'Arabo*'s activities. Members of the man's personal staff were in jeopardy from a vendetta conducted by a Middle Eastern rival. At the word '*vendetta*' there was a glimmer in the elderly couple's eyes, an echoing whisper from the old woman: This was a concept they understood and treated with proper respect.

'Just yesterday, I saw the body of a young woman who . . .' Belknap broke off. He noticed the couple's widening eyes, shook his head. 'It's too horrible. *Very* upsetting. There are certain images that stay with one forever. And when I think what they did to that young woman, a beautiful young woman just like your daughter, I can't help but shudder.' He stood up. 'But I've done all I could here. I have to remember that. You must remember it, too. Now I will leave you in peace. You will not see me again. Nor, I fear, your daughter.'

Signora Zingaretti placed a clawlike hand on her husband's. 'Wait,' she said. Her husband shot her a glance, but it was clear that she was in command of this household. She stared at Belknap, making her own assessment of his character, his probity. Then she made a decision. 'You are mistaken,' she said. 'Lucia is safe. We speak to her regularly. We spoke to her last night.'

'Where is she?' Belknap asked.

'This we do not know. This she does not tell us.' The vertical lines on her upper lip were like the tick marks on a ruler.

'Why not?'

The potbellied man said, 'She tells us it's a very nice place. But the location is confidential. She cannot say. Because of . . . terms of employment.' *Termini di occupazione.* He gave an uncertain grin – uncertain because he could not know whether his words had refuted the worries the American had expressed or given fuel to them.

'Lucia is a clever girl,' said her mother. Her face was drawn with fear; it was as if there were ashes in her mouth. 'She knows how to look after herself.' She was trying to reassure herself.

'You spoke to her last night,' Belknap repeated.

'She was fine.' The old man's beefy hands shook as he folded them in his lap.

'She will take care of herself.' The crone's words were a defiant pledge, or maybe just a hope.

As soon as Belknap was back on the cobblestone street, he called an old *carabiniere* contact, Gianni Mattucci. In Italy – and Italian law enforcement was no exception – you got things done through friends, not formalities. He quickly conveyed his request to Mattucci. Lucia might have been

119

just as close-mouthed as her parents had claimed, but the phone records would surely be more forthcoming.

Mattucci's voice was as astringent as a young Barolo, and as rich. '*Più lento!* Slower,' he prompted. 'Give me the name and the address. I'll run the name through the city database, get her INPS code.' That was the Italian equivalent of a Social Security number. 'Then I'll take that to the municipal phone registry.'

'Tell me this won't take long, Gianni.'

'You Americans – always in such a rush. I'll do my best, okay, my friend?'

'Your best is usually pretty good,' Belknap allowed.

'Go have an espresso someplace,' the Italian police inspector said coaxingly. 'I call you.'

Belknap had barely walked a couple of blocks when his cell phone buzzed: It was Mattucci again.

'That was fast,' Belknap said.

'We just got a report about the very address you mention,' Mattucci said. He sounded agitated. 'A neighbor reports gunfire. We've got a couple of squad cars on their way. What's going on?'

Belknap was thunderstruck. 'Oh, Christ,' he breathed. 'Let me check it out.'

'Don't,' Mattucci implored, but Belknap clicked off, already racing toward the ground-floor apartment he had left only minutes before. As he rounded the corner, he heard the sounds of squealing tires – and his heart began to shudder in his chest. The entrance had been left unlocked, and he strode into a room riddled with bullets and spattered with blood. He had been followed: There was no other explanation. He had spoken to the elderly couple of protection, yet had only brought death in his train.

More tires, skidding on cobblestone: this time the sound of arrival. It was a coupe, dark blue save for its white roof. On the roof was a stenciled number meant to be visible to helicopters, along with three lights. The world CARABINIERI was lettered on the side, in white, a red racing stripe above it. It was the real thing, and so were the two police officers who, scrambling out of the vehicle, ordered Belknap not to move.

Out of the corner of his eye, Belknap saw another police car coming. He gestured frantically in the direction of a side street, signaling that the assailants had gone in that direction.

Then he ran.

One of the policemen gave chase, of course; the other had to secure the crime scene. Belknap hoped that he had sown enough confusion to discourage his pursuer from shooting at him: They had at least to consider the possibility that he, too, was in pursuit of the *criminali*. Belknap dashed around metal trash canisters, around Dumpsters and parked cars – anything to obscure the sightline between him and the policeman. The line of sight.

The line of fire.

He could feel his muscles burning, his breath coming in gulps, as he sprinted wildly, with the zigzagging movements of a fleeing hare. He was scarcely aware of the ground beneath his rubber-soled leather shoes. Within a few minutes, though, he had climbed into his vehicle, a white windowless van emblazoned with the logo of the Italian mail service: SERVIZIO POSTALE. It was one of various vehicles that Consular Operations had at its disposal, and though Belknap did not have authorization, he had little trouble gaining access to it. It was the sort of vehicle that normally attracted little notice. He hoped that would be the case now.

As he started up the van and sped away, however, he saw, in his rearview mirror, another police vehicle – a Jeep-style *carabinieri* car with a boxy top, meant for holding prisoners. At the same time, his cell buzzed again.

Mattucci's voice, even more agitated than before. 'You must tell me what is happening!' he said, almost shouting. 'They say this elderly couple has been massacred, the apartment shot up. Evidently the bullets are semi-jacketed U.S. special-op hollowpoints. Do you hear me? The scalloped-copper jackets you happen to favor. *Not* good.'

Belknap spun the steering wheel sharply to the right,

making a last-minute turn. To his right was a green tramcar with four rubberized expansion joints, half a block in length. It would block him from the view of anyone on the opposite lane. 'Gianni, you can't possibly believe that – '

'A fingerprint technician will be arriving shortly. If they find your prints, I won't be able to protect you.' A pause. 'I can't protect you now.' This time it was Mattucci who clicked off first.

Another police car was pulling up behind Belknap. He had to have been spotted getting into the van, and it was too late to change vehicles now. He steadily increased the pressure on the accelerator pedal as he veered through the traffic on the Piazza San Calisto and onto the faster-moving viale de Trastevere, speeding toward the river. Now the police car behind him had activated its own siren and flashing lights. By the time he crossed the via Indumo, he had picked up another cruiser – a Citroën sedan emblazoned with the word polizia in backward-slanting capitals of blue and white. There was no room for ambiguity. He was being chased.

Something had gone very wrong.

He pressed the accelerator to the floor, veering around slower vehicles – taxis, ordinary motorists, a delivery truck – and, blaring his horn, shot through the light at the Piazza Porta Portese, slewing through lanes of traffic. He had lost the *carabinieri* Jeeps, at least. The limestone buildings to his left and right became blurred dirty-gray silhouettes; the pavement in front of him became everything – the small shifting portals between moving vehicles, gaps that appeared and disappeared in rapid flux, openings that would close if not seized at the right instant. High-speed driving was an entirely different activity than ordinary lawful motoring, and, as he crossed the Ponte Sublicio over the dark-green Tiber, toward the Piazza Emporio, Belknap had to hope that the old reflexes would kick in when they were needed. There were hundreds of ways to go wrong, a very few ways to go right. The second cruiser, the Citroën sedan, suddenly found a clear pathway and shot ahead of Belknap.

The box was beginning to form.

If, as seemed likely, a third cruiser were to appear, Belknap's chances of evasion would drop precipitously. He had been hoping to enter the higher-speed thoroughfare that wrapped along the Tiber, along the high, tree-mounded, brick-and-concrete embankment. That was too risky now.

Abruptly he swung the steering wheel to the right, and his vehicle swerved onto the Lungotevere Aventino, the road that ran along the Testaccio side of the river. He felt his torso hurtled toward the left, restrained only by the seat and shoulder belts.

Now he made another sharp turn, onto the café-cluttered via Rubattino, and then took a breath and swung the van back onto the via Vespucci – this time driving the wrong way, against traffic. He only had to traverse a few hundred yards of it before he could turn onto the fast-moving Tiber-side road – assuming he could avoid collision on the Vespucci.

The horns of a dozen cars shrilled and blared as motorists frantically tried to avoid the white postal van that was rushing toward them.

Belknap steered with hands slick with sweat. The task of swerving this way and that to maneuver the van through a stream of motorists facing the opposite direction required him to anticipate their own evasive swerves. A single miscalculation would result in a head-on collision with the summed force of their opposing velocities.

The world was reduced to nothing more than a ribbon of pavement and a swarming constellation of cars, every one a potential deadly weapon. The underbody of the postal van, with its low-riding chassis, bounced, scraped, and sparked as it descended too fast onto the ramp leading back to the fast-moving embankment road, but he made it over the next bridge, the Ponte Palatino, and, with another sharp, skidding turn, onto the Porta di Ripagrande.

Now he could breathe, he told himself, as he powered the van on the straightaway past grand anonymous buildings. Yet when he looked in his rearview mirror, he saw half a dozen police cruisers. How had they materialized so quickly? Then he remembered the large police station located near the

Piazzale Portuense. He steered onto the left road shoulder, gutterballing down it and peeling off onto the Clivio Portuense, one of the faster streets in the area. Once again, only the restraint belts kept him from being flung across the vehicle.

The cruisers swept past him, unable to slow down in time to catch the turn. He had lost them – at least for the moment. He powered down the streets until he reached the via Parboni, and took a left.

Yet what was that ahead of him? He could scarcely hear himself think above the blaring siren, the straining motor, the squealing tires.

It seemed impossible! Ahead of him, at the corner of the via Bargoni, he saw a roadblock. How had they put it up so fast? He squinted, saw that it was made up of two cruisers and a portable wooden barricade. He could try to crash it . . .

Except that, behind him, roaring up seemingly from out of nowhere, was an unmarked car from the *polizia municipale*'s highway-patrol unit, a three-liter-turbo-engined Lancia sedan especially equipped for high-speed vehicular apprehension.

Belknap gunned the van fully, watching four *carabinieri* standing at the roadblock – large men with sunglasses and arms folded on their chests – scramble out of the way. Then he jerked the gearshift into neutral and seized the parking brake at the exact same moment he gave the steering wheel a half-turn toward the left. The car had slewed around perpendicular to the road, and the tires of the high-powered Lancia screamed as it veered off to the side of the road to avoid colliding with the postal van, shuddering to a halt as its front crumpled into a fire hydrant.

Now Belknap released the parking brake, floored the accelerator, and straightened out the steering wheel. The vehicle juddered, and a loud clattering noise told him that the pressure on the sidewalls had caused the hubcaps to fly off. At the same time, the torque on the transmission had caused oil to surge into the system, and in the rearview mirror he could see a cloud of thick black smoke pouring from his exhaust. But he had reversed direction without pausing. Now he was skimming the wrong way down via Bargoni, except this time the street was nearly empty. By blocking it off at the other end, the police had unwittingly done him a favor. He turned left on the via Bezzi, whipped onto the speedy viale de Trastevere, past the Autorità per la Informatica nella Pubblica Amministrazione – and lost his pursuers.

Ten minutes later, he was seated at a café, where he finally ordered the espresso Gianni Mattucci had recommended. He disguised his exhaustion as the ennui of a bored tourist, but phoned his *carabiniere* contact at first opportunity.

'Now we can talk,' Belknap said quietly, keeping his voice conversational. Many fugitives swiftly gave themselves away by their anxiety; they were keyed up in a way that invariably brought them attention. Belknap would not make that mistake.

'*Ma che diavolo!* Do you have any idea what I'm dealing with right now?' Mattucci's voice was beyond strained. 'You must tell me what you know!'

'You first,' said Belknap.

CHAPTER SIX

'I'm serious,' Hank Sidgwick was saying over the telephone, and Andrea Bancroft realized, with a sinking feeling, that he was. 'I'm telling you, this guy could really use the bucks.'

She could picture him at his desk. Sidgwick, pushing forty, retained his all-American looks: blue eyes, blond hair, the body of a middleweight wrestler, though the sun-reddened furrows of his forehead foretold a less-than-flattering middle age. Somehow he always smelled like fresh laundry. He was a friend and colleague at Coventry Equity Group, but she had first met him years earlier, when he was dating a girlfriend of hers in college.

'You know the most interesting people,' she said carefully. She had always enjoyed Hank's company and was at first pleased by his call. He had, in turn, been fascinated by her recounting of her first foundation meeting. Now, though, she wondered whether she should have been so forthcoming. Hadn't she promised, strictly speaking, to treat the foundation's proceedings as 'privileged and confidential'? But what really took her aback was how callow Hank's response had been when she told him about the test that Paul Bancroft had put her to. Hank's wife had a friend who was an independent documentary maker. 'He could put twenty million to good use,' Hank had told Andrea: his first response. Evidently the filmmaker wanted to complete a documentary about East Village performance artists who engaged in bizarre body-modification practices. Andrea glanced at the door, unconsciously signaling her impatience. She had been talking about saving lives, and all Hank could think of was this trivial endeavor?

'Just something to mull over,' Sidgwick said in a fake offhanded tone as he stood up to go.

'Of course,' she said automatically.

Didn't anybody get it? Yet she would not let herself express her indignation. She was self-conscious about coming across as a snob. It was important to her, somehow, that everyone saw her as the same old Andrea, unchanged by sudden fortune.

But I'm not, she reflected. *That's the truth. I'm different now.*

Yes, it was time to stop pretending, she decided. Everything was different.

Almost as soon as she hung up, the telephone rang again.

'Miss Bancroft?' the caller asked. A voice that sounded slightly hoarse and somehow smoky.

'Yes,' she said, instantly feeling a pang of unease.

'I'm calling from the Bancroft Foundation, the security desk. Just wanted to make sure you were clear about the details of the nondisclosure agreement.'

'Of course.' A silly, paranoid thought came to her: *It was as if they knew.* As if they'd heard her speaking indiscreetly and were calling her to account.

'And there are other security protocol and compliance issues. We'll be sending someone to you shortly, if that's all right.'

'Sure thing,' Andrea said, still spooked, and when she put the phone down, she realized that she was hugging herself for warmth.

Something small and disquieting was beginning to bud in the back of her mind, so she forced herself to think about other things. She once again found herself walking – trudging – in a dreamlike state through her small home. *Welcome to your new life*, she thought.

But she wasn't going to live for herself alone. That was the thing. She was going to be part of an incredible project – something truly large, truly important. Merlin's assurance: *On your say-so.*

What project would be deserving? So much needed to be done. Water and sanitation was a life-or-death issue for many, and so were diseases like AIDS and malaria, conditions like malnutrition. Then there were issues like global warming. Endangered species. There were so many challenges, so many unknowns, so many partially knowns. How to target the funds for maximal results – the biggest bang for the buck? It was hard, all right, damned hard. Because, really, you had to do the math and think five steps ahead, as Paul Bancroft had explained. Twenty million was too much for some problems, way too little for others. As different scenarios filled her mind, she found that her appreciation for what Paul Bancroft had managed to achieve mounted.

There was a knock at the door, and her thoughts dissipated like smoke rings. At the door was a man she did not recognize, a man whose well-tailored suit failed to conceal how heavily muscled he was: To her, he looked like a cross between a banker and a . . . bouncer.

'I'm with the Bancroft Foundation,' the man said.

No surprise there.

'You'd asked to have certain case files delivered,' he went on.

She noticed he had a briefcase in one hand, and remembered the request that she'd made the day before. She had been expecting a courier service, or a UPS deliveryman. 'Oh, of course,' she said. 'Please come in.'

'And there are various security details to review. I hope someone called before to say I was coming.' His steel-gray hair was combed in a knife-sharp part. He had a square face with undistinguished features. He was at some indeterminate point of middle age; she wasn't even sure which decade.

'Someone called, yeah,' Andrea said.

He stepped inside, his movements like those of a jungle cat; muscles seemed to ripple beneath costly fabric. He opened the briefcase and handed her a clutch of folders. 'You have any questions about procedure at the foundation? Protocol's been laid out?'

'Everything's been carefully explained.'

'Good to know,' he said. 'You have a shredder?'

'Like for cheese?'

The man did not smile. 'We can supply you with a DoD-grade crosscut shredder. Otherwise we'll ask you to be sure that the contents of these files, photocopied or otherwise, are returned to the foundation offices.'

'Okay.'

'Just the procedure. You're new, so I'm supposed to remind you about the terms of the nondisclosure agreement you're party to.'

'Look, I was in finance, I get the nondisclosure thing.'

His eyes seemed to study her face. 'Then you understand that you're forbidden to discuss any foundation business with outsiders.'

'Right,' Andrea said nervously.

'Easy to forget.' The man spoke the words with a twinkle, but not, it somehow seemed to her, a friendly twinkle. 'Important not to.' He began to make his way to the door.

'Thank you. I'll bear that in mind.' Andrea tried not to let it show, but, again, she was spooked. Was it really possible that the foundation had her under surveillance? That it knew about the conversation she'd had just a little earlier? Had her house been bugged?

Nonsense. It was all nonsense, the paranoid imaginings of an unsettled mind, she assured herself. But was there something about the way the man looked at her: a hint of a smile, a certain curious familiarity? No, she was being paranoid again.

Andrea was about to ask him whether they had ever met before when, just before he stepped onto her porch, he offered a terse explanation. 'You look a lot like your mother.'

The way he said it chilled her further. She thanked her visitor politely, formally. 'I'm sorry – I forgot what you said your name was,' she prompted.

'I didn't,' he replied blandly. As he turned and walked to an idling Town Car, the phone rang again.

Cindy Lewalski, a realtor with the Cooper Brandt Group, was returning a call Andrea had almost forgotten she had made.

'So I gather you're interested in looking at apartments in

Manhattan,' the woman said. A whiskey voice, businesslike but friendly.

'That's right,' Andrea said. She had always dreamed of a loft in New York, and, darn it, now she could afford it, with twelve million dollars earning two percent interest in her savings account. She didn't want to put on airs, but she wasn't fooling anybody, and she wasn't going to martyr herself by staying 'humble' – that would be the worst affectation of all. She could make an all-cash offer on a place in the big city, get something nice. Something *really* nice.

Cindy Lewalski took down Andrea's basic information as she opened a client file on her computer, establishing a price range and the features that Andrea was looking for – size, neighborhood, and so forth. She verified the spelling of Andrea's name. 'You wouldn't happen to be one of *those* Bancrofts, by chance?' she asked.

Andrea replied without a flicker of hesitation. 'You've got my number.'

West End, London

To the world, he was Lukas. The Edinburgh-born rock star had sported the mononym since his early days with the band G7; and the first of the four platinum albums he had recorded since starting a solo career was, as the industry had it, 'self-titled.' Someone charted the frequency of babies named Lukas and showed a sharp upturn that began with his hit-making career. Hardcore fans knew he was born Hugh Burney, but the knowledge never stuck. Lukas was the truer identity. He had come to look like Lukas, even to himself.

The sound studio, tucked away in what had once been a girls' school on Gosfield Street, was gleaming and state-of-the-art, a far cry from the places he had been used to before his career took off. But certain aspects of the enterprise remained the same. For instance, the headphones were getting itchy, as often happened after twenty or so minutes. He pulled them off, put them on again. His producer, Jack Rawls, played another sequence of bass lines.

'Too heavy, man,' Lukas said. 'Still too heavy.'

'You don't want it to fly away,' Rawls protested mildly. 'This song, it's like a picnic blanket in a windstorm. You need to weight it down with a heavy object. A curling stone, like.'

'Yeah, but you've given us a boulder. It's just too much. You feelin' me?' This wasn't the glamorous part of the business. The air inside the recording studio was getting stuffy – 'fuggy,' as Rawls would say – because mechanical ventilation produced noise. Rawls was seated before an array of synthesizers. These days, the line between producers and instrumentalists was getting blurry, and Rawls, a former keyboard player, combined both roles. Lukas was aiming for an atmospheric soundscape – an ambient electronic groove. When Lukas and Rawls were at the Ipswich Art School together, they experimented with using tape recorders as instruments. The hiss of a blank tape itself could be a powerful sonic element. Lukas was aiming for something like that now.

'How about we try it both ways?' Rawls said, in an agreeable tone of voice that meant he was determined to get his way.

'How about you just dial it back a titch?' Lukas grinned, displaying his famously dazzling smile. *Not this time, Jack.*

It was his first album in two years, and Lukas was fastidious about every detail. He owed it to people. His fans. Lukas hated the word 'fans,' but there it was. What did you call the people who bought not just the albums, but the singles, too? Who traded so-called basement tapes with one another? Who knew his music even better than Lukas himself did?

An assistant, wildly pantomiming outside the glass: *telephone.*

Lukas made a blow-off gesture in return. He'd told them that he wasn't taking phone calls. He was working. The Pan-African tour was going to start in just two weeks, so he didn't have a lot of time at the recording studio. He had to make the most of the sessions he had scheduled.

Now the assistant reappeared holding the phone, pointing to it. 'You'll want to take this,' she mouthed.

Lukas took off his headphones, stood up, and retreated to the jury-rigged office he had made for himself across the hall.

'They said yes!' His agent, Ari Sanders, crowing.

'What are you talking about?'

'Eighty percent of the house. Madison Square Garden. You're wondering: How did Ari Sanders swing this one? Yes, you are. Well, forget about it. A magician never reveals his secrets!'

'I'm a slow Scotsman, Ari. You need to break it down for me nice and easy. I have no idea what you're talking about.'

'Okay, okay, I can refuse you nothing. We got word that the Garden had to cancel the hip-hop gala because of insurance problems. Can you believe? Suddenly, they've got a humungous hole in their schedule. A Friday night and they're dark, can you believe it? So that's when your faithful knight commits armed robbery. A daylight hijacking. I tell the manager, There's one guy who can sell out the house in four days, and that's *my* guy. Am I right? You put an ad on the radio saying Surprise Lukas Concert! So the goniff's practically wetting himself. He wants it. This is headline news, right?'

'News to *me*,' Lukas said warningly.

'Oh, but I had to play it this way. I got his balls in my hand. Then I squeezed, hard. I say, Lukas hasn't performed a live concert in the United States for a long, long time. But if you want him to break his goddamn self-denying ordinance, you have to do right by him. Eighty percent of the house. That's what I said. The bastard starts bellyaching, about how they've never given more than fifty percent, on and on. I said, 'Fine. This conversation is over.' He says, 'Hold on a sec.' I'm counting to myself: one Mississippi, two Mississippi . . . And he caved. Can you believe it! He caved! New York, make some noise for . . . Lukas!'

'Listen, Ari,' Lukas said. An eel of unease squirmed through his innards. 'I just don't know whether – '

Ari Sanders steamrollered on with his customary manic energy. 'You're a saint! A goddamn Scottish saint! All those

benefit concerts you've been doing for the past three years –
I mean, it chokes me up to think about it. All those orphans
and widows you've helped. It humbles me. It *humbles* me.
Your Children's Crusade? Truly an inspiring thing. Like *Time*
magazine says, nobody has done more to draw the world's attention to the worst off among us. A rock star with a social
conscience – I mean, who would have figured? But Lukas?'

'Yeah?'

'*Enough's enough*. Oh, sure, widows and orphans – you
gotta love 'em. But the secret to life is balance. You gotta
show love to the hordes of Lukas fans out there. And you
gotta show love to little Ari Sanders, who's been busting his
heinie for you out on the front lines every day.'

'A twenty percent cut's not enough, all of a sudden?'

'Do this,' Ari said. 'I made history today. I made history
for *you*. Eighty percent of box office receipts – the Pope
doesn't get that.' He paused to take a breath. 'Then again,
how many Grammy Awards has *he* won?'

'I'll think about it, okay,' Lukas said weakly. 'But I've got
these benefit concerts all lined up, and – '

'So they'll be heartbroken in Ouagadougou for a day.
Change your plans. You cannot say no to this.'

'I'll – I'll get back to you.'

'Jesus, Lukas, you sound like someone's got a gun to your
head.'

Lukas clicked off. He noticed that he was sweating.

Moments later, his personal cell phone chimed its Jimi
Hendrix ringtone. 'Lukas here,' he said.

It was an all-too-familiar voice: electronically altered,
eerily devoid of humanity, of affect. 'Stick to the plan,' the
voice said. If a lizard could speak, Lukas thought, this is what
it would sound like.

He swallowed hard. It felt as if there was a stone lodged
in his throat. 'Look, I've done everything you told me to – '

'We still have the videotape,' the voice said.

The videotape. The goddamn videotape. The girl had
sworn she was seventeen. How could he have known that
she was exaggerating by three crucial years? Which made it

statutory rape. A criminal offense. Deadly to his endorsement deals, his career, his reputation, his marriage. Lukas needed reminding of none of this. There were some musicians who could weather a revelation like that, especially the ones who deliberately cultivated a bad-boy image. That wasn't Lukas's way, though. If anything, a few had even accused him of sententiousness, of a holier-than-thou streak: They would pounce on the slightest weakness. And if he were prosecuted? He could readily imagine the headlines: LUKAS TO FACE THE MUSIC. ROCK STAR JAILED ON CHILD MOLESTING RAP. CHILDREN'S CRUSADER ARRAIGNED ON KIDDIE SEX CHARGES.

Maybe there were some who could survive that. Lukas wasn't among them.

'All right,' Lukas said. 'I get it.' What sickened him the most was the rapidity with which the call had followed Ari's. His every call was evidently monitored, and must have been for the past three years. Indeed, he could only guess at how much of his life was under surveillance by these faceless manipulators. There seemed no limit to what they knew about him – whoever 'they' really were.

'Stick to the plan,' the voice repeated. 'Do the right thing.'

'Like I have a choice,' Lukas replied shakily. 'Like I have a friggin' choice.'

Dubai, the United Arab Emirates

It was a skyline out of Jules Verne: the Arabian sands sprouting vast structures of glass and steel, contours undulating like spacecraft. Ancient souks huddled in the shadow of vast new shopping malls; dhows and abras nestled besides vast freighters and cruise ships; low, crowded street markets displayed DVD players and karaoke machines alongside rugs, leather goods, and trinkets. Dubai was a place that had everything – except mailing addresses. A building was on Sheikh Zayed Road, and on some official map that building had a number. But mail was delivered according to P.O. boxes, not street numbers. At Dubai International Airport, an area larger than the city center, Belknap took a tan-colored metered taxi, paying for the three empty seats at the driver's voluble insistence.

The man, evidently a Pakistani, wore a local-style keffiyeh of white-and-red checked fabric, like the tablecloth of an old-fashioned Italian restaurant, and rattled off one sales pitch after another. But he had to repeat his chief mid-trip sugges-tion three times before Belknap was able to understand him: 'You want to go Wild Wadi Waterpark?' It was evidently a tourist attraction, twelve acres of water rides, and the driver probably got a finder's fee for bringing visitors over.

Between the blast-furnace heat and the bleaching dazzle from the sun overhead, Belknap felt he had arrived at a planet that did not naturally support life, and had to move from one oxygenated pod to another. Certainly most of Dubai's superstructure was devoted to creating a wholly arti-ficial environment: an oasis of freon and steel and polarized glass. It was a place of portals, and yet curiously guarded, if your interest was not in shopping or the luxuries of a resort existence: Depending on the nature of one's pursuits, one would find it to be a place of a thousand welcome mats or a thousand locked gates. In Rome, Gianni Mattucci had sup-plied the address that corresponded to the number from which the Italian girl had telephoned. In Dubai, Belknap learned that the address led him to no residence or hotel, but rather a commercial post office that handled mail for several of the swank hotels along the beach.

If it weren't for the gentle azure of the Gulf, he could have been in Las Vegas in summer: There was the same garish display of affluence, the sleek pop-modernism of the construction, the boundlessness of human greed emblema-tized in architecture. And yet in the real wadis and escarp-ments nearby were Koranic holy men who sought to establish a global *ummah*, and to unhorse what they regarded as the American imperium. Dubai existed for the delectation of foreigners in an arid country that dreamed fervently of their humiliation. The serenity that obtained was as perishable as a rainbow.

'No Wild Wadi Waterpark,' Belknap grumbled warningly when the driver had brightened with the thought of another tourist snare. 'No Dubai Dinner Cruise. No Dubai Desert Class Golf. *No.*'

'But Sahib – '

'And don't 'Sahib' me. I'm not some colonel out of Kipling.'

The taxi driver reluctantly let him off at the small mail-sorting facility. Belknap stepped out of the car, was struck by a riptide of sheer heat, and ducked back inside. 'You wait here,' he instructed the driver, handing him another sheaf of pink and blue dirhams, the currency of the Emirates.

'I take dollars,' the driver said hopefully.

'Of course you do. Isn't that what Dubai exists for?'

A sly look crept over the man's face. Belknap was reminded of an Arab proverb: Never seek to know what the camel thinks of the camel driver. 'I wait,' the man said.

The facility was a white-painted, low-slung concrete box, windowless except for the grated front. It was infrastructure, not superstructure: one of those buildings designed not for public display but for serving those that were. It received mail addressed to many separately designated post boxes, and made deliveries up and down the small rear lane that serviced the gargantuan pleasure palaces on the beach roads.

Belknap would rely upon an air of officialdom, his unwrinkled blue tropical-weight suit and white shirt. He knew immediately upon entering that the establishment was not set up for visitors. There was no receptionist, nobody minding a counter. Instead, an expanse of grip-textured laminated flooring – the kind one found in sweatshops that did not use heavy machinery – opened onto a space where workers sorted mail into wire-mesh bins. They looked, at a glance, to be Filipinos; it took Belknap just a few moments to determine who the manager was. It was a fat man, a local, it seemed, who held an unlighted cigar in his sausage-like fingers and sat on a high stool in a corner, with a clipboard on one knee. The fat man's nails gleamed under the overhead fluorescent lights; they had been buffed, perhaps even lacquered with a clear polish. Thick rings puckered his fingers like the neck-bands on Chinese fishing cormorants.

Belknap would take advantage of his anomalousness. Holding his cell phone to his ear, he wrapped up a fictitious, official-sounding conversation: 'That's right, Inspector. We appreciate your help, and please do send our best to the deputy governor. We don't anticipate any problems with this. Bye.' Then, with an officious hand gesture, he summoned the plump bejeweled Arab. He would get what he needed not by pretending to fit in but by emphasizing his foreignness. He would be the imperious American, a government agent who expected all foreigners to be at his beck and call, his extraterritorial privileges paved by hundreds of obscure treaties and bilateral agreements.

The manager padded over to him with a look hedged between obsequiousness and annoyance.

'I'm Agent Belknap,' the American intoned. He solemnly handed the man his Virginia driver's license, as if it were the keys to the city.

The Arab pretended to look at it before handing it back. 'I see,' he replied, affecting an air of responsibility and efficiency.

'With the DEA, as you saw,' Belknap went on. 'Joint service request.'

'Yes, of course.' The manager was still deciding whether to call for a superior to come over, Belknap could tell.

'P.O. Box 11417,' Belknap announced, a man with no time to waste. 'Tell me the physical location.' His face was stern, the request made with no 'please,' no apologies, no concessions to courtesy whatsoever. The very preemptory nature of his approach would place it above suspicion, or beneath it. He was not wheedling, appealing to the man's discretion, as someone would who was trying to gain information that was not his by right. Nothing suggested that the Arab had even the right to decide whether to comply with the request. On the contrary. Belknap was demanding something owed him by virtue of his office. The effect was to alleviate the manager's uncertain and anxiety: He could not make the wrong decision because he had not been invited to make a decision at all.

'Ah,' the manager said, given an easy question where he feared a hard one. 'That would be the Palace Hotel. About two kilometers past the Al-Khaleej Roundabout.' The man made a flowing gesture with his hand, and Belknap realized he was describing the hotel's distinctive shape, a sort of glass whale with a central tower shaped like a waterspout.

'That's what I needed to know,' Belknap said. The manager looked almost grateful: *Is that all?*

When Belknap returned to the cab, he saw the manager peering out at the front door, looking puzzled to see the beige vehicle. He had obviously been expecting something more official. Yet it was unlikely he would discuss what happened with anyone. If he had indeed erred, it was better that nobody knew it.

'Now we go Wild Wadi Waterpark?' the driver prompted.

'Now we go Palace Hotel,' Belknap replied.

'Very good,' the driver said. 'You will have whale of a time.' His wide smile was gap-toothed and khat-colored.

The driver took a shortcut through a fish souk, where turquoise-clad migrant workers gutted fish with metronomic regularity, and then onto Sheikh Zayed Road, which was lined with enormous glittering edifices, one glass-skinned leviathan after another. The Palace was among the more recent and outlandish of them. The 'tail' functioned as a porte-cochère over the entrance, and, as the cab stood a discreet distance away, Belknap strode into the lobby like a man on a mission.

What now? The Palace Hotel probably had upward of seven hundred rooms. Although the Italian girl's call had been routed through a central switchboard, the hotel itself kept a record of outgoing calls. But the managers of the Palace would be vastly more sophisticated than the man at the back-office mail center; they were accustomed to dealing with visitors, valued a reputation for discretion, knew what the authorities could and could not require them to do.

Inside the lobby, he looked around and swiftly took the

measure of the place. In the center of the vast space stood a large blue-tinted aquarium. Rather than any exotic sea creatures, the tank featured a scantily clad woman in a mermaid suit and waterproof pasties who swam in slow circles to tinkly synthesized New Age music, her disciplined motions designed to look lazy and undirected; at intervals, she took breaths from an air pipe painted seaweed green. If a Muslim fundamentalist were ever to enter the lobby, the scene would confirm his worst suspicions of Western decadence. But that was extremely unlikely. Distance, in the modern world, was not measured in miles or kilometers but in units of social removal. The enclave belonged to a world that included Cap d'Antibes, East Hampton, Positano, and Mustique. Those were its true neighbors. An enclave like the Palace had no connection to the geopolitical territory known as the Middle East, save by merest accident of geography. The building had been designed by a team of architects from London, Paris, and New York; its restaurant was supervised by a Spanish chef with an international reputation; even the desk clerks and concierges were British, though, of course, able to converse in the major European languages.

Belknap sat down on a dark-blue upholstered ottoman in a corner of the lobby and placed a cell-phone call, a real one. It went through in a matter of moments. He could remember when international calls were invariably marred by a burble of distortion and static, as if one could hear the watery currents through which the transoceanic cables had been laid. These days, the signal from one affluent part of the world to another was crystal-clear – indeed, clearer than a local call made from one neighborhood of Lagos to another. Matt Gomes's voice was instantly recognizable when he picked up, and Gomes instantly recognized who was calling him.

'Word is,' the junior officer said, 'you got in a major pissing match with Wild Bill Garrison. When something like that happens, the rest of us think it's raining.'

'Into each life some rain must fall,' Belknap replied. 'Just like Pat Boone says.'

'Pat Boone? How about the Ink Spots, my brother?'

'Need a favor, little man,' Belknap said, his eyes scanning the lobby. Inside the wide, shallow tank, the mermaid kept up her ostensibly lazy circles, no doubt counting her hourly wages in her head. Her blissful smile was beginning to look strained.

'All calls may be monitored for quality assurance,' Gomes said, a casual warning.

'Do you know how many years of digital tape they've already accumulated? Recording is easy, because it's automated. As for listening, nobody ever has enough man-hours. I'll take my chances that nobody's taking a special interest in you.'

'Your chances, or my chances? 'Cause 'when I think of you, another shower starts.''

'I just need you to do what Pat Boone did: Cover for me.'

'Can you assure me that this is strictly pursuant to an officially authorized operation?' There was a wink in Gomes's voice.

'You took the words out of my mouth,' Belknap said. Then he told Gomes what he needed him to do. As to favors owed, the junior officer needed no reminding.

At all the international hotel chains, there was always someone who served the American spy agencies as a facilitator when some special service was required. It was the nature of a business that provided temporary habitation for tens of thousands of travelers that criminals, even terrorists, would occasionally seek refuge among them. In return for the informal alerts, the CIA would sometimes provide the hotels, on an equally informal basis, background checks, information about prospective security risks, and the like.

Gomes would not call anyone at the Palace directly; he would call someone at the Chicago headquarters of the holding company that owned it. That person would then call the hotel manager at the Palace. Five minutes later, Belknap's cell phone silently vibrated. It was Gomes with the name of an assistant manager who had been reached and given to understand that he was to give Agent Belknap his full cooperation.

And he did. His name was Ibrahim Hafez, and he was a small, well-educated man in his thirties, probably the son of an hotelier who managed another of the emirate's stately pleasure domes. He was neither overimpressed nor sullen in the American's presence. They conferred in a small office, hidden away from the guests. It was a tidy nook, with neat stacks of envelopes and two photographs, evidently of Hafez's wife and infant daughter. The wife was slender, with luminous black eyes, and she smiled at the camera with an expression both brazen and somehow abashed. For the assistant manager, she must have been a necessary reminder of what was real in a realm of simulacrum.

Hafez seated himself before the terminal and keyed in the Rome exchange numbers. Moments later, the screen displayed the search results. The number had been called half a dozen times.

'Can you tell me what room number these calls originated from?' The girl had told her parents that she was 'someplace nice,' which was, if anything, an understatement. If she were a guest of the Palace, she was being royally treated indeed.

'A room number?' The assistant manager shook his head. 'But – '

'Each time, a different room number.' He tapped on a column of digits with the capped point of a pen.

How was that possible? 'So the guest has checked into different rooms?'

Hafez looked at him as if he were dense. A small headshake. He clicked on a few room numbers, opening data fields that showed the name of each registered guest and the duration of his or her stay. Each name was different; each was male.

'Then you're saying that . . .'

'What do *you* think?' It was a statement, and not the most polite one. Lucia Zingaretti was working as a prostitute – an 'escort' – and, given that she was frequenting the Palace, undoubtedly a high-priced one. If she occasionally made a phone call from the rooms she visited – perhaps while using the bathroom – her clients were unlikely to raise a fuss with hotel management about the extra charges.

'Can you give me the names of the girls who work the place?'

Hafez looked at him blandly. 'You must be joking. The Palace Hotel does not condone such activity. How could I have any knowledge of it?'

'You mean you turn a blind eye to it.'

'I turn no eye to it at all. Rich Westerners come here to play. We accommodate them in nearly every way possible. You will have noticed in the lobby natatorium that we have a *sharmuta* swimming around all day.' *Sharmuta* was Arabic slang for slut or whore, and Hafez almost spat the word with unconcealed distaste. He had made a profession of catering to the fantasies of his guests, but he would not pretend that he approved of them. He noticed that Belknap was looking at the photograph of his wife, and, with a fluid movement, he placed the picture facedown. It was not that he had taken offense: It was that the unveiled face of his wife was not meant to be seen by strangers. Belknap suddenly realized the significance of her slightly abashed expression. This was a woman who would appear in public only in a veil. The exposure of her full face and hair was something of a transgression, akin to a nude picture, for her and for him. 'We wash your soiled sheets and clean the toilets and the filthy leavings of your menstruating women, yes, we do all this, and smile even so. But do not ask us to enjoy it. Grant us that much dignity.'

'Thanks for the fatwa. But I need names.'

'I have none.'

'The name of someone who does, then. You're a professional, Ibrahim. There's nothing that goes on in this place you can't find out about.'

Hafez sighed. 'There's a bellhop who will know.' He pressed a five-digit extension from his telephone console. 'Conrad,' he said. 'Come to my office.' Again, he did not disguise his disapproval. Undoubtedly Conrad was one of the European employees foisted upon him by the foreign owners. Hafez clearly placed him in the same category as soiled sheets and used sanitary napkins.

An Irish voice could be heard on the console speaker: 'Be right there.'

Conrad was a jockey-sized young man with curly red hair and a too-quick smile. 'Yo, Bram,' he said to Hafez, with a mock salute from his visored Palace Hotel cap.

Hafez did not deign to respond. 'You will answer this man's questions,' he told the bellhop severely. 'I leave you two together.' With a curt bow, he did so.

Conrad's smile faded and reappeared with offputting rapidity as Belknap questioned him, his expression shifting from puzzled and solicitous to conspiratorial and lascivious, equally obnoxious from Belknap's point of view. 'So what kind of hoochie are you looking for, my friend?' he finally asked.

'Italian,' Belknap said. 'Young. Dark.'

'My, my,' said Conrad. 'You're mighty particular. A man who knows what he wants. Gotta respect that.' He was obviously confused by Hafez's involvement, however.

'You know anybody who fits the bill?'

'Well.' Conrad's eyes were calculating. 'As a matter of fact, I've got just what the doctor ordered.'

'When can I see her?'

Conrad sneaked a peek at his wristwatch. 'Soon,' he said.

'Within the hour?'

'I could swing that. For a consideration. If you're having a party, by the way, you might want some party favors. Ecstasy, blow, sensimilla, whatever – just say the word.'

'She's in the hotel now?'

'Now why would you be asking me that?' Conrad said, a clumsy feint. The answer was yes.

'What room number?'

'If it's a threesome you want . . .'

Belknap took a step toward the small Irishman and grabbed him by the collar, lifting him a few inches into the air. He pressed his face near Conrad's. 'Tell me the goddamn room number,' he barked. 'Or I'll have you rendered to the goddamned Egyptians for interrogation. You got me?'

'Bejabbers!' Conrad flushed, beginning to understand that he was in over his head.

'You want to interfere with an international investigation, I suggest you get yourself lawyered up. And when our Egyptian friends offer you the option of scrotal electrodes, say yes. Because the alternative is even worse.'

'Fourteen-fifty, sir. Floor fourteen, straight to the left from the main elevators. All I ask is that you leave me the hell out of it.'

'You gonna call and warn them?'

'After what you were saying about scrotal electrodes? I don't think so, mate.' A forced guffaw was meant to convey nonchalance but conveyed the opposite. 'Those were the magic words. Quite vivid.'

Belknap just held out a hand. 'Master key,' he demanded.

Reluctantly, the bellhop handed over his keycard. Then he hovered, in a way peculiar to the serving professions, as if expecting a tip. 'Scrotal electrodes': Belknap mouthed the words as he brushed past him.

Less than four minutes later, he was outside Room 1450, two-thirds of the way up the hotel's central tower. He paused at the door, could hear nothing. The Palace was a well-engineered building, constructed of premium materials. He placed the card in the slot, watched the light blink green, and turned the knob. On the other side of the door he would find Lucia Zingaretti: his one thread. *Hang on, Jared*, he silently urged. *I'm on my way.*

Andrea Bancroft had meant to clear out her desk at Coventry Equity Group, but as she sat there she had another thought. The office's resources would be helpful to her. Her colleagues were sorry to see her go; they would hardly begrudge her the right to spend her last day as she wanted to.

There was something else, too. She kept thinking about what her nameless visitor had said: *You look a lot like your mother*. What was the significance of that? Was she becoming undone by suspicion? Perhaps it was the result of some delayed grief reaction from her mother's death, the jolting abruptness of the Bancroft bequest, perhaps – but no, she wasn't some hysteric. That wasn't the kind of person she was. Except that she wasn't sure she knew what kind of person she was anymore.

You're a professional. Do what you're trained to do. The foundation was ultimately another organization – a nonprofit corporation – and she had expertise in doing due diligence on corporations, in researching companies both public and private, in peering beneath the glossy assurances of their brochures and press releases. She might as well take a closer look at the Bancroft Foundation itself.

Seated before the networked computer terminal at her desk, she roamed through a series of arcane databases. A nonprofit entity that was chartered in the United States – even a private one like the Bancroft – had to abide by various statutes and regulations; mandated federal filings included the original charter, bylaws, and employee identification numbers for certain senior officers.

After peering through digitized documents for two hours, Andrea worked out that the foundation was – at least formally – a complex of separately incorporated entities. There was the Bancroft Estates, the Bancroft Philanthropic Trust, the Bancroft Family Trust, and on and on. Funds seemed to slosh through them as through the pipes and valves of a manifold.

All around her she saw her colleagues – *former colleagues*, she corrected herself – working busily at their stations. They seemed dronelike, in a way that she'd never noticed before; seated at desks, fingering keyboards, speaking on telephones – performing hundreds of tasks through about three or four basic motions that were repeated all day long.

What makes me any different? she thought. *I'm doing the same thing.* It felt different from inside, that was all. It felt different when you knew that what you did truly mattered.

Her phone purred, intruding on her thoughts.

'Hey, girl!' Brent Farley's smooth baritone was dialed up to its most ingratiating pitch. 'It's me.'

Her voice was tundra-dry. 'How can I help you?'

'How much time you got?' he breezily replied. 'Look, it's just that I hated the way we left things. We need to talk, okay?'

'And what would this be in regard to?' Maintaining the secretarial permafrost took surprisingly little effort.

'Hey, don't be that way, Andrea. Look, I got us a couple of tickets to – '

'I'm just curious,' she cut in. 'Why is it that you're calling me out of the blue? Why now?'

He stammered. 'Why – why am I calling? No special reason,' he lied. At that moment, she knew for sure: The word had reached him. 'I just, like I said, I just thought we needed to talk. Maybe start over again. But, however it goes, we really need to talk.'

Because suddenly the 'small-time' girl is worth more than you'll ever make?

'We did need to talk,' she replied calmly. 'And, thank goodness, we just have. Good-bye, Brent. Please don't call again.'

She hung up, feeling vindicated, excited, and, oddly, tired.

She walked over to the coffee machine, waved at Walter Sachs, the firm's tech guru, who seemed to be in the middle of a riff with an assistant on the subject of granola bars. He was a brilliant guy, really, and a classic underachiever. Sachs, oddly, took satisfaction in being absolutely indifferent to what he did for a living; he did it well, but found it entirely undemanding, which was to his liking.

'Hey, Walt,' she said. 'Working hard or hardly working?'

He turned his long, rectangular head toward her and blinked hard, as if there was something stuck in his contact lenses. 'Running the systems here is something I can do in my sleep and with my left hand or, come to think of it, with my left hand asleep. The 'or' is inclusive, not exclusive: My claim, in its strongest form, is that the tingling left hand of a sleeping Walt Sachs would suffice. Sorry, Andrea, I'm feeling very Boolean today. I blame granola-bar intoxication. Did you realize that granola bars are essentially conduits for com syrup? Do you know how many products on the super-market shelves are essentially conduits for corn syrup?' He blinked again, a hard, windshield-wiper-style clench. 'Consider, of all things, ketchup.'

'See you, Walt,' she said, and returned to her desk with a Stryrofoam cup of coffee.

She downloaded more documents, more digitized filings. The honeycombed intricacy of the foundation's structure presented an intellectual challenge. She tried to be alert both to small irregularities and larger patterns. As she paged through the federal filings over the past decade, she was taken back to find that the officers of the principal founda-tion once included her own mother, Laura Parry Bancroft.

It was startling. How was it that her mother, so deeply disaffected with everything to do with the family she mar-ried into, had once served as a foundation officer? Andrea peered at the document more closely and noticed something even stranger. Her mother had resigned her position just one day before the car accident that killed her.

Dubai, United Arab Emirates

In one corner of the darkened room, a man was seated on an overstuffed blue velvet chair; seated upon the man, in turn, was a lissome young woman. At the sound of the door closing behind Belknap, the man – sixtyish, with a sun-reddened, smooth-shaven head, white-blond hair chest hair, and sagging pectorals – sat upright with a jolt, threw the woman off him, and scrambled to his feet.

'The girl's under new management,' Belknap growled.

'What the hell?' The man spoke with a Swedish accent. His assumption was that he was being set up, that the whore was in cahoots with the intruder. It was the assumption of a worldly man who was experienced with the sex trade and had no illusions about the limits of human knavery. 'Get the hell out of my – '

'Why don't you make me?' Belknap replied, cutting him off.

The older man sized up his opponent swiftly; he was a businessman, someone used to assessing the odds and acting accordingly. Making a swift decision, he grabbed his wallet and a couple of items of clothing and bolted from the room. 'You're not getting another Euro out of me, you hear?' he hissed to the girl on his way out.

When Belknap turned back to the girl, she was no longer sprawled on the floor, but had put on a silk robe and stood with her arms crossed.

'Lucia Zingaretti?' he asked.

A look of shock passed across her face. She knew it would be pointless to deny it. 'Who are you?' she demanded in a throaty Italian accent.

He ignored her question. 'Your parents have no idea, do they?'

'What do you know of my parents?'

'I spoke to them yesterday. They were worried about you.'

'You spoke to them.' Her voice was deathly.

'As have you. Except you ply them with lies only. Not exactly the daughter they imagine.'

'What do you know about them, or about me?'

'They're good people. Trusting people. The sort people like you take advantage of.'

'How *dare* you judge me!' the Italian girl spat. 'What I do, I do for them!'

'Does that include killing Khalil Ansari?'

The girl blanched. She lowered herself to the blue velvet chair and spoke in a quiet voice. 'They promised great sums of money. My parents struggled every working day of their lives, and what can they afford? They said if I did what they asked, I would be able to set them up in luxury for the rest of their lives.'

'They?'

'They,' the girl repeated defiantly.

'And you, too, no doubt. Where did they end up taking you?'

'Not a place like this,' the girl said quietly. 'Not like they said. Not like any place fit for human being. Like for animals.'

She seemed bewildered that they had failed to live up to their promises. Yet to Belknap, the greater perplexity was that they had even allowed the girl to live. Why were they so confident she would maintain her silence? 'This came as a surprise?' he asked mildly.

She nodded grimly. 'When they fly me to Dubai, they say it is for cooling-off period. Just to stay out of the way for a while. To keep me safe. Then when I come, they say I must work. I must earn my keep. Otherwise I will be on the street or killed. No money. No papers.'

'You were a prisoner.'

'After one day, they take me out of hotel. They take me to this . . . *magazzino*, this . . . warehouse. On outskirts of Dubai. They say I must do this thing. Customers must never complain. Otherwise . . .' She faltered, a victim of sexual servitude who had sought to repress the degradation she had been forced to accept. 'But they say that at the end of one year, I can go free. After one year, they say, Lucia write her own ticket. Set up for life. All of us.'

'You and your parents,' Belknap said. 'Set up for life, they told you. And you believed them?'

'Why I not believe them?' the Italian girl demanded stormily. 'What else can I believe?'

'When they had you poison Ansari, they never told you that you'd end up a high-class whore, did they?'

Her silence was her assent.

'They lied to you once. You really think they're not lying to you now?'

Lucia Zingaretti said nothing, but he could see the contending emotions in her face. Belknap could easily imagine what had happened. It was a phenomenon that plagued nested organizations, each part of which had its own particular needs. In Dubai, the girl's beauty meant that she could be of great value to those who provided sexual services to rich visitors. What's more, she was, after all, a mere servant girl: Many Arabs would be inclined to think that such a girl was likely to be a *sharmuta* anyway. Nor was she in any position to bargain, as she acknowledged: They knew what she had done. The deed did not put them in her debt, as she had supposed; it put her in their power.

'And still you protect them, the very people who have forced you into a life of degradation.'

'It is not for you to say what is *degradazione*.' Lucia Zingaretti pouted and rose to her feet. 'Not for you.'

'Tell me who they are,' Belknap said steadily.

'It is not for you to interfere.'

'Tell me who they are,' he repeated, more urgently.

'So that I should be in your clutches rather than theirs? I think I take my chances. Yes, I think I take my chances, thank you very much.'

'Goddammit, Lucia . . .'

'What must I do to make you go away?' the girl asked. Her voice was breathy, sultry. 'What can I offer you?'

With a shrug of her shoulders she let her robe fall to the floor. Now she stood naked before him. He could feel the heat of her body, could smell the scent of her honeyed skin. Her breasts were smallish but perfectly shaped.

'There's nothing you can offer me,' Belknap replied contemptuously. 'That body can pay for a lot. But not in any currency I accept.'

'Please,' she said, purring, taking a step toward him, caressing her breasts with one hand. Her gestures were sensual, but motivated by sheer survival. Her eyes narrowed to slits, vampishly – and then, suddenly, they blinked open.

Belknap saw a red dot blossom in the center of her forehead a split-second before he heard a quiet popping noise from behind him. Time became viscous as Belknap dived to the floor and rolled behind the large, skirted bed.

A silenced shot had been fired.

Silencing Lucia Zingaretti forever.

He flashed back to what he had glimpsed of the assailants, forced himself to piece together visual fragments into a whole. There had been . . . two men at the door, each armed with a long-barreled, sighted handgun. Both had short dark hair. One, wearing a black nylon warm-up jacket, had the dead eyes of a hammerhead shark – obviously a combat-seasoned veteran, and a marksman of considerable skill. A precise head shot from a handgun across a room lay beyond the competence even of most professionals. On the base of a shiny brass floor lamp, Belknap caught the reflection of the two men. They were moving their handguns in sweeping arcs, but had stepped only a few feet into the room. They were cautious, more cautious than Belknap would have been in their situation. At least one of them should have seized the opportunity of surprise and pushed clear across the bed-room.

Yet their movements made one thing plain. They were hunting him. Their mission would not be complete until there was a slug in Belknap's brain as well.

Belknap snake-bellied himself under the bed until he was within arm's length of one of the gunmen. Now he lashed out with an arm curved like a grappling hook, striking with all his might.

A risky move: He had just given away his position.

The man fell heavily to the ground. Belknap grabbed his weapon, firing it at him a second later. Close-quarters combat was like speed chess. You stop to think, you lose. Swiftness of response was paramount. He could feel his face wetted with a spray of warm blood. No matter. Where was the second assailant, the one who had moved to get an angle on the rest of the room?

Belknap seized the torso of the slain man and hoisted his body into the air. The sudden movement drew gunfire, as he had expected, a quick reflexive *rat-a-tat* that must have emptied the gun – and that identified the other man's exact firing position. Belknap set his newly acquired pistol to single-shot action and squeezed off a returning round. Accuracy of gunfire counted more than volume. Better to have to squeeze a few times than to be caught with an empty chamber.

The man's cry told him that the bullet had connected – but not with a vital organ.

Then he heard the sound of glass shattering, and another pair of men stepped into the room from the balcony outside. Belknap rolled the corpse over himself, drawing the limp body over him like a saddlebag. He was conscious of the slain man's body heat, the acrid smell of his sweat. The members of his unit could not be certain that he was dead – at least not at first – and would not fire freely toward him.

It would buy Belknap only seconds, but seconds were all he needed.

One of the late arrivals – tall, husky, muscled – was wearing a combat vest and holding a Heckler & Koch MP5, a compact automatic weapon known as a 'room broom.' He directed a spray of bullets into the mattress. Nobody hiding beneath it could have survived. It was a sensible precaution, Belknap thought as he squeezed a carefully aimed shot into the sternum of each balcony boy. Two rounds spaced by a second-long interval. Conveniently, they were almost exactly the same height; the adjustment between shots was slight.

Belknap heard the other man slam a new magazine into his pistol – the one he had wounded, the one he had forgotten about. *Dammit! A mistake he could not afford.*

With lightning rapidity, he swept his gun arm around and squeezed the trigger, knowing that success or failure would be determined in the next two-tenths of a second. He watched as his one remaining round punched through his assailant's neck, and the man slumped to the ground. Had Belknap been two-tenths of a second slower, the round would have been fired by his victim, and Belknap, not him, would have been the last man down.

Unsteadily, Belknap rose to his feet and looked at the dizzying carnage around him. Here, in a well-appointed hotel bedroom, were four bodies of powerful young men – nourished and exercised for well over two decades, trained at considerable expense. Dead. So was a beautiful girl, scarcely out of adolescence, doted on by hardworking parents to whom the world had never given a break, not one. Dead. Human lives transformed into jointed meat. If they were outdoors, not protected by the air-conditioned sanctuary of this glass-skinned whale, botflies would have already started to hover and alight. Belknap had just taken on four well-armed gunmen and survived. Close-quarters combat was a rare art, and he was more experienced at it than his opponents. Yet he felt no sense of conquest, no sense of triumph. He felt only a bone-deep sense of waste.

If we do not treat death with respect, Jared used to say, *it will reciprocate in kind.*

He spent the next three minutes searching the combat vests of the slain men. There were wallets stuffed with faked identity cards – generic in nature, identities designed to be swiftly adopted and swiftly discarded. Finally, in an interior pocket in the combat vest of the skilled marksman, he found a torn scrap of paper. The kind that came on narrow rolls, like a cash-register receipt. In a simple sans-serif font was a typed list of names.

Belknap rinsed the blood from his face in the bathroom and hastened from the hotel. Only after he had rented a rugged SUV from a nearby Hertz office and motored off did he scrutinize the list.

He recognized a few of the names. A recently slain investigative reporter for *La Repubblica*, the Italian newspaper. A Paris-based magistrate whose murder had also made the papers recently. Marked for death? Most of the other names were a bewildering jumble of personages who were unknown to him. One name, however, was Lucia Zingaretti.

Another was his own.

CHAPTER SEVEN

Driving to the Bancroft Foundation headquarters in Katonah on her own was an entirely different experience from being driven there. Andrea Bancroft was glad she had paid close attention to the sequence of turns when she was riding there in the backseat. Even so, she made a few wrong turns, and the trip took longer than it should have.

At the main door, she was greeted cordially by the woman with the stiff copper hair, who seemed slightly puzzled at her appearance.

'Just here to do research,' Andrea said. 'Preparing for the next board meeting, you know. I remember you had that very impressive library on the second floor.' She *was* a trustee, after all. Her real purpose was to research possible projects for the twenty-million-dollar challenge that Paul Bancroft had set to her, but she judged that it would be better not to discuss with others the special grant he had allocated. It might be seen as favoritism of some sort. Reticence, at this point, seemed the wisest course. 'Also, I'm returning the files you guys delivered to me yesterday.'

'You're so very conscientious,' the woman told her with a set smile. 'That's wonderful. I'll get you some tea.'

One by one the foundation officers appeared from their offices, greeted her, offered to assist with whatever questions she might have. They were nothing if not solicitous.

A little too solicitous, perhaps? A little too eager to help her in her researches, as if intent on monitoring her? For the first couple of hours, Andrea did some strenuous data-foraging, getting numbers about sanitation projects in the less-developed world. The range of information resources available there were, she had to admit, impressive, and impressively displayed. In the research rooms, books and binders were shelved in elegant walnut cases sturdily erected above the dark wood flooring. At one point, she walked through the 'reading corner' of the library and saw a boy with curly blond hair and apple cheeks. Brandon. On his lap was a stack of books: some sort of tome on natural history, what looked like a Russian treatise on number theory, and a copy of Kant's *Groundwork of the Metaphysics of Morals*. Not your average thirteen-year-old! His eyes lighted up when he saw her. He looked tired; there were smudges beneath his eyes.

'Hey, you.' He grinned.

'Hey, you,' she returned. 'A little light reading?'

'Actually, yeah. You know anything about the lancet liver fluke? Way cool. It's this tiny wormy creature, and its life cycle is pretty awesome.'

'Let me guess. It commutes every weekday to an office in New York until retirement, and then moves to Miami to run out the clock.'

'Wrong species, lady. Naw, it gets snails to excrete it so that ants, which love snail poop, will eat it, and then when it's inside, it goes to the ant's brain and basically lobotomizes it. So now it programs the ant to climb to the top of a blade of grass and then paralyzes the mandibles, so the ant just stays there all day, so that it can make sure it gets eaten by sheep.'

'Hmm.' Andrea made a face. 'It programs the ant to get itself eaten by sheep. Interesting. I guess everybody has his own idea of a good time.'

'It's really about survival. See, the sheep's intestines is where the lancet fluke reproduces. So when the sheep takes a dump, you get millions of them out in the world. All ready to sneak inside more ants and program them for destruction. Lancet liver flukes *rule*.'

'And I have a hard enough time wrapping my mind around the birds and bees,' Andrea said to him, shaking her head.

A little later, she was reshelving a box of CD-ROMs filled with morbidity and mortality data from the World Health Organization when a white-haired clerk gave her a lingering look.

Andrea nodded pleasantly. The woman looked to be in her sixties, her white hair offsetting a pink, slightly puffy face. Not someone she had seen before. On a desk in front of her was a sheet of library-style adhesive labels that she had been affixing to various disk boxes.

'Excuse me, ma'am,' the clerk said diffidently, 'but you remind me of someone.' She hesitated. 'Laura Bancroft.'

'My mother,' Andrea said, feeling her face prickle. 'You knew her?'

'Oh, certainly. She was a good person. A breath of fresh air, I always felt. I liked her a lot.' The woman sounded as if she might have come from Maryland or Virginia – her voice had a hint of Southern, but little more. 'She was the kind of person who *notices* people, you know what I mean? She noticed people like us. With some people – her ex-husband, for one – clerks and secretaries are like pieces of furniture. Like, you'd be sorry if they weren't around, but you don't really focus on them. Your mother was different.'

Andrea recalled the words of the gray-suited man who had visited her: *You look a lot like your mother.* 'I guess I hadn't really realized how active she was in the foundation,' she said after a pause.

'Laura never minded upsetting the apple cart. Like I say, she was a noticing kind of gal. And I think she truly cared about the work. So much so that she refused to take any money for it.'

'Really.'

'Besides, since Reynolds had cycled off the board, it wasn't like they'd be running into each other.'

Andrea sat down beside the white-haired clerk. There was something grandmotherly about her, some quality of undemanding sympathy. 'So they asked her to serve as a foundation officer. Even though she was just a Bancroft by marriage, she fulfilled the family quota, was that it?'

'You know that the charter has all these rules about that. So yeah, that was pretty much the shape of it. I'm guessing she hadn't mentioned it to you.'

'No, ma'am,' Andrea said.

'Doesn't surprise me much.' The woman glanced down at her adhesive labels. 'Wouldn't want you to think we're all gossips here, but we'd heard a thing or two about that marriage. It's no wonder she wanted to keep you protected from the mess – she figured Reynolds would just find a way to make you feel bad about yourself, same as he did to her.' She stopped. 'Sorry – I know they say you shouldn't speak ill of the dead. But if we don't, who's gonna? You don't need me to tell you that Reynolds was a piece of work.'

'I'm not sure I understand, though. About my mother's concern.'

The woman looked at her with cornflower-blue eyes. 'Sometimes, when you've got a kid to take care of, you try to make a clean break seem a little cleaner than it really is. Too much to explain otherwise. Too many questions. Expectations get raised and crushed. I'm a divorced mother of four, all grown now. So I got my own perspective on it. What I think is, your mom aimed to protect you.'

Andrea swallowed hard. 'Is that why she finally resigned?'

The woman looked away. 'I guess I'm not sure what you're talking about,' she said after a while. There was a slight cooling of her tone, as if Andrea had overstepped a boundary. 'So, anything I can help you with?' Her face was professional, now, and somehow closed, as expressionless as polished slate.

Andrea thanked her quickly and returned to her carrel, but she felt a prickling again, and something else, some deep, glowing disquiet. It was as if embers that had smoldered for years were suddenly fanned.

Laura never minded upsetting the apple cart. A tribute to her character, surely, nothing more. *She was a noticing kind of gal.* But what did that really mean, other than she wasn't any kind of snob? Andrea berated herself for her paranoia, her inability to manage her own emotions. *Passion must be within reason*, Paul Bancroft had said: She ought to be able to subordinate what she felt to hard demands of rationality. But, hard as she tried, she could not eradicate the suspicions that now swarmed around her. They were like yellow jackets at a picnic, small yet persistent, and no matter how she swatted at them, they would not be banished.

She tried to direct her attentions to a page from a W.H.O. almanac, but it was no use. Her mind kept returning to the Bancroft Foundation itself. It undoubtedly kept archives of its activities at hand, and they would be at a level of detail far in excess of the federally required reports. If there were answers to be found, they might well be in the basement archives, where older documents relating to the foundation's operations were stored.

As she made her way out of the library wing, she saw Brandon again, and something lifted in her as he caught her eye.

'You know, they don't have a hoop at this place or I'd challenge you to a little one-on-one,' he said, giggling sweetly.

'Next time,' Andrea said. 'I've got some archive-trawling to do right now, I'm afraid. The boring basement kind.'

Brandon nodded. 'The good stuff's shut in cages. All locked up like dirty magazines.'

'And what would you know about such things?' she asked, mock-censorious.

The boy's face split open into another one of his joyful grins. He was nothing less than a genius; but he was also just a boy.

Cages: They would indeed be standard in unsupervised low-use archives. She needed to get to those caged archives, and this time she would actively solicit help. But not from a senior officer. Rather, she would enlist a younger, low-level employee. She wandered through one of the smaller offices outside the library wing, past a water cooler and a coffee machine, and introduced herself to a twenty-something man who was sorting through a pile of mail. The man – moon-pale, with short mousy hair and nicotine-stained fingernails – recognized her name, had heard that she was a new trustee, and seemed delighted that she would take the time to make his acquaintance.

'So,' Andrea said, after the initial pleasantries, 'I'm wondering if you can help me. If I'm being a bother, you let me know. All right?'

'No bother at all,' replied the man, whose name was Robby.

'It's just that I've been asked to sort through various documents, you know, trusteeship stuff, and I've locked myself out of the basement archives,' she said, with a low cunning she hadn't known was in her. 'So embarrassing.'

'Not a bit!' the man replied heartily, grateful for a reprieve from the letter opener. 'Not a bit! I could . . . I bet I could help you.' He looked around the office. 'I'm sure one of these good people will have a key.' He rummaged through desk drawers until he found one.

'You're such a blessing,' Andrea said. 'I'll get this back to you in two shakes.'

'I'll come with you,' the man said. 'Easier that way.' No doubt he was hoping for a quick smoke outside while he was at it.

'I hate to make myself a bother,' Andrea cooed.

But she was glad that he showed her the way, because instead of the exposed main staircase, he took her down a narrower rear staircase that descended to the basement in a few steep zigzags. The basement wasn't very basement-like; it was elegantly appointed, steeped in the fragrance of lemon furniture polish, of old paper, even, faintly, of ancient pipe tobacco. The walls were wainscoted; the floors carpeted with a Wiltshire broadloom of evident distinction. The archives were divided into two sections, one of which was secluded behind a metal grate, just as Brandon had told her. The man let Andrea in and then took the stairs up, not entirely hiding the eagerness of someone craving a nicotine fix.

Andrea was left alone with the foundation's archives. Black laminated boxes with coded alphanumeric labels stretched before her in long rows. There were hundreds of them, and Andrea did not know where to begin. She pulled the box nearest to her, riffled through the pages. Photostats of bills – physical-plant repairs, groundskeeping expenses from fifteen years earlier. She reshelved the box and started on another shelf. It was like taking soil samples. When she came to the bills that corresponded to the month in which her mother was killed, she took her time, scrutinizing every detail, hoping that something would pop up, announce itself as unusual. Yet nothing did.

The fifth box she looked through contained itemized telephone bills made from the Katonah headquarters, as did the one beside it. She located the box at the end of that shelf and kept going until she found another box that contained bills from the period when her mother died. Again, she saw nothing that, on the face of it, seemed worth a second glance. Finally, she opened a carton that contained telephone bills from the past half-year. Without having anything particular in mind, she took the list of telephone calls from the last month and slipped it into her handbag.

She turned to another section, opened another box, then another. Intriguingly, she encountered a couple of references to a facility in Research Triangle Park, North Carolina. Now she scanned the other shelves swiftly, stopping when she found a series of document boxes with labels prefixed by the letters RTP.

What was this facility? She crouched down and sampled documents from the RTP boxes on the lowest shelves. A few budget lines for seemingly minor items suggested that it was lavishly funded. Lavishly funded – yet never mentioned during the board meeting. What could it be for?

She looked up, still musing, and was startled to see the powerfully built man who had visited her at her house in Carlyle.

He was standing with arms akimbo. He must have just arrived – but how had he known to do so? Andrea resolved to maintain an icy composure even as her heart hammered in her chest. She rose slowly to her feet and extended a hand.

'I'm Andrea Bancroft,' she said with great deliberateness. 'As I'm sure you remember. And you are . . . ?' Her way of taking the offensive.

'Just here to help,' the man replied blandly. She could feel him looking right through her. He was obviously there to keep an eye on her.

'You're too kind,' Andrea returned freezingly.

The man seemed distantly amused by her ploys. 'Just kind enough,' he assured her.

A long pause ensued. She did not have the mental fortitude, just then, for an extended standoff. She needed to speak to Paul Bancroft. She had questions. He would have answers. Yet did he himself know everything that was going on in the foundation? It would not be the first time that an idealist was exploited by others with less lofty objectives.

Don't get ahead of yourself, Andrea.

'I was actually just about to have a word with Paul,' she said, using her intimacy with the great man as a weapon. She gave him a tight smile. *And one thing we'll be discussing is whether he really wants to have people like you in his employ.*

'He's out of town.'

'I know,' Andrea lied. 'I was going to give him a call.' Already she was conscious that she was over-explaining. She didn't owe this man any reasons.

'Out of town,' the man responded, imperturbable, 'and unreachable. As they should have explained.'

Andrea tried to meet his steady gaze, but, to her chagrin, was the first to look away. 'He'll be back when?'

'In time for the next board meeting.'

'Right,' Andrea said, deflated. 'Anyway, I was just leaving,' she said.

'Then let me escort you to your car,' the man said with studied formality.

He did not speak again until they reached the graveled parking lot where she had left her car. He pointed to some drips of motor oil beneath the undercarriage. 'You should have that looked at,' he said. His tone was kindly, yet his eyes were like slits.

'Thank you, I will,' Andrea replied.

'A lot of things can go wrong with a car,' the man persisted. 'Things that can get you killed. You of all people should know what can happen.'

Getting into her car, Andrea felt a shivery wave of cold pass over her, as if she'd been licked by an alligator. *A lot of things can go wrong with a car.* It was, on its face, friendly advice.

Why, then, did it feel like a threat?

Dubai, United Arab Emirates

'So what did you find?' Todd Belknap demanded. He gripped the cell phone tightly.

'Almost all those names on that list have something in common,' Matt Gomes said. Belknap could tell that he had his lips close to the mouthpiece of his phone and was speaking softly. 'They're dead. And all in the past couple of weeks, too.'

'Murdered?'

'Causes of death are all over the map. Some straight-up homicides. Two suicides. Some accidental. Some natural causes.'

'If I'm betting my money? They're all homicides. Some of them better hidden than others. And Gianni?'

'Massive heart attack. Just a few minutes ago.'

'Christ on a raft,' Belknap roared.

'You tell me all the names on that list?'

'Damned straight,' Belknap said, hanging up. All of them except one name: Todd Belknap.

What did it mean? The natural assumption was that they were people whom the Ansari network, or its new masters, regarded as a threat. But why, exactly? Had there been an internal coup within the network? If so, how did it connect to Jared Rinehart's abduction, if it did at all?

Belknap's scalp tightened with apprehension. *The list.* It bore all the signs of a mop-up. The sort of housecleaning that was typically performed before a make-or-break operation. It could mean that he had even less time than he'd feared to find Pollux.

It could mean it was already too late.

Something else gnawed at Belknap's mind. Given the

obvious ruthlessness of those in charge, it was even more perplexing that the Italian girl hadn't been killed immediately, back in Rome. Why had they waited until his arrival forced the issue? Was she of potential value to them in some way that eluded Belknap? It seemed impossible. As confounding as her treatment was, however, it represented a wisp of hope – the hope that Pollux, too, had been allowed to live.

The Italian girl said she had been staying at a place past the Dhow Building Yard, on Marwat Road. He would drive there now in the rented SUV. Perhaps there were others there in whom she had confided. Perhaps the master of the establishment would have the information he needed.

The cell phone he had lifted from the death-squad leader purred. He answered with an ambiguous half-syllable: 'Ya.' The voice at the other end, he was surprised to hear, belonged to a woman.

'Hello, is this . . . ?' The woman – an American – trailed off.

Belknap said nothing, and a second later the woman hung up with a murmured apology. The squad's controller? A wrong number? From the caller-log function, he could tell that the call originated from the United States. It was no random misdial; he was sure of it. Once more, he enlisted Gomes's help.

'I'm not your freakin' back office, Castor,' Gomes groused, as Belknap read him the digits. 'You feelin' me?'

'Look, help a brother out, okay? I'm in kind of a hurry here. Need you to step up and represent. Just ID the goddamn number, would you?'

Half a minute elapsed before Gomes got back to him. 'Okay, man, I got Jane Doe's name, did a quick records search, too.'

'Chances are good she's the goddamn princess of darkness,' Belknap said grimly.

'Yeah, well, her civilian handle is Andrea Bancroft.'

Belknap paused. 'A *Bancroft* Bancroft?'

'No duh. She just became a trustee of the Bancroft Foundation.' Cockily, he added, 'Who's your daddy now?'

163

Andrea Bancroft. How was she involved in the killings? How high up was she? Could she know something about – have been complicit in – the disappearance of Jared Rinehart? There were too many questions, too many uncertainties. But Belknap didn't believe in coincidences. This wasn't any wrong number. All indications were that Andrea Bancroft was a dangerous customer, or, at the very least, keeping dangerous company.

Belknap made a call to a retired operative he hadn't spoken to in years. No matter. The man's field name was Navajo Blue, and Navajo Blue owed Belknap one.

A few minutes later, a cinderblock structure came into view. Hidden from the road, near a series of industrial buildings, the building was dun-colored, just shy of derelict, and almost seemed to vibrate in the heat. As the Italian girl had described the setup, it was basically a warehouse for prostitutes. The place had doubtless seen all sorts of people from all walks of life. But it had never seen anyone like Todd Belknap.

Andrea Bancroft pulled over again and dialed another one of the most-frequently-called numbers on the phone bill. That one turned out to be a nursery in New Jersey, probably part of the ground-maintenance detail. She crossed it off. She had to be more systematic; she wasn't going to get very far just by calling numbers and seeing who answered. In the case of the international cell-phone number, the person who answered hardly said anything at all – which was suspicious, to be sure, but hardly informative. She tucked the phone bill away and let her mind drift. Something was nagging at her – some odd detail.

What was it?

It was morbid of her, no doubt, but she could not help going over the painful teenage memory of her mother's death. The policeman at the door . . . ready to break the news. Except she had already been informed by – who was that caller? It had happened more than a decade before. Yet someone had phoned to tell her that her mother had been killed. And then it came to her: what it was about the man with the hoarse smoky voice – the foundation officer who'd telephoned about security protocols and compliance issues – that made her blood run cold.

It was the same voice as the man who called that night.

At the time, she'd assumed it was someone from the police – yet the policeman at the door seemed puzzled when she mentioned the call. Maybe she was wrong. Maybe she was imagining things. And yet ... something about that night had always bothered her, like a lash under her eyelid. Her mother, she was told, had a blood-alcohol level of 0.1 – yet she didn't drink. When Andrea said so, the kindly patrolman had asked a perceptive question: Had she once been an alcoholic? Yes, but her mother had joined AA, hadn't had a drop for years. The policeman nodded; he admitted that he was a recovering alcoholic himself. One day at a time. Still, almost everyone falls off the wagon at one point or another. Andrea's protests had been quietly, gently set aside, the indignation of a protective daughter unwilling to face the truth.

When did it happen? the seventeen-year-old Andrea had asked. *About twenty minutes ago*, the patrolman explained. *No*, Andrea said, *it must have been* earlier – *they called me at least half an hour ago*.

The patrolman had given her a strange look. She remembered little else, because then everything had been washed away by an ocean of grief.

She had to tell Paul Bancroft. She had to talk to him, she resolved. Yet what if he knew already? What if he knew far more than he was letting on? Her head began to pound.

As Andrea motored along the Old Post Road, she turned on the windshield wipers before she realized that nothing was obscuring the view except the tears that had welled up in her own eyes.

You're losing it, Andrea, she scolded herself. Yet another voice, darker and deeper, spoke in contradiction: *Maybe you're finding it, Andrea. Maybe you're finding it.*

*

Nimble fingers roamed across the computer keyboard. Fingers that knew their destination, that executed a complex series of directives with precision and celerity. In a flurry of quiet clicks, an e-mail message was composed. A few more keystrokes and the message was encrypted, then dispatched to an offshore anonymizer service, where it would be stripped of all identifying codes, decrypted, and rerouted to its ultimate recipient, one with a senate.gov suffix. In less than a minute, a computer in the office of a United States senator would ping. The message would have arrived, and with it its signoff.

Genesis.

In the next few minutes, other messages were sent, other instructions dispatched. Strings of digits shifted money from one numbered account to another, moving levers that would move still other levers, pulling strings that would pull still other strings.

Genesis. For some, it was indeed the beginning. For others, it meant the beginning of the end.

Tom Mitchell ached all over. It was the way he felt after a bout of unaccustomed exercise or after an alcoholic binge. He had not taken any exercise. Process of elimination, right? Blinking hard, he peered into the garbage pail by the sink. It was heaped with beer cans – 'tinnies,' as his Australians friends called them. How many six-packs had he gone through? His head hurt when he thought about it. His head hurt when he didn't.

The screen door banged noisily in the breeze, like a concussion bomb, he thought. A wasp buzzed in the doorway, and to him it sounded as if a Second World War fighter plane was overhead. And when the phone had rung a little earlier in the day, it had sounded like an air-raid siren.

Maybe it *was* an air-raid siren, of sorts. Castor had called, and it wasn't to borrow a cup of sugar, either. Didn't matter. He wasn't someone you said no to, and Tom Mitchell – Navajo Blue had been his field name, when he had been in active deployment – figured he ought to be grateful for a chance to repay a debt. You didn't want to get on the Hound's bad side, that was for sure. Because the Hound had teeth, and his bite was worse than his bark.

The serenity of Tom's New Hampshire idyll was killing him, anyway. He wasn't cut out for the quiet life, that was the long and short of it, and it was asking too much from the booze to supply all the excitement that was missing from his daily routine.

Sheila had found the place. Post-and-beam construction, whatever the hell that meant. Wide plank floors under the particleboard – she crowed at the discovery as if she'd unearthed King Tut's tomb. Just a little down the road of them to either side were ratty A-frames and piece-of-shit bungalows and car-killed raccoons, each with their own blowfly cloud. But there was enough land in back that he could take out his Ruger snubby for a spin once in a while and blast a few squirrels out of the trees, squirrels being the Vietcong of the rodent family, as far as he was concerned. The bird feeders were strictly designated for creatures of feather: A tree rat messed with their supply lines at its peril.

But that wasn't the hardy-har-har part of the whole Simple Life thing. Thirty years of gallivanting all over the godforsaken planet in the service of the US of A – including month-long sojourns out of radio contact – and Sheila loyally sticks it out. Thirty years – thirty-one and a half, more precisely. His wife through thick and thin. Always overjoyed when he came back, but careful not to lay a big guilt trip on him when he had to set off again. So now, the payoff for all those years of patience: She gets her husband full-time, the way it ought to be, right? They get the rural hideaway they've always talked about. A few green acres, mostly paid for. Paradise at last, if you didn't mind the blackflies in the summer.

Sheila lasted for just over a year of it. That was all she could take. Probably saw more of him during that time than she had in the previous three decades. Which evidently was the trouble.

She tried to explain. She said she never got used to sharing her bed, somehow. She said a lot of things. Eight acres of New Hampshire wilderness and she complained that she Needed Her Space. Neither were great talkers, but they had talked a fair amount the day before Sheila headed off to Chapel Hill, where her sister lived and had found her a condo. She said: *I'm bored.* He said: *We could get cable.*

Tom would never forget the look she gave him then. Pitying, mostly. Not angry, but disappointed, the way you'd look at an incontinent old dog when it made a mess. Sheila called him once a week, and there was something nurselike about her conversations. She was acting like the responsible adult, checking to make sure he was okay, was keeping himself out of trouble. The truth was, he felt like a car rusting away on cinderblocks. A common sight in these parts.

He took a carafe from the coffee machine and filled a mug on which was emblazoned the once humorous logo DOES THIS BODY MAKE ME LOOK FAT? He poured a heaping spoonful of sugar into it. No Sheila glares to worry about, right? He could have all the sugar he wanted. Like the state motto said: Live free or die!

The Dodge pickup truck started up just fine, but two hours down the turnpike later, the coffee seemed to have turned into piss and stomach acid. A couple of rest stops took care of one problem; a roll of Tums was contending with the other. His ass was going to sleep, something to do with the springs in the seat, maybe. He should have invested in one of those special seat pads, the kind that hemorrhoidal truck drivers always seemed to have.

It took a good four hours before he reached Carlyle, Connecticut, and he was in a foul mood. Four freaking hours of his life. When he could have been doing – what? Still. Four hours. 'Just nip over,' Castor had said. Four hours wasn't any kind of a nip.

The job would be a cakewalk, though. By the time he'd made a few reconnoitering runs along Elm Street, he was sure about that. The Carlyle police were a joke. And the lady in question lived in a doll's house of a Cape Cod. No visible security measures whatever. A screen porch. Ordinary glass on the windows. No house-hugging shrubbery that might have concealed security devices by the foundations. He wouldn't be surprised if she didn't even lock her doors.

Still, this trip was strictly business, not pleasure; he was a professional. Castor would not have tasked him for no reason. Which meant it was time for the Navajo Blue show.

He parked his truck across the street and a few hundred yards away from the house. When he finally emerged from the truck – and there was relief in stepping away from his own funk and flatulence – he was wearing a generic-looking handyman uniform: a Dickies-style silver-gray shirt and pants with a small embroidered pocket patch that said SERVICE MASTER, a leather tool belt. Generic service guy: That's how it would read. Nobody you took a second look at, unless you were the guy who had called him. Elm Street was filled with nicely mown rectangular yards with one-from-column-A-one-from-column-B shrubs: red barberries, blue junipers, flat-topped yews, forsythia – all varieties had become indigenous to the suburban sprawl that was the greater Northeast. He craned his head, looked at the houses on both sides of the street, as far as he could see. Four kinds of plants, four styles of houses. Everybody's special in the US of A, right?

Navajo Blue saw an empty garage, no car in the driveway. Nobody in view from any of the windows. Nobody at home. He went to the door, rang the bell, prepared to pretend he had come to the wrong house if someone answered. As he expected, nobody did. He walked around to the rear of the house, found the place where the telephone and coaxial cables entered the house. Nothing could be easier than to place a listening device on the line. The one he would use – like a lot of retired ops, he kept a trick bag of such devices – was nothing special, but it was road-tested and reliable. He got down on his knees and took out what looked like a cable tester, a small black plastic gizmo the size of a garage opener with an LCD display, and reached under the cable cluster. He felt a small oblong object, a little like a small battery, and a lot like a signal-intercept device.

169

What the hell?

He squinted at it, visually confirming what he had felt. Someone had got there before he had. There already was a tap on the line, and it was a better model than one that he had. Now he let himself in the back – it took fifteen seconds with a couple of stiff bristles inside the keyhole, not his personal best, but not bad, either – and wandered through the place. Nicely but modestly furnished; a girl's place but not a girly girl's. Nothing too pink or fluffy. On the other hand, nothing that suggested it was a lair of iniquity, either.

There were a number of good places for secreting audio-surveillance instruments, in his professional estimation. An ideal location had to meet two tests. It had to be a place where it wouldn't be detected, but also where it would be capable of getting a high-quality feed. Stick a bug in a pipe and nobody would find it, but you wouldn't pick up a goddamn thing, either. And it had to be someplace that wouldn't get moved or thrown out, the way a floral arrangement would be. He figured he'd have no problem finding good homes for half a dozen of the devices, starting with the chandelier in the dining room, which was close to ideal. He stepped on a chair and examined the inner brass circle around which was a circle of flame-shaped bulbs. Out of sight, there was a recessed spot where the wiring came through, and that would probably leave room for . . . Navajo Blue blinked. Once again, someone had beaten him to it. To most people, the thing would look like an extra, capped-off wire. But he knew exactly what it was – starting with the fact that the top of the cap was actually sieve-textured glass.

Over the next fifteen minutes, he identified several other prime locations for surveillance devices. Each time he found that one had already been planted there.

His nerves were now sparking at him, and it wasn't the hangover anymore. The fact was, 42 Elm Street was wired up like a goddamn studio. Something was very wrong.

His instincts might have grown muzzy, but they told him to get out of there fast, and he did so, walking out the back door and rounding to the street. He thought he caught a glimpse of something out of the corner of his eye – someone watching from a neighboring yard? – but when he turned for a second look, whatever he saw was gone. Now he strode the half-block to his truck and drove off. Castor said he'd check in within a few hours. Castor was going to get an earful.

The AC was blasting away – he hadn't remembered leaving it on – and he reached over to fiddle with the knobs on the dashboard, which suddenly seemed far away, as if someone had stretched everything out. The afternoon sun seemed to flicker and dim, which meant that a cloud had passed over it, except that the light got dimmer and dimmer and no cloud could turn day into night and it was definitely night, it was midnight-blue, and he had some thought about turning on the headlights and another thought that the headlight thought didn't really make sense, and he just managed to pull the truck over to a halt on the side of the road before the weird nocturnal vision turned into inky blackness. Then he had no more thoughts at all.

A tinted-glass navy sedan glided to a stop just behind the van. The two men who emerged from it – both of medium height and medium build, medium brown hair at medium length, wholly unexceptional save for their hatchet-like countenances – were efficient in their movements. Someone who met them might have taken them to be brothers, and they were. One of them lifted the truck's hood and removed a spent flat canister from the air-conditioning system. The other opened the driver's-side door to the truck and, taking care not to inhale, pulled the lifeless body out of it. His companion would drive the truck back to the address they had in New Hampshire, but first he helped carry the dead man into the trunk of the sedan. The body, too, would be returned to the man's home and arranged in some plausible position there.

'You realize it's going to be a four-hour drive,' said the first man, hoisting the body from beneath its arms.

'It's the least we can do,' his companion replied. Together, they arranged the body in the trunk so that it would

171

not slide around in transit. Before the trunk was closed, Navajo Blue's body was curled around a spare tire as if it were hugging it. 'After all, he's in no condition to drive.'

CHAPTER EIGHT

Hang on, Pollux, Belknap silently urged. *I'm coming to get you.*

But the course would not follow a straight line – for reasons Jared Rinehart understood better than anyone.

The shortest distance between two points, Jared had once ventured, *is frequently a parabola followed by a ellipse followed by a hyperbola.* He meant that in the world of espionage, indirection and obliquity were just as likely to provide a shortcut as blunderbuss directness, and he had been cautioning Belknap when he said so. Not that Belknap had any other choice at the moment.

The dun-colored building could have been a distribution center for industrial components. There was a halfhearted stretch of barbed wire around the property, which seemed mainly for show, a way of discouraging casual visitors. Belknap drove his SUV through the main drive and parked off to one side. Stealth wasn't possible with a building like this one, and Belknap wasn't going to attempt it. Such an approach would signal that he had something to hide, that he was in a position of weakness. They were the ones who had something to hide. Belknap would make more progress by being bold and fearless in his approach.

He stepped outside the SUV, instantly enrobed in kilnlike heat, and he hurried to the nearest door before he began to perspire. Not the garage-style hinged door leading to the tarmac drive, but the white enameled steel door to the left of it. The door pushed open, and, as his eyes adjusted from the dazzling white outside to the gloom within, he had the sense that he had stumbled across a small refugee camp.

The space was cavernous, poorly lit, with sleeping bags

and thin mattresses scattered pell-mell. A row of open shower stalls was at one end of the space; water dripped from leaky faucets. There were food smells: cartons of cheap local stews. And everywhere there were people – girls, boys, many shockingly young. Some were clustered around pillars, some slumped, dozing, off on their own. They were a strikingly international crew. Some seemed to have arrived from Thailand, Burma, or the Philippines. Some were Arab. A few were from sub-Saharan Africa; others might have been village kids from India. A handful might have been from Eastern Europe.

What he saw did not surprise Belknap, but it nauseated him all the same. Young girls, younger boys, all driven by indigence into sexual slavery. Some must have been sold by their parents; others would have been fortunate even to have living parents.

Coming toward him slowly was a jowly, swarthy man in a white gauzy shirt and denim cutoffs, with a long, curved knife in one belt holster and a radio communicator in another. The man walked with a slight limp. He was nothing more than a watchman, a caretaker. For that was the ugliest part of it: Those who run such establishments did not need guards to keep these boys and girls in captivity; they required no locks, bars, shackles. And Belknap couldn't have set them free if he wanted to. For these children, the true shackles were forged of poverty. Even if they were left to wander freely through Dubai, they would only be picked up by another such establishment. Physical beauty was their one saleable asset; the rest reflected the cold inexorable logic of the marketplace.

Belknap's nostrils filled with a harsh chemical scent, overwhelming the human fetor; the drains in the concrete floors indicated that the place was hosed down regularly, and doubtless mopped with some industrial-grade disinfectant. Factory-farmed swine were kept in better conditions.

The man with the knife growled at him ineffectually, saying something in Arabic. When Belknap did not respond, he came closer and said in heavily accented English, 'You are in the wrong place. You must go now.' It was clear that he considered the radio communicator on his belt – his ability to summon backup – his real weapon.

Belknap ignored the fat man and continued to look around. This was a Hades of sorts, an underworld that few of its inhabitants would ever leave, at least not with their souls intact. Of the dozens of people in the building, few were over twenty, he reckoned. A fair number were probably no older than twelve or thirteen. Every one a story of an everyday tragedy.

Amid the heat, he felt cold. His had been a lifetime of heroics, of derring-do with guns and spycraft, yet what did it amount to in the face of such horrors? In the face of the grinding poverty that drove children into a place like this, and made them feel grateful that they at least were able to fill their bellies? For there was no humiliation like want, no degradation like hunger.

'I say, you must go!' the jowly man repeated, his breath garlicky and stale.

There was a noise from a group of somber-looking teenage girls, and the man turned around and scowled at them. He brandished his knife and shouted a string of multilingual curse words. Some rule of local etiquette had been breached. Then he turned back to Belknap, the knife now in his hand.

'Tell me about the Italian girl,' Belknap demanded.

The fat man looked blank. The girls were livestock to him; he did not distinguish among them save by the grossest characteristics. 'You go!' he bellowed, coming closer to Belknap.

The man reached for his radio handset and Belknap grabbed it from his chubby hand. Then, with a swift blow, he drove rigid fingers into the man's soft throat. As the man sank to the ground, helplessly clawing at his rapidly swelling larynx, Belknap kicked him hard in the face with a heavy shoe. The fat man sprawled motionless on the floor, breathing in fast puffs but unconscious.

There were dozens of eyes on Belknap when he turned around, neither approving nor condemning, but simply interested to see what he would do next. There was something sheeplike about them, and he felt a surge of contempt.

He turned toward a girl who looked to be around Lucia Zingaretti's age. 'You know an Italian girl? A girl named Lucia?'

The girl dazedly shook her head. She neither moved away from him nor met his gaze. She just wanted to get through the day. For someone like her, mere survival was an achievement.

He tried again with another girl, and again; the responses were the same. These were people who had been taught that whatever they did would be futile; the lesson of helplessness was not easily unlearned.

Then Belknap made his way across the main floor until he noticed, through a slatlike window, a small cinderblock storage facility at the rear of the property. He barged through a back door and made his way across yards of sand and scrub until he reached the small cinderblock shelter. He noticed that the main door was designed to take a heavy security padlock, and that such a padlock had been used recently. The paint was scratched in spots, exposing glinting steel. No evidence of corrosion yet, which meant that the scratches were recent.

He pushed through the steel door and, pulling a penlight from his pocket, he investigated the gloom. The space was basically a shack, the sort of structure that was normally made of sheet metal, not heavy cement blocks. There was dust on the concrete floor, but there were also areas where the dust had been wiped away – further evidence of recent activity.

It took him nearly five minutes before he saw it.

A small inscription, easy to miss, about a foot above the floor on the rear wall. He knelt down and peered, holding his penlight very close to it.

Two words, in small painted letters: POLLUX ADERAT.

It was Latin for 'Pollux was here.' Belknap could hardly breathe. He recognized the neat, almost crabbed handwriting – unmistakably Jared's – and he recognized something else as well.

176

The words had been written in blood.

Jared Rinehart had been there – but when? And, most crucially, where was he now? Belknap raced back into the main building and started demanding of everyone he came across whether they had seen a man in the past few days, a tall American. All he aroused was mute indifference.

As he made his way back to his SUV, hair now sweat-pasted on his forehead, he heard a boy's voice. 'Mister, mister,' the child was calling out.

He turned around to see a kohl-eyed Arab, who was maybe in his early teens, maybe not yet. The urchin's voice had not yet broken. A specialty taste.

Belknap gazed at him, mute, expectant.

'You ask about your friend?' the boy asked.

'Yes?'

The boy was silent for a moment, staring up at the American as if to scrutinize his character, his soul, the possible danger he presented and the possible help he could offer. 'A trade?'

'Go on.'

'You take me back to my home village in Oman.'

'And?'

'I know where they took your friend.'

That was the boy's trade, then: information for transport. Yet could he be trusted? If he were desperate to be returned to his Omani village, a crafty boy could concoct a story on the spur of the moment.

'Where?'

The boy shook his head, his fine black hair gleaming in the sun. The makeup they had applied around his eyes was doubtless a regional specialty. But his delicate face was resolute, his large eyes were solemn. The terms of the exchange had to be honored first.

'Talk to me,' Belknap said. 'Give me a reason to believe you.'

The boy – perhaps four foot six in height – tapped on the hood of the SUV. 'You have air conditioning?'

Belknap gave him a hard stare. Then he got into the driver's seat and opened the door opposite; the Arab boy climbed in. He started up the engine, and within moments cool air bathed them both.

The boy smiled, a dazzling white smile, as he pressed his face to the nearest AC vent. 'Habib Almani – do you know this princeling?'

'Princeling?'

'He calls himself 'princeling.' An Omani gentleman. Very rich. Big man.' The boy gestured with his hands to describe someone of considerable girth. 'Owns much property in Dubai. Owns stores. Owns trucking firm. Owns dhow business.' He pointed toward the dun-colored building. 'Owns this, too. Nobody knows.'

'But you know.'

'My father owe him money. Almani is also a *Beit*, a clan chieftain.'

'So your father gave you to him.'

The boy shook his head vehemently. 'My father never do that! He refused! So Habib Almani's men take his two children. Zip, zip, in the darkness, he steals us away. What can my father do? He does not know where we are.'

'And my American friend?'

'I see him brought here blindfolded, in Habib Almani van. They use his trucking service. They use his building for the rent boys and girls. Habib Almani does all this for them. Then they take the tall American away. The princeling knows, because he is the one in charge!'

'How do you figure that?'

'My name is Baz. Baz means falcon. Falcons see much.' He gave Belknap an intent look. 'You are an American, so this is hard for you to understand. But poor is not the same as stupid.'

'Point taken.'

The drive that the boy described would involve traveling through the desert, and on some poorly trafficked terrain. If Baz were lying to him . . . but the boy seemed to understand the risks as well as the rewards. Too, there were details in his story that made a sickening kind of sense.

'Take me with you,' the boy implored, 'and I'll take you to him.'

At the Portland headquarters of the SoftSystems Corporation – a sprawling campus of redbrick and energy-efficient glass that the *New York Times* architecture critic had called 'Portland postmodern' – there was never any cause to complain about the coffee. William Culp, its founder and CEO, liked to crack that a programmer was a machine for turning coffee into code. In the great Silicon Valley tradition, sophisticated coffee machines were available throughout the offices, and the brew was an upscale blend of specialty beans. Still, William Culp's own brew was, well, first among equals. Kona or Tanzanian Peaberry was all very well, but he'd developed a fondness for Kopi Luwak beans. They cost six hundred dollars a pound, and only five hundred pounds were harvested every year, all from the Indonesian island of Sulawesi. Most of it was snapped up by Japanese gourmets. But Culp made sure he had a regular supply.

What was special about Kopi Luwak? Culp relished the explanation. The beans had actually been eaten by a tree-dwelling marsupial that always went for the ripest coffee cherries, and then excreted them whole, still layered in their mucilage but subtly altered by the animal's digestive enzymes. The locals gathered the marsupial's droppings and carefully washed them to retrieve the beans, as if panning for gold. The result was the most complex java in the world – heavy-bodied, rich, musty, with caramel flavors and a hint of something he could only describe as 'jungly.'

He was enjoying a freshly brewed cup right now.

Bob Donnelly, his chief operating officer, a man with the broad shoulders of the college fullback he had once been, regarded him with amusement. He wore an open-collared pale blue shirt with the shirtsleeves rolled up. SoftSystems generally adhered to a dress-down ethic – if you saw anyone wearing a tie, it was invariably a visitor – and preserved the conventions of Silicon Valley informality. 'Another cup of your crappuccino?' he asked wryly. They were sitting together in a small conference room adjacent to Culp's private office.

'You'll never know what you're missing.' Culp smiled. 'Which is fine with me.'

Donnelly wasn't one of the 'OGs,' as they liked to call themselves – he wasn't one of the six boys from Marin County who, decades back, had monkeyed around with old Atari consoles in their garages and had come up with the prototype of the computer mouse. What was patentable wasn't the mouse itself – the 'hardware peripheral' – but the software that made it work, that integrated it with a visual interface. In the years that followed, nearly every software package on the shelf licensed intellectual property that Culp and company had patented. SoftSystems got big. Culp had given his parents a chunk of stock, and they sold it for a hefty sum once the price broke a hundred. Culp privately scorned their fearful attitude toward financial risk. The stock would triple in just another five years, making Culp a billionaire before his thirty-fifth birthday.

But over the years, most of the other fellows from the old days peeled off to do their own thing. Some started their own companies; others spent their days with costly toys – speedy yachts and jets. Culp stayed the course. He replaced the garage boys with MBA types, and, apart from a nasty and narrowly dodged antitrust trial, SoftSystems had gone from strength to strength ever since.

'So what do you say we acquire Prismatic?' Donnelly asked.

'You think we can make it profitable?'

Donnelly ran a hand through his short reddish hair, as thick as boar bristles, and shook his head. 'Strictly as a B&B.' A B&B was their shorthand for 'buy and bury.' When Soft-Systems analysts stumbled on a company with a technology that might pose a competitive threat, it would sometimes acquire the company, and thus its patents, simply to take them off the market. Retooling SoftSystems programs with the superior algorithm could be a costly proposition. 'Good enough' was, often, all that the market really required.

'You work up the financials?' Culp took another sip of the rich brew. He looked like an aging schoolboy, with wire-rim glasses that had scarcely changed since college, a thatch of sandy brown hair that still hadn't receded a millimeter. Close up, you could see the lines around his eyes, the way it took a while for his forehead to uncrinkle when he had raised his eyebrows. The truth was that he had never really been boyish when he was a boy. There had been something middle-aged about him even when he was an adolescent, so it was maybe only fitting that there was something adolescent about him now that he was middle-aged. It amused him sometimes when people pretending to be his intimates referred to him as 'Bill'; the people who really knew him knew that he had always been 'William.' Not Bill, not Will, not Billy, not Willy. William. Two syllables separated by a hint of a third.

'Got 'em here,' said Donnelly. He had boiled them down to a single page. Culp liked his executive summaries to be truly summary.

'I like what I'm seeing,' Culp said. 'An equity swap – think they'll go for that?'

'We can do it either way. We'll make a richer offer in equity, but if they want cash, no problemo. And I know their angel investors – Billy Hoffman, Lou Parini, guys like that. They'll insist on a quick payday. Force the managers' hand if they have to.'

'I'm so sorry,' said Millie Lodge, one of Culp's personal assistants. 'Urgent call.'

'I'll take it here,' Culp said absently.

Millie silently shook her head – a small gesture, but one that caused Culp's stomach to clutch.

He took his coffee with him to his office, and picked up the phone: 'Culp here,' he said, suddenly hoarse.

The voice that greeted him was sickeningly familiar. A creepy, electronically altered sound. It was whispery and raspy and harsh and heartless and eerily insistent. The way it would sound if an insect could speak, he sometimes thought.

'Time to tithe,' the voice said.

Culp broke out in a cold sweat. From experience, he knew that the call would have been placed via Web-based telephony and was impossible to trace. It could have emanated from the floor below him or from some hovel in Siberia; there was simply no way to know.

'More money for those goddamn savages?' Culp asked between gritted teeth.

'We're looking at a document composed on October seventeen, another series of e-mail exchanges from that afternoon, another internal document from October twenty-one, and a confidential communication sent to Rexell Computing, Ltd. Shall we forward copies to the S.E.C.? In addition, we have documentation relating to the formation of an offshore business entity called WLD Enterprises, and – '

'Stop,' Culp croaked. 'You had me at hello.' Any hint of rebellion or defiance had been crushed. Each one of those documents by itself could spur the S.E.C. and the Justice Department into a fresh investigation of antitrust activities, and a legal morass that could cost billions to deal with and dent the company's market capitalization for a long time. There was even the looming danger that the company would be broken up, spun off into parts – which would be the greatest disaster, because the parts were decidedly less valuable than the whole. Nobody needed to belabor the consequences. They were crystal-clear.

That was why he had already been forced to give away vast sums, through the William and Jennifer Culp Charitable Trust, toward the treatment of tropical diseases. If the whole goddamn continent of Africa just sank beneath the waves one day, Culp wouldn't give a good goddamn. But he was running an empire here: He had responsibilities to it. And his enemies were formidable and intelligent and unsympathetic. Culp had spent a shitload of cash trying to track them down, and with nothing to show for it save a few denial-of-service attacks on the corporate Web sites.

People thought he was the master of his domain. Nonsense. He was a goddamn *victim*. What did he really control, after all? He glanced through the glass at his COO. Donnelly had a whitehead on the side of his nose, a small pustule, and Culp felt a sudden urge to pop it, or poke it with a needle. A twisted grin appeared on his face. *Imagine what would happen if I did that.* He caught Millie Lodge's eyes; Millie Lodge who knew so many of his secrets and was every inch a loyalist, he had no doubt. But that goddamn reeking perfume she always wore. He'd meant to say something to her about it, but somehow it never seemed appropriate – he could never figure out a sufficiently offhand way to bring it up, without devastating her, and now, all these years later, it would be just too goddamn awkward to broach the subject. So there! William Culp, a prisoner of her Jean Tatou cologne or whatever the hell it was.

But maybe – maybe Millie herself was somehow behind the shakedown! He looked at her again, tried to size her up as a potential conspirator. It didn't make sense, somehow; she just wasn't that crafty. He continued to steam, silently. *Here I sit, William Culp, No. 3 on the Forbes Four Hundred, and these bastards have my goddamn sack in their fist! Where's the justice in that?*

'The European Commission would look askance at your proposed acquisition of Logiciel Lilles,' the voice from hell prompted, 'if it was made aware of your draft marketing scheme for – '

'Just tell me what you want from me, for the love of God,' Culp said with bitter resignation. It was the snarling of a defeated animal. 'Just tell me!' He took another sip of his cooling brew and made a face. The flavor was actively unpleasant. Who was he kidding, anyway? It tasted like shit.

Oman

The horizon line was serrated with crags and swales and the occasional stunted acacia tree. Half-shrouded in the distance, to the north, was the irregular crest of the distant Hajar Mountains. The one-lane road was often powdered over with the reddish sand, so that it blended into the surrounding desert. Finally, the road lurched through a rocky pass and into a green arroyo. There were date palms along the ravine, desert oleander, and scrubby grasses.

For intervals, he allowed himself to be dazed by the beauty of the landscape, his mind emptying out into the barren majesty of his surroundings. Then thoughts of Jared Rinehart began to intrude.

He was failing a man – he could not shake the feeling – who had never failed him. A man who had not only saved his life on more than one occasion, but who had stepped in on occasion to keep him from harm's way. He remembered the time when Jared had warned him that a woman he had been getting close to – a Bulgarian émigrée who worked at Walter Reed – was a suspected mole, the subject of a clandestine FBI probe. The dossier Rinehart showed him had been devastating to Belknap. Yet how much more devastating would it have been if Belknap hadn't learned the truth? The FBI generally guarded its domestic investigations from the other agencies; Belknap's own career could have been destroyed, and perhaps, given his carelessness, it should have been. But Rinehart would not hear of it. Through every kind of travail, he always kept an eye out for Belknap, as much a guardian angel as a friend, Belknap sometimes thought. When a close friend of Belknap's – a friend from childhood – died in a car accident, Rinehart had traveled all the way to Vermont to attend the funeral, simply to keep Belknap company, and make it clear he was not alone, that when he grieved Rinehart grieved as well. When a girlfriend of Belknap's was killed during an operation in Belfast, Rinehart had insisted that he be the one to break the terrible news to him. He remembered how he struggled not to fall apart, how he struggled not to weep, until he looked up and saw that Rinehart's own eyes were moist.

Thank God I still have you, Belknap had told him. *Because you're all I've got.*

And now? What did Belknap have?

He was failing the one true friend he had. Failing, yes, the one man who had never failed him.

The SUV juddered as he drove over a crested ridge of fissured road, and his gaze drifted away from the crenulated mountains in the distance, the shades of ochre and yellow in the earth and stones. He had filled the tank two hours earlier, and now he gave the gas gauge an occasional glance. Up ahead, a cluster of mud-brick houses was sheltered by a cliff. A few birds circled overhead.

'Falcons!' Baz said, pointing.

'Like you, Baz,' Belknap said, to show that he understood. The boy had been chatty at the onset of the journey, and then subdued, and Belknap wanted to be sure that he would hold together if there were troubles ahead. As soon as they were out of Dubai, he had peered at himself in the mirror on the reverse side of the sunshade, and started rubbing at the kohl around his eyelids. Belknap gave him his handkerchief for the job. Now that it was almost gone, it was easier to see who the boy had been before being dragooned into the services of Habib Almani. Baz told him that his father wanted him to be an imam, that his grandfather had taught him to memorize scripture from a young age. The grand-father, once a trader from the coast, was also the one who had taught him English. Baz was fascinated by the radio in the dashboard, and during the first half hour of the trip he had avidly, marvelingly, switched between stations.

At the base of an escarpment, across from the wasp-nest village of mud houses on a wadi, was a large tentlike structure. The fabric – a cream-colored silk, it seemed – rustled in the faint breeze.

'This the place?'

'Yes,' Baz confirmed. There was tension in his voice.

The Omani princeling would be inside, holding court. Outside was a loose line of six or seven men in turbans and dishdashas, some sun-wizened, all lean, nearly to the point of emaciation. Baz had said that Almani would be on one of his regular visits to his region of tribal origin, and plainly he was – doling out gifts to the local chiefs and village elders. That was how the essentially feudal social order worked in places like Oman.

Belknap pushed his way into the tent and found himself walking on silk carpets. An attendant looked dismayed and heckled him in Arabic, gesturing excitedly. Belknap realized that the man was upset because he had not removed his shoes. *The least of your problems*, he thought.

Baz told him that the princeling was a man of considerable girth, but that was an understatement. He was corpulent. He was perhaps five-eight and must have weighed three hundred pounds. All of which made it easy to recognize him. He sat on a woven-cane seat, as if it were a throne. On a rug beside him was a heap of gaudy trinkets, obviously for bestowing upon the visiting elders. One of them, clad in dusty muslin, was walking away on bare feet as he clutched some bauble of gold foil.

'You're Habib Almani,' Belknap said.

'My dear sir,' the man replied with an elegant sweep of a hand, his eyes widening. On his fingers were jewel-encrusted rings that glinted and flashed. A diamond-studded *khandjar*, a small L-shaped ceremonial scabbard, drooped from a sash around his waist. He spoke in the plummiest of British accents; Belknap could have been at the Athenaeum Club. 'We come across so few Americans here. You must excuse the humble and temporary nature of my establishment. This is not exactly Muscat! And to what do we owe the pleasure of your company?' His small hard eyes belied his elaborate courtesies.

'I'm here for information.'

'You come to this humble Omani princeling for information? Driving directions, perhaps? How to get to the nearest . . . discotheque?' He started to guffaw, the very image of debauchery, and stole a leering side glance at a girl, perhaps thirteen, who silently huddled in the corner. 'You'd enjoy a night at a discotheque, wouldn't you, my little rosebud,' he cooed to her. Then he turned to Belknap again. 'I'm sure you know about Arab hospitality. Everywhere we are renowned for it. I must ply you with goodies, and take pleasure in doing so. But, well, you see, I am curious.'

'I'm with the U.S. Department of State. A researcher, shall we say.'

A small twitch was visible on the man's porridgy face. 'A spy. Lovely. The Great Game. Just like in the old days of the

Ottomans.' The self-described princeling took another sip from a silver teacup. Belknap was close enough to smell liquor – Scotch, in fact. Probably the expensive stuff. The princeling was plainly the worse for drink. He did not slur his words; he enunciated them with the emphatic precision of someone determined not to, which was no less of a give-away.

'An Italian girl came into your possession recently,' Belknap said.

'I'm afraid I don't know what you're talking about.'

'She was employed by an escort service you own.'

'By the beard of the Prophet, you shock me to the core, you cut me to the quick, you rock me to the foundations, you shiver my timbers and – '

'Don't try my patience,' Belknap said in a low, menacing voice.

'Oh, hell, if you're looking for an Italian *putta*, you've really gone out of your way. I can offer you other satisfactions. I can and I will. What's your speed? Name your poison? You want – yes, my little rosebud?' He gestured toward the cowering girl. 'You can have her. *Not* for keeps. But you can take her for a test drive, shall we say – a test drive to paradise!'

'You disgust me,' Belknap said.

'A thousand apologies. I understand. You steer the other course. You drive on the other side. No need to explain. You see, I went to Eton, where buggery was practically a school sport, like the Wall Game. You know about the Wall Game? Only played at Eton. You must go to the St. Andrew's Day game one year, watch the Collegers and the Oppidans have it out. Rather like football. Rather. But rather different, too. I believe the last time a goal was scored on a St. Andrew's Day match was in 1909, if you can believe it.'

'Believe *this*, you bastard,' Belknap growled in a voice only loud enough for Almani to hear. 'I'll rip your arm out of its socket if you don't come clean.'

'Ah, a taste for rough trade!' The voice was jeering beneath its obliging tone. 'We can accommodate that as well.

Whatever lights your torch! Whatever charges your battery! Now, if you'll just turn around and head to Dubai, I'll be able to provide you exactly – '

'With one phone call I can scramble a couple of helicopters that will take you and your goddamn entourage to a very dark place from which you may never emerge. With one phone call I can – '

'Oh, poo!' The bejeweled Omani downed the contents of his goblet and exhaled boozily. 'You know something? You're the sort of person Dr. Spooner would have called a shining wit.'

'I warned you.'

'The wop wench – what about her? It was a favor, that was all. Not my cuppa, I'll tell you that for nothing. Someone wanted to get her out of the way.'

'Someone connected with the Khalil Ansari group.'

Suddenly the princeling looked uncomfortable. With a sloppy sweep of his arm and a few words of guttural Omani Arabic, he ordered the others away, including two glowering burly men who had stood to either side of him and whose *khandjars* looked more than merely ornamental. Only the silent, cowering girl remained.

'Loose lips sink ships!' Almani scowled.

'Who?' Belknap pressed. 'Tell me who.'

'Khalil Ansari's dead,' the man said sullenly. Wariness had entered his voice; a man like him did not dismiss his guards cavalierly. He must have placed great weight on the risk of untoward revelation.

'You think I don't know that?'

'Not that it'll make a goddamn bit of difference now, will it?' the drunken Omani went on. 'He wasn't really in control of the business anyway, not toward the end. New management. New maestro.' He pretended to be an orchestra conductor. 'Tum-tee-tum, tum-tumity-tumity-tum,' he burbled, a snatch of some tune Belknap didn't recognize. 'Anyway, it wasn't like I had any choice. You CIA types never understand that. You're always picking on us pawns and leaving the kings, queens, bishops, and rooks to their own devices!'

Abruptly, he had turned maudlin and self-pitying. 'What did I ever do to *you*?'

Belknap took a menacing step closer. Almani, he inferred, had been on the CIA payroll at one time or another. It affected the way he dealt with the American: made him desperate to buy him off, lest evidence of his past associates compromise his standing with his current associates. In the Gulf, it was not an uncommon situation among middlemen like this glorified princeling.

'It wasn't just the Italian girl,' Belknap said. 'Tell me about the tall American. Tell me about Jared Rinehart.'

Habib Almani's eyes widened, his cheeks puffed out as if he was about to be sick. Finally he blurted, 'I had no bloody choice, did I? There are some people and some powers to whom you just can't say, 'Sod off!' I had no bloody choice.'

Belknap grabbed hold of the man's pudgy soft hand and began to squeeze hard, then harder. Pain was visible in the princeling's contorted face.

'Where is he?' Belknap asked. Then he put his face inches from the Omani's and bellowed the question: 'Where is he?'

'You're too late, aren't you?' Almani sneered. 'He's not here. Not in the Emirates at all. Not any longer. He had been in Dubai, yes. They wanted to put him in my safekeeping and all that. But next thing you know, they put the long fellow on a private bird, you see. Your friend has flown away.'

'*Where*, goddammit?'

'Somewhere in Europe, I'd guess. But you know how it is with private jets. They file flight plans – but then they don't always stick to them, do they?'

'I said where?' Belknap lashed out with an open hand and struck the Omani across the face.

The man reeled drunkenly, and then settled into a half-crouch, breathing hard. He was obviously debating whether to summon his guards, and then, just as obviously, thought better of it. Almani was debauched and vainglorious; he was not rash. His temper quickly cooled to a wounded dignity.

'I told you,' Almani said, 'I don't know, you son of a dog and a camel. It's not the sort of thing you ask, now is it?'

'Bullshit.' Belknap placed both his hands around Almani's fat, pulpy throat. 'You don't seem to know who you're dealing with. You want to know what I'll do if you don't talk? You want a taste? Do you?'

The Omani's face colored deeply. 'You're out of your league,' he coughed. 'You've had your twenty questions. But if you think I would cross – '

Belknap punched him hard. Knuckles met cheekbones through an inch of adipose.

'You're *insane* if you think I would tangle with Genesis,' Almani said in a low voice, hushed with intensity. A spark of lucidity glinted through his drunkenness and affectation, like a voice at the bottom of a well. 'You're insane if *you're* thinking of tangling with Genesis.'

Genesis? Belknap threw out an arm and slammed his elbow into the Omani's jaw.

Blood appeared in a small rivulet from the corner of the man's mouth, dripping from his thick lips, as if someone had tried to draw a lopsided frown on his face. 'You are wasting your energies,' the man gasped. Not his words but the finality on his face made Belknap stop. The finality, and the fear.

'Genesis?'

Breathing heavily, Almani managed a twisted smile despite the pain, the blows. 'He's everywhere, don't you know?'

'He?'

'He. She. It. They. The hell of it is, nobody knows for sure, except for a few unfortunates who have reason to wish to Allah that they didn't. I say 'he' for convenience. He has his fingers everywhere. His confederates always among us. Perhaps even you.'

'Oh, you think?' Belknap grunted.

'No, not really. You're too bloody obvious in your moves. You're a two-plus-two-equals-four guy. Not a connoisseur of complexity. No match for Genesis. But then who is?'

'I don't understand you. You live in holy terror of a person you've never seen?'

'As have men throughout the millennia. But seldom for such good reason. The princeling will take pity on you. The princeling will tell you the facts of life, you silly ignorant naïf. Call it Arab hospitality. Or don't. But never say I didn't warn you. There are those who say that Genesis is a woman, the daughter of a German industrialist who fell in with the radicals of the nineteen-seventies – Baader-Meinhof, the June Two Movement – and then out the other side. Some say Genesis has a public profile as an orchestra conductor, a maestro, who travels around the world from one engagement to another, while stealthily maintaining discipline among those who have no idea of his true identity. Some say he's a giant of a man, others, that he's a midget, literally. I've heard that she's a ravishing beauty, and I've also heard she's a wizened crone. I've heard it said that Genesis was born in Corsica, Malta, Mauritius, and various points east, west, north, and south. Some say he's descended from a family of samurai, and spends more of his time in a Zen monastery. Some say his father was a poor ranch hand in South Africa, and that he was adopted by a rich Boer family with mining interests, which he then inherited. Some say he's Chinese, a onetime intimate of Deng. Some say he is a professor at the School of Oriental and African Studies in London, but nobody knows which. Yet others – '

'Stop it, you're gibbering.'

'My point is merely that there are many stories and no validated truths. He rules over a shadowland that encompasses the globe, yet he – or she, or it – remains forever out of sight, like the dark side of the moon.'

'What the hell . . . ?'

'You're hopelessly over your head. I suppose we both are. But at least I know it.'

'I'd just as soon kill you as spit on you, you do know that, don't you?' Belknap snarled.

'Sure, you could kill me. But Genesis could do worse. Inconceivably worse. Oh, the stories I've heard. The legend of Genesis is not inconsiderable.'

'Campfire tales!' Belknap scoffed. 'Rumors based on super-stition – is that what you're talking about?'

'Stories that are passed along on the lower frequencies. Rumors, if you like – but rumors I have good reason to credit. Campfire tales, you say? Genesis knows a thing or two about fire. Let me tell you about another princeling – a member of the Saudi royal family in fact. It was said that an agent of Genesis passed along a request to him. A request from Genesis. The foolish man had the temerity to refuse. He thought he could defy Genesis.' Habib Almani swallowed hard. His forehead gleamed in the sunlight filtered through the layers of silk and muslin. His soft round hands clutched each other. 'He disappeared for a week. Then they found his body in a Dumpster in Riyadh.'

'Dead.'

'Worse,' Almani said. 'Alive. He remains alive in a Riyadh hospital to this day, I'm told. And in precisely the same condition as when he was discovered.' The Omani leaned forward with a look of horrified intensity. 'You see, when they found him, he was paralyzed from the neck down – the cervical spinal cord had been carefully severed. His tongue had been surgically cut out. And then a state of permanent blepharospasm was induced, apparently through the injection of a neurotoxin. Do you follow? His very eyelids were paralyzed, permanently clenched shut. So he cannot even communicate by blinking!'

'The man was otherwise intact?'

'Which is the really horrifying thing. He lives on, perfectly conscious, utterly immobile, locked into his midnight existence, his own body the ultimate crypt . . . as a warning to the rest of us.'

'Jesus Christ,' Belknap breathed.

'*Allahu Akbar,*' the Omani echoed.

Belknap narrowed his eyes. 'If you've never seen him, how do you know *I'm* not Genesis?'

A measuring gaze. 'Could *you* do such a thing?'

The look on Belknap's face was answer enough.

'And then there was a famously handsome Kuwaiti. Heir to a petrol fortune. A great ladies' man. So beautiful, it was said, that when he entered a room people would fall silent.

192

Then one day he defied the will of Genesis. When they found him – still alive – his entire face had been flayed. Do you understand? The very skin from his face was – '

'Enough!' the American barked, cutting him off. 'Goddammit, I've heard enough. Are you telling me that Pollux is in the clutches of this Genesis?'

Habib Almani shrugged elaborately. 'Are we not *all* in his clutches?' Then he lowered his face and cradled it in his hands, retreating into a fugue of fear. A place beyond reach.

'Goddammit, you'll answer my questions or I'll slice your throat open, rip your balls off, and shove them down your gullet. Nothing fancy, but I find it usually does the trick.' He took a folding blade from his pocket and held it at the man's throat.

Almani just stared off, spent. 'I have no more answers,' he said miserably. 'About Pollux, about Genesis? I have told you all I know.'

Belknap searched the man's face. He was, Belknap could tell, speaking the truth. The operative would learn no more from him.

The boy was waiting for him in front of the SUV when Belknap emerged, looking solemn. Dust from the desert breeze was already beginning to dull Baz's lustrous black hair.

'Get in,' Belknap grunted.

'There is one more thing you must do,' the boy told him.

Belknap just looked at him, suddenly conscious again of the baking heat, rising in waves from the earth itself.

'In the tent, you saw a girl, thirteen years old, kept by the princeling?'

Belknap nodded. 'An Arab girl.'

'You must go back and get her,' Baz instructed. He clasped himself with his slender arms, a pose of resolve. 'You must take her with us.' He took a deep breath and looked up at the American. For the first time, his eyes were moist. 'She's my sister.'

CHAPTER NINE

An hour's drive outside of Buenos Aires, the Casa de Oro was a cross between a classic hacienda and a Renaissance villa, with large arches everywhere and no shortage of gold-flecked marble. This morning, the guests were assembled at the far end of its formal, gently sloping lawns, to watch a polo match that was taking place on an adjacent field, ten fenced-off acres in size. Waiters in morning coats continually circulated with fruit drinks and canapés. A wizened man in an electric wheelchair was attended to by an Asian youth. An older woman with surgically tightened cheeks and bleached teeth that seemed to belong to someone else's mouth, the mouth of someone much younger and much larger, emitted shrill squeals as a white-haired eminence told stories.

Few of the guests paid much attention to the players, with their yellow jackets, white helmets, and long mallets. The ponies snorted as they made tight turns, their breath forming wraiths in the chill morning air.

A man in his early fifties adjusted his summer formal wear – a white swallowtail jacket and a crimson sash – and inhaled deeply. From the field drifted a whiff of sweat, both equine and human. He was an international businessman whose assets included telecom companies that stretched across much of the South American continent, and it was second nature for him to wonder how much the entire property would cost to acquire. The villa, the three hundred verdant acres surrounding it. He had no reason to think that Danny Munoz, their host, was interested in selling, and no real need to add to his own real-estate holdings. Yet he couldn't help wonder. It was his nature.

One of the waiters – older than the others, but a last-minute replacement had been needed – approached the middle-aged telecommunication mogul. 'Refresh your drink, sir?'

The man grunted.

With a smile, the waiter poured some of the lime-and-melon punch into his glass. The light blond hairs on the back of his hand glistened in the morning sun. Then he stepped behind a row of tall Italian cypresses and quietly dumped the rest of the liquid onto the soil. He had almost returned to the villa when the sounds of commotion – first a sudden silence, then random shrieks and hollers – told him that the mogul had been stricken.

'*Ataque del corazón!*' someone yelled.

Yes, a very good guess, mused the man in the waiter's attire. It would have seemed like a heart attack. Even the coroner would come to the same conclusion. He'd make sure that help was summoned. No reason not to. Especially since the target was assuredly beyond helping.

Andrea Bancroft unzipped a black nylon carrying case and set the laptop computer it contained on the square, paper-topped table. She and Walter Sachs were sitting together at the back of Greenwich's second-best vegan diner. It was a place Sachs seemed to favor just so he could mock it. The place was nearly empty; the waitress on duty looked over occasionally to make sure she wasn't needed, but mostly had her nose in a paperback copy of *Great Expectations*.

'You just buy this?' he asked. 'It's a pretty good model. You could do better for the price, though. Should have asked me first.'

Walter Sachs had taken to wearing his gray-brown hair short on the sides and long on top, which made his long, rectangular face look even more so. His cleft jaw conveyed a sense of strength that was slightly discordant with his narrow chest. He had – it embarrassed Andrea that she noticed, but there it was – a flat butt. He wore his trousers hitched up almost to his navel, but they bagged a little in the back. As if to combat the stereotype of the bespectacled computer geek, he wore contacts, but he had obviously never quite grown accustomed to them. His eyes were always slightly reddened, slightly irritated. Maybe he had dry eyes, or maybe the curvature of the lenses wasn't quite right. Andrea wasn't going to ask.

'It's not mine.'

'Got it,' Walter said lightly. 'Receipt of stolen goods.'

'Sort of,' Andrea said. 'As a matter of fact.'

Walter gave her a look. 'Andrea . . .'

'I'm asking you for a favor here. There are files on this computer, and I'd like to read them. Only they're encrypted. That's the situation. How much more do you really want to know?'

Walter stroked his chin and gave her a marveling look. 'As little as possible,' he said. 'You're not doing something you shouldn't be doing, right?'

'You know me, Walter.' Andrea smiled wanly. 'When have I ever done something I shouldn't?'

'Fine. Say no more.'

How could she even begin to explain? She couldn't even explain it to herself.

Maybe her suspicions were groundless. Yet those red ants continued to swarm. She had to do something to get rid of them – or else follow them to their destination. The decision she made was impetuous; the manner of executing it was anything but.

It had been something of a shot in the dark, replacing the Hewlett-Packard laptop belonging to the Bancroft Foundation's comptroller with an identical model whose hard disk she had wiped. The natural assumption would simply be that the disk had crashed; the data would be backed up, and that would be that. Unplugging the machine from the Ethernet and power cord had taken less than ten seconds. The fellow was eating in a lunchroom on the floor below. It was child's play. Except for the telltale heart hammering in her chest as she made her way back to the parking lot with the stolen object in her knapsack. She wasn't just entering a different world; she was a different Andrea Bancroft. She did not know what she would discover about the foundation. But she had already discovered a great deal about herself, and she wasn't sure it was entirely heartening.

Walter was already rummaging through the computer's root directory. 'Lot of stuff here. Data files, mainly.'

'Start with the most recent,' she directed.

'They're uniformly encrypted.'

'As I said.' She poured herself more Tissane of Tranquility – apparently some sort of chamomile tea, except that, this being a vegan diner, everything was given a cute name. Her earthenware mug felt unpleasantly sandy against her lips.

Walter rebooted the computer while holding down a combination of keys – Shift, Option, a couple of others that Andrea didn't catch. Instead of the usual startup screen, a bare command line was visible. Walter was working at the machine-code level. He keyed in a few lines and then nodded sagely. 'Pretty standard crypto,' he said. 'Commercial-strength RSA.'

'Easy to crack?'

'Like opening a sardine can,' Walter said, blinking furiously. 'With your fingernails.'

'Yikes. How long?'

'Hard to say. I'm gonna have to C-plus-plus the sucker. Wire it up to my Big Bertha. There are some pretty decent can openers out there in shareware land. I'll upload a dozen of these files and keep throwing shit at it. Kinda like smashing a window so you can unlock the front door. I mean, we're basically talking about reversing a one-way hash algorithm in order to get an entering wedge that'll pull up the modulus between two 1024-bit primes, which is what makes it a little hairy.'

Andrea tilted her head. 'I have no idea what you just said.'

'Then I guess I'm just talking to myself. Wouldn't be the first time.'

'You're a darling.'

'You wouldn't be landing me in hot water, now, would you?'

'Of course not. I'd never do that. Tepid, sure. *Warm*, maybe. Warm's okay, isn't it?'

'You're a deep one, you are, Andrea Bancroft.'

'How do you mean?'

Walter pursed his lips as he peered at the machine code that had started to crowd the screen. 'Who said I was talking to you?'

He *had* to be dead. Navajo Blue had agreed to what Castor had asked of him, and he had been killed. It was the likeliest explanation for the man's failure to leave a message at the appointed time, let alone his failure to respond to calls on any of his numbers. A combination of nausea and fury welled up in Belknap, and he noticed he was traveling at a dangerous speed. What had he done today? More harm than good? He had – in the plus column, he hoped – dropped off Baz and his sister at their village, which clung to a ledge of rose-colored rock like a gray lichen. He could hear ululations and joyous cries among the villagers as he drove off, and his thoughts returned back to the princeling and his baubles. Such exploitation. Such depravity. Such disrespect for human life in a sun-parched region where any kind of life was a kind of miracle. And what would become of twelve-year-old Baz? Would he grow up to be an imam, as his grandfather hoped? Would his life be claimed in the next round of cholera or typhoid? A round of interclan violence? Would he become a terrorist or a caregiver? Would the evil visited upon him bear malignant fruit in his own later life – or would it increase his resolve to work for good? No guarantees. The boy was clever, well-spoken, clearly better-educated already than most of the villagers among whom he lived. Perhaps he would escape the obscurity that surrounded him. Perhaps his name would come to be far better known than the names of his kith and kin – but known for ill or for good?

There were some who would say that the answer depended on who you were; they would point out that the most notorious terrorists were frequently heroes among their own people. *There are some who would say that you and I are terrorists*, Jared told him once. Belknap had been indignant: *Because we do violence to evildoers?* Jared had shook his head: *Because they think we are the evildoers.*

Not that Jared had never been tempted by easy relativism. There were lies and there were truths. There were facts and there were forgeries. *If someone shows you a penny with two faces, you know you've been given a fake penny*, he once said. *But you know something else, too.*

What's that? Belknap had asked.

Jared gave him a sleepy smile. *You should bet on heads.*

His thoughts returned to what the Omani had told him about Genesis – about the fantastic penalties he had exacted from those who crossed him. Could Jared really be in the hands of this monster? Belknap shuddered. And how had someone managed to keep his or her identity so closely guarded, even while wielding so much power? *A shadowland that encompasses the globe.*

Acid spurted in the back of Belknap's throat as he pulled his SUV over and tried calling Gomes for the third time in the past hour; the junior agent was evidently in meetings, and Belknap wasn't going to leave a message with anybody else. This time Gomes was in, and, when Belknap had gotten him on the phone and explained the situation – no response on any of his numbers – the junior agent had swiftly confirmed the worst. Navajo Blue – Thomas Mitchell – was indeed deceased. A squad car from the township of Wellington, New Hampshire, had been sent to his house and confirmed it. He was dead. Estimated time of death was seven hours earlier. Cause as yet unknown. No evidence of foul play. No evidence of anything.

Except that Belknap had sent him to his death.

He had sent him to put Andrea Bancroft under surveillance, but he had underestimated her wiles, her ruthlessness – or that of those protecting her.

Because of his mistake, a man was dead.

Gomes, as requested, gave him a fuller report on Andrea Bancroft. The seeming innocence of the public-life details might have only attested to her skill at fabrication. She clearly was highly intelligent, had enormous resources at her disposal.

Could she be Genesis?

Belknap rattled off the names of a dozen federal data-bases. 'Here's what I need to know,' he said to Gomes.

This time, the junior analyst made no protest. Navajo Blue's death would not go unavenged. The woman would be brought to justice.

Or Belknap would visit brutal justice upon her.

PART TWO

CHAPTER TEN

Andrea Bancroft tried to doze during the two-hour flight from Kennedy to the Raleigh-Durham International Airport in North Carolina, but her mind raced throughout. It was evening before Walter Sachs was able to give her a gigabyte CD-ROM with decrypted files. At her home computer, Andrea had peered into them until her eyes burned. She found a few staff memos, dozens of Excel spreadsheets, files relating to 'asset life-cycle management' in an Oracle format. Andrea had no difficulty opening any of them. Parsing them, properly, however, took time and attention.

The real puzzle was to be found among the financial transactions recorded: Hundreds of millions of dollars had been funneled to a nameless facility in Research Triangle Park, and – to go by the clearance codes – the transfers had been authorized directly by Dr. Paul Bancroft. Indeed, buried beneath a dozen legal shelters, it was, effectively, the biggest budget item for the entire foundation. Yet, as she quickly ascertained, the facility appeared on no maps. One Terrapin Drive was the address she found in the foundation's records, and she suspected it would indeed be found in the seven-thousand-acre expanse of pine forest known as Research Triangle Park. But it was not to be found on any map.

Research Triangle Park itself was something of an anomaly. Its motto was 'Where the minds of the world meet.' But it was not clear whom it belonged to. The United States Postal Service regarded it as a town or municipality, and though Durham claimed some authority over it, it was not itself part of any neighboring township. It included some of the largest supercomputing facilities in the world, some leading pharmaceutical research campuses, various think tanks as well. But it was, technically, neither public nor private, but a kind of nonprofit entity in its own right. It was created more than forty years ago by an obscure plutocrat – a Russian émigré who had supposedly made a fortune in textiles, and who had acquired the vast parcel of land. Carved into the forest were large campuses for high-tech companies and policy institutes, but officially most of it remained undeveloped, virgin forest.

Was the truth, in fact, more complicated? If only she could speak to Paul Bancroft – but nobody at the foundation could tell her when he would return, and she could wait no longer. The dreams and nightmares increasingly focused on the mystery surrounding the facility at Research Triangle Park. A foundation within the foundation? If so, did Paul Bancroft know about it? Had her mother learned about it? Too many questions, too much uncertainty.

Once again it seemed that ashed-over embers had been fanned and reignited. Something drew her toward them. *Like a moth to a flame?*

Doing nothing was maddening. Maybe it was insanity to go to Research Triangle Park herself, yet sitting on the sidelines was turning into another form of insanity. Maybe the plain banal facts would put to rest her feverish imaginings once and for all; it was altogether possible that there was a boring explanation that she had overlooked. Yet she would find no reassurance in dwelling on the anomalies she had discovered. Inaction would not bring calm.

One Terrapin Drive.

It was her mood, but once she landed everything struck her as ominous, even the giant sign with 'RDU' in huge blue letters. The airport, scarcely distinguishable in its sterile modernism from hundreds around the country, was a terrazzo jungle.

She was, if she were honest with herself, suffering from a bad case of nerves. Almost every face she saw seemed suspicious. She actually found herself peering into a baby stroller to make sure it wasn't just a prop used by someone doing surveillance. The baby gurgled at her, and she felt immediately ashamed. *Get a grip, Andrea.*

She had packed light, stowed her one piece of luggage in the overhead compartment. Now she wheeled it ahead of her as she pushed toward the ground-transportation exit. A gaggle of men with hand-lettered signs loitered by the glass, enjoying the air conditioning. Andrea had arranged to be picked up by a driver, but didn't see anyone with a sign for her. She was about to give up and head for the taxi stand when she saw a latecomer holding up a piece of paper lettered A. BANCROFT. So the man was a few minutes late. She waved at the driver, willing away her trivial sense of annoyance. The driver – a ruggedly handsome man, she noticed, with gray eyes – nodded and took her case, leading her to his dark-blue Buick. In his mid-forties, he was bulky, but light on his feet. No, not bulky, exactly; Andrea corrected her first impression. He was just heavily muscled, perhaps a fitness buff. His forehead was reddened, as if he had recently been out in the sun.

She gave him the address of her hotel, a Radisson in RTP, and the man silently and fluidly navigated the Buick through the outflows of airport traffic. For the first time, Andrea allowed herself to relax a little. Yet the thoughts that came to her were anything but serene.

How quickly a dream could curdle into a nightmare. Laura Parry Bancroft. Seeing the name neatly typed onto the registry forms had come as a shock, and the memory still had the power to transfix her with grief. Her mother's death had cast a shadow over her life. Yet how far could she trust her own feelings, her own suspicions? Perhaps she was in the sway of a maternal disaffection – a maternal delusion – out of love and loyalty and grief. Had the Bancrofts really done her any harm, or had she harmed herself because of her own frustrated anger? How well did she really understand her own mother? There were so many questions she wished she could ask her. So many questions.

Questions that her mother would never be able to answer. So much had perished in that car crash. And Andrea ached –

ached with her whole body – whenever she thought about it.

The car seemed to be driving over bumpy terrain, and Andrea opened her eyes and looked out for the first time. They were on a nearly deserted two-lane country road, and the car was gliding across the right lane to the shoulder, slowing, and –

This was wrong.

She was thrown abruptly to the side, her shoulder belt snapping and yanking at her, as the car slewed at a sharp angle and swerved off the shoulder and behind a dense road-side copse. Oh Christ . . . *It was a trap!*

Had the driver scouted out the area ahead of time, and driven her to this hidden spot knowing that she wouldn't get wise to what was happening until it was too late?

She saw the driver's face in the rearview mirror, saw a look of fury and hatred that almost took her breath away.

'Take my money,' she pleaded.

'You *wish*,' the driver scoffed, with chilling contempt.

She felt an icicle of fear touch her neck. She realized that she had been optimistic in thinking that it was only money he was after. And he was a powerful specimen indeed. All she had at her disposal was the possibility of surprise. And the likelihood that she would be underestimated.

What was the heaviest article she had? Hair brush, cell phone, a Cross pen that her mother had given her years ago, and . . . what? She commanded herself to focus, reached down to her ankle with her left hand. When she looked up again, the man was climbing over the front seat toward her. For a brief moment, his arms would be occupied while he negotiated the awkward passage. She made herself look small, surrendered, harmless.

Clutching her stiletto-heeled shoe in her right hand, she suddenly lashed out, heel forward – lashing toward his face, toward his eyes, and at the same moment she let out a piercing shriek.

Almost. With the stiletto just an inch away from his eyes, he grabbed her wrist with a steel-like hand, slamming it away while – thinking took too long – she smashed her other hand toward his nose. She remembered being told by a roommate taking martial-arts lessons that victims were frightened of hitting an assailant in the face – that they became victims by their own fear of aggression. *You gouge their eyes, you smash their nose, you do as much damage as you can* – that was the common sense that all the training came down to. *Your greatest enemy is yourself*, Alison always said.

Yeah? *Bullshit.* Her greatest enemy was the son of a bitch who was trying to kill her – and who had turned his head just in time to avert her second blow. *Whatever happens to me*, she thought, thrashing ferociously as she tried to unlock the door, *at least nobody will say I went easy.*

But the man was unstoppable, powerful, able to anticipate her every move. Pinning her down beneath him, he roared a question.

'Why did you kill Tom Mitchell?'

Andrea blinked, uncomprehending, but the monster persisted with a barrage of mystifying questions. Mitchell. Navajo Blue. Gerald – or was it Jared? – Rinehart. A fusillade of names, accusations.

It made no sense.

'*How* did you kill him, dammit?' With a quick motion, he reached into his jacket and pulled out a blued-metal handgun. Then he placed it to her head. 'I'd like to shoot you,' he said in a voice of immaculate hatred. 'Try giving me a reason why I shouldn't.'

Todd Belknap glowered at his captive. She had been wild, a hellcat, had left bruises he would undoubtedly feel tomorrow. But it was purely a matter of animal spirits; there was no evidence of training. That was just one of several discordant elements. Another was that she seemed genuinely bewildered by his questions. She could have been a superb liar; nothing he had learned ruled out the possibility that she was Genesis, or one of his confederates. But nothing gave support to that hypothesis, either.

He scrutinized her closely as he held the pistol steady. Another question surfaced obscurely in his mind, like a fish in a muddy pond. Hadn't it all been just a little too easy? She had purchased the airplane ticket under her own name, ensuring that it would appear in the FAA databases. She'd used the concierge service of her platinum charge card to arrange for a car to pick her up, again under her own name. Getting rid of the actual driver had been child's play, requiring no more than a fistful of cash and a good story about a surprise birthday. If she was indeed a professional, she had to be bizarrely confident that nobody was likely to be after her. Perhaps, then, she was merely unskilled labor – a cutaway, someone to be used on occasion, but not trained, someone whose very amateurishness would provide bona fides of her innocence. Or perhaps it was all a mistake. But then why had a call been placed from her cell phone to that of the leader of the squad in Dubai?

The woman struggled to control her breathing. She was, he noticed, an attractive woman, and quite possibly a former athlete. Someone used as bait?

There were too many questions. He needed answers.

'I have a question for you,' the woman said, returning his glare. 'Who sent you? Are you with the Bancroft Foundation?'

'You're not fooling anyone,' the operative barked.

She gulped air, winded with fear. 'If you're going to kill me, I think I have the right to die knowing the truth. Did you people kill my mother, too?'

What the hell was she talking about? 'Your mother?'

'Laura Parry Bancroft. She died ten years ago. In a car accident, they said. I'd always believed it, too. But I'm not sure I believe it anymore.'

Belknap could not stop a look of puzzlement from spreading across his features.

'Who *are* you people?' she demanded, a sob in her voice. 'What are you after?'

'What are you talking about?' Belknap asked. He was losing control of the situation.

'You know who I am, right?'

'You're Andrea Bancroft.'

'Correct. And who ordered you to kill me? It's my final goddamn request, okay? Like a last cigarette. Don't you hit men have a goddamn code of honor?' She blinked away tears. 'Like in the movies, when they say, 'Since you're about to die, I may as well tell you . . .' That's all I'm asking.' She smiled through her tears, but she was obviously struggling to fend off collapse.

Belknap just shook his head.

'I need to know,' she whispered. 'I need to know,' she repeated. Now she was hyperventilating and she was yelling at the top of her lungs, no longer begging but demanding. *I need to know.*

Numbly, Belknap returned the pistol to his shoulder holster. 'Yesterday afternoon, a man drove down from New Hampshire and went to your house, on my instructions. He was dead before sunset.'

'On your *instructions*?' Andrea asked incredulously. 'For what?'

Belknap pulled out the cell phone that belonged to the slain commando, brought up its log of received calls, and dialed the one that had arrived from the United States. Inside her handbag, another cell phone began to trill. Belknap clicked off the call. The trilling ceased. 'This cell phone belonged to the leader of a death squad. I had an encounter with him in Dubai. Now, why did you call him?'

'Why would I call? But I didn't . . .' Andrea faltered. 'I mean, yes, I might have dialed the number, but I had no idea who I was calling.' She opened her handbag and started to scavenge through it.

'Not so fast!' he roared, brandishing the pistol again.

The woman froze. 'Do you see that folded sheet?'

Belknap looked into the handbag, retrieved the sheet with his left hand, flipped it open with a snap of his wrist. A list of telephone numbers.

'Was it you who I called?'

Belknap just shook his head.

'I dialed all those numbers, in order,' the woman said insistently. 'The first dozen of them, anyway. If you don't believe me, you can check out my cell phone, see the list of dialed calls, the times.'

'Why?'

'I . . .' Again she broke off. 'It's complicated.'

Belknap bit off the words as he replied. 'Then make it simple.'

'I'll try, but . . .' She took a deep, unsteady breath. 'There's a hell of a lot I don't know yet. A hell of a lot I don't understand.'

Belknap's gaze softened a little. *That makes two of us*, he thought. 'I don't know whether I should believe you,' he replied warily, but he reholstered the pistol. 'You called, I answered, you hung up. Let's start there.'

'Yeah, let's. Someone hangs up on you, so you travel halfway around the globe and hunt them down with a gun.' Andrea held his gaze. 'I'd hate to see what you do when someone steals your parking space.'

Despite himself, Belknap laughed. 'You've got the wrong idea.'

'Maybe we both do,' she said.

'And maybe,' Belknap said, tension entering his voice again, 'there's a way to sort things out.'

She shook her head slowly: marveling, not dissenting. 'Let me get this straight. You sent someone to my house in Carlyle. Um, checking to see if I removed a mattress tag illegally? Sorry, I'm still not getting this.'

'I had to know whether you were behind Jared Rinehart's abduction.'

'And Jared is . . . ?'

'Jared?' He stopped.

'Because it's hard to follow without a scorecard.'

Belknap grimaced with impatience. 'You know what? It doesn't really matter if you understand.'

'Doesn't matter to whom?'

'What matters is that we figure out why this cell number appears on that phone bill. That's what I'm going to need your help with.'

'Of course,' she said with a brittle smile. She tossed her

curtain of blond hair back and gave him a hard look. 'Now, you want to remind me again why I should give a shit?'

Belknap stared at her, anger mounting. 'Goddammit,' he started. Yet she had a point to make: she had no idea what his concerns were, and he had no idea what hers were, either. 'Okay, listen. There are security issues involved here. Highly classified information. I wish I could say more.'

'You're trying to say that you've got government clearance and I don't.'

'You got it.'

'What kind of an airhead do you take me for?'

'Huh?'

'You heard me. You're supposed to be some secret agent man? Give me a goddamn break. I really don't think U.S. intelligence officers run their operations this way. Like, where's your team? Why are you by yourself? Best I can tell, you've got some Charles Bronson *Death Wish* thing going on and I just got caught in the middle of it. On the other hand, if I'm wrong, I'd be happy to meet you at your government offices and hash the whole thing out with your superiors.'

Belknap exhaled heavily. 'Maybe we got started off on the wrong foot.'

'Oh, you *think*? What little social faux pas of yours did you have in mind? The part where you waved your pistol in my face and threatened to blow my brains out? Or the part where you practically crushed both my collarbones? Why don't we check Amy Vanderbilt's etiquette guide, see if either one violates any of her little rules?'

'Please listen to me. I'm not in the service right now. You called that right. But I *was*. A career operative, okay? I don't expect any of this to make a lot of sense to you. I know a certain amount about you. You don't know anything about me. But maybe, just maybe, we can help each other.'

'How sweet. That makes everything all right, then.' Andrea Bancroft spoke with heavy sarcasm. 'A goddamn psycho thinks we can be of mutual assistance. Break out the champagne.' Anger glinted from her eyes.

'You honestly think I'm a psycho?'

She stared at him for a long moment, then looked away. 'No,' she said quietly. 'Oddly enough, I don't.' She paused. 'How about you? You honestly think I'm part of some conspiracy to kidnap your friend?'

'You wanna know the truth?'

'Might make a nice change.'

'I think probably you're not. But I also think it's a little too soon to say.'

'A man who's afraid to commit.' A mock simper. 'The story of my life.'

'Tell me more about this foundation,' Belknap said. 'What does it do, exactly?'

'What does it do? It's the Bancroft Foundation. It does . . . good deeds. Global public health, that kind of stuff.'

'Then why did you ask if I was from the foundation?'

'What? I'm sorry, I can't even think straight just now.' She put a hand on her forehead. 'All of a sudden I'm feeling a little dizzy. I need to step out, just walk for a few minutes, breathe some fresh air, or I'm going to pass out. This has all been a lot to deal with.'

'Fine,' Belknap said mistrustfully. 'Take some air.' Maybe she was telling the truth, but he had serious doubts. She might well be trying to collect herself while she contemplated a countermove. He would keep an eye on her as she walked through the copse of firs, alert to any sudden movements. At the same time, he did not want her to feel that she had been taken prisoner; if her account was honest – and his instincts told him that, for the most part, it was – he might indeed need to gain her confidence.

She had her back to him, was walking, shoeless, in a steady, deliberate gait, and when she finally circled back, he could tell from her face, instantly, that something had changed. In his mind, he replayed what he had seen, and not seen, and, in a flash, he knew. She had her purse with her, had dialed 911 from her cell phone, had murmured a distress call into it.

'Shall we go?' Belknap asked her.

'In a few minutes,' she said. 'My stomach, you know. All this stress. I just need to settle down. Do you mind?'

'Why should I mind?' He took a step toward her and, in a sudden movement, plunged a hand into her purse and retrieved her small cell phone. He mashed two keys, got the dialed calls log to display. Just as he thought: The first number to appear was 911. He tossed the phone to her. 'Summoning the cavalry?'

Again, she held his gaze. 'You said you needed help. I figured we'd get some professionals on the case.' There was only the faintest quaver in her voice.

Dammit! From a distance – but not a great distance – he heard the siren of a patrol car.

He threw the car keys on the ground.

'Did I do something wrong?' she asked, a trace of a taunt in her voice. She turned toward the highway.

The siren grew louder.

CHAPTER ELEVEN

Raleigh, North Carolina

Andrea Bancroft finally checked into her hotel two hours later than she had expected to. *The trip from hell*, she thought mordantly.

She remembered how relieved she felt when she heard the sirens, how she had turned toward the highway, and how, when she turned back, the burly man had vanished. It was eerie: She hadn't heard a thing, no sounds of a man scrambling, no huffing or puffing. One moment he was there; the next moment he was gone. It was like a conjurer's trick. No doubt it could all be easily explained. For one thing, she noticed that the ground was covered not with leaves but pine needles, which dampened sound while making hardly any noise when stepped on. Plus, the man had claimed to be an 'operative,' whatever that was, exactly. Maybe this was the kind of thing they were trained to do.

'Your credit card, ma'am,' prompted the woman at the desk – auburn hair teased high, a sprinkling of light acne on her cheeks.

Andrea took the card back and signed the form she was given. Not at the Radisson, where she had planned to stay, but at the Doubletree. There seemed little chance that the man would chance another meeting – if he had any sense, that was the last thing he'd want – but the elementary precaution seemed prudent.

The police made every appearance of being helpful, but they clearly regarded her account with a certain skepticism, which only deepened when they tried to check it out. She had claimed that she had been picked up by a driver, and yet they were able to determine, with just a couple of phone calls, that the car was actually a rental. *Not only that, but the records say you're the one who rented it, Ms. Bancroft.*

They started to ask questions that seemed designed to elicit a 'relationship' with the stranger. And some of the details she reported did not go over well. *You're saying he just disappeared?* And how was it that she didn't get his name, if she seemed to know so many odd facts about him? After an hour in the District 23 police station on Atlantic Avenue, she almost felt that she had been the suspect, not the victim. The policemen's Southern politeness scarcely wavered, but she could tell that she represented an unwelcome kind of anomaly. Further inquiries would be made with the rental car company, they promised. Prints would be taken from the vehicle, and her own prints would be recorded for elimination purposes. They were to let her know if there were any developments. But it was plain that, from their point of view, the likeliest explanation was that they were dealing with a hysteric.

At the fifth floor, she let the bellhop point out the bathroom and closets and let him go with his tip. She unzipped her overnight bag, hung its contents in the closet near the door, and then turned back to the window.

She felt her heart miss a beat an instant before she realized why.

The man. The burly man with the gun. *He was in her room.* Silhouetted by the window. Arms folded on his chest.

She knew she should run, should turn around and race out of her hotel room. Yet the man was standing perfectly still, not posing an obvious threat. She fought down the panic fluttering in her chest. She could remain another few seconds without worsening her odds, and perhaps she might learn something of value.

'Why are you here?' she asked stonily. She could have asked him *how* he got there, but she had a better chance of working that out on her own. He must have been hiding behind the heavily lined drapes gathered to one side of the window when she came in. He could have called all the major hotels in the area, learned that she was staying here,

215

and obtained her designated room by means of some simple ruse. No, how was not the hard question. The hard question was why.

'Just picking up where we left off,' the man replied. 'We weren't introduced properly. The name's Todd Belknap.'

Andrea felt another jolt of panic. Her eyes widened. 'You're a stalker.'

'What?'

'You've got some kind of sick sexual fixation – '

'Don't flatter yourself.' The man cut her off with a contemptuous snort. 'You're not my type.'

'Then – '

'And you're not a very good listener, either.'

'The whole abduction-at-gunpoint thing was kind of distracting.' Her eyes narrowed. Curiously, her sense of fear was ebbing. She could turn around and flee – she knew that. Yet somehow she felt no direct sense of threat. *Play out the line a little*, she told herself. 'Look, I'm sorry I called the cops,' she lied.

'Are you? I don't know that I am.' The man's deep baritone was calm and commanding. 'It told me something.'

'How do you mean?'

'It's exactly the kind of damn-fool thing that a clueless civilian would do. I don't think you're duping me. Not anymore. I think *you've* been duped.'

Andrea was quiet, but her thoughts were loud, clamoring for her attention. Finally she spoke. 'I'm listening now. Tell me again who that cell phone belongs to. The one whose number I got from the foundation's records.'

'It belonged to a man who was in the killing business. A professional, combat-seasoned killer.'

'Why would anybody at the Bancroft Foundation call anybody like that?'

'You tell me.'

'I don't know.'

'Yet you don't seem utterly shocked.'

'I am shocked,' she said. 'Just not . . . utterly.'

'All right, then.'

'You said you were a career operative. Who can I call at whatever your place of employment was?' A tight-lipped smile.

'You want references?'

'Something like that. Is that a problem?'

He gave her an appraising look. 'First, why don't *I* call the Bancroft Foundation? Ask what you're doing here down here. More specifically, Research Triangle Park. Your initial reservation was at the RTP Radisson, after all.'

'That might not be a good idea,' Andrea said.

A chilly smile. 'Then we seem to be at an impasse.'

'This conversation is over.'

'Is it?' Again, the man did not move. It was as if he realized that his absolute stillness was the only thing that convinced her to postpone flight. 'From where I stand, it hasn't really started. In the past couple of hours, I've had a chance to think some about our encounter, starting with different premises. A man threatens you with a gun. You ask him whether the Bancroft Foundation sent him. What does this tell me? That there's something about this institution that worries you. Something that makes you fear the worst. Whatever that is, it stands to reason, is connected to this sudden trip to RTP. You booked the tickets the same day you boarded the flight. That's a little irregular. You're looking for something, same as me.'

'What I'm looking for isn't the same as what you're looking for.'

'There could be a connection.'

'Maybe yes, maybe no.'

'Until I know more, I'm bound to agree with that. Let's explore the 'maybe yes' possibility.' The man gestured toward a nearby chair. 'May I sit down?'

'This is crazy,' Andrea said. 'I don't know who you really are. You're asking me to take chances I have no reason to take.'

'My friend Jared used to say, 'Roll the dice, or you're not in the game.' Let's say you and I go our separate ways. We never see each other again. And so we missed our one

217

chance to set things right for both of us. My point is, missing a chance is another way of taking a chance, and sometimes the worst one.'

'I'll let you sit down,' Andrea finally said, 'but you can't stay here.'

'Got news for you, Andrea Bancroft. You better not stay here, either.'

The couple who checked into a nearby Marriott used neither the name Bancroft nor the name Belknap, and the shared room resulted not from intimacy but the simple demands of security. The two, for all their lingering mistrust, had recognized each other as fellow seekers; the conversation had to continue.

Communication did not result in clarity, however. Any hope that the two accounts would match like two adjoining pieces of a jigsaw puzzle soon evaporated. Instead of answers, they found themselves confronting a deepening mystery.

Paul Bancroft. Was *he* Genesis? Going by her account, he struck Belknap as a figure of extraordinary benevolence, or perhaps the opposite. The resources he commanded, not to mention his intellectual capacities, could make him an incredible ally or adversary.

'So Genesis was the code name of the guy who started this Inver Brass,' Belknap repeated.

'Or more like a title. It referred to whoever happened to be in charge at any time.'

'Inver Brass – could someone have revived it?'

Andrea shrugged.

'Could Paul Bancroft have done so?'

'I guess so. Though he sounded pretty disapproving when he talked about the whole organization, pretty disapproving when he talked about Genesis. Not that that proves anything.'

'A friend of mine liked to say that all saints must be considered guilty until proven innocent,' Belknap mused. He had stretched out on one of the two beds.

'He was quoting Orwell.' Andrea had seated herself on a fake antique chair by a fake antique secretary desk. By her elbow was a scattering of colorful pamphlets about activities in the nearby cities of Raleigh, Durham, and Chapel Hill. The phrase 'family fun' received a considerable workout. 'I'm going to have to reserve judgment. Maybe there's an innocent explanation. Maybe it's all some big misunderstanding. Maybe . . .' She gave him a sharp look. 'It's on your say-so, about the man in Dubai. Maybe you're making it up.'

'Why would I?'

'How the hell would I know? I'm just enumerating possibilities. I'm not taking sides.'

'Well, stop.'

'Stop? Stop what?'

'Stop not taking sides.'

The set of the woman's jaw suggested resolve and displeasure. 'Listen, it's late. I'm going to take a shower now. Why don't you order room service for us? We'll eat, and then – we'll figure something out. But dammit, if you're going to keep me prisoner, at least give me my own cell.'

'Not gonna happen. And it's for your own good, believe me. You could be in danger.'

She knitted her brows. 'For the love of God . . .'

'Don't worry. I'm not going to use your toothbrush.'

'That isn't what I'm talking about, and you know it,' she snapped.

'I just prefer knowing you're where I can see you.'

'Is that what you prefer? How about what *I* prefer?' Andrea slammed the bathroom door behind her.

As he heard the shower start, he picked up a phone and called an old contact of his at Cons Ops sig intel. Her name was Ruth Robbins, and she had started out at the State Department's INR, the intelligence and research bureau. It was Belknap who had gotten her a promotion and arranged to have her transferred to the more exclusive conclave that was Consular Operations. He had recognized her wit, her judgment, instincts that went beyond the mere ability to collate and compare. In some ways, he recognized a kindred spirit, even though her natural domain was not the field but the office, the realm of cables and transmissions and computers.

Now in her fifties, she was a heavyset woman with a sensibility as astringent as witch hazel. She had raised two boys on her own – her husband, a military man, had been killed in a training exercise – and had a maternal eye for the foibles of the male-dominated establishment in which she had made her career.

'Castor,' she said when she heard his voice. 'Always meant to ask – was it the *oil* you were named for?' There was warmth beneath the witticism. It was irregular to have phoned her at home, but she understood the urgency at once. 'Just a sec,' she said, and though she was obviously covering the mouthpiece with her hand, he could still hear her call out, 'That's enough television, young man! Time to march yourself to bed, and no back talk!' A brief pause. Then she got on the phone again: 'You were saying?'

Quickly, Belknap mentioned a few key words, a few indices of his current conundrum. At the name Genesis, he could hear her sharp intake of breath.

'Listen, Castor, I can't talk on the phone. But yes, we do have that term in our databanks – there's a history there. And yes, we've recently intercepted some chatter having to do with Genesis after years of silence. You know the procedures in our shop – I couldn't get in after hours if I wanted to. But when I'm logged in tomorrow morning, I'll do an all-sources review. Not something to be discussed over an open line – I'm probably already in violation.'

'We need to meet, then.'

'I don't think so.' There was unease in her voice.

'Ruth, please.'

'It would be my ass. If I'm spotted having lunch with you, the way things are, I could get decertified. End up sorting underwear at one of the training facilities.'

'Noon tomorrow,' Belknap said.

'You're not hearing me.'

'Rock Creek Park. A public, safe meet, okay? A brief encounter. Nobody will ever learn about it. Remember the bridle trail by the ravine at the east? I'll see you there. Don't be late.'

'Dammit, Castor,' Robbins said, but there was acquiescence in her voice.

Ruth Robbins was a riding enthusiast, he knew, and often spent her lunch hour on the trails in Rock Creek Park – two thousand forested acres in northwest Washington. It was prudent to choose a regular haunt of hers: There would be nothing out of the ordinary for anyone to notice, and she could give a truthful account of her movements if there were ever an inquiry. But it was also a location where they were unlikely to be observed.

He could take an early flight into Ronald Reagan or Dulles and be there in plenty of time. He stretched out on the sofa and willed himself to sleep; his field-honed ability to sleep at will was proving less reliable these days. He lay awake in the darkened room, conscious of Andrea Bancroft's breathing in the bed several feet away. She was pretending to be asleep, as was he, and what seemed like hours passed before consciousness waned. He dreamed of loss. Of Yvette, taken from him before she was truly his own. Of Louisa, blown up during an operation in Belfast. A procession of faces flitted through the recesses of his mind: friends and lovers he had survived, friends and lovers who had left him behind. Only one had stayed with him through the years, Pollux to his Castor.

Jared Rinehart, the one who had never let him down. The one who he was letting down even now.

Belknap imagined him now, captive, tortured, desolate – but not, he hoped, deprived of all hope. Pollux had saved Castor's life more than once, and so long as Castor breathed, he would scheme and struggle to save his friend. *Hang on, Pollux. I'm coming to get you. The road may twist and turn, but I'll follow it wherever it leads.*

The next morning, he explained to Andrea what he had planned.

'That's fine,' she said. 'Meanwhile, I've got to find Terrapin Drive. I want to know what my mother knew.'

'You can't be sure that it had anything to do with this.

You're taking a shot in the dark.'

'Wrong. I'm taking a shot in the daytime.'

'You're not trained for this, Andrea.'

'Nobody's trained for this. But only one of us is a foundation trustee. Only one of us has a legitimate excuse to be there.'

'This isn't the right time.'

'So we're on your schedule now?'

'I'll go with you. I'll help you, okay?'

'When?'

'Later.'

Andrea gave him a hard stare. Abruptly, she nodded. 'We'll do it your way.'

'I'm on a nine a.m. flight; I'll be back by midafternoon,' he said. 'Keep out of trouble until then. Order room service, keep a low profile, and you'll be fine.'

'Got it.'

'Important that you play by the rules.'

'I'll do exactly what you say,' Andrea told him. 'You can count on that.'

I'll do exactly what you say, Andrea had told him blandly, craftily, and the man, Todd Belknap, seemed to believe her. There was something in his gaze that told her he would not be swayed by her priorities, that nothing would stop him from pursuing his own to the exclusion of everything else. The arrogance of the musclebound lug seemed boundless, but it would not deter her. This was her *life* they were talking about. And what was he, anyway? His official status was anything but clear. For all she knew, he'd been bounced out of the intelligence community for good reason. Still, she believed him about the basic facts. Someone at the Bancroft Foundation had called a very, very bad man. It was consistent with the notion that the foundation was harboring someone, or some element, that was operating according to a separate set of exigencies. The crucial question remained whether Paul Bancroft himself knew about it.

At the moment, she was too determined to be scared, or

222

maybe the encounter with Belknap in the car yesterday had drained most of the fright juice out of her system. Now, in a purple rented Cougar, she drove along the roads that crisscrossed Research Triangle Park, looking for a small lane marked 'Terrapin.'

The Bancroft Foundation's parcel of land here was more than a thousand acres in size; it was impossible to hide anything that big. Impossible to hide a thousand acres of pine forest . . . except, of course, among seven thousand acres of pine forest.

It was maddening! She sped along a major throughway and then motored down the small roads that connected the various R&D facilities. Back and forth she went. She knew it wasn't along the major state routes or the interstate. The southern section of the triangle was the most developed. Which meant it was probably to the north. Here, small lanes branched through the land like capillaries, many of them signposted only very occasionally. She had the distinct sense that she was no longer driving on public roadways, that she was trespassing. She had been driving for hours and yet had traveled almost nowhere. Finally, after endless turns and doubling-backs and roundabouts, she saw a gravel road with an emblem of a green turtle on it. A terrapin, in fact – a freshwater turtle with webbed feet. But the sign that seemed truly confirmatory was the one that said no entry.

She turned onto it. The road wound through mature forest; at every tenth of a mile or so, another sign of prohibition was posted. No entry. No hunting or fishing. No trespassing. The signs were impossible to ignore.

Andrea ignored them. The gravel quickly gave way to a narrow, winding, but immaculately paved lane. Yet still she saw nothing around her save virgin forest. Could she have been mistaken? She would not be deterred. She had gone through a quarter-tank of gas simply driving along this uncharted lane, making turns at random, hoping that sooner or later, by sheer chance, she would happen upon the place.

And now – no mistaking it – she had.

She instantly recognized something about the building

she saw; it wasn't the same style as that of the Katonah head-quarters, and yet there was something similar about the way the building related to its surroundings. It was a low-slung structure of brick and glass, and impressive in a way that was hard to pinpoint. As with the Katonah structure, you could be very near and not see it – doubtless it was entirely concealed from overhead observation – but once you did, it was impossible to miss the subtle grandeur of the place. As with the foundation headquarters in Katonah, there was a sense of quality and magnitude without ostentation. They both represented an architecture of discretion.

The throaty growl of a powerful engine told her that she was not alone. A large black Range Rover loomed in her rearview mirror, and then swerved to her left. Another hard turn and the Range Rover was inches away from her vehicle. It was impossible to see into the vehicle – perhaps because of the angle of the sun's reflection, perhaps because of the tinted glass. But the powerful vehicle was now forcing her small sedan into the drive that led to the brick-and-glass facility. Her heart was in her throat. Yet this was what she had been looking for, wasn't it?

Be careful what you wish for . . .

She could gun the motor and – what? Ram into an SUV that weighed twice as much as her small car? They wouldn't dare hurt her, would they? The Range Rovers looked like security vehicles; they must have taken her for an intruder of some sort, yes? Andrea told herself these things: She did not quite believe them.

Moments later, two stocky men climbed out of the Range Rover and ushered her out of her car, in a manner one could take for either politesse or coercion.

'What the hell are you doing?' she demanded. An air of presumption would help her more than one of timidity. 'Do you have any idea who I am?'

One of the men stared at her appraisingly. Andrea shuddered at his blotchy skin and bat-wing eyebrows.

'Dr. Bancroft is waiting for you,' the other man told her, gently but firmly guiding her to the facility's door.

CHAPTER TWELVE

And so he was.

As the glass door sucked closed behind her, Paul Bancroft stepped around a corner and beamed, holding his arms open as if to embrace her. She did not come to him. She saw the smile on his face, crazing his delicate skin with fine lines, the unclouded warm gaze, and she did not know what to believe.

'My goodness, Andrea,' the philanthropist exulted. 'You never cease to impress me.'

'Wherever you go, there I am,' Andrea said dryly. 'Like a bad penny.'

'There are no bad pennies. Only misunderstood ones.' Paul Bancroft chuckled merrily. 'Welcome to the factory.'

She studied his face for a trace of ire or menace, saw none. Instead, he was brimming with bonhomie.

'I don't know whether to be more impressed by your curiosity, your hardheadedness, your determination, or your resourcefulness,' the gray-haired savant told her.

'Curiosity will do,' Andrea said carefully. 'That part's real enough.'

'I see genuine leadership potential in you, my dear.' With a wave of his elegant, long-fingered hand he dismissed the stocky men who had accompanied her to the door. 'And, at my age, you start looking around for a successor.'

'A regent, anyway,' Andrea said.

'While Brandon's still a minor, you mean. I'm still hoping my boy will take an interest in the family business, you know, but there are no assurances. So when you find someone with the right stuff, attention must be paid.' His eyes sparkled.

Andrea's mouth was dry.

'Let me show you around,' he said, in a cordial tone. 'There's a lot to see.'

It had to have been a good ten years, Todd Belknap decided, since Ruth Robbins tried to persuade him that riding on the back of a horse – a vehicle without shock absorbers or air conditioning – might be something to be done as recreation rather than as a last resort. He had never been a convert, never came to enjoy horses, but he did enjoy his time with Ruth. She had grown up in Stillwater, Oklahoma, daughter of a high school football coach in a place where high school football coaches were royalty of a sort. The sort who occasionally got loaded onto tumbrels. Her mom, a Quebecoise, taught French at another high school. Ruth had a knack for languages – first French, from her mother, and the other Romance languages, Spanish and Italian. But after she spent a summer in Bavaria as a fourteen-year-old, she got a decent handle on German, too. She was nuts about soccer – loved it as much as American football – and brought a mixture of high spirits and dry irony to everything she did. When she went riding, it was always in a Western-style saddle; not for her the affectations of the Eastern equestriennes. She was a people collector; something about her made people just naturally open up. Teenage girls would tell her about their love lives; women in their thirties would tell her about their marital issues; old women would tell her about their financial problems. She sassed but she didn't judge, and even her most cutting remarks were delivered with kindness.

At almost exactly noon, Belknap heard the *clop-clop-clop* of equine hoof against packed earth. He stirred himself from the rocky ledge beside the trail and waved lazily as his horse-mounted contact came into sight. Her face was drawn as she dismounted and tied one of the bridle straps to a slender tree trunk. There were eleven miles of bridle trails, and this was probably the most secluded area to be found along them.

Ruth Robbins once cracked, not inaccurately, that she didn't have breasts, she had a *bust*. She wasn't fat, exactly, but

226

she was heavyset in an old-settler way, like one of those nineteenth-century mothers of eleven kids who set off for the West in a covered wagon. There was even something Old West about her attire, though he'd be hard pressed to put his finger on exactly what. It wasn't that she wore petticoats or hoops.

She dismounted and stood near him, though without facing in his direction. They could each scan a hundred-and-eighty-degree vista, alert to any anomaly. 'First things first,' she said, without preamble. 'The Ansari network. We really know zip. Unconfirmed intercepts, though, are pointing to some unidentified Estonian tycoon.'

'How many of those can there be?'

'You'd be surprised.' A dry chuckle. 'Might be one who hasn't come onto our sig-scope yet. But there's some logic to it. The Soviets left behind enormous caches of weaponry when they yanked up the empire – and it mostly didn't end up in the hands of the Estonian army, I can tell you that.' A breeze rustled through the pin oaks, wafting the scent of loam and horse sweat.

'Why did they want to have an Estonian arsenal in the first place?'

Now she turned to face him. 'Remember your geography. The Gulf of Finland was considered strategically vital. All goods shipped into St. Petersburg – Leningrad, I should say – had to pass through that gulf. And for two hundred or so miles, it's Finland to the north and good old Estonia to the south. Estonia was on the playbooks for the Gulf of Riga, too – the whole Baltic Sea, for that matter. Anything naval in the Baltics was going to have to involve Estonia. So you had a goddamn enormous Soviet naval base there, and nobody was better at commanding munitions and military resources than the Soviet navy. Probably came down to Kremlinological office politicking more than solid strategic arguments, but when it came to handing out the goodies, the Russian sailor was always given pride of place.'

'I assume that the privatization of the Estonian arsenal wasn't exactly official policy.' His gaze settled on an old

227

walnut tree that was being slowly strangled by kudzu. The vine draped over its boughs like a tarp.

'It was wholesale larceny during a time of chaos, when a lot of people in the East didn't quite grasp the difference between capitalism and theft.'

'So what are we dealing with here? You're saying that Genesis is an Estonian oligarch? Or just works through one? What's the picture?'

'I've told you what I know, which isn't much. Hints and guesswork, you understand. Funnily enough, the Ansari network has never seen fit to send us a nice company brochure in the mail.'

'How does Genesis fit into the picture?'

Ruth winced slightly. 'My dad used to be an amateur photographer. Had his own darkroom in the basement. Once in a while, one of us kids would barge in while he was developing his negatives. Turn all his great shots of hurtling footballs into blobs of shadow and fog. He used to tan our hide but good. Point is, we don't have a goddamn picture here. We've got shadows and fog.'

'And I just want to know whose hide to tan,' Belknap pressed. 'Talk to me, Ruth. Tell me about Genesis.'

'Genesis. Lot of stories associated with that legend. See, there's kind of a mystique there. There's a story about someone who crossed Genesis and was held captive for two years in a steel crypt shaped around his body, kept alive by IV nutrition. All the while he couldn't move any part of his body more than an inch or so. After two years, he just atrophies, major lost muscle tissue, and that's how he died. Can you imagine? There's a real Poe-like imagination here. I'll tell you another story. Came from Athens sector. The story is, one of the victims was a member of a powerful Greek shipping family. But the story's not really about him. It's about his mother. Apparently the mother was inconsolable. Time's supposed to heal all, but not in this case. She wanted to see the person who took her son's life, and she wouldn't shut up about it. She talked about nothing else.'

'She wanted revenge. That's understandable.'

'Not even that. She knew she couldn't get revenge. She just wanted to see the face of Genesis. Just wanted to gaze into this person's eyes. Just wanted to *see*, to see what nobody was known to have seen. And she was so persistent, so badgering, that one day, a message arrived for her.'

'A message from Genesis?'

'Message was that Genesis had heard her demand, and that she could get her wish. But at a price. And the price would be her life. Those were the terms. She could accept or she could decline. But those were the terms.'

Belknap shivered, and it wasn't because of the gentle breeze.

'So the mom, who was hysterical with grief, agreed,' Ruth continued. 'She agreed to the condition. And I guess she was given a cell phone and series of instructions that took her to a procession of isolated places. Her body was found the next morning. She had tucked a statement into her brassiere, a statement written in her own hand, something to the effect that she had indeed seen the One Whom None Could See and Live. So everyone knew that Genesis had lived up to its side of the bargain. And the weird thing is – or so the story goes – nobody could determine a cause of death. She was just dead.'

'That's unbelievable.'

'I'm inclined to agree,' the Consular Operations analyst told him. 'It's like a goddamn urban legend. We've all heard these stories, but we've never been able to verify them. And you know me. I don't trust where I can't verify.'

'There are more things on heaven and earth . . .'

'Maybe so. Maybe so. But I count only what I can count. If a tree falls in a forest and Ruth Robbins gets no reliable confirmation from signals intelligence, then that tree's still standing as far as I'm concerned.'

Belknap gave her a sharp look. 'Tell me about Inver Brass.'

Ruth Robbins blanched. Suddenly, there was something dead in her gaze.

It took few seconds – and the appearance of a rivulet of blood from the corner of her mouth, like a misplaced stroke of lipstick – before he realized why. Her body crumpled, but she had been dead even before she hit the ground.

The crimson rivulet winked in the midday light.

Paul Bancroft's pride in his North Carolina facility was boyish, exuberant, unabashed. He strode commandingly down hallways of lacquered slate, along walls and floor dividers of frosted glass. Yet what *was* this place? Andrea wondered. Why was he here? She saw shelves filled with paper documents, clusters of computer terminals, a hum of preparedness like at a NASA command station. The light was low but of a constant intensity, reminding her of a rare-book-and-manuscript library. At regular intervals, stairs to a lower floor were visible: wood and steel railings, slate landings. Much of the building was no doubt underground. Seated at computers, men and women in business attire glanced up casually as the two passed.

'I've assembled a truly formidable team of analysts, if I do say so myself,' Paul Bancroft declared as they reached a central area. Slatted skylights allowed a carefully titrated amount of sunlight through filtered glass.

'And hidden them well.'

'It *is* rather secluded here,' the maven allowed. 'You'll understand why when I explain.'

He stopped and gestured around him. Surrounded by a semicircular bank of monitors and chairs, half a dozen people were apparently conferring at a U-shaped table. One of them – a slight man with a neatly trimmed black beard who was wearing a dark, lightweight navy suit but no tie – stood up as Bancroft approached.

'What's the latest from La Paz?' Bancroft asked him.

'We're just collating the analyses now,' the bearded man replied in a fluting voice. His hands were delicate, almost feminine.

Andrea looked at the men and women at the table. She was getting that Alice-Through-the-Looking-Glass sensation again.

'I'm just giving my cousin Andrea here a bit of a tour,'

Paul Bancroft explained to the others. He turned back to her. 'Most of those terminals are connected to a massively parallel system of computer processors – not just one Cray XT3 supercomputer but a roomful of them. The fastest computer in the world today is probably the one in the Department of Energy's Livermore National Laboratory. The second is said to be IBM's BlueGene system in Yorktown. Ours would probably come in third, neck and neck with one at Sandia and another at the University of Groningen in the Netherlands. We're talking about machine clusters that can execute hundreds of teraflops per second – hundreds of trillions of calculations. Take all the calculations that were done anywhere during the whole first half-century of modern computing – this cluster does more in an hour. Machines of this computational power are used to do genomic and proteomic analysis, or to predict chaotic seismic activities, to model nuclear explosions – events of that nature. What we're modeling is no less complex. We're modeling event horizons and event cascades affecting the seven billion inhabitants of this planet.'

'My God,' Andrea breathed. 'You're trying to work out the greatest good for the greatest number – the calculus of felicity.'

'It's always been a pretty phrase. Nobody had ever been able to make a decent attempt at actually calculating it. The counterfactuals are simply too complex. Computational explosion remains a problem. But we've made real headway, with real results. It's been a dream of great minds since the Enlightenment.' His eyes gleamed. 'We're turning morality into math.'

Andrea was speechless.

'You know, they say that human knowledge doubled in the fifteen hundred years between, say, the birth of Christ and the Renaissance. Between the Renaissance and the French Revolution, it doubled again. In the century and a quarter spanning that revolution to the acme of the industrial revolution, with the birth of the automobile, knowledge once more doubled. By our best estimates, Andrea, these days human knowledge doubles every two years. At the same time, our moral faculties remain unevolved. The technical prowess of our species has vastly outstripped our ethical prowess. These computational resources that we've enlisted are, in effect, a sort of mental prosthesis, extending our intellectual capacities by artificial means. But what's ultimately more important is that the combination of our algorithms and analyses and computer models can produce the equivalent of a moral prosthesis. Nobody objects when NASA or the Human Genome Project assembles scientists and computers in order to solve certain engineering or biological problems that confront us. So why not tackle the welfare of our species more directly? That's the challenge that we've taken up here.'

'But what do you mean exactly? What are you saying?'

'Small interventions can have big consequences. We're trying to plot out those event cascades so that we can gauge such intervention. Forgive me, this is still too abstract, isn't it?'

'You could say that.'

The look he gave her was kindly but firm. 'I'll have to trust your discretion. The program couldn't work if its activities were made public.'

'Its activities. You're still speaking in code.'

'And you no doubt suspect the secrecy,' Paul Bancroft observed. 'You would be right to, as a general rule. You're wondering why I've hived off this group, kept it all below radar – quite literally off the map. You're wondering what I've got to hide.'

Andrea nodded. Questions teemed in her mind, but she knew that for the moment she would do best by saying least.

'It's a delicate matter,' he said. 'But when I tell you how it all started, I think you'll understand why it was necessary.'

Paul Bancroft led her to a quiet alcove overlooking a lushly verdant garden. Through the filtered glass, she saw a bubbling creek running through bushes and banks of flowers.

'Necessary,' she repeated. 'A fraught word.'

'Sometimes the only way for benevolent projects to succeed in corrupt regimes is to identify malefactors, obstructionists, and persuade them to step aside, perhaps by the threat of public exposure. That's how it started, you see.' His burnished, mellifluous voice was soothing, almost hypnotic. He leaned back in the chrome-and-leather chair, looking off into the middle distance. 'It was many years ago. The foundation had just completed work on a costly waterworks project in the Zamora-Chinchipe province of Ecuador, a project that was going to provide sanitary drinking water for tens of thousands of poor villagers, Quechuas for the most part. Then, out of the blue, we found out that a notoriously venal government minister had decided to commandeer the land. It quickly emerged that he wanted to sell it to a mining company that had been a reliable source of kickbacks to him.'

'That's lousy.'

'Andrea, I had been there personally. I had walked through clinics filled with children – four, five, six years of age – who were dying, needlessly, because of contaminated drinking water. I looked upon the tear-stained faces of a mother who had lost all five of her children to waterborne parasites and pathogens. And there were thousands and thousands of mothers like her. Thousands and thousands of children who were regularly stricken, debilitated, killed. All needlessly. All *preventably*. You just had to give a damn. Which, apparently, was too much to ask.' His eyes were moist as he looked directly at Andrea. 'A program officer on the ground, based in Zamora, happened to have personally damaging information about the minister. She took the information to me. And, Andrea, I took a deep breath, and I made a decision.' His brown eyes were intent, warm, steady, unabashed. 'I decided to use it as she had hoped I would. We neutralized the corrupt minister.'

'I don't understand. What did you do?'

He waved a hand vaguely. 'A whispered aside. A word to the right intermediary. We took a step forward. He took a step back. And thousands of lives were saved that very year.' He paused. 'Would you have done something different?'

Andrea's response was unhesitating. 'What choice was there?'

He nodded approvingly. 'Then you understand. To change the world – to increase the sum of human well-being – philanthropy must be worldly. It must be strategic, not just well-intentioned. Gathering that sort of strategic information – and, when necessary, acting on it – is beyond the competence of the traditional program officers. That's why this special facility had to be created, housing a special division.'

'And nobody knows.'

'Nobody can know. It would interfere with the results we've been trying to achieve. People would try to predict and anticipate our interventions – and then to predict what others were likely to predict, and then to predict what others were likely to predict others were likely to predict. And then we would indeed have computational explosion. The hazy horizons of causality would be completely opaque.'

'But what is this division, exactly? You still haven't said.'

'The Theta Group.' Paul Bancroft's gaze was watchful but warm. 'And welcome to it.' He stood up. 'You remember what you were saying about perverse consequences. About the well-intended deed with malign results. That's the problem that my task force here has devoted itself to. But on a level of granularity – of detail and precision – never before attempted. You're a tough-minded young woman, Andrea, but not because you don't have a heart. On the contrary, it's because you do have a heart, and a head, and you know that each is useless without the other.' There was something saintlike about his visage, serenity combined with an acute sensitivity to the suffering of others. *The man is for real –* every instinct she had told her so. Yet something Belknap said returned to her: *You've been duped.*

Andrea stared at him hard and made a decision. A reckless one, perhaps, but a calculated one all the same. 'You talked about interventions. Would this be related to contacts between the Bancroft Foundation and a paramilitary-squad leader in the U.A.E.?' She tried to keep her tone cool, though she could feel a hammering in her chest.

Paul Bancroft looked bemused. 'I don't think I'm following.'

Andrea handed Bancroft a photocopy of the last page of the phone list. She indicated the number that was prefixed by 011 971 4, the Dubai calling code. 'Don't ask me how I came to have this. Just explain this call. Because I called the number, and I think it went to the cell phone of . . . what I said. Some sort of paramilitary type.' Her words were deliberately vague, but involuntarily faltering. She did not want to tell him about Todd Belknap. Not yet. She was haunted by too many uncertainties. If Paul Bancroft were complicit, he would probably concoct some story about a misdialed number. If he were not, he would be as determined to learn more as she was.

He squinted at the number and then at his cousin. 'I won't ask how you know that, Andrea. I trust you and I trust your instincts.' He rose, looked around, and with a gesture summoned a dark-suited man.

Not one of those who sat around the U-shaped table, but someone else, someone Andrea hadn't even noticed before. Wheat-colored hair, a tanned face, a broken nose, and a gait that was close to a glide.

Bancroft handed him the page with the international telephone number on it. 'Scanlon, I'd like you to do a database search of that Dubai number. Let me know what you come up with.'

The man nodded mutely and glided off.

Bancroft returned to his chair and gave his cousin a questioning look.

'That's it?' Andrea asked.

'For now.' He directed another measuring gaze toward her. 'Someone mentioned to me that you'd taken an interest in the foundation's archives. I think we both know why.' There was no reproach in his voice, not even a display of disappointment.

Andrea said nothing.

'It's about your mother, isn't it?'

She looked away. 'There's so much about her I never really

knew. So much I'm just starting to find out. Her role at the foundation.' She paused, watched his expression as she spoke the next words. 'The circumstances of her death.'

'So you've learned what happened,' Paul Bancroft said, and he lowered his head sorrowfully.

How to play this? She hoped that she wasn't flushing as she responded with careful ambiguity. 'It's been pretty upsetting.'

Paul Bancroft now placed a hand on her wrist, gave it a pastoral squeeze. 'Please, Andrea. You mustn't blame her.'

Blame her? What was he talking about? Emotions churned inside her, scraping one another like rocks in a tumbler. She remained silent, hoping her silence would serve as a prod.

'The truth is,' the aging savant said, 'we're responsible for what happened.'

CHAPTER THIRTEEN

Andrea felt dizzy and more than a little sick. 'When she resigned from the board . . .' she began.

'Exactly. When the board voted to ask for her resignation, nobody had any idea that she would respond the way she did. But they *should* have. It breaks me up when I think back to it. During a weekend retreat of the trustees, she went on a bender. Fell off the wagon. I wasn't there, but I heard the accounts. I'm sorry. This kind of thing must be so hard to hear.'

'It's important to hear *you* say it,' Andrea choked out. 'I need this.'

'And so the vote was taken. Precipitously, in my view. Laura was an incredibly vibrant and insightful human being. She brought so much to the board. And if she had a weakness, well, who among us does not? But the request for her resignation must have seemed punitive to her. She was angry and upset, and who could blame her? She responded just the way they should have anticipated. We don't keep the liquor under lock and key at Katonah. She drank herself into a state of advanced intoxication.'

Andrea's head was throbbing. *The Balm of Gilead* was what her mother had jokingly called it once upon a time. All those tumblers filled with ice cubes and vodka. But she had quit. She was clean and sober. She had put it behind her. Hadn't she?

'As soon as someone discovered that she'd taken her car keys and had driven off, we sent a member of our security staff after her. To try to stop her, bring her back safe.' He looked stricken as he spoke. 'But it was too late.'

The two sat together in silence for a while. Paul Bancroft seemed to understand that she could not be rushed, that she would need some time to regain her composure.

The tanned man with the wheat-colored hair – Scanlon – returned with the sheet of telephone numbers.

'Registered to a Thomas Hill Green, Jr., sir,' he told Bancroft briskly. 'Public-affairs officer of the U.S. Consulate General in Dubai. We'll work up a bio on him.'

Bancroft turned to his cousin. 'Does that seem possible?' Taking in her quizzical expression, he said, 'Let's call it now, why don't we?' He gestured toward a compact black telephone console on a low table nearby.

Andrea pressed the SPEAKER button and then pressed the digits carefully. After a few seconds of fuzz and burbling came the purring tones of a ringing phone.

A friendly, almost chipper voice. 'Tommy Green here.'

'I'm calling from the Bancroft Foundation,' Andrea said. 'We're trying to reach the public-affairs officer of the Consulate General.'

'You're in luck,' said the voice. 'How can I help? This about the education conference tonight?'

'I'm sorry, Mr. Green,' Andrea said. 'Mix-up on my end. I'm actually going to have to call you back.' She ended the phone call.

'The foundation does support some educational work in the Gulf,' Bancroft said cautiously. 'If he'd been called, I assume it was to do with coordinating our Emirati programs. But I can look into it further if you like. We do hear reports about cellular numbers being 'cloned' by lawbreakers of various sorts. A way to stick other people with their phone bill.'

Andrea's gaze drifted over to the bubbling creek. 'Please don't bother,' she said. She had been planning to ask him about the nameless man. Yet in the clear light of day, she was at a loss to say exactly what that man had done or said that was so troubling. When she even tried to frame the complaint in her head, it all seemed so hysterical, even to herself. The words died in her mouth.

'You know you can always ask me anything,' he said. 'Whatever questions you have.'

'Thank you,' she said mechanically.

'You're feeling foolish. Don't. You did what I would have done. Someone hands you a gold coin, you grip it between your teeth, see if it's real. You came across things that puzzled you. You needed to find out more. And you wouldn't be put off. If this was a test, Andrea, you passed with flying colors.'

'A test. Is that what this was?' Despite herself, she spoke with a flare of heat.

'I didn't say that.' The philosopher pressed his lips together, hesitated. 'But we *are* tested – every day, every week, every year. Decisions confront us. Judgments must be made. And there are no answers in the back of the book. That's why stupidity, like incuriousness, is a vice. A form of sloth. In the real world, decisions are always made under conditions of uncertainty. Knowledge is always partial. You act, there are consequences. You don't act, there are consequences.'

'Like with that runaway trolley car of yours.'

'Ten years ago I *failed* to act, and we lost somebody I cared for very much.'

'My mother.' Andrea swallowed hard. 'Did she know about . . . ?'

'Theta? No. But we could have used someone like her.' His eyes were bright. 'I know how much you must wonder about this part of her life. But you mustn't be disappointed by what's in the official record. You mother's contributions were very real and very significant, more so than those sorts of documents could ever capture. Please know this.' He took a deep breath. 'Laura. I think I loved her, in a way. I don't mean that there was anything between us, anything romantic. It's just that she was so alive, so vital, so *good*. Forgive me, I shouldn't be troubling you with this.'

'I'm not her,' Andrea said in a small voice.

'Of course. And yet the first time I saw you, I knew who you were, because I could see her in you.' His voice cracked, and he paused before continuing. 'And when we had dinner, at first it was like a ghostly afterimage on an old television set. I somehow felt her presence. Then it faded, and I was able to see you for who you were.'

Andrea felt that she was about to cry, and was determined not to. What to believe? Who to trust? *I trust your instincts*, Paul Bancroft had said. But could she?

'Andrea, I'd like to make a proposal to you. I want you to join my inner council as an adviser. With your knowledge and insights – with your background in economic history – you're perfectly equipped for the challenge. You could be useful to us. To the world.'

'I doubt that.'

'You've discovered I have feelings. *Mirabile dictu.*' A wan smile. 'But I reverence reason. Make no mistake: My proposal is a rational one. Besides, I'm not exactly a spring chicken, as the boffins here regularly remind me. You see me here the host at an estate where I will soon no longer be the master. The ranks have to be replenished with those of the next generation. And we can't simply take out an ad in the newspaper, can we? As I say, nobody must know what we do here. Even in the foundation proper, very few officers would fully appreciate the exigencies we deal with here.'

'*Exigencies.* I need to know more about what really happens here.'

'Soon you will. At least, that's my hope. It's a stepwise process. You can't throw algebraic topology at a student before he's done geometry. Education is about sequence. We can't make sense of information if it comes out of order. Knowledge builds on knowledge. But I have no worries. As I've had reason to remark, you're a fast learner.'

'Then shouldn't you start by explaining your worldview?' Andrea said, allowing herself a hint of sarcasm.

'No, Andrea. Because it's already your worldview. The Bancroft strategy – you've already articulated it about as well as anyone ever has.'

'I feel like I've wandered someplace far away. We are definitely not in Kansas anymore.'

'Listen to me, Andrea. Listen to your own arguments, the

voice of reason in your own head and heart. *You've come home.*'

'Home?' She focused now. 'You know, I listen to you and everything sounds right as rain. Everything has the rightness of two plus two equals four. But I have to wonder.'

'I *want* you to wonder. We need people who wonder and who ask hard questions.'

'A secret organization that does secret acts. What I want to know is, where are the boundaries? What is it that you *won't* do?'

'In pursuit of the good? Trust me, these are issues we constantly wrestle with. As I say, each of us is tested, all the time.'

'That's an awfully abstract reply.'

'To an awfully abstract question.'

'So give me some details.'

The response was gentle but unyielding. 'When you're ready.'

Andrea stared at the flowing water through the sheltered glade, saw the sun sieved through the needles of tall pine trees. Their vast branches, she realized, concealed the facility from aerial view.

So much here was concealed from view.

Indeed, much was doubtless still concealed from her.

Exigencies. Activities. Interventions.

Andrea herself had something to conceal. Paul Bancroft's reasoning was plausible, but disturbing to her as well. He was not someone who would shy from the logical conclusions of his own premises. And the steely logic of his doctrines would easily lead to actions that were outright unlawful. Would Paul Bancroft really hesitate to take the law into his own hands? Did he recognize the authority of any rules that did not arise from his own intricate system of morality?

'I'm not going to debate you,' she said finally, making a decision. She was half-persuaded by Bancroft's words; she would pretend to be a good deal more. Her only chance to gain further information – enough to settle her doubts, in one direction or the other – was to be on the inside. Who knew what truths might repose in Paul Bancroft's hidden empire? 'Look, I don't know if I'd really fit in,' she added. *Don't acquiesce too readily. Feign reluctance – let him win you over.*

'Then we'll need to learn how to fit in with you. Personal styles will vary. And that's fine – so long as the Bancroft strategy remains constant. Will you at least think about it?'

Part of her felt guilty for deceiving him. Yet if she decided that he was the moral paragon she had first taken him to be, she would have done no real harm. 'I'm unlikely not to.'

'Just remember,' the spry savant said, arching an eyebrow. 'Doing the right thing isn't always easy.'

She recalled his remarks about bad acts with good consequences. *Ecrasez l'infame!* – Crush the horror! But too often, she knew, the effort to crush the horror became itself another horror.

'I guess my real worry is that I'll disappoint you,' she lied. She tried to keep her voice from trembling. 'You have these expectations of me. I don't know that I can live up to them.'

'Are you willing to try?'

She took a deep breath. 'Yes,' she said. 'I am.' She forced a smile.

Bancroft smiled back, yet there was now something elusive and guarded about his expression. Had he fully accepted her display of enthusiasm? She would have to be careful. She could well find herself under surveillance. Bancroft's team wouldn't trust her yet: She could tell that much. She had been entrusted with a secret. That made her a potential asset – or a potential threat. She could not afford to do anything to alarm them.

The ambiguous admonition of the nameless man in Katonah returned to her, and the words were like a dark cloud passing over the sun: *You of all people should know what can happen.*

CHAPTER FOURTEEN

Washington, D.C.

Will Garrison's quilted cheeks stretched into a grimace of fury and frustration. 'I blame myself,' the senior Cons Ops manager fumed. 'I should have had the bastard locked up when we had the chance.'

A voice of mild demurral came from Mike Oakeshott, the deputy director for analysis. 'The Hound – '

'Needs to be put down!' Garrison roared.

Both men were in the office of the Director of Operations, Gareth Drucker, whose own gaze kept drifting down to the dispatch on his desk. A veteran Cons Ops analyst struck down on her lunch hour. The news would have rocked him even if he had not been personally fond of Ruth Robbins. As it was, the news came as a double blow. Gareth picked up a pencil, about to scribble a note, and instead snapped the pencil in two.

'On my goddamn watch!' Drucker's eyes darted wildly. 'It happened on my goddamn watch!'

'But, forgive me, *what* exactly happened?' The spindle-shanked senior analyst jumped up from the chair where he had sprawled himself, keyed up with frustration. He tugged at his nimbus of gray hair. Ruth Robbins had been a mainstay of his team; the loss was his, and on some elemental, playground level, it annoyed Oakeshott that Garrison was somehow appropriating his own tragedy.

Garrison turned to him like a bull lowering its shoulders for a charge. 'You know goddamn well – '

'Who was killed, sure.' He caught Drucker's eyes. 'But how what why . . .'

'Don't make this more complicated than it is,' Garrison growled. 'Obviously Belknap has become unhinged.'

'Deranged by grief, is that it?' Oakeshott hugged himself, spider arms clasping a reed-narrow torso.

'Jonesing for vengeance, more likely,' Garrison snapped, irritated by the interruption. 'And he's going on some sort of goddamn global killing spree. He's delusional, but the son of a bitch is killing anyone and everyone he imagines is connected to Rinehart's disappearance. From that Italian girl to poor Ruthie Robbins. Christ almighty! Who's safe from this bastard?'

Oakeshott looked unsettled and unconvinced, but Garrison's rage had its own persuasive force. 'Not you,' the senior analyst said.

'Let that scumbucket try,' Garrison bellowed.

Gareth Drucker looked at the two, drumming his fingers. 'We've got to separate supposition from fact,' he said. A vein pulsed in his forehead. 'The exam boys are still studying the video from the CCTV cams at the park's entrances and exits. Firming this up – it's going to take time.'

'Time that we can't spare,' Garrison protested.

'Shit,' the Director of Operations said, an expletive of assent. 'My call is, we've got enough to activate a retrieval team. I want him brought in and interrogated, using all necessary means. But no beyond-salvage orders. We all need to be clear on that. Because everything has to be by the book.'

'The goddamn Kirk Commission,' Garrison said. 'Don't I know it.'

Drucker nodded. 'We're following the Queensberry rules. Ever since the probe started, 'beyond salvage' has been taken off the table. Proper administrative procedures. Act like anything you do could be read into the Senate record, because for all we know . . .'

'Ops isn't my department, so don't let me talk out of school,' Oakeshott said. 'But you know that a lot of the guys here have beaucoup respect for Castor.'

'What are you saying?' Drucker demanded. 'You're telling me operatives would disobey an official directive?'

'Because they don't know what he's been up to,' Oakeshott put in.

Drucker shook his head firmly. 'I don't think so. I'm still running this goddamn show.'

'I'm just saying you'll want to proceed with some care,' Oakeshott went on. 'He's got friends. Friends tip off friends. They might give him a heads-up. For a lot of the junior guys, especially, he's a goddamn folk hero.' He looked at Drucker. 'And you're just the sheriff.' He held up his elongated hands, a gesture of appeasement. 'I'm merely saying you need to be aware of unit-discipline issues.'

'One more thing I can't afford with that goddamn Senate probe hovering overhead.' The director of operations stared miserably into space. 'You think one of his allies could spill to the commission?'

'I'm not saying that,' Oakeshott began. 'I'm just saying be careful.'

Drucker frowned. 'Then we'll cabin it as a special-access program. Use S.A.P. staff down the line. That way, nobody else here needs to know about it.'

'Belknap's done plenty of S.A.P. work himself,' Oakeshott cautioned.

'Which is why we'll use muscle from nonoverlapping S.A.P. operations only. That goes for support staff, too. Different programs, different firewalls. Ergo, no cross talk.'

Oakeshott tilted his head. 'Doesn't give you a huge pool to choose from. Manpower-wise.'

'We'll keep it lean and mean. Probably better that way. We need this op to go like clockwork. Because Kirk's loaded for bear, the son of a bitch. That's one thing I learned at the interagency lunch today.' He crooked a smile. 'Another is that it's been a long downhill slide since Edgar Hoover. If you're thinking the FBI's gonna come up with some dossier and make the revered Senator Bennett Kirk stand down, then dream on.'

'Those Feds are a bunch of pansies nowadays,' Garrison growled. 'Couldn't find their butts with two hands and a periscope.'

'Nobody's saying Kirk's the driven snow,' Drucker continued. 'He's just not particularly dirty. Besides, there are too many moving parts to this thing now.'

'Double your pleasure, double your fun,' Garrison said heavily. He did not need to elaborate on the fact that Kirk was coordinating the efforts of both an independent counsel and a Senate investigative team. Kirk's speeches about how he intended to root out abuses within the U.S. intelligence community, as well as the businesses and NGOs they had been dealing with, had galvanized the media. He had too much momentum to be turned back. In the spy agencies, long-term survival was the priority. Intelligence officers were all on their best behavior these days . . . or busily trying to erase evidence of their bad behavior.

'There's no way I'm going to ink my name on any piece of paper I don't want Kirk to get his hands on,' Drucker murmured. 'Just so we're clear.' He peered again at Ruth Robbins's personnel file and then his gaze settled upon the mottled, livid countenance of Will Garrison. A long moment passed. 'I'm authorizing a retrieval. S.A.P. designation. Nothing more.'

'If the retrieval team fails, I'll take him out myself,' Garrison vowed grimly. It was a matter of professional pride at this point. He raised his chin slightly, eliciting tacit assent from Drucker's silence. 'Your hands will be clean, Gareth. It was my bad. If need be, I'll make good on it.'

Research Triangle Park, North Carolina

'Listen, Paul, can we have a moment?' asked the man with the well-trimmed black beard.

Paul Bancroft stopped and joined him at the U-shaped conference table.

'Certainly. What is it?'

'Ms. Bancroft is – '

'Being escorted back to her hotel.'

'I hope you're right about her,' the bearded man, George Collingwood, said.

The maven was usually tolerant of forthright comment and criticism. But this was a family matter. One stepped carefully when it came to family – even with Paul Bancroft.

'We'll know for sure soon enough,' the gray-haired philosopher replied. 'We can't rush the . . . acclimation process. It's got to be one step at a time. As it was with you.'

'You make it sound like brainwashing.'

'Into the cult of reason. Whose brain couldn't stand a little cleansing?'

'This whole Nancy Drew bent of hers doesn't worry you?'

'On the contrary. She's had suspicions, and she's had the opportunity to air them. Now she's in a position to move on. To put these matters behind her. That's a good first step toward becoming an initiate.'

'An initiate in the cult of reason.' Collingwood seemed to savor the phrase. 'Well, you know her best. It's just that the Kirk Commission looks to me like a hovering storm cloud, and just one seed crystal could loose a hailstorm on our heads.' He glanced at a dossier on the senator from Indiana that a colleague of his was studying.

'I understand,' Paul Bancroft replied, imperturbably, 'and I grant that I could be wrong about her. But I'm hopeful.'

'With reason, let's trust.' Collingwood flashed a quick, bleak smile.

A husky woman with spiky black hair pressed several buttons on a nearby console and, with a low hum, a narrow metal platform rose up from the level below and slotted into an adjacent cabinet. Her name was Gina Tracy, and she was the most junior member of the team. She rested her hand on a recessed glass panel until its bio-identification scanner had approved her handprint. Then the side panel swung open and she retrieved a set of dossiers. The documents were printed on paper that would blacken immediately in the presence of small quantities of ultraviolet light, even the quantities emitted by regular incandescent and fluorescent fixtures. The illumination within the Theta facility was carefully filtered, eliminating all wavelengths shorter than indigo.

If stolen, the facility's internal documents would be immediately rendered useless, like a film negative exposed to light.

'We've already got a squad en route to La Paz,' she said, handing out the dossier on the land-reclamation project based there. 'There's a fake community activist who's been holding strikes, gumming up the works. Turns out he's on retainer from the local representative of a French conglomerate.'

'No surprise there,' Paul Bancroft said, nodding.

'We're going to burn him – circulate copies of his financial records, show the exact amounts disbursed into his bank account. It was done incredibly crudely. His name's on everything. He'll be instantly discredited.' She smiled. 'GGGN, asshole.' GGGN – it was Theta shorthand for the prime objective: the greatest good for the greatest number.

'Excellent,' Bancroft said with a savoring air.

'The African loan-forgiveness question has been trickier, because the bureaucracy for the European Union is so messy. We've zeroed in on an obscure Belgian policymaker, though. He's low down on the totem pole, but apparently he has an inordinate influence on the higher-ups. He's smart and opinionated and hardworking, and he's won their trust. And he's vehemently opposed to any form of Third World debt forgiveness. A real ideologue. Burgess has the personal stats.' She turned to an associate – a sharp-featured man whose blond hair was so pale it appeared nearly white.

His name was John Burgess, and he had spent ten years at Kroll Associates as a manager of investigations before joining the Theta Group. 'He's not just an ideologue. He's also a bachelor,' he said. 'No kids. One surviving parent with Alzheimer's. We've run the models. Verdict is, we put him out of his misery – or anyway, other people's misery.'

'No disagreement here?' Bancroft asked.

'Both teams ran the numbers separately,' said Collingwood, 'and both teams came to the same conclusion. He doesn't wake tomorrow, and the world's a better place. GGGN, right?'

'Very well,' Bancroft said somberly.

'As for the banking official in Indonesia?' Collingwood

went on. 'We've had a win there. He got a phone call last night, and he's just submitted his resignation.'

'Tidy,' Bancroft commended.

In the next half-hour, more dossiers were reviewed. A recalcitrant mining director in South Africa, a religious activist in Gujarat, India, a communications mogul in Thailand: Each was the source of significant, avoidable suffering. Some would be forced to resign or shift their behaviors; where blackmail was not an option, however, an elite execution team would do its work, typically making the deaths appear to be the result of accidental or natural causes.

On infrequent occasions, to be sure, members of the Theta Group had resorted to spectacle, as when they had arranged the assassination of Martin Luther King, Jr. – a tragic necessity, all agreed – in order the bolster the civil rights movement. Or as when they had arranged a couple of NASA shuttle disasters in order to promote the defunding of the wasteful, pointless program. The loss of a handful of lives meant thousands of lives saved, billions of dollars for worthier programs.

But they had to be careful. Though the models were ever more sophisticated, they all knew that such models could never be infallible, however potent the computer power harnessed.

Finally, Bancroft and the members of his executive team came to the final operational dossier, and the thorniest one. It involved a complex political carom shot that would require the deaths of an entire national soccer team. A regional governor had arranged to have the soccer team – the subject of delirious adulation since their World Cup victory three days earlier – come as guests to his private estate, and to a celebration party he was having. At his insistence, they were to be flown over on his private airplane, a prized and lovingly polished vintage specimen that dated to the Second World War and was meant to recall the wartime heroism of the governor's father. A midair explosion that took the lives of the celebrated young men would cast a pall over the nation in the short run. But it would also doom the governor's

249

chances in the national election to be held the following day, for the common folk would blame him for the tragedy. It was the one way to avert a disastrous administration and ensure the success of a reformist candidate. A soccer team would be destroyed; a handful of lives would be wasted. It was not a decision to be undertaken lightly. But the country would prosper. Thousands of lives would be saved as foreign investment surged and the country's economic development was accelerated.

Bancroft paused for a long time. It was not something to authorize lightly. His eyes sought out those of the oldest analyst at the table, Herman Liebman. 'What do you think, Herm?' the philosopher asked quietly.

Liebman ran his hand through his thinning gray hair. 'You've always looked to me as the guy who remembers when things didn't work as planned,' he said mordantly. 'There's no question that the governor's a kleptocrat. Definitely bad news. Then again, I can't help but remember Ahmad Hasan al-Bakr.'

'Who?' Tracy asked.

'A real hard-on. A truculent Iraqi leader who governed together with another Sunni secularist in the seventies. Before your time, Gina. But Paul remembers. We tussled with the problem, and all the analysts were convinced that al-Bakr was the worse of the two. So we sent a team of operatives to Iraq. This was in 1976. Technically, it was a beautiful job. They chemically induced a myocardial infarction. Complete control was promptly assumed by his partner. Saddam Hussein.'

'Not one of our finest moments,' Paul agreed.

'Not one of mine,' Liebman persisted. 'Because – and Paul's too polite to point it out – I was the one who had been lobbying the hardest to get rid of al-Bakr. All the models seemed to back me up.'

'That was a long time ago,' Bancroft said gently. 'We've fine-tuned the Theta algorithms since then. Not to mention the fact that we're employing today's vastly greater computational power. We're not perfect, never have been. But in the long run, we've made this planet a better place. Men and women are now alive and living good, productive lives who would have died in infancy if it weren't for Theta. What we're doing is surgery, Herm – you know this as well as anyone. A scalpel to the body: That's a kind of violence. You don't make a deep cut without having reason to. But sometimes survival depends upon surgery. Cutting out malignancies, clearing blockages, and sometimes just finding out what's really going on. People die from surgery all the time. But a lot more people die from the lack of it.' He turned to Burgess. 'It's funny – I watched that final World Cup match. An incredibly spirited group of players. And when Rodriguez scored, the look on his face . . .' He smiled at the memory. 'But we've done the math. The opportunity to affect national governance in a country where bad policies have been laying waste to entire communities, entire generations – we can't pass that up. It may be among the most important decision we make all year.'

'Just for the sake of argument, let's spare another thought for the twelve men who will be on that plane.' Liebman wasn't challenging him; he knew that Bancroft counted on him to spell out the immediate consequences as well as the distant ones they hoped for. '*Young* men.' He tapped a finger on the second page of the dossier. 'Three of whom have wives. Including Rodriguez – his wife has already borne him two girls, and she's pregnant again. They're hoping for a boy. And the men have parents, grandparents in most cases. The pain will be terrible and lingering for these people. Indeed, the whole nation will experience an intense bout of grief.'

'And all these factors have been carefully accounted for in the computer models,' Bancroft said softly. 'We wouldn't be contemplating it if the upside weren't greater still. The people of that beleaguered nation – the children of that nation – are owed our best judgment. They won't know what really happened, and they certainly won't know why, so they'll never thank us. But in four or five years, they will have cause to give thanks.'

'GGGN,' Burgess murmured in a soft undertone, like a prayer.

'Oh, here's something that will brighten your day,' Collingwood fluted, holding a copy of a press release that had just been issued from the Culp Foundation. 'William Culp is funding a new round of AIDS vaccine trials in Kenya.'

'And the bastard gets all the glory,' Tracy remarked wryly. 'It's so unfair.'

'Glory is not why we're here,' Bancroft replied with asperity. Still, he knew not to make too much of the occasional cynical crack; the men and women of Theta were idealists through and through.

He turned to Liebman. 'Regarding the soccer team – do you think I made the wrong decision?'

Liebman said nothing for a moment, then shook his head. 'On the contrary, I know you made the right one. The best decisions – the smartest ones, the ones that really change things for the better – are often the ones that hurt most. You taught me that. You taught me a lot of things. And I'm still learning.'

'As am I,' Dr. Bancroft said. 'You know, Plato claimed that all learning was really remembering. Which certainly feels true in my case. Because it's so easy to forget how morally blinkered humanity can be. Governments will pursue policies that result in tens of thousands of deaths – *foreseeably*, as with misconceived public-health policies. Yet they will spend millions to investigate a single assassination.' He looked off. 'Worldwide mortality from AIDS is the equivalent of twenty fully loaded jumbo jets crashing every day, and leaders barely lift a finger. Yet the death of a single silly archduke can mobilize entire nations for war. One baby is trapped in a well, and the attention of the world is riveted for days on end. Yet mass starvation can decimate entire regions and the news is crowded out by celebrity misbehavior.'

'It's amazing.' Tracy nodded.

'It's monstrous, actually,' Bancroft said, his cheeks coloring.

'What's pathetic is that the Theta Group should have to do its good deeds in secret,' said Collingwood, 'instead of being heralded by a grateful world. I mean it.' He turned to Dr. Bancroft. 'Has humanity ever had a benefactor like you? That's not flattery, just fact. The Cray cluster downstairs would confirm it. I mean, really and truly, has any organization ever done more good than the Theta Group?'

Burgess spread his hands on the Bennett Kirk file. 'Which is exactly what makes self-protection so important. To do what we do, we need to be left alone. And let's face it. There are a lot of people who would like to put us out of business.'

'In some cases,' Dr. Bancroft replied in a voice that was both calm and relentless, 'our obligation to the greater good means putting *them* out of business.'

CHAPTER FIFTEEN

Washington, D.C.

The Hart Senate Office Building, between Constitution Avenue and Second Street, provided a million square feet of office space, all nine stories of which were devoted to the United States Senate and its staff. The number of senators was fixed when the republic was founded, at two per state; but the number of staffers was not, and would come to exceed ten thousand. A gratelike marble facade shielded the building's windows from the mid-Atlantic sun; inside, a large skylit atrium featured Alexander Calder's mobile *Mountains and Clouds*, a monumental work of black steel and aluminum. The atrium was surrounded by elevators and circular stairs, and bridged by walkways.

The duplex suite belonging to Senator Bennett Kirk occupied space on the seventh and eight floors. The offices were handsome but short of luxurious – the Oriental carpets were of the standard elephant's-foot variety, the paneling in the reception area was of stained oak, not walnut – but they had a certain solidity that lent itself to the hush of power. The senator's own office was grander, and darker, but also vaguely impersonal: Its furnishings somehow announced that they had been passed down to the senator from his predecessors, and would be passed down, in turn, to his successors.

Philip Sutton, the senator's chief of staff for more than a decade, watched a C-SPAN broadcast of proceedings in the building's Central Hearing Facility, five floors below him. He sometimes found it easiest to track down his boss by watching television, especially these days. Sutton glanced at his watch; the senator had left the hearing a minute ago, would probably reappear in his suite in a couple of minutes more. He turned off the small television set, caught a glimpse of himself in the dead screen: short, pudgy, balding – not exactly ready for prime time. His nails were bitten close to the quick. Men like him couldn't get elected dog-catcher. He was a natural lieutenant, not a leader, and it was a fact he accepted with neither bitterness nor regret. If he wanted to know what it was that he lacked, he just had to take a look at Bennett Kirk, and it was all on display. He could see the senator now, in fact, entering the suite with his distinctive loose-limbed lope, broad shoulders, the narrow, almost delicate nose, the head of silver hair that seemed to come with its own key light.

Senator Kirk was smart, earthy, and short-tempered, and he wasn't devoid of vanity, either. Sutton knew the man's every flaw and foible, but they detracted not at all from his admiration. What Bennett Kirk had going for him wasn't just the senatorial looks; he also had something like clarity of purpose, integrity. Pretentious words that would make Senator Kirk cringe, but it was hard to find another way to put it.

'Phil, you look tired,' Senator Kirk said gruffly, putting an arm around his shoulders. 'Actually, you look like you've been getting your meals out of the vending machines. When you gonna learn that Lunchables are not the fifth food group?'

Sutton studied the older man's face carefully, but, he hoped, discreetly. He didn't want the senator to be self-conscious about the state of his health, and so far the illness was scarcely detectable. Sutton had helped him manage the ambitious investigation for many weeks now, but the senator himself was doing a lot of the heavy lifting. Too much of the heavy lifting. It would take a toll even on a healthy man.

'Want to hear about your latest opportunities?' Sutton asked. 'You've never had so many people aching to do you favors.'

'Lead me not into temptation, boy.' The senator eased himself onto a leather wing chair that faced away from the windows. He took a small brown plastic bottle from a trousers pocket, palmed it open, and dry-swallowed an oval yellow pill.

'Let's see, now. This morning, a call came from Arch Gleeson – you know, former congressman, now a registered lobbyist for the National Aerospace Industries Association. They've developed a sudden interest in helping you raise funds for future campaigns.'

'Ah, those defense-industry lobbyists. About as shy as a coon in a Dumpster.'

'Oh, he delicately mentioned the caveat that, if you weren't interested, they'd make the same offer to any plausible opponent. 'We just want to be helpful,' he kept saying. Help me help you – or else. That's what it came down to.'

'They're worried about what the committee probe might rumble onto. Or how big a stink we'll raise once we do. Can't blame 'em for looking after their interests.'

'Mighty Christian of you,' Sutton shot back with a sardonic grin. 'Another firm has offered to hire Amanda as a vice president for corporate communications.' The senator's wife was a high-school English teacher; it was another transparent attempt at reaching the man leading the Senate probe.

'I can guess what Amanda's likely to say,' he chuckled. 'I guess they're not aiming at subtlety.'

'A big salary, too. They actually mentioned a range.'

'See if they'd take me instead,' the senator said waggishly. Ever since the Kirk Commission was established, such veiled threats and bribes had been arriving every day.

Kirk was no kind of saint; Sutton wrinkled his nose at the senator's support for ethanol programs, a political favor for a major agribusiness supporter, though, like any Senate staffer, he also recognized the political exigencies involved. But the senator had generally kept his nose clean.

And now he had his eyes on the prize. What none of the influence-peddlers realized was that he was beyond deterring or swaying at this point. Aside from his closest aides and his wife, Bennett Kirk had kept the diagnosis to himself.

Nobody needed to know that Bennett Kirk had been diagnosed with an aggressive and treatment-resistant variety of lymphoma. It had already reached stage four at the time of diagnosis. He was not going to be alive to run again. All he cared about now was his legacy; and the kind of legacy Senator Kirk cared about was the kind of legacy a man could not buy.

Sutton only occasionally got inklings of the chronic pain the senator was in, as when a subtle facial twitch or not-wholly-concealed wince made a fleeting appearance. For the most part, however, Bennett Kirk was determined to ignore or overcome any and all symptoms of the disease, until the disease burst the floodgates of stoicism.

'There's something else, isn't there?' Kirk said, his eyes meeting Sutton's. He rearranged himself on his chair, crossing and uncrossing his legs, trying to get comfortable. But no position was comfortable. The bone metastases made sure of that. 'I can tell. You got another one of those message thingies.'

Sutton paused, then nodded. 'Another communication from Genesis, yes. Via e-mail.'

'And you take this bogeyman seriously?'

Solemnly, his chief of staff nodded. 'We've been through this. From the earlier messages we've received, it's clear that Genesis is privy to all sorts of buried secrets. I grant we're dealing with a pretty vaporous figure, but we've got to take Genesis very seriously indeed.'

'So what's this bit of ectoplasm saying now?'

Sutton handed the senator a printout of the latest e-mail. 'Genesis is promising to supply us with information – including names, dates, possible witnesses and perpetrators. Quite a gift.'

'Remember my philosophy: Always look a gift horse in the mouth. But if the horse is invisible, you can't give it a dental exam, can you?'

'We can't walk away from this. It's too good. Too valuable. Stuff we'd never be able to get on our own, no matter how many investigators we threw at it. We'll be able to unveil and dismantle a conspiracy that's been under way, it appears, for longer than you've been in the Senate.'

'Or we'll be left holding our breeches in a rainstorm. I mean, this could be the mother of all practical jokes.'

'There's too much knowledge here. Too many verifiable – and verified – details.'

'In politics, you know, there's a saying: Consider the source. I don't like communicating with spirits. This thing unsettles my stomach.' Senator Kirk gave Sutton a level stare. 'I need to know who Genesis is. Have we made any progress toward finding out?'

Sutton shrugged uneasily. 'We're in an awkward position. Normally it would be a problem to be kicked over to the investigative and espionage services. Except, of course, those are the agencies you're investigating.'

Kirk grunted. 'I bet some of those bastards would love to get their hands on this Genesis before I did.'

'Word has it,' his chief of staff put in, 'that he'll let people see him . . . if they'll let him kill them afterward. Most folks just aren't that curious.'

'Kee-*rist*, I hope you're just yanking my chain.' The senator's mouth was smiling, but his eyes were not. 'And I hope Genesis isn't.'

Eastern Uruguay

Javier Solanas patted his full belly, drained the last of his mug of beer, gazed around the table, and decided that he was probably as happy as he had ever been, and perhaps as happy as a man should be.

His modest ranch outside Paysandú was nothing special; there were thousands bigger and more prosperous in Uruguay. But he had built it all, had pieced it together from three small plots of land – he, the son of a goatherd! The party wasn't even for him; it was for his wife of forty years, Elena, whose birthday it was. But that made it all the better. It meant that his pride was not inviting a visit from the evil eye. And nobody, not even the evil eye, could begrudge

Elena anyway. Five children – three girls, two boys – Elena had borne him, and all full-grown, all with children of their own. He had three sons-in-law, and he actually liked two of them! Who was so lucky?

The table was filled with plates and platters, half empty. Slabs of fine Uruguayan beef had been grilled in the parilla, slathered with chimichurri sauce. Javier had made his own specialty, morcilla dulce, or blood sausage made with walnuts and raisins. Then there was Elena's special stuffed sweet peppers. All ravenously consumed. Along with a fair amount of Javier's beer.

And how about the face of his pretty dark-eyed Elena when he presented her with the pair of plane tickets! She had always dreamed of visiting Paris, and now they would. They would leave tomorrow.

'You shouldn't have!' Elena had cried out, her beaming countenance saying, *Thank God you did.*

This was what it was to be a man: to be surrounded by children of all ages, children and grandchildren, to be in a position to feed them all so well that they could not swallow another bite! No, not bad for a goatherd's son!

'A toast!' Javier called out.

'You've already proposed seven toasts,' his daughter Evita said.

'Papi!' her older sister Marie said. She was nursing her infant while keeping an eye on her toddler. 'We've run out of baby food. Pedro loves the strained carrots.'

'We've run out of beer,' said Evita's husband, Juan.

'No more Pepsi!' called Evita.

'I'll go to the store,' Juan offered.

'In whose car?' Javier demanded.

'Yours?' The response was a sheepish interrogative.

Javier gestured toward the three empty bottles of lager by Juan's dinner plate. '*I* go,' Javier said.

'Don't go,' said his wife.

'I'm back in five minutes. You won't notice.' He raised himself to his feet and walked over to the back door. When he and Elena were married, he had a flat belly, flat like the pampas; now he couldn't see his own feet without making an effort. Elena told him, 'More of you to love,' but Javier wondered whether he should take more exercise. A pater-familias had an obligation to his family. He had to set a good example.

When he reached the green-painted garage – a converted chickencoop, not that anybody could tell – he closed the narrow side door behind him and turned on the lights. Then he jabbed at the button that would raise the rolling door.

Nothing happened. He tried again. Still nothing. He would have to lift up the rolling door himself. He took a step and felt odd. He took another deep breath, and another. But no matter how much he breathed, he could not catch his breath.

The lights flickered and went out. Javier thought it odd. He was aware of himself blacking out, losing muscle control, slumping gently to the concrete floor. He was aware of himself lying there, flesh, food, blood, bones. Aware that a fly had settled on his forehead, that others were coming to feed on him. Aware that soon he would not be aware at all. It had to have been a heart attack, yes? Or a stroke? But it wasn't the way he thought such things would be. Not that he had given the eventuality of death a great deal of thought.

His mind drifted, eddied. *So this is what it's like*, he thought. *I wish I could go back and tell the others. It's not so bad, really. The main thing is not to be afraid of the dark.*

Then consciousness began to evaporate like morning dew, and the flies gathered in a thick cloud.

From just behind the berm line of a wheatfield across the road, two men peered with binoculars.

'Do you think he felt much pain?' one of them asked.

'Nitrogen asphyxiation is about the kindest way you can take a life,' the other, who was more experienced, said. He called himself Mr. Smith, at least when he was on assign-ment. 'You don't feel breathless, because there's no carbon dioxide buildup in the blood. You run out of oxygen, but you don't know what's happening to you. It's like someone has turned out the lights.'

'I think you always know when you're dying,' said the other, a tall man with sandy hair, who went by the name Mr. Jones.

'Marco Brodz didn't.'

'No,' his companion agreed. 'A large-caliber bullet to the head. He never had time. I think *that's* the kindest way.'

'They're both kind. Even fast-acting poisons are kind compared to what nature has in store for us. Cancer, with its jaws munching away at your gut. That's how my mom went, and it was rotten. Even the horrible crushing sensation of a heart attack – my dad told me about how it felt, the first time he had a coronary. Natural death is a bitch. Really, it's much better this way. Our way.'

'How did you know that Javier would go to the garage, not anybody else?'

'What, and let another person drive his brand-new sedan? A man like that? You obviously don't know these parts very well.' He pressed the button of an augmented radio-frequency transmitter; two hundred yards away, a garage door rolled up.

Replacing the air in the garage with a pure nitrogen from the tank of liquid gas had taken nearly half an hour. Now the atmosphere would equilibrate in less than a minute.

Mr. Jones looked through the binoculars, adjusting the focus until he saw the stricken man on the concrete, an area of urine darkening his crotch, a fog of flies darkening his face. 'There's never any real dignity in death,' he observed. 'But he does look peaceful, don't you think?'

The second man, Mr. Smith, took the binoculars and peered carefully. 'Does he look peaceful? It's hard to tell. He certainly looks dead.'

Raleigh, North Carolina

The images kept cycling through his head as Belknap re-turned to the hotel. Ruth's sightless, staring eyes, the rivulet

261

of blood glistening from the corner of her slack mouth. One moment she was talking, breathing, reasoning; the next moment she had simply ceased to exist, leaving behind only insentient tissue. No, she had left behind more than that. There were her two young boys, now orphaned, and there were the memories that others had of the woman's unique and precious existence. An existence that blinked out when someone had squeezed off a carefully aimed bullet.

A sniper's bullet, obviously from a considerable distance, given its soundless arrival, and therefore demonstrating considerable marksmanship. Belknap himself might have been next, had he not dived into the brush as soon as he realized what had happened. Why was the sniper dispatched? Who had done so? How had they been shadowed? Belknap tried to be analytical, but he felt the rage grow within him, wrapping tendrils around his stony heart. How many of his friends had he seen die? And then there was his beloved Yvette: a memory he had tried to bury as deep as he could, like nuclear waste canistered and interred in a desert salt mine. Part of him – a dream of the man he might have been – had been struck down along with his bride. Where there is beauty, one finds death.

He appeared punctually at the lobby of the Raleigh Marriott at precisely four, and there was Andrea Bancroft, equally punctual, drinking from a white china cup at one of the chair-and-low-table clusters to the right side of the lobby. He hoped that she had followed his instructions and stayed at the hotel. After what had happened at Rock Creek, he had to worry about her own safety as well as his own.

By reflex, he let his gaze wash over the rest of the lobby, a second-long glance that slid like a windshield washer over slick glass. His neck prickled. *Something was wrong.* To try to warn Andrea was to endanger her; it would plant a target on her within sight of his enemies. She wasn't their objective, or she wouldn't be there.

He had to act before he could analyze, act in a manner that was swift, erratic, and difficult to anticipate. *Don't turn back: They'll have thought of that. Go in!* Todd did not break stride as he made his way through the lobby.

Out of the corner of his eye, he saw Andrea leap up. She assumed he didn't see her, was coming after him.

Exactly the wrong thing to do.

He whipped his head around, tried frantically to signal her with his eyes, by looking at and yet past her: *Do not acknowledge me, as I am not acknowledging you. Pretend we are strangers.*

He kept race-walking across the lobby, and – rather than stopping at the front desk or waiting by the elevator bank – immediately pushed through the unmarked swing door behind the concierge desk. Now he was in a luggage-storage area. The fleur-de-lis carpet immediately gave way to hard Congoleum flooring, chandelier lights gave way to fluorescent tubes; racks of suitcase lined either side of the long alcove.

Even as he ran, an inward eye reviewed his threat assessment. What had he seen in the lobby, exactly? A man – an ordinary-looking man, maybe forty, in an ordinary gray suit – reading a newspaper in one of the hotel wing chairs. Diagonally across an unmarked centerline, a man and a woman, both in their late twenties or early thirties, sitting together at a small table. A white porcelain tea server, two white cups. Nothing that would be noticed by a nonprofessional. What alerted Belknap was that neither the man nor the woman at the table near the door looked up when he walked in. A typical couple would have responded to the arrival of a stranger with a flicker of the eye at least. But this couple did not need to; they had already registered his arrival through the glass adjoining the extra-wide revolving door. Instead, the woman glanced, fleetingly, at the older man, who was holding the newspaper just a little lower than he would if he had actually been reading it. Then there was the matter of footwear. The older man was sitting with his legs crossed at the ankles, such that the soles of his shoes were visible, and visibly discordant with his expensive leather shows: textured black rubber, not leather. The woman was dressed fancily – a pale blouse, a dark skirt – and yet her shoes, too, had thick rubber soles. Her makeup was careful, her hair pinned up above her neck, her attire elegant: The rubber-soled shoes she wore were an incongruous element. Belknap had picked up on these things at a glance, instinctively; spelling them out, naming them, took longer. He knew these people: not personally, but professionally, generically. He knew how they were trained; he knew who had trained them. People like him.

They were enemies, but worse still, they were *colleagues*. Members of a Consular Operations retrieval team. They had to be. Highly trained professionals, carrying out orders. They were not used to failure; they had no reason to be. Belknap had been on just such a detail more than once in his own career. Never had the operation ended in anything less than swift success. How did they know where he was going to show up? he wondered – yet there was no time for such questions.

There was another swing door with a small glass window toward the end of the space; Belknap pushed through it and into an industrial-looking kitchen. A row of small brown men with straight black hair were cleaning or doing prep work, but nobody heard him over the faucet noises, the clattering of aluminum pots on the range grates. Cans of vegetables the size of small oil drums were stacked on wheeled steel carts. There was a rear entrance – but it would be watched. Instead, he found a small elevator, no doubt used for room service.

From behind him, he heard the clattering of unmuffled footsteps: Andrea had gone chasing after him.

Exactly the wrong thing to do. She was no professional, had understood nothing of what he had tried to signal.

Another sound: the *snick-click* of a pistol being readied. A small, wiry man stepped out of a recessed area next to the service elevator, an M9 pistol trained at Belknap.

Dammit! She was not the only one to miscalculate. The team was well deployed; an operative was stationed by the service elevator as well.

Andrea was tugging on Belknap's arm. 'What the hell is going on?'

The small, wiry man – iron eyes in a broad, weathered face – stepped closer to them, moving his pistol from one to the other. 'So who's your friend?' he barked.

Andrea gasped. 'Oh, Jesus. This isn't happening. This isn't happening.'

Three in the lobby. Not five or seven. Three. That meant that they were staffing the operation with S.A.P. operatives only – veterans of special-access programs, with the very highest level of security clearance. Three in the lobby meant that the man with the dull black pistol in his hand was on his own. He would call in the others momentarily – but had not done so yet. *He wants to get credit for the capture,* Belknap thought. *He'll want it to be absolutely clear that he'd already taken charge of the target when the others arrive.*

'I said, who's your friend?' the gunman snarled.

Belknap snorted. 'My *friend*? For three hundred dollars an hour, the bitch better be my friend. She'll be your friend, too.'

Belknap saw something on Andrea's face. A glint of comprehension.

'Screw you,' she yelled at Belknap, suddenly vehement. 'And give me my goddamn money!' She punched Belknap hard in the shoulder. 'You think you can get away with not paying, you asshole?' Then she turned to the gunman. 'What the hell are you looking at? You gonna help me or not? Help me get his wallet. I'll split it with you.'

'You're out of your tree,' the gunman said, startled and unsettled. Belknap saw him reaching for his communicator.

'Didn't Burke send you?' Andrea asked him. 'Get on the goddamn stick.'

'You move again, bitch, you'll get a breast implant of bullets,' the gunman snarled at her. 'Both of you – you better freeze. I ain't saying it again.'

One gunman. One gun. Belknap stepped in front of Andrea, keeping his body between her and the gun. If his orders were to shoot, he would have done so already. Therefore shooting was to be resorted to only in the event of likely mission failure. He took a long step toward the gunman, plunging both his hands inside his own trouser pockets. 'You want my wallet? That what this is about?'

He saw the uncertainty in the other man's eyes. An operative's most important weapon was his hands; no professional would encumber his hands the way Belknap had by sticking them in his pockets. Had Belknap approached him with his hands raised to shoulder level, the wiry operative would instantly have recognized the gambit; he would have been trained to employ it himself. Even with hands raised high in the air, Belknap would be identified as a threat. An opponent becomes more dangerous when he's within an arm's length of you.

'You tell Burke that if he wants a john to pay up, he better make sure his honeys are putting out.' Belknap's voice was confiding, as if he were trying to appeal to the other, man to man.

'Don't take another goddamn step!' The man's command was taut, yet his uncertainty was visibly growing. Was this, in fact, the correct target?

Belknap ignored him. 'Put yourself in my situation,' Belknap went on, and came closer still. He was close enough to smell cigarettes and sweat on the man. 'Because I'm going to tell you a secret about your boss I don't want this bitch to hear.'

With a sudden movement, Belknap scissored his torso and smashed his forehead into the other man's face, then wrested the pistol from his grasp before he crumpled to the ground.

'Andrea, listen to me,' he told her urgently. 'There were three operatives in the lobby, and they would have made you. Chances are at least one of them will be here in maybe fifteen seconds. The others won't recognize you. You need to do precisely what I tell you.'

He knelt down, rummaged through the fallen man's pockets until he found a pack of Camels, half-empty, and a disposable lighter.

Andrea was breathing hard now. She had momentarily staved off her terror, lost it in the mad intensity of her performance. Soon, he knew, it would return.

'Keep it together, okay?' He handed her the cigarettes and lighter.

She nodded mutely.

Belknap looked into her eyes as he spoke, as if to verify that she was absorbing his words. 'You leave the back way, like you're a manager taking a cigarette break. Five paces away from the door, stop. Turn and face the hotel. Open your purse. Take out a cigarette. Light it. That cigarette is like oxygen to you. Then you start to wander off the lot and toward the street, like you need to buy more cigarettes. You keep going. There's a hotel a block south with a taxi line. Get a taxi there, get yourself to downtown Durham, stay in public places like shopping areas.'

'Please,' she whispered. 'Come with me.'

He shook his head. 'I can't go out that way. They're waiting for me.'

'Then what's going to happen to you? That man, he was going to – '

Belknap heard footfalls from the corridor where the luggage was stored. 'You're craving a cigarette,' he said in a low, urgent voice. 'The smoke is like oxygen to you. Now *go*!'

Her shoulders stiffened slightly, and he saw that she grasped the situation. She put the cigarette pack into her purse, and, without another word, let herself out the rear entrance. If she were given a role, he knew, she could play it. He had given her one. She would be safe.

He had no such confidence about himself.

Now he jabbed the button to the service elevator. He could hear the sound of luggage being tossed around. One person, plainly, had been detached from the lobby unit to search the internal spaces of the floor. A sound move: The agents watching the other exits must have reported in that the target had made no appearance so far.

He jabbed the elevator call button again. It would take just seconds before the operative satisfied himself that Belknap was not hiding with the luggage, and pushed toward the rear of the hotel.

The elevator cabin opened and Belknap stepped in. He pressed the button, almost randomly, for the fourth floor. The doors closed jerkily and the cabin started to move.

He closed his eyes, calmed his pulse, reviewed his options. He had to consider the strong possibility that he had been glimpsed stepping onto the elevator – in which case others may well be in pursuit, taking other elevators to the fourth floor, or simply bounding up the stairs. He raced down the hallways, looking for a maid's towel-laden cart, an open door. His head start, if he had one, could be measurable in seconds.

An open door. He found one: a room being turned down, the bolster pillows removed from the headboard, the spread and blanket folded back. The maid, moving stiffly in her pale blue uniform, greeted him with a Spanish accented 'Good afternoon, sir,' as he entered, taking him to be the guest. 'Just finishing up,' she added.

Suddenly she shrieked, and Belknap knew that his luck had run out. When he whirled around he saw that two armed men had raced into the room. One of them spun the maid around and shoved her out of the room before standing post at the door.

Belknap forced himself to breathe normally as he sized up the two operatives. Neither was from the lobby; indeed, neither was anybody he had ever seen before. One of them looked vaguely Filipino, though with the long limbs and well-developed musculature of a corn-fed American. Child of an army base marriage, Belknap figured. The other was denser, and dark-skinned, with a shaven skull that gleamed like ebony. Both held short-barreled automatic weapons, polymer grip, long curved magazines beneath the stock. Thirty rounds of 9mm ammunition each. At full fire, the weapon could probably discharge all thirty rounds in a few seconds.

'Lie flat on the floor.' The black man spoke first. His voice was light and eerily calm. 'Clasp your hands behind your head. One ankle over the other. You know the drill.' He could have been a driving instructor telling a student to release the clutch. 'Do it now.'

Rinehart was always dismissive when Belknap spoke of good luck. *Has it ever occurred to you that your 'good luck' consists of getting you out of fixes that your bad luck got you into?*

'I'll repeat the instructions – once,' the man said. Again, he sounded utterly calm.

I'd feel calm, too, if I was aiming a powerhouse machine gun at a man with a pistol stuck in his pocket.

'No need,' Belknap said. 'Speaking as a colleague, I gotta say you guys have done a bang-up job so far. If I were writing up a post-action report, though, I might raise a question about the ammunition. Hotel walls are famously thin. I assume you're using standard NATO cartridges. That means one round could punch through half a dozen walls. You got those things set at triple burst? Or single shot?'

The two men traded glances. 'Full fire,' the black man said.

'Oh, see, that's not good.' A chink in the armor: The man had responded to him. They had the well-founded confidence of their overwhelming firepower. Belknap's only hope was to find a way to use that confidence to his own advantage. 'You didn't work out the backstopping issues.'

'On the ground now, or I *will* fire.' The black man spoke the words with the air of someone who had killed enough men to regard it as little more than an inconvenience. At the same time, pride kept him from adjusting his weapon's firing rate; he wasn't going to lose face in front of a colleague.

An S.A.P. retrieval team. Belknap knew that his best chance of surviving was to surrender. But S.A.P. retrievals did not end in court hearings or newspaper items. Once 'retrieved,' he would probably face incarceration for an indefinite number of years at a clandestine facility in West Virginia or a black-site location in rural Poland. He did not value his own survival highly enough for surrender to be an appealing option.

'First, it's highly irresponsible for you to use full fire in an environment dense with nontarget civilians,' Belknap said, adopting the tone of a training instructor. 'When I started in this business, you two were still sucking on pacifiers, so listen to the voice of goddamn experience. Full fire against hotel drywall? The post-action report practically writes itself. Classic tyro's mistake: Job like this, you need a fine camel-hair brush, not a goddamn paint roller.' As he spoke, he walked over to the window. 'So let me help you out here. What we've got here is a window.'

The man who looked part-Filipino snickered. 'Oh, you noticed? No other hotel guests out in the air, now are they?'

'Who the hell trained you?' Belknap demanded. 'Please don't tell me it was me. No, I think I'd recognize your ugly mugs. Now, then, before you find yourself trying to explain to Will Garrison why two guys with machine guns were forced to terminate a retrieval and blast away at an unarmed man' – he slipped the lie in with a name they'd recognize – 'which we can all agree is a suboptimal mission outcome, let me ask you a question. How far will a nine-millimeter bullet travel through the air?'

'We ain't your goddamn students,' the larger gunman sneered.

'High-velocity plinker like you got there, could be more than two miles. Over ten thousand feet. Even if you reset to triple burst, you need to expect that the third bullet is essentially traveling through thin air, following the opening punched out by the first two. Now, let's take a closer look at where the natural trajectory is going to lead.' He turned his back to them and slid open the floor-to-ceiling window, which let onto a narrow balcony.

'Hey, Denny,' the corn-fed Asian said to his partner, 'I know what I'm gonna write in the post-action report. Target was terminated because he was so goddamn *annoying*.'

Belknap ignored him. 'As you may have noticed, we're in a fairly built-up and densely populated region.' He gestured toward a glass-and-steel office building across the nearby highway, but his own attention was focused on the large out-door pool that the balcony overlooked. A tall privacy hedge of rhododendrons screened the pool from a busy street nearby.

With an easy grin, the black man lowered himself into a

crouch, keeping the gun aimed at center-body mass, but at an upward angle. 'Easy enough to change the trajectory, now isn't it? That's some bullshit you're talking.'

'You should have taken a closer look,' Belknap said, undeterred. 'Should have done what I'm doing.' He stepped onto the balcony, gauged the horizontal distance between it and the pool.

'Sucker thinks he can run out the clock,' the second gunman said with a nasty laugh.

'I'm just trying to teach you kids a thing or two,' Belknap went on. 'Because if you're firing from that rice-paddy crouch of yours, Denny, you'd ideally want your target in a more elevated position.' As if to demonstrate, Belknap turned his back to the operatives again and stepped onto the four-foot steel trellis, its exact measurement doubtless in compliance with some child-safety law. *What about the safety of fleeing adults?* Balancing himself precariously, he sprang forward with all the coiled strength of his legs, forward and into thin air.

He heard a spurt of gunfire, like a chainsaw exploding into life: full fire depleting their magazines at eight hundred rounds per minute, or a little over two seconds for a thirty-round clip. *If you can hear it, it didn't hit you.* They had failed to anticipate his move, and their surprise must have delayed their reaction by a critical instant.

Belknap was hurtling downward – yet, in freefall, he felt as if he were motionless, and that the ground was hurtling toward him, growing bigger and bigger and closer and closer. He had perhaps three seconds to right himself, to stretch his body into a blade, knife though the surface tension. At these heights, one did not dive headfirst. He could not waste time peering downward: If he had miscalculated and was going to hit cement, then nothing he did mattered. He had to assume that he was going to fall where he had aimed himself, at the deep end of the pool. To a body falling from a height of twenty yards, water was not a soft and yielding substance: It was stiff and resistant, and the more surface area exposed to it – the broader the area of impact –

the harder the water would hit him. In training, he had learned the basic equation: shape factor multiplied by water density multiplied by the square of velocity. It was like someone taking a two-by-four to your bare feet, he recalled a professional cliff diver reporting. He would be traveling at almost forty miles per hour when he reached the water. *The problem isn't the falling*, the cliff diver had said. *It's the stopping*.

Belknap could not affect his velocity; he could not change the fact that water was more than eight hundred times denser than air. All he could do was reduce his shape factor – to place his feet together, angled *en pointe*, raise his arms above his head, straight, palm to palm. He glimpsed cars on the adjacent roadway and, though they had to have been traveling at least forty miles an hour, they looked to him as if they were inching along, scarcely moving at all. At the last moment before hitting the water, Belknap inhaled deeply, filled his lungs, and prepared for what could not be prepared for.

The jolt ran through his body, an impact that rippled through his very skeleton, his spinal cord, his every joint and sinew.

He'd thought it would never come, and yet, paradoxically, it had come sooner than he had expected. He had done all he could, and yet felt utterly unready. After the concussing shock of impact, he grew conscious of other sensations, like a sense of coolness all over his body, and the way the water, having struck the first blow, now cushioned him, as if to make amends, gentling his course to the bottom. Coolness became warmth, uncomfortable warmth, and then the sensation of temperature was swamped by a mounting breathlessness. A warning chimed in his head: *Don't inhale*. He could feel solid ground beneath him – the bottom of the pool. He sank down further, bending his knees all the way, and then he shot upward, toward the surface, fourteen feet above him. Only when he could wave a hand freely in front of his face, proving that he was no longer underwater, did he allow himself to take a breath of air. *No time!* He clambered over the side of the pool and rolled himself onto the stone coping.

He did not bother to look up at the window from which he had jumped. The gunmen there were equipped for close-quarters combat. Neither was a marksman, nor equipped with a distance-accurate rifle, and there were too many civilians in the pool area for a burst of automatic fire to be a permissible action.

With great effort he struggled to his feet. His entire lower body felt like a giant bruise. His muscles jellied, and no sooner was he upright than he sprawled to the ground. *No!* He would not give in. Adrenaline surged through his viscera, tightening every muscle fiber as if someone were twisting the pegs of a violin. He lurched into a run – he was not sure he could walk, but he could *run* – and found a small opening in the rhododendron hedge. His sodden clothing added at least ten pounds to the weight he had to carry, and – as he realized only when he nearly stepped into the path of a whizzing and, to him, noiseless car – he was deafened: Pool water had evidently filled both ear canals. His legs were now pincushions; he could not feel the asphalt underneath his feet: In place of physical sensation, tactile awareness, there was only a needling pain, and then pulses of searing heat.

Yet he had not been captured. Not yet. He had not been 'retrieved.' His adversaries had failed – so far.

Belknap darted across the busy road, testing the limits of a two- or three-second interval between vehicles – if he stumbled, took just a second longer than he hoped, he would have met the bumper of an oncoming van – and then through another intersection.

A block later, he reached a row of small houses with separate garages; most looked dark, shuttered, waiting for their owners to get home from work. Belknap scooted into a garage through an unlocked side door and stretched out behind a pile of tires. As his eyes adjusted to the gloom, he made out a silhouetted statuary of gas-powered gardening gizmos – a leaf-blower, a weed-whacker, a tiller with its tines plugged by ancient sod. Evidence of a fitful enthusiasm. The toys were no doubt purchased after a great deal of care and comparison shopping, used a couple of times, and left to gather dust. He inhaled the familiar smells of decaying tire rubber, motor oil, and tried to make himself comfortable. He would stay here until his clothes dried.

There were too many places he could have gone to make it rational for the retrieval team to stay in place, especially after the burst of gunfire and the unwanted attention it would attract. The team would disperse until the next sighting. Belknap simply had to stay still for the next six hours, with no companion but the pain, which assaulted him like a violent, whole-body toothache. Still, nothing was broken, nothing torn. Time would heal the bruising, and, as Belknap reviewed what had happened, he knew that the physical agony would be overtaken by the one thing that had always proved its equal: rage.

CHAPTER SIXTEEN

Los Angeles

'I'm sorry, sir,' said the burly black-clad man standing at the velvet ropes in front of the ultra-hip nightclub on Sunset Boulevard near Larrabee Street. He combined the functions of doorman and bouncer. 'There's a private party tonight.'

The Cobra Room was the most exclusive club in L.A., and it was his job to ensure that it stayed so. Its main habitués were celebrities and the very rich. The presence of gawkers, hangers-on, and wannabes could quickly make the environment uncomfortable for the clientele. The hulking doorman spent most of the evening repeating, with firm politeness, variations on the standard formula: a private function, no admittance. Only people who won the approval of his discerning gaze would be allowed in, whisked past the crowds of failed supplicants, and they were very much the exception.

'I'm sorry, miss,' the man said. 'Private function tonight. Can't let you in.' And: 'I'm sorry, sir. Private party. No admissions.'

'But I'm meeting a friend,' the would-be entrants pleaded, as if this ploy wasn't trotted out dozens of times each evening.

A brisk headshake. 'I'm sorry. No exceptions.'

A bleached blonde with a low-cut dress and knockoff Jimmy Choos dug through a tiny black purse, trying to get in with a tip. 'Thank you, no, ma'am,' the doorman preempted her. The hair was obviously a do-it-yourself job; a good salon would have produced more natural-looking results. 'You need to move along.'

The man who called himself Mr. Jones observed the

activities at the Cobra Room door for half an hour, from the tinted glass of a town car parked on the other side of the street and further down the block. Mr. Smith, his companion, had already prepared the ground for him. He glanced at his watch. He was wearing black thin-wale corduroys, a ribbed cotton sweater from Helmut Lang, a silk zippered jacket, vintage black sneakers. The costume – typical of the dressed-down yet lavishly expensive garb of L.A.'s glitterati – would not do the trick by itself, but it would not count against him. He had the driver drive around the block and pull up just in front of the Cobra Room. Then he donned a pair of Oakleys and walked casually toward the door.

The doorman's wide-spaced eyes missed little, but this was clearly a tough call. Suddenly, the blonde darted over to Mr. Jones.

'Omigod, you're Trevor Avery!' she squeaked. 'I've got to tell my girlfriends. We just *love* you.' She started to grip the man in the Helmut Lang sweater, clasping his arms in squealing excitement. 'Stay here for a sec! Please, oh, please!'

'Ma'am,' the doorman said in a warning tone.

'Don't you watch *Venice Beach*?' she asked the doorman, referring to a television show popular among teenagers.

'No, I don't,' the doorman said sternly.

'*Please*, couldn't you take a picture of us together with my cell-phone cam? That would be *soooo* awesome!'

Mr. Jones turned to the doorman. 'Hate when this happens,' he muttered.

'Step right in, sir,' the burly man said, unhooking the velvet rope from a brass stanchion and smiling at his new guest. The decision had become easy. '*You*, ma'am' – a stare that would freeze meat – 'need to move along. Now. Like I said, it's a private function.'

The blonde sullenly retreated, opening her little purse and no doubt fingering the hundred-dollar bill that Mr. Smith had slipped her.

Mr. Jones was in. As soon as his eyes adjusted to the dim lighting inside, he saw the L.A. developer Eli Little at one of the black vinyl booths. His white hair gleamed under the blood-red track lights. With him was a young film director who had just won a Sundance prize, an old-school studio exec, a big-time music mogul, and an actress who had her own HBO series. The rumors that connected the developer to organized crime made him only more alluring to Hollywood folk, who were fascinated by anything that savored of the dark side.

Mr. Jones looked genial as he crossed the small lounge space to get a better look at his target. The developer, who was usually protected by a veritable cordon of security, was expansive in his gestures, relaxed, and very comfortable, like a fish in its own aquarium.

He had no idea that a shark had just entered the tank.

Lower Manhattan, New York

Andrea Bancroft sat at the diner sipping at the third cup of the dishwater-weak coffee that was grudgingly sloshed from the Pyrex carafe. She kept her eyes peeled on the sidewalk. Aside from the diner's signage – the swooping Greengrove Diner logo; an open plastic-laminated menu taped to one side of the door – it was easy to see through the plate glass. This wasn't a place she would have selected for privacy, but Belknap had his own ways.

She was rattled; there was no way to hide it. She was entering another world. A world of ruses and snares, a world where guns were casually drawn and casually fired. A world where life was cheap and truths were costly. She noticed that she was clutching her coffee cup with a white-knuckled grip. *Keep it together*, she urged herself. *Keep it together.* It was Belknap's world, and he knew how to function there. But it was not her world.

Or was it?

Uncertainty and fear battered at her like ocean waves against a pier. Could she trust Belknap? Could she afford not to? She remembered the way he had inserted himself between her and the gunman, rescuing her with his actions and his words. Yet he was the one they were after – and why was that? His answers had been maddeningly vague, but amounted to the claim that he had been set up. Which was what suspects always maintained. She had no reason to believe him. But for some reason, she did.

And what about Paul Bancroft? Could the foundation really be involved with the kidnapping that Belknap was obsessed with? Paul had assured her that the Theta Group's sole purpose was to do good. And for some reason she believed him, too.

'I'm surprised you showed up.' Belknap's voice.

She turned around, and saw that he had slipped into the banquette next to her. 'You mean, after all the fun times we had together?' Her words were sarcastic, but her heart wasn't in it.

'Something like that.' He shrugged. 'How long have you been nursing that cuppa joe?'

'Nursing? I'd say the coffee was definitely beyond resuscitation.' She took another sip. 'I didn't see you come in.'

Belknap head-pointed toward the back, the employees-only door. 'I'm hoping nobody else did, either.' His tone was impassive, almost smug, and yet Andrea could tell that he was keyed up; his eyes darted around the place, swept across the sidewalk outside, roamed across the other table and banquettes inside. *God sees the little sparrow fall*: The words of the old spiritual came to her. She had an idea that he would see the little sparrow fall, too.

'What happened at the hotel – I'm sorry, I can't even wrap my mind around it.' She wanted to add, *Thank God you're all right*, but held back. She did not know why.

'The hotel reservations were under a certified field name,' Belknap said in his low, gruff voice. He was wearing a knit polo shirt, olive-green, and she could see the outlines of his heavy muscles beneath the fabric. 'A field legend. Protects you from your enemies who come from the outside world. It doesn't protect you from your enemies *inside* the agency. This was an official Consular Operations retrieval team.'

Another sip of the hot, flavorless fluid. 'That guy in the back of the hotel. I really thought he'd shoot me. People like that . . .' She shook her head.

'A special-access-program operative. S.A.P. is way beyond the usual security classifications. S.A.P. means nothing leaks beyond the immediate players. With some S.A.P.s, there could be five or six people in the entire government who know about it.'

'This includes the president?'

'Sometimes yes. Sometimes no.'

'So those are the kinds of trigger-happy brutes you're up against. I guess I'm starting to have some sympathy for you.'

Belknap shook his head. 'Maybe you shouldn't. You saw some S.A.P. brutes in action, and you were appalled.'

'Damn right,' she put in sharply.

'Whereas the fact is I'm one of them myself. Just not right now.'

'But – '

'It's best that you know exactly what I am. I've done what they were doing. I could have been any one of them.'

'Which raises an obvious question. If your own colleagues don't trust you, why the hell should I?'

'I never said they didn't trust me.' His slate eyes appeared almost guileless. 'Their job was to hogtie me and put me into a cage. That doesn't mean they've decided I'm un-trustworthy. For all they know, maybe it's because I'm *too* trustworthy. They're not the ones who make the decisions. They're the ones who carry out the decisions. I've got no hard feelings toward them. Like I say, I've *been* them. Only difference is, I'd probably have done the tracking solo. Possibly the capture, too. And I've have done it right.'

'Tracking?'

'It's what I do, Andrea. I find people. Usually people who don't want to be found.'

'You good at it?'

'Probably the best,' he said. There was nothing boastful about the way he said it. He could have been reporting his height or date of birth.

'Your colleagues share that assessment.'

He nodded. 'They call me the Hound. Like I say, it's what I do.'

A wave of cheap drugstore fragrance announced the arrival of the waitress. Strawberry-haired and slender, except for her pointing, melon-heavy breasts; the shirt of her uniform was open to the third button. 'What would you like?' she asked him.

'Benny in the back?'

'Yup.'

'Ask him to make the thing he does with the French toast stuffed with mascarpone,' Belknap said.

'Oh, that's *fantastic*,' the waitress shrilled. 'I've had that. I'll ask him, okay?'

'You do that,' Belknap told her, winking. 'We'll have two.' Then he spoke to her in a low voice. Andrea couldn't make it all out – something about a guy he was trying to avoid, about how she could do him a solid.

'I'll keep an eye out,' she returned in a low voice, and winked. Her tongue was coral-pink in the corner of her mouth, like a sugar rosebud on a cupcake.

'You have a gift for making friends,' Andrea said, surprised that she sounded slightly nettled when she spoke. She couldn't have been jealous, could she?

'We don't have a lot of time,' Belknap said. His eyes seemed to linger on the waitress, but when he turned to her, he was all business. For some reason, Andrea felt disappointed. Quietly she relayed her experiences of the previous day. The muscled operative listened without expression. Only when she told him about the phone call to Dubai did he lift an eyebrow.

'So what's your explanation?' Andrea asked. 'What's to say you're not full of shit?'

'A trunk-line redirect. If they've got access to the ISDN computers, it would take all of thirty seconds. How much time elapsed between when you gave them the number and when you placed the call?'

'Longer than that,' Andrea allowed. 'Christ, I don't know

what to think. It isn't as if I have any better reasons for believing your story.'

'It happens to be true.'

'So you say.' She looked down, peering into her coffee cup as if it contained secrets. 'And what he told me about my mother – it's perfectly possible. More plausible than the alternatives, rationally speaking. What haunts me is, what if he's right, and all I'm doing is shadowboxing with figments of my own imagination? I don't even know what I'm doing here with you.'

Belknap nodded. 'You shouldn't be. Rationally speaking.'

'Then you agree.'

'You've been given good, solid, well-crafted explanations. Why not take them at face value? Believe everything they told you and live a long, happy life. Buy that loft in Tribeca you told me about. You ought to be talking to an interior designer right now, talking about swatches and samples. Instead you're talking to me.' He leaned forward. 'Why do you think that is?'

Andrea felt a prickling on her face. Her mouth was dry.

'Because,' Belknap pressed, 'you didn't *believe* him.'

She took a sip from her glass of ice water, and the sip turned into a long gulp. The glass was empty when she put it down.

'There's something we've got in common. A second sense for when things only *seem* to add up. They gave you a sound, orderly explanation. But somehow it didn't wash with you. You're not sure what's wrong with it. You're just sure that something is.'

'Please don't pretend you know me.'

'I'm just saying. A lot of true things are unreasonable. You know this. Someone tried to give you a logical explanation of what had been preying on your mind. And the fact is that, on some intuitive level, you're still not convinced. Because otherwise you wouldn't be here, drinking the worst coffee in lower Manhattan.'

'Maybe,' she replied shakily. 'Or maybe I was feeling grateful.'

'You know better than that. If it wasn't for me, you wouldn't have needed rescuing in the first place.'

Andrea studied Belknap's face, tried to imagine how he would look to her if they were meeting for the first time. She would see someone who was ruggedly handsome, strapping, and, yes, intimidating. His dense, heavy muscles weren't the kind produced by a health-club membership; they weren't toned, they were knotted, muscles for work, not for display. And there was something else about him, too: the willed control of someone who could, if he chose, go out of control. A brute? Yes, in some sense. But more than a brute. There was something forceful about his very personality.

'How come every time I try to think well of you,' she said after a while, 'you try to set me straight?'

'There's a lake, and its waters are very deep and very dark. And your boat is very small. And you're told that the only things in the lake are nice little fish. But one some level, you don't believe this. You think there's something big and scary down there.'

'A lake,' Andrea mused. 'Like Inver Brass. So what do you think? Has Paul Bancroft somehow reconstituted Inver Brass? Is *he* Genesis?'

'What do you think?'

'I wonder.'

'Look, you've got to assume that everything he's told you is a lie.'

'Except I don't,' Andrea said. 'It would be overly obvious, in a way, and Paul Bancroft isn't an obvious man. I think a lot of what he's told me is truthful. Truthful, maybe, in ways we're not fully capable of grasping.'

'You're talking about a flesh-and-blood human being, not some sort of Greek god,' Belknap snapped.

'You don't know him.'

'Don't be so sure. I've spent twenty-five years hunting down all kinds of assholes. When you get down to brass tacks, they're pretty similar.'

Andrea shook her head. 'He's not like anybody you've ever known. You need to start with that.'

'Spare me. I bet he puts his trousers on one leg at a time.'

'Oh, real subtle, Todd,' she said, with an odd surge of bitterness. Andrea felt herself flushing; she realized it was the first time she had called him by his first name. She wondered whether he had picked up on it, too. 'Paul Bancroft is the most brilliant man either one of us is ever likely to meet. When he was at the Institute for Advanced Study, he used to chat with world-historical figures – Kurt Gödel, Robert Oppenheimer, Freeman Dyson, even Albert Einstein, for God's sakes – and they talked to him as one of them. They spoke as equals.' She paused, but only to take a breath. 'Maybe you find it comforting to reduce other men down to your own level, but you really don't know how ridiculous you sound when you talk about Paul Bancroft like that.' She was surprised at how heatedly she spoke. Maybe she was still hoping that Bancroft would be vindicated – that her fears and suspicions would prove to be misplaced. But if they weren't, and if Belknap made the mistake of underestimating Paul Bancroft, he was already lost.

'Calm the hell down,' Belknap said. 'Whose side are you on, anyhow? It sounds like the Great Brain has gotten to you. He must know what buttons to push.'

'Screw you,' Andrea said. 'Did you take in anything I told you about the Theta Group?'

'I took it all in, and it gave me the creeps, okay? Find *that* comforting?'

'Inasmuch as it suggests you're in at least distant contact with reality, yes.'

Belknap's countenance darkened. 'You're describing some mastermind with more money than Scrooge McDuck and some wacko visionary plan for the betterment of mankind. People like that usually do more damage that people who set out to do wrong.'

Andrea nodded slowly, relenting. In truth, it was Dr. Bancroft's very utopianism that chilled her most. What Belknap said, in his crude way, wasn't far from the mark. The grand theory, the big idea: They became motive forces of history. For the sake of a paper utopia, thousands of Peruvians had been slaughtered by Sendero Luminoso; millions had perished on the killing fields of Cambodia. Idealism had killed as many as hatred. 'I'm not sure what he wouldn't do if he thought the ends justify it,' she said.

'Exactly,' said Belknap. 'My bet is he's crossed a line, probably did it a long time ago. He's rigging the race, he's stuffing the ballot boxes of human destiny. And, just like you say, he'd do anything, anything at all, that his theories tell him might be justified.'

'But I still don't think he's Genesis.'

'You have no grounds for saying that.'

'You think I'm wrong?'

'No,' he said, his eyes roaming the street outside. 'I think you're right. I also think he's part of the picture somehow. There's some kind of connection here – friend or foe, collaborator or nemesis or something else entirely. But there *is* a connection. Probably a complex web of connections. And one way or another, Jared Rinehart got tangled in that web. Maybe your mother, too.'

Andrea shuddered. 'But if my cousin isn't Genesis, who is?'

Belknap's gaze swept across their surroundings again. 'When I was in Washington, a friend of mine told me a few things about Genesis,' he said slowly. 'They think he may be an Estonian. A mogul, the kind of gangster who became a billionaire when the state industries were privatized. More than that, he's someone who seized control of a hefty chunk of the Soviet arsenal. We're talking about a major-league arms dealer.'

'An arms dealer?' That sounded wrong to her. She worried that Belknap was, once again, reducing the adversary to his own level.

'We're talking about the kind of person who has tentacles across the world. A person with a truly global reach, and global ambition, okay? This is a business that crosses national borders as easily as the birds in the sky, the fish in the sea. Who would be better placed? That's our Genesis.'

'And the Theta Group? Maybe you should ask your

friend about how the Theta Group might fit into this.'

Belknap reacted as if he had been slapped. 'I can't.' Breathing hard, he explained, 'She was killed in front of me.'

'Oh, my God,' she said softly. 'I'm so sorry.'

'There's somebody else who's going to be sorry one day.' Belknap's voice was arctic.

'Genesis.'

A fractional nod. 'Maybe the Theta Group has been trying to bring him down. Maybe they want to join forces. Who the hell knows? One way or the other, I'm going to hunt the bastard down. Because he'll know where Jared Rinehart is. Sooner rather than later, I'm going to get my hands around the neck of this monster, and I'm going to squeeze, and if I don't like what I hear, I'm going to wring his neck like a chicken's.' He held his beefy hands before him, his fingers bent at the knuckles.

'A velociraptor's, maybe.'

'Doesn't matter. Every vertebrate's got a neck.'

'Estonia's a long way away,' she said.

'Genesis is a globetrotter. Like the Bancroft Foundation itself. Makes them natural allies. Or adversaries.'

'You think Genesis has confederates inside the foundation?'

'I think it's likely. I'll have a better idea when I get back from Estonia.'

'You'll let me know, right?'

'Fair's fair,' he said. 'Meanwhile, stay the hell away from any on-the-lam operatives you come across. We're nothing but trouble.'

'So I've noticed. But I'm going to be doing some digging of my own. See, I talked to a friend of mine who works for the New York State Department of Taxation and Finance.'

'And this is someone who has friends?'

'The foundation is chartered in New York, so I figured that paperwork had to be filed with this department.'

Belknap craned his head once more, evidently peering for anything out of the ordinary. Had he noticed something? 'And?' he prompted.

'I didn't strike gold or anything. But he said that there would be decades' worth of paperwork in storage.'

'In storage where?'

'It's all in an iron-mountain facility in Rosendale, New York,' Andrea said.

'So what? Fake papers get filed all the time.'

'No question. It's different, though, when you're dealing with private filings that are audited closely. These will be authentic records, and they'll have to be truthful, at least up to a point. They won't contain the whole truth, obviously. But there may be enough solid data points here to start with.'

The waitress brought two plates. The special French toast he had ordered. 'Sorry for the delay,' she said. 'Benny went across the street to get some mascarpone. He didn't want to let you down.'

'Benny has never let me down,' said Belknap.

'She thinks you're a cop, doesn't she?' Andrea asked after the waitress left.

'She thinks I'm some kind of cop, she's not sure which. A federal investigator, maybe. I've always kept it vague. Point is, they like cops over here.'

'Because they don't have anything to hide.'

'Or because they do.'

'So Doug is going to help me get access to this place in Rosendale.'

'Ooh, paperwork.'

'Somewhere in the past of this foundation, there's got to be a chink. A giveaway. A clue. Some weakness that can be exploited. Something. There's always something.'

'Yes, in books and in movies. In real life, there's often nothing. Hate to be the one to break it to you. Stories are one thing. Life's another.'

Andrea shook her head. 'I think we live by stories. We organize our lives around stories. You ask me who I am, I tell you a story. But stories change. I told myself one story about my mother. When that story started to fall apart, I started to fall apart. You have a story about Jared Rinehart, about all he's done for you – and that story makes it imperative that you rescue him even at the cost of your own life. There's no experience outside of narrative.'

'You ever think you spent too many years in the classroom?' Belknap looked at her with amusement. 'I owe my life to Jared Rinehart. And that's that. Don't try to complicate it any more than that.' He gave her a stern look. 'Try the French toast.'

'Why? *I* didn't order it. This is such typical male behavior. Imposing dominance through food.' She blinked. 'Christ, I *am* turning into a college-town shrew.'

Suddenly he stiffened. 'Time to go.'

'Says who?' Andrea demanded. Then she caught the expression on his face and felt chilled.

'FedEx guy across the street.' Belknap spoke through gritted teeth. 'Making a delivery.'

'So?'

'Wrong time of day. FedEx doesn't make deliveries at four o'clock.' He put cash on the table and stood up. 'Follow me.'

Belknap gave the waitress a broad wink, then strode through a swinging door, past the kitchen, and out the back, a small paved area where a stack of recyclable bottles was awaiting pickup. A little beyond was a narrow alleyway. They squeezed past a Dumpster and made their way to an adjacent street. At the end of the block, Belknap craned his head around. Then, seemingly reassured, he bent down and keyed open the door of a dark-green Mercury. 'Get in,' he said.

Moments later they had turned the corner and, after a few more turns, blended in with the traffic on West Street.

'Your car was parked at a fire hydrant,' Andrea said finally.

'I know.'

'How did you know it wouldn't be ticketed or towed?'

'You didn't notice the ticket book on the dashboard. But someone who worked for the city would have. Means it's a cop car. You leave it alone.'

'This is a cop car?'

'No, and it's not a real ticket book, either. But it always does the trick.' He glanced at her. 'You holding up okay?'

'I'm fine. Stop asking me that.'

'Whoa. Why don't you save the "I am woman, hear me roar" thing for some other occasion? I get it. You are strong. You are invincible. You are woman.'

'Okay, I'm scared out of my wits. How the hell did your buddies – ?'

'Not my buddies, I don't think. Yours.'

'What?'

'Didn't have the hallmarks of a Cons Ops dragnet. Looked more like a stand-and-survey deal. My guys would have used a U.S. Postal Service truck, and there'd be more than one.'

'So what are you saying?'

'My guess is, after your visit to One Terrapin, your colleagues have decided to keep an eye on you. Nonviolent monitoring. Keep tabs on an uncertain situation.'

'I was careful,' she protested. 'I had an eye out. I don't know how they could have tracked me here.'

'They're professionals. You're not.'

Andrea blushed. 'I'm sorry.'

'Don't be sorry. Just live and learn. Or, more to the point, learn and live. You want to get to Rosendale, right?'

'I was going to overnight at a hotel nearby.'

'I'll take you there.'

'It's a two-hour drive,' she warned.

He shrugged. 'The car has a radio,' he said.

But they never turned it on as they motored over the Major Deegan Expressway north and onto Interstate 87. The car was as anonymous a model as he could get his hands on; nobody was following them, he assured her, and nobody had any reason to anticipate their movements, she told herself.

'We could have been killed yesterday,' she said as he adjusted his rearview mirror for what seemed the tenth time. 'It's stupid, but I can't get it out of my head. We could have died.'

'You don't say,' he returned heavily.

Andrea stared at him, again trying to make sense of the man. He was all coiled muscle and rage, a visage that conveyed shades of frustration and anger, thick fingers, thickened nails – hands that had experienced a great deal of punishment, and surely had meted out no little punishment as well. He seemed hopelessly crude and unsubtle, and yet . . . there was also an acuity of perception here, an acuity that had so far eluded her. He was rawboned, coarse, blunt, and yet wily. What did they call him – the Hound, wasn't that it? She could see it. He had a certain canine ferocity.

'So something like this happens – a close call, a near miss, the grim reaper flashing his scythe – and you think, what, 'Yes, I like the way I lived my life.' Or you think something else?'

Belknap turned to face her. 'I don't think.'

'You don't.'

'That's right. Top operative's secret to success. Don't think too much.'

Andrea fell silent. He wasn't auditioning for the Algonquin Round Table after all. She stole another look, noticed how the fabric of his shirt stretched around the bicep of his upper arms, how the hand that lightly grasped the steering wheel seemed at once battered and powerful. She wondered, idly, what he would have made of Brent Farley. The muscle-bound operative might have earned Brent's flared-nostril contempt, but then he could probably have reduced Brent to jelly by clasping his hand too hard. She smiled at the thought.

'What?' he prompted.

'Nothing,' she said a beat too quickly.

What did he make of her? Some spoiled Connecticut lady in over her head? Some overgrown grad student only recently out of Birkenstocks?

'You know,' she said, a few minutes later, 'I'm not really a Bancroft.'

'You explained.'

'My mother – she wanted to protect me from all that.

She'd been hurt, didn't want me to get hurt. But there was part of being a Bancroft that she really valued. That's what I never understood. That foundation meant something to her. I wish we could have talked about it.'

Belknap nodded but said nothing.

She was thinking out loud, and she doubted he was even taking it in, but neither did he seem to mind. Anyway, it was marginally better than talking to herself. 'Paul said he loved her. 'In a way,' he said. But I think he did. She was beautiful, but not the porcelain-doll kind of beautiful. She was a live wire. Irreverent. Funny. High-spirited. And troubled.'

'The drinking.'

'But I really thought she put it behind her. It started with Reynolds. But a year or so after they got divorced, she made a pledge. And that was that. I never saw her with a drink after that. Then again, there was a lot I never knew about her. So much I wish I could ask her.' She felt her eyes grow moist, tried to blink it away.

He gave her a stony gaze. 'Sometimes the questions are more important than the answers.'

'Tell me something. Do you ever get scared?'

Another stony gaze.

'I'm serious.'

'All animals know fear,' Belknap said. 'You see a mouse or chipmunk or a hog or a fox. Does it think? Beats me. Does it have self-consciousness? I'd guess not. Does it laugh? Doubt it. Can it feel joy? Who can say? But one thing you know. You know it experiences fear.'

'Yes.'

'Fear is like pain. Pain is productive if it tells you you've touched a hot burner or you've picked up a sharp object. On the other hand, if it's a chronic condition, just feeding on itself, it's not doing you any good. It's just eroding your ability to function. Fear can save your life. Fear can also destroy your life.'

Andrea nodded slowly. 'It'll be the next exit,' she said after a while.

Three miles later, they approached the Clear Creek Inn,

where she had made reservations for the evening. She felt a jolt of terror, blinked, and saw why. Standing in the parking lot, leaning against a car, was the unmistakable bulk of the nameless man from the Bancroft Foundation.

Christ, no! Her heart started to hammer, fear and outrage vying within her. They wanted to intimidate her, she realized, and the realization made her indignant.

'Keep driving,' she said in a level voice. She was scared, yes, but she was resolute, too. She would *not* be intimidated. Her mother deserved more. She deserved more, dammit.

He complied without a moment's hesitation. Only after they had returned to the interstate did he give her a questioning look.

'I thought I saw someone I recognized.'

'Please don't tell me you made reservations under your own name,' Belknap said in a rush.

'No, no – I used my mom's maiden name instead.' She had a sinking feeling even as she said the words.

'Like *that's* going to throw them a curve. And then you probably gave them your own credit card.'

'Oh my God. I didn't even think.'

'Jesus Christ, woman,' Belknap said. 'We've been through this. Would you use common sense?'

Andrea massaged her temples with her forefingers. 'I'm in a car with someone who may well be a dangerous enemy of the state, someone the United States government is trying to apprehend. Exactly where does common sense come into this?'

'Don't talk.' Belknap's voice was like the growling of a double bass.

'And interrupt the patriarchal edict of silence? Never.'

'You want to pull over and have a consciousness-raising session? Be my guest. I'm sorry you're stuck with me. I'm sure Simone de Beauvoir would be more your speed, but she doesn't seem to be available.'

'Simone de Beauvoir?'

'She's – '

'I know who she is. I'm just surprised you do.'

'When I'm not rereading the SIG-Sauer owner's manual, you know . . .' He shrugged his bulky shoulders.

'Whatever. Listen, I just – oh, hell, I don't know.'

'The one true thing you've said for some time.' He reached into his trouser band and pulled out an oblong object; she flinched, and he gave her another look. It was, she realized, a cell phone.

Todd Belknap dialed the Clear Creek Inn. 'I'm calling for Ms. Parry,' he said, in a voice that sounded somehow servile, almost effeminate. 'No, I realize she hasn't checked in yet. She's asked me to let you know that she's been delayed, and won't be arriving until quite late. Around one in the morning. Could you please hold the room? Yes? Thank you.' He clicked off.

She was going to ask him why, but hazily saw the wisdom in it: If there was someone stationed to look for her, it was better that the person remain in a place where she definitely wasn't going to be.

'Listen and learn, okay?'

Andrea shook her head miserably. 'I know I need to get used to this. But I wish to God I didn't have to.'

The look Belknap shot her seemed almost pitying. Suddenly, the car slewed across a lane and Belknap took an exit, ending up at a slummy-looking roadside motel. He turned to her, and the halogen light outside the motel cast a harsh, raking light on his square jaw and blocky features, his deep chest and callused hands and a gaze that, most of the time, barely registered her existence except as a convenience, an instrument in his own investigation. 'Here's where you sleep tonight.'

'If I get fleas . . .'

'Fleas you can get rid of. Bullet holes, not so easily.'

He guided her to the long Formica counter, behind which an Indian man stood on a stool.

'Can I help you?' the man asked. There was more than a trace of Hindi in his voice.

'One night,' Belknap said.

'No problem.'

'Great,' said Belknap. He spoke in a rush. 'The name's Boldizsar Csikszentmihalyi. B-o-l-d-i-z-s-a-r. C-s-i-k-s-z-e-n-t-m-i-h-a-l-y-i.'

The clerk stopped writing after a few letters. 'I'm sorry, I didn't quite . . .'

Belknap gave him a reassuring grin. 'Nobody ever does. It's Hungarian, I'm afraid. Here, let me write it all out for you. Believe me, I'm used to it.'

Reluctantly the clerk ceded him the guest registry. With a flourish, Belknap wrote out the name. 'Room forty-three?' He saw the key hanging on the key rack behind the clerk.

'That's fine, but I can – '

'Not to worry,' Belknap said. 'I used to manage a hotel myself.' Making a show of checking his wallet, he pretended to write the number of his driver's license in the adjoining box. Barely lifting his pen from the paper, he filled out the time of arrival, the number of occupants, a credit card number. Then he returned the clipboard to the Indian man with a cheerful wink. 'It's the same everywhere.'

'I can see that,' said the clerk.

And we'll be paying with cash. Eighty-nine plus the tax comes to 96.57, we'll round to a hundred if you don't mind.' He immediately leafed five twenty-dollar bills on the counter in front of the clerk. 'Now, if you'll pardon an unseemly rush, my good wife is bursting – she couldn't bring herself to use the john at the gas station. So if you'll get us a room key . . .'

'Oh, my goodness, right away.' The man handed him the key, and Andrea found herself miming the condition Belknap had described.

Moments later they were in a room, alone. The highway traffic sounded like a rainstorm, surging and ebbing. She could smell stale cigarette smoke in the room, the hair pomades of strangers, the chemical scent of cleaners.

'My hat would be off if I wore a hat,' Andrea said to Belknap. 'You're a bullshit artist of the first order.'

'A LeRoy Neiman rather than a Leonardo. I mean, let's not exaggerate.'

'You're a man of many surprises,' Andrea said, and took a

deep breath. Now she could smell him, the liquid soap he had used on his hands and face at their last rest stop, the laundry detergent of his shirt, and somehow it lessened the bleak foreignness of the dimly lighted room.

'A pretty crappy place for an heiress, huh?'

'I keep forgetting,' she said dryly. But it was true.

'Best that you do,' Belknap said soberly. 'For the time being. That money is a homing beacon. If the Theta security people have anything on the ball, they'll know about any withdrawal you make, and they'll know precisely where you were when you made it. It's not like you're using a numbered account in Liechtenstein. So until things are sorted out, consider it radioactive.'

'Root of all evil. Got it.'

'This isn't a joke, Andrea.'

'I said I got it,' Andrea replied, a little testily. She didn't meet his eyes. 'So what now? Are you going to take a load off your battered feet? Linger a bit before hitting the road?' She knew it was irrational: Her association with him had put her into jeopardy, and yet she somehow felt safer when she was around him.

Belknap, however, took her invitation as mere sarcasm. 'Is that what you're afraid of?' The strapping operative shook his head. 'No worries. I'm out of here.

That's not what I meant, she thought. But what *had* she meant? Did she even know?

He stepped out of the door, then, before closing it, turned to her, his slate eyes intent. 'You find something I need to know, you tell me soon as you can. I'll do the same for you. Deal?'

'Deal,' Andrea echoed in a hollow voice. The door clicked shut and, through the window, she watched the man lope back to the car; they agreed that it would be safest for her to call for a taxicab in the morning. She somehow felt at a loss. He was, she realized, a dangerous man who brought trouble in his wake. And yet when she was around him, she had felt safer. Again, she fully appreciated that it made no sense, but that was how she felt.

The density of all that battered flesh, the scar tissue, the muscle that seemed almost to drop over his upper body like a poncho of hard flesh, the quick, alert eyes, vigilant to every menace. She still found herself choking on fear; he had somehow worked past it, was able to use fear. Or so she imagined. Tomorrow, though, she would be off to the archives, where the greatest risk was surely tedium. What else could befall her? Death by a thousand paper cuts?

Better get some sleep, she told herself. *You have a long day tomorrow.*

From her motel window, she watched the taillights of his car grow smaller and smaller as he drove off, until they were nothing more than pinpricks, and then nothing more than a memory.

CHAPTER SEVENTEEN

Todd Belknap was thirty thousand feet over the Atlantic, but his mind kept returning to his last sight of the Bancroft woman at that roadside lodge. There was, he knew, a good chance that they'd never see each other again. It would prove to be another brief encounter in a lifetime of brief encounters, if stormier than most. He had not opened the car windows right away as he drove off from the motel. He could still smell her light, citrusy fragrance in the vehicle, and he did not want the night air to push it away just yet. It somehow kept a damp feeling of despondency at bay. Dimly, he recognized that he was developing inappropriate and unreciprocated feelings toward Andrea Bancroft. They were not feelings he welcomed; too many people he let into his life ended up dead. Violence shadowed him, and, with uncanny sadism, picked off those he held closest to his heart. Yvette's voice came to him like a distant echo: *Where there is beauty, one finds death.*

Andrea had asked him whether he felt fear; right then, he was feeling fear for her.

The sleep that finally overtook him offered little respite. Images crowded his unconscious, as vaporous as wraiths, and then as solid as real-time experience. He was back in Calí, reliving something that had happened half a decade earlier as if it were happening now. The sounds, the smells, the sights. The fear.

The mission was to intercept a truckload of weaponry en route to a cartel of Colombian narcoterrorists. But the targets had been tipped off. One of their informants, it appeared, had been playing both sides. Men with bandoliers of .308-caliber full-jacketed rounds suddenly appeared from the back of a flatbed, spraying bullets at the positions where the Americans had been lying in wait. None of them was prepared for this. Belknap had been laying low in an ordinary sedan, unarmored – and now the car was being perforated with explosive bursts of the high-velocity rounds.

Then – from someplace behind him – Belknap made out the distinctive round of a long rifle. There were *crack*s, spaced perhaps two seconds apart, and the torrential buzzing of the machine guns ceased. A glance at his cracked rearview mirror told the story: Each of the Colombian gunmen had fallen. Four gunmen, their torsos still draped with bandoliers. Four head shots.

Silence had never been so welcome.

Belknap craned his head to the roadside area where the rifle shots had been fired. Saw, outlined against the darkening sky, a lean, almost elongated figure holding a scoped rifle. A pair of binoculars hung from a strap around his neck.

Pollux.

He approached with his long stride, swiftly assessed the situation, and then turned to his friend.

'I have to say, my heart's in my throat,' Rinehart told him.

'Imagine how *I'm* feeling,' Belknap said, unembarrassed by his gratitude.

'You saw it, too, did you? Amazing, isn't it! A flame-rumped tanager. I'm *positive* – the black head, the short beak, the incredible red oval on the wing. I even got a glimpse of the yellow breast.' He extended a hand, helped Belknap out of the car. 'You look skeptical, my friend. Well, I'd show you, if only our Colombian friends hadn't made such a racket. I swear, they've flushed every finch in earshot. What were they thinking?'

Belknap couldn't stop himself from smiling. 'What are you even doing here, Jared?'

Later, Belknap figured out what had happened: The operation's B team had taken a wrong turn, reported their delay to the Calí station; Rinehart, monitoring the situation from the local consulate, had feared the worst, that the key informant wasn't just incompetent, but treacherous. Yet that wasn't the explanation Rinehart had given at the time.

Instead, he simply shrugged and said, 'Where else can you hope to find a flame-rumped tanager?'

Now Belknap opened his eyes, peered through the fog of slumber, felt the stream of air from the nozzle overhead, fingered his lap belt, and remembered where he was. He was on a chartered jet that was taking the Empire State Chorus to an international music festival in Tallinn, Estonia. Todd Belknap – no, he was Tyler Cooper now – was tagging along as an official with the State Department's cultural-exchange program. Belknap's old ally and former colleague – 'Turtle' Lydgate – knew the chorus master somehow and had arranged it. Lydgate had pointed out that chartered flights were less carefully monitored than those of the international carriers – and that, it being the week of Estonia's annual choral festival, a goodly number of such chartered planes would be arriving at Tallinn, Estonia's capital. Among the chorus members, there were vague intimations that the cultural-programs officers at State might provide funding for the chorus as an item in a new 'civil society and the arts' initiative. They were to treat him as an honorary member of the chorus. In the event, they were both courteous and intimidated in his presence, which suited Belknap fine.

He was following new rules: The near miss in Raleigh had jolted him into proper caution. No government-authorized documents any longer. He would have to dig into his cache of truly off-the-book identity papers. All deep-cover agents he knew had them – not because they had plans to live off the grid, or to defect, but simply because paranoia came with the job. 'Tyler Cooper' was one of Belknap's best-hidden and best-crafted legends, and tonight that was who Belknap was.

He tried to return to sleep, but over the sound of the engines, he heard – oh, God, more of their infernal singing.

The chorus master, Calvin Garth, had a helmet of orangey Grecian Formulated hair, an oddly full mouth, plump and delicate hands, and a little whinnying laugh. Worse, he was hell-bent on using the flying time for further rehearsals.

When some of the choristers groused, he whipped himself into a lather of indignation that would have done Patton proud and made Bear Bryant envious. 'Do you people realize what the stakes are?' he demanded, pacing down the aisle. 'You may think you're veterans of the touring circuit. Paris, Montreal, Frankfurt, Cairo, Rio, and so on – those concerts weren't the big time, kids. For the choral arts, places like those are strictly minor-league. All that was warmup, nothing more. No, *this* is the big time. *This* is the make-or-break. In just twenty-four hours, your audience will be – the whole entire world! Years from now, you'll realize this is probably the most important thing you ever did. This was the moment you stood up to sound the chords of freedom, and you *will* be heard.' His plump hands wriggled in the air, expressing the ineffable. 'Take it from me. You know I'll travel *anywhere* to keep up with what's happening in the vocal realm. Well, when it comes to the choral arts, the Estonians don't just *play*. What ice hockey is to Canadians, what soccer is to Brazilians – that's what the chorus is to Estonia. They are a deeply choral people. So folks, you "gotta *represent*". Jamal here knows what I'm talking about.' He gave a tender glance at a tenor with cornrows and a gold hoop earring. 'Tallinn is hosting choirs and choruses from fifty countries around the world. They're going to be singing from here' – he clutched his diaphragm – 'and from here' – he pounded his heart – 'and they're going to be giving their all. But guess what. I've heard what you ladies and gentlemen are capable of. Some may think I'm too much of a perfectionist. Well, listen up. I'm a bear because I *care*. We're arriving at the choral Olympics. And together' – an ethereal smile crept over his face – 'together we will make sweet music.' He plucked a piece of lint from his tan jacket.

When Belknap surfaced again, three hours later, the chorus master was still at it, cuing the altos and basses; the young men and women in the chorus were seated according to their section. '*Ar-tic-u-late*, ladies and gentlemen!' Garth implored. 'Now, again! This is the Empire State Chorus anthem, so it's got to be perfect!'

The passengers watched his downbeat carefully, and then began as cued:

> *We've traveled round the planet giving freedom a voice*
> *So the chorus of nations knows it's time to rejoice!*
> *Because freedom is part*
> *Of every human heart –*

The fussy man in the tan jacket cut them off. 'Not good enough! Eighty soloists put together do not a chorus make. Adam, Melissa, you're *ruining* the attack. This passage must be *allargando*. We're slowing, we're broadening – watch my right hand. Amanda, turn that frown upside down! Eduardo, you're pressing against the beat as if it were marked *affrettando*. I mean, really – is there someplace you need to be? Next week, Eduardo, you go back to work managing the perfume counter at Saks Fifth Avenue and then you can coast. But this week you represent the United States of America, am I right? This week you represent the Empire State Chorus. I meant what I said. You're all going to make *yourselves* proud. Eduardo, you're going to make your adopted country proud, too. I know it.'

'Adopted?' A voice of confusion from several rows back. 'I was born in Queens.'

'And what an amazing journey it's been, hasn't it?' Garth replied implacably. 'You inspire us all. And if you can just learn to come in on the downbeat with everybody else, you'll soon be singing in the world capital of the choral arts. Speaking of which, we need to do one more run-through of the Estonian national anthem. "My Native Land." That's part of the program, too, remember.' He hummed a snatch of melody. His voice was reedy, nasal, and unpleasant. *Those who can't sing*, Belknap decided, *lead choruses*. The sopranos started in:

> *Mu isamaa, mu õnn ja rõõm,*
> *Kui kaunis oled sa!*

My native land, my joy, delight,
How fair thou art and bright!

Belknap suddenly sat up, his heart pummeling in his chest. It was the draggy, marchlike tune that the corpulent Omani princeling had sung in his drunken way. He struggled to remember the context. Something about how Ansari had begun to lose control of his arms network, something about *new management*. The drunken Omani had pretended to be a conductor. *New maestro* – that was something he had said, too.

The Ansari network had fallen into the hands of an Estonian. An Estonian who, if Robbins's intelligence was accurate, had already seized control of a vast Cold War arsenal. Genesis? Or merely one of Genesis's powerful confederates?

I'm coming for you, Belknap thought grimly. *The Hound has caught your scent.*

A long time passed before the operative got to sleep again.

When the plane landed at the Tallinn airport, after nine hours in the air, Cal Garth jogged him awake. 'We're at the gate,' he said. 'And it's going to be a *madhouse* in there. You'll see – Estonia's annual choral festival is practically the Olympics of the vocal arts. Did you know that a majority of Estonians belong to a chorus? It's in their blood. More than two hundred thousand choristers congregate here, and Tallinn's population is only about half a million. So it's, like, this is our town. 'We're the Empire State Chorus, and we're keeping it real.'

As Belknap joined the others in a queue in front of a handful of overloaded customs-and-immigrations booths, he saw that Garth was not exaggerating. Around him were hundreds of foreign arrivals, just off full-to-capacity planes, some clutching sheet music, most having that unmistakable chorister's twinkle. It was already obvious to Belknap that the customs officers weren't seriously scrutinizing the flocking choristers; Tyler Cooper, ostensibly a member of the Empire State Chorus, was essentially waved through with no more than a cursory glance at his passport.

'It was something of a miracle,' Calvin Garth was telling him as he gathered his troops at the airport's ground-transportation deck, 'but we did manage to wangle a hotel room for you at the Reval, near the sea docks.'

'I'm much obliged,' Belknap said.

On the bus to the hotel, Garth sat next to Belknap. 'We were all going to stay at the Mihkli Hotel, but the Latvians stay there and they are *killers*,' he explained in his loudly voluble manner. 'I didn't want to worry about their ears being pressed against the walls when my people rehearse their numbers. I swear, you have no idea the level of deceit and trickery those Baltic chorus boys get up to. They'll put saltpeter in your tea if they think it'll give them a leg up in the competition. You can't be too careful.'

Belknap kept gazing out of the window, saw windmill farms give way to the familiar city-outskirt structures: gas stations, vast tanks of oil and natural gas. 'Sounds pretty sordid,' he grunted.

Tallinn Old Town was now coming into view. Clusters of red-roofed baroque buildings; spires and clock towers of churches and an old town hall, cafés with blue or red awnings. A blue streetcar swept past on tracks set into the cobblestone. He caught a glimpse of a furled Union Jack projecting over a bar. A sign below read NIMETA BAAR, with the words 'Jack Lives Here' inscribed in cursive on the plate glass. A feeble attempt at appealing to nascent Anglophilia. It was another instance of a phenomenon ubiquitous in developing regions: nostalgia without memory.

'You have no idea, Tyler,' Garth said in his penetrating nasal voice, gesticulating with his hands. 'The seamy underbelly of song. I've heard tales that would *shock* you.'

The young woman seated behind them got up and joined a friend a few rows away. Belknap wondered whether she found Garth's voice as headache-inducing as he did, especially after the wearying flight.

'That so?' Belknap said.

'Really, it's better that you remain innocent of what some of these folks get up to. But I have to counsel caution when

I'm talking to my people. I hate to act like a den mother, but the stakes, you know, the *stakes*!'

Belknap nodded gravely. There was something in his voice that made him wonder whether the chorus master wasn't pulling his leg. 'I'm very grateful to you, as I say, for accommodating me. Very helpful as we rethink our cultural-exchange programs . . .'

Garth looked around before he replied. 'Tertius asked me to do whatever I could for you,' he said quietly. It was an entirely different voice this time, devoid of the lilting vowels, the exaggerated animation, the hissing sibilants he had previously displayed. His hands were still, his face impassive. The transformation was startling.

'Appreciate it.'

Garth leaned closer to him, as if pointing out a feature of the cityscape. 'Don't know what your plans are, don't want to know.' Again, the voice was low and gruff. 'But bear in mind a couple of things. The Estonian intelligence service was set up and organized by the Soviets, like you'd guess. These days it's basically a wind-up clock without a key. Underfunded, understaffed. It's the NSP, the National Security Police, that you need to watch for. Better funded and more aggressive because of the organized-crime factor. Do not mess with them.'

'Understood.' Belknap found himself marveling. A globetrotting chorus master: the perfect cover – though for what? Lydgate had given him no hints, but Belknap could guess. He knew of retired spooks who had offered their services to a corporate clientele, helping firms clear the way for branch offices and subsidiaries in regions of the world where the rule of law wasn't exactly ascendant. Regions of the world where the kind of local knowledge possessed by an experienced spy could prove its worth. Such post-service careers were condoned by the official spymasters as long as certain boundaries were observed. 'Understood,' Belknap repeated.

'Then understand this, too.' Garth's voice was a quiet rumble, and his eyes grew hard. 'If you get burned, don't come to me. Because I don't want to know you.'

Belknap nodded gravely, then turned and gazed out the window again. The sky was a piercing blue; residents of a sun-starved nation were out, soaking up as much of it as they could, as if it could be banked and metered out during the long dark months. There was beauty here, and spirit, and history. Yet those long dark months made it a perfect incubator for those merchants of death, men who thrived on darkness and who profited through the convergence of two ineradicable features of human nature: violence and greed.

A darkened room, no illumination save what emanated from the screen. The soft crackle of a keyboard, caressed into service by agile fingertips. Strings of alphanumeric characters rippled from the keyboard to the screen and disappeared into cryptographic algorithms of extraordinary complexity before reconstituting themselves in far-off lands, to faraway recipients. Messages were sent and received. Directives were discharged and verified.

Digital instructions decanted money from one numbered account to another, pulled strings that would pull other strings that would pull yet other strings.

Once more, Genesis reflected on the simple key-cap labels: CONTROL. COMMAND.

But also OPTION. And, of course, SHIFT.

To shift the course of history would require more than a keystroke. But a string of keystrokes – the right ones, at the right times – might very well do it.

To know for sure would take time. A very long time. A very, *very* long time, really.

Perhaps as long as seventy-two hours.

Tallinn was more than 40 percent Russian – the residuum of empire. Russians were not just among the privileged classes; they were among the worst-off as well. Ethnic Russians were Mohawk-haired punk youths with safety pins in their cheeks; they were waiters in restaurants and redcaps in train stations; they were bureaucrats and businessmen. More than a handful were former apparatchiks who regarded the place as a picturesque province of a rightful Russian empire, and some – like the man Belknap set out to meet – were KGB men who had been stationed in Tallinn and, when they retired, found it a more restful prospect than the available alternatives.

Gennady Chakvetadze was a retired KGB man who was of Georgian ancestry but who grew up mainly in Moscow and had spent twenty years at the Tallinn station. He had started out a flaps-and-seals man, humble stuff, as befitted someone with a two-year degree from a provincial technical school and few connections with the nomenklatura. He had rubbery, peasant features: a bulbous nose, cheekbones invisible beneath pudgy, wide-spaced eyes, slightly recessed jaw. But only fools underestimated him because of his manners and appearance. He did not stay in flaps-and-seals for long.

When Belknap first made his acquaintance, they were on opposite sides of the great geopolitical divide known as the Cold War. Yet even then, the great states had common enemies: terrorism and insurgencies led by those who were hostile to the existing world order. Belknap had been looking for POSHLUST, the code name for a Soviet weapons scientist who had – on the 'informal' market – been selling information to the Libyans and other unlicensed customers. The Americans had no name, just the coded legend, but Belknap had the idea of following a Libyan delegation to a scientific conference at the resort town of Paldiski, thirty miles west of Tallinn. There Belknap recorded a rendezvous between a man whom he knew, from his facebook, to be a member of Mukhabarat, the Libyan state-security services, and a Russian physicist named Dmitri Barashenkov. During a panel discussion at which Bareshenkov was present, Belknap let himself into the physicist's room – the participants were put up at a slightly decrepit spa – and conducted a swift search. He found enough to confirm the identification. When he left the room, however, and made his way down the hallway, amber-and-white tiles set in discolored grout, he found himself accosted by a KGB man with peasant features and a look of exhaustion: Gennady. Later, Belknap realized that Gennady could have come with a full entourage but chose to appear alone in order to be less threatening. To the Soviets, POSHLUST was nothing less than an embarrassment – one of their own who had wandered off the reservation and was making side deals irrespective of state policies and official diplomacy. Their failure to have identified him over the past twenty-four months had been galling – as was the way they finally had done so.

'Would I be speaking to Mr. Ralph Cogan, science administrator from the Rensselaer Institute of Technology?' Chakvetadze had asked him.

Belknap had given him an uncomprehending look.

'G. I. Chakvetadze,' replied the Russian. 'But you can call me Gennady.' He smiled. 'At least if I can call you Todd. I think we are, in fact, colleagues. If you are an employee of RPI, I am with the Kiev Gas Company.' He put an arm around Belknap, who tensed. 'May I say thank you? On behalf of the Soviet people?'

'I have no idea what you're talking about,' Belknap replied.

'Come, we shall have tea in the lobby,' the slovenly KGB man replied, the buttons on his cheap navy jacket straining at his belly, his too-short tie askew. 'Tell me, have you ever gone hunting for wild boar? Great sport in the republic of Georgia. You must use dogs. Two kinds, at least. Track dogs, which have the gift of scenting out and tracking down the wild hog. But once the boar has been located, then what? You bay them up. Then what? That's when you need catch dogs. The catch dogs sink their teeth in its nose and hang on. A lesser skill? No doubt. But an indispensable one.'

The two were walking down the stairs together. There was no point in putting up further resistance. 'We look for POSHLUST, but never find. Then we learn that the fabled Mr. Belknap is coming to a seaside resort here in Estonia. How? From you, Todd, I have no secrets, save the secrets that I have. Not your fault. One of your legend clerks gets sloppy. They accidentally doubled up on 'Ralph Cogan' documents. There's a Ralph Cogan in Bratislava as we speak.

The Estonian processor is puzzled, and the photo ID is kicked upstairs, and the determination is made. This is none other than Todd Belknap, the one they call *sobak*, the Hound. Who is he looking for? Could it be the one we look for? We wait and see.'

Once they had reached the ground floor, Belknap decided he would indeed have tea with the KGB man, take his measure as the other did the same.

'So we are grateful to you. But you now have reason to thank us. After all, what were you going to do with this swine once you had bayed him up at the corner of a tree? You Americans are too dainty to be comfortable with *mokry dela*, with 'wetwork.' Yet you must eliminate him. The problem is solved. At the conclusion of the panel, the errant physicist will be whisked off into the world of Soviet criminal justice. Your job is done, your track-dog paws are clean. You leave the unpleasant work of the catch dog to us, yes? You did confirm that Dmitri Barashenkov is POSHLUST, yes? If you tell me yes, I have him apprehended. So, your conclusion is – what?'

Belknap took a long time before he answered.

The two had stayed in touch at irregular intervals over the succeeding two decades; each time was memorable. Belknap knew that the KGB agent wrote reports of their meetings; he also suspected that those reports were not complete. And when the Soviet empire shriveled up and the KGB was scaled down, Belknap assumed that the Georgian had retained his position, though he had so many guises that Belknap could not be certain. Sometimes, a legend was converted into reality: There were cases in which someone set up by the KGB to play a businessman would detach himself from his superiors and simply pursue his cover career in earnest. Belknap did know that Chakvetadze was retired now; the man was in his mid-seventies, after all, and the years of hard drinking had told. He also knew that Chakvetadze would have held on to a kit bag from his old trade; the ex–KGB officers all did, the way Second World War infantrymen often held on to souvenir sidearms.

Chakvetadze's lakeside cottage, by Lake Ülemiste, was just a couple of miles south of Tallinn Old Town. It was not exactly a picture of arcadia; the airport was not far, and the sound of jets was as omnipresent as birdsong. It was a spare, bungalow-like house, a one-story structure of semicircular shingles, a redbrick fireplace sprouting from the center like a handle.

Perhaps as a point of pride, Chakvetadze did not admit to surprise at hearing from his old friend. 'Yes, come, come,' he had said with a Slavic garrulity that had never been chastened by Estonian reserve.

Immediately upon Belknap's arrival, the Russian ushered him through the house to a concrete patio, where there were a couple of worse-for-wear canvas-backed chairs and a table of silvered wood. Then he returned with a bottle of vodka and two glasses, and began pouring with little ceremony.

'I'm afraid I've got a long day ahead of me,' Belknap said.

'It will be longer if you don't have some of this lighting fluid in your belly,' the Georgian said. 'I'm sorry you didn't come earlier. I could have introduced you to my wife.'

'She out of town?'

'I meant a few years earlier, *durak*, not a few hours. Raisa's been dead for two years.' He settled down, took a generous swallow, and gestured toward the lake, from which wisps of fog arose like steam from soup. 'You see that great boulder in the middle of the lake there? It's called Lindakivi. According to Estonian folklore, the great king Kalev married a woman born of a hen's egg, named Linda. When he died, Linda was supposed to carry great boulders to his grave, but one fell off her apron. So she sat on it and cried. Hence Lake Ülemiste. The tears, you know.'

'Do you believe that?'

'All national epics are truthful,' Gennady replied stoutly. 'In their way. It is also said that Ülemiste the Elder lives in this lake. If you meet him, he asks, 'Is Tallinn ready yet?' and you must always answer, 'No, much remains to be done.''

'What if you answered yes?'

'Then he would flood the city.' The Georgian chortled

merrily. 'So you see, *disinformatzia* is a very old Estonian occupation.' He closed his eyes, turned to face the lake breeze. There was a sound like the whine of a distant gnat as an airplane came in for a landing.

'It *is* a powerful tool, disinformation,' Belknap allowed. 'I am in search of others.'

Gennady opened one eye, and then the other. 'I can deny you nothing, old friend, save what I must deny you.'

Belknap looked at his watch. It was a good start. 'I thank you, *moy droog.*'

'So.' The Russian's eyes were watchful, but his smile was unforced. 'What outrageous requests have you come to make?'

The depository on Binnewater Road, Rosendale, just north of New Paltz, was an old mine that had been converted into a high-security storage center. As her cab pulled up to the address, little was visible from outside, other than a vast black plastic mat – a moisture barrier – that was stretched over a sandy knoll. She showed her ID to a guard in a booth, and a steel gate was raised, enabling the cab to pull into the large parking lot – a parking lot without a building, so it seemed, for the storage facility was underground. The terrain, she'd learned, had once been rich with veins of limestone, especially sought after because it was low in magnesium, making it desirable for the manufacture of cement and concrete. Indeed, much of the physical structure of modern Manhattan had been extracted from the county. It was in the remains of one of these 'cement mines' that the Archival Storage facility had been built. Despite its colloquial designation as an 'iron mountain,' it was, in fact, a steel-lined mine.

At an entrance area her photo ID was carefully scrutinized. Her friend at the New York State Department of Taxation and Finance had called ahead and authorized her visit; ostensibly she was an independent auditor contracted by the state for special research. Seated at a wood-veneer counter by the entrance was a pear-shaped man with deep-set eyes, broad sloping shoulders, and receding glossy black hair. He looked to be in his late thirties. Despite his bulky torso, his face was oddly fatless; his cheeks were grooved, almost gaunt, skin taut over a death's head. Finally, almost reluctantly, the man gave her a special badge with a magnetic strip.

'The badge activates all doors and elevators,' he said, in the tone of someone who had regularly issued the official cautions. 'It's good for eight hours from stamp date, by the clock. You must return before that interval has elapsed. On any future visit, you must fill out the same form and get your badge reissued or recharged. The badge must be with you at all times.' He tapped it with a long fingernail. 'That bad boy there turns on the lights automatically for the segment where you're working. Be sure to keep an eye out for staffers on the electric carts. They beep, just like the trolleys at the airport. You hear beeping, step aside, because those carts can zoom by pretty fast. On the other hand, if you need vehicular transport, you use one of the internal phones and call in the request. Number, letter, all that good shit. Righty-ho? If you've visited an iron-mountain type facility before, you're probably familiar with the system. If not, it's better to get your questions answered now.' When he stood up, Andrea saw that he was shorter than she had thought.

'How big is this installation?'

He returned to his college-tour voice. 'More than a hundred thousand linear feet, on three levels. Atmosphere is monitored, with automatic CO_2 correction and humidity control. This ain't no town library. Like I say, you really don't want to get lost, and you really don't want to misplace your badge. There's a computer console at every stop of the elevator that you can use to get location coordinates for your research needs. There are numbers or letters corresponding to level, sector, row, rank, and shelf. I always say, it's easy once you get the hang of it, but almost nobody ever gets the hang of it.'

'Appreciate the vote of confidence,' Andrea said wanly. She knew such facilities were big, but she had no conception of just how big until she entered the slow-moving glass

310

elevator and gazed through the sides as she descended to the bottom level. It was like an underground city, some expressionist conceit, something out of Fritz Lang's *Metropolis*. A catacomb for the digital age. Microfiche, microfilm, paper files, medical records, backup tapes, every storage device known to man: everything that companies and municipalities were legally required to retain, and much more. It all ended up here, neatly catalogued and preserved in facilities like this one, vast cemeteries of the information age.

She felt a heavy bleakness descend on her, perhaps because of the dimness of the light or a curious interaction between the normally opposite anxieties of agoraphobia and claustrophobia – the sense of being encrypted in a vastness. *Let's just get this over with*, she coached herself. Now she walked across a seemingly endless concrete floor, following a white line, numbers in stenciled light-blue paint: 3l 2:566-999. The badge around her neck silently announced her presence, flicking on lights; some sort of electronic chip embedded inside must have responded to radio signals in a certain way. The air was curiously dustless, and it was cooler than she had anticipated; she was already sorry she hadn't brought a sweater. All around her were vast steel shelves, extending all the way to the fourteen-foot ceilings. Small collapsible ladders were available at the end of each six-foot-long shelf segment. The place was really designed for spider monkeys, she decided.

She rounded the corner and turned down the next aisle; once again, a series of lights startled her by blinking on, activated by her badge sensor. It took her a good fifteen minutes of walking and searching before she located the first tranche of papers she was looking for. Having located it, she spent another hour before she came upon something that looked peculiarly like a loose thread.

Foreign-exchange data. Most people would have made nothing of it, but she knew better. When organizations were making a sizable conversion of U.S. currency into foreign currencies – in preparation for purchases or payments in other countries – they often established a hedge to protect themselves from adverse swings in currency valuation. At irregular intervals, the Bancroft Foundation had done so.

Why? Ordinary acquisitions of property or infrastructure used the standard protocols of international banking, facilitated by the major institutions of global finance. These currency hedges suggested large-scale cash infusions. To what end? In the modern economy, large amounts of cash suggested activities that were extralegal. Graft? Or something else entirely?

She was starting to feel like a Mohican tracker. She could not see the forest creature, but she could see a few broken twigs, an odd deposit of spoor, and she knew where it had been.

A hundred feet above her, the man with the deep-set eyes keyed in the woman's badge number, and the multipaneled video screen in front of him lighted up with feeds from the cameras that operated in her immediate vicinity. He zoomed in with a few clicks of the mouse, then rotated the image so that he could read the type on the page. The Bancroft Foundation. He had standing instructions in a case like this. Probably this was no big deal. Probably this was one of their own – the honey's name was Bancroft, after all. But they weren't paying him to think. They were paying him to give them the heads-up. *Yo, Kev, that's why you get the big bucks*. Okay, not big maybe, but compared to the pittance he got from Secure Archive Inc., it was damn generous. He picked up his telephone, his finger hovering over the number pad. Then he returned the handset to the cradle. Better not to leave a record at work. He took out his cell phone and placed the call.

It was that evening that Belknap's bogus chorus affiliation proved its true worth. That evening, a reception, in honor of the international choral festival, was held at the residence of the country's president. The Empire State Chorus was among the groups that were scheduled to perform at a goodwill concert following it. For top-level Estonian ministers, attendance was obligatory. For Belknap, a plan foggily drafted would now be made concrete.

Logy from too little sleep and a heavy meal of fried pork and kali, Belknap was the last one on the bus that was taking the chorus to its destination, Kadriorg Palace, on Weizenbergi Street, in the northern district of the city. He sat next to a straw-haired young man with puppy-dog eyes and a wide elastic grin who endlessly repeated the words 'tender as a poem, tough as steel,' pouncing on the t's with saliva-spewing force. Behind him, a pair of altos were singing 'how fair thou art and bright.'

Belknap was wearing the same Empire State Chorus badge that everyone else had on. He concentrated on blending in, adopting that slightly dazed, slightly dazzled expression that they all seemed to have, not to mention the hair-trigger grins.

The Kadriorg park, like so much of Estonia's grandeur, was a legacy of Peter the Great: Russian richesse in the wake of Russian domination. Many of the pavilions had been turned into museums and concert halls, but the main part of the palace remained an official residence of the president, used for occasions of state – and, for Estonians, an international choral festival certainly counted as that. The largest building was two stories – two extremely grand stories, a baroque fantasy of white pilasters on red stone. Just up the hill, in a matching but somewhat simplified style, was the presidential palace, built in 1938, a year when, even as darkness overtook much of Europe, Estonia thought it saw a new dawn. A freshly inked constitution promised to guarantee democratic freedoms after four years of dictatorship; it did not last the year. Nor did the desperate attempts to preserve Baltic neutrality. The building enshrined illusory hopes; perhaps, Belknap mused, that was why it was so handsome.

Outside the palace was a tented makeshift vestibule, providing what passed as security in Tallinn. He saw Calvin Garth conferring with a blue-suited security officer, flashing documentation. Then the members of his chorus were waved through. Belknap made sure that his badge was prominently displayed as he fell into step with the others. Though he was more than a decade older than any of the real chorus members, he plastered a bemused grin on his face and was not stopped for additional scrutiny.

The foyer was lavishly decorated with intricate stucco work and plaster ornaments that rose to the level of sculpture. He exchanged glances with the young men and women in the chorus and pretended to be as overawed as they were. The banquet hall, where the reception was held, was already crowded, he was relieved to see. Now, stepping toward a wall, he pretended to examine a painting of the Empress Catherine while removing the badge from his jacket. This was the tricky part: Arriving as one person, he swiftly had to become another.

Not just anybody, either. He was now Roger Delamain, of Grinnell International. He replaced the soapy grin on his face with a look of slightly imperious suspicion, and quickly glanced around. Though he had previously studied the faces of the country's high-level ministers, he would still have to wing it. The president was easily distinguished: With his bushy eyebrows and mane of white-silver hair, he was the very type of the ceremonial head of state, the well-educated man with a gift for making orotund pronouncements. He shook hands in a practiced squeeze-and-smile motion, although the real skill, as Belknap now saw, was in his ability to detach – for the man had to remove himself from one guest in order to greet another, swiftly, invisibly, having a moment of conversational significance that did not allow for entanglement. Belknap drifted closer. Flypaper questions were treated as witticisms, eliciting appreciative chuckles, or, depending upon tonal clues, as somber reflections that the president would surely take to heart. Handclasp, eye-lock, smile, dismiss. Handclasp, eye-lock, smile, dismiss. He was a virtuoso; the Estonian parliament did not go wrong in elevating him to this post.

The prime minister was, like most of his cabinet, dressed in navy blue. Less skilled at detachment than the president, he was nodding with exaggerated enthusiasm, trapped in conversation with a stout woman – doubtless some notable in the music world – even as his eyes were desperately sending out distress flares to his aides. The minister of culture – a man with a suet complexion and what looked like grease-paint eyebrows – was talking expansively to a group of Westerners, evidently in the middle of a joke or humorous anecdote, because he kept interrupting himself with pants of laughter. The man Belknap was looking for – the deputy trade minister – had a rather different mien. The glass in his hand, with a small wedge of lime on one side, probably contained nothing stronger than seltzer. His eyes were small and shadowed beneath a prominent, widow's-peaked forehead. He was not speaking, but nodding, and spent little time with any one group.

Andrus Pärt was the deputy minister's name, and, by Gennady's reckoning, it would be worth Belknap's while to get to know him. The logic was elementary. The mogul he was seeking was big. The nation of Estonia was small. Andrus Pärt, Gennady assured Belknap, had contacts with all the major figures of Estonia's private sector, licit and illicit. Nobody operated in a small Baltic republic without reaching an accommodation with high-ranking members of the government. Andrus Pärt would know the players; he would know the man Belknap was hunting. As soon as the operative laid eyes on him, indeed, he felt all the more certain of it. *The nose of the Hound*, he mused.

Now came the hard part. Belknap drifted through clusters and crowds, across costly carpet and costlier parquet, until he was a few feet from the deputy minister. He wore an expression distinct from the usual ingratiating smiles at a reception like this one; he was a man on business. To a politician, the overly unctuous smile was a signal to move right along. But Belknap could not be discourteous, either. A tight, wary smile flashed on his face as he turned to the deputy minister.

'The honorable Andrus Pärt, if I'm not mistaken,' Belknap said. His accent was flat, ambiguous, the English of someone who had learned it as a foreign language but at posh schools.

'That's right,' the deputy minister said blandly. Yet Belknap could tell he was intrigued. This was not a gathering of people conversant with Estonian politics, and Belknap's level gaze was not that of the usual partygoer.

'Curiously, we've never met,' Belknap said carefully. Another morsel that would prolong the man's interest: It was a statement that suggested that there might have been reason for them to have met. A glimmer of interest appeared on Pärt's face, doubtless for the first time this evening. 'I've been asked to remedy this.'

'Have you?' The Estonian's hooded eyes betrayed little. 'And why is that?'

'Forgive me.' Only now did Belknap extend a hand, and he did so with an air of noblesse. 'Roger Delamain.'

The deputy minister's eyes began to scan the room. 'Of Grinnell International,' Belknap added meaningfully. The name belonged to an actual managing director of Grinnell; if the man looked him up, he would find a corporate biography, though no photograph.

'Grinnell,' the Estonian repeated. He gave Belknap a look that spoke volumes, all of them in a foreign language. 'Really. Are you developing a musical division, then?' A quick, twitchlike smile. 'Military music, perhaps?'

'It is my great passion,' Belknap said, gesturing around him. 'The Estonian traditions of singing. This is not an occasion I could pass up.'

'It fills us with pride,' Pärt replied automatically.

'I'm devoted to other Estonian traditions as well,' Belknap said quickly. 'I'm afraid I'm not here strictly due to my amateur interests. You understand. It is the nature of Grinnell's operations. Unpredictable, sudden demands. They arrive with little notice and the company's directors, like myself, must scurry to cope with them.'

'I only wish I could be of service.'

Belknap's smile was almost tender. 'Perhaps you can be.'

After two hours of perusing small type, Andrea's eyes were becoming hot and scratchy, and her head was starting to throb. Battling mid-afternoon fatigue, she had jotted down several columns of digit and dates on a small piece of paper.

Maybe it meant nothing. Maybe it meant something. She had to go on instinct at this point, do more research when she returned to planet Earth. She checked the time, and made a spur-of-the-moment decision to track down the archives from the April when her mother died. *The cruelest month*. Well, *her* cruelest month, anyway.

The archived corporate records contained nothing that made reference to it. She leaned against the shelves, scanning the black plastic clad boxes of the bank opposite, lost in thought. There was a movement in her peripheral vision, and she turned to see an electric cart driving toward her at top speed. *Aren't they supposed to beep?* she wondered fleetingly, as adrenaline pulsed through her and she stepped out of its path.

Yet the cart now veered, tracking her movement. It was – *impossible!* – as if the driver *wanted* to hit her. She let out a shriek as she realized that the man on the cart was wearing a motorcycle helmet with a full tinted visor and face-shield. She could see only a reflection of herself when she looked at him, and somehow the image of her own terror just compounded it. At the last moment, she leaped up, sprang as high as she could with all the strength she had, and then, gripping a high shelf, pulled herself up and out of harm's way. *Oh, dear Lord!*

The cart skidded to halt, and the man on it swiftly dismounted. Now Andrea raced down the end of the bank of shelves, turned left, and plunged down another long corridor. The maze of shelving would conceal her, wouldn't it? She ran down another corridor and made a series of erratic turns that took her deeper into the vast, dimly lighted space. She ran, her knees pumping high into the air, her crepe-soled shoes squeaking against the concrete flooring only occasionally. Finally, winded, she slid to the floor behind a support pillar at row K, rank L, and – *dammit* – suddenly a bank of halogens sparked on, flooding the section with light. She might as well have put a homing beacon on her head. The badge – the security badge – was designed to turn on the lights wherever she went. Listening carefully, she could hear the soft whine of the electric cart: The man in the helmet had to have been motoring after her.

She heard footfalls, perhaps twenty feet away. Someone else, then. She craned her head, caught a glimpse of another figure, dressed in paramilitary garb, obviously armed. Not here to help her. It was a difficult Gestalt shift; for her entire life, men with guns – policemen, usually – had been on *her* side. They worked for her. She realized this was not everyone's experience of the world, but it was hers. Now they were working against her, and the realization clashed with so many of her settled assumptions. The badge. She gripped it, tugged on its lanyard. The badge was betraying her. She had to leave it behind. Or was there a way to enlist it?

With a sudden burst of speed, she darted down the end of the row and zigzagged across a few sections. She was now somewhere in P rank. She hid her badge inside a document-storage box and, just as the halogens blazed, she climbed up to the very top shelf, scuttled over a long row of metal canisters, the kind that held film or magnetic tape, and kept moving until she was at the other end of the row, where the reading lights remained dark. Had she been quiet enough? She stretched herself out on the top shelf, invisible, or so she hoped. Then she pulled out one of the heavy canisters so that she would have an angle of vision on what was happening on the floor, twelve feet beneath her.

The man in the paramilitary garb arrived first. Not seeing her, he darted to the aisles to either side. With a look of frustration, he returned to the lighted section, scanning the shelves, looking either for her or for her badge. Then he spoke into a handy-talkie.

'Bitch ditched the badge,' he said in a voice like gravel. 'A goddamned risky strategy. We have kill clearance yet from Theta?'

As he spoke, he walked further down the P-rank aisle, closer to Andrea. Timing was everything. Now she held the heavy steel canister in both hands, waiting for the shadowy figure to get to the spot she was visualizing on the floor beneath her, and – *now!* – she let it drop.

She heard the man's strangled yelp, then peered down to see him sprawled on the ground, the steel canister lying awkwardly on his skull.

Oh, Christ what have you done, Andrea? Oh, Christ!

A surge of nausea and revulsion rippled through her. This wasn't her world. This was not what she did, not who she was.

But if her assailants thought she would not resist with every fiber of her being, they had underestimated her. *We have kill clearance yet?* The words returned like an arctic wind.

A fist of rage hammered in her chest. *No, asshole, but I have.*

She swung down, like a child on a jungle gym, and fell on the slain man. There was a gun holstered on his belt. The sides were flat, not curved, so it was probably a pistol. She grabbed it and, by the light of the distant halogens, examined it.

She had never held a handgun before. How hard could it be, though? She knew which was the business end, and that was a start, wasn't it? She knew that rap artists in music videos liked to hold their guns sideways, though she couldn't imagine how that made any difference to a bullet's trajectory. She had seen too many movies where a gun didn't go off because someone didn't know about the safety. Did the gun have a safety? Was it even loaded?

Dammit. It didn't come with handy instructions printed on the handle, and she didn't have time to read anyway. The truth is, she had no idea what would happen if she squeezed the trigger. Maybe nothing. Maybe it needed to be cocked or something. But maybe the guy had left it in point-and-shoot mode.

One or the other. Probably the gun would do her more harm than good. The guy in the polarized-glass helmet would hear her squeeze the trigger, and nothing would happen, and he'd take her out. She scampered to the end of the bank of shelves and watched as the helmeted man raced over in the electric cart.

Then the man surprised her, getting out of the cart, stepping behind a pillar and – *where was he?*

Half a minute passed; still no sign of the man. She curled up on the lower shelf, concealing herself as best she could, and simply listened.

Then she heard him, and slowly craned her head. Her stomach dropped: The man had found her. He was walking toward her slowly. She remained stock-still, feeling like a frog that did not know it had been spotted.

'Come to papa,' the man said, walking slowly toward her. He held a black plastic device; electricity arced from one end of it menacingly. Some sort of stun gun, or Taser. He tossed a pair of plastic handcuffs at her. 'Here, you can put the cuffs on yourself. Make things easy for you.'

Andrea still didn't move.

'I can see you, you know,' the visored man said almost playfully. 'There's nobody else here. Just you and me. And I'm not in any great rush.' The electric wand arced and sparked as he strode closer to her. With his other hand, he loosened his leather belt, began massaging his crotch. 'Hey, baby. Boss says it's all about the greatest pleasure.' He took a few steps closer to her. 'Yo bitch, why don't you maximize *my* pleasure today?'

She squeezed the trigger without thinking, was shocked at the loudness of the report. The man in the visor stopped walking, but he did not fall to the ground or make a noise. Had she missed?

She squeezed the trigger again, and again. The third round shattered the man's face-shield, and he finally fell backward in a heap.

Andrea clambered down to the floor, standing on wobbling legs. She walked over to the man she had shot. She recognized him, recognized the bat-wing eyebrows, the blotchy skin. He was one of the men who had taken her from her car at the Research Triangle Park. *We have kill clearance yet?* A shudder ran through her entire body. Then she saw the lifeless eyes of the man at her feet, and she suddenly doubled over and retched, the hot acid contents of her stomach streaming from her mouth, splashing on the man's face, and, when she saw what had happened, she retched again.

A beefy arm reached around the Estonian minister's shoulders. 'Andrus!' boomed an overly hearty voice. A heavyset, boisterous man with an unshaveable beard shadow. His breath had the anise smell of a popular Estonian schnapps. 'Come meet Stephanie Berger. She's from Polygram. Very interested in the prospects of setting up a studio in Tallinn. Perhaps a distribution center, even.' He addressed the deputy minister in English out of deference to his English-speaking interloper.

Andrus Pärt turned to Belknap with an apologetic look. 'This is unfortunate. You should have told me you were visiting Estonia.'

'My colleagues, on the contrary, think it's very fortunate. That I happened to be in Tallinn when the crisis arose. Fortunate for us, that is.' He lowered his voice. 'Perhaps fortunate for you?'

The deputy minister gave him a curious, unsettled look. 'I will be right back, Roger . . .'

'Delamain,' Belknap said.

He drifted toward a long table draped in white lace, where servants busily took and fulfilled beverage requests, but he kept Andrus Pärt in the corner of his eye. The deputy minister listened to the woman with head nods and flashes of porcelain teeth. He clasped the upper arm of the boisterous man – a businessman, no doubt, and probably one of the underwriters of the affair – and made we'll-continue-this-conversation-soon gestures. But he did not circle back immediately, Belknap observed. Instead, reaching for a cell phone, he disappeared into an adjoining room. When he returned, a few minutes later, he was decidedly more upbeat than before.

'Roger Delamain,' he said, giving the name a French pronunciation. 'Thank you for your patience.'

So he had made brief inquiries, had at least asked an aide

to verify the name and its connection to the global security firm Grinnell International. 'Either pronunciation is fine with me,' Belknap replied. 'Among Anglophones, I pronounce it one way, and I knew you spoke English. Among French speakers, the French way. I'm highly adaptable, just like my company. Our clients have their own demands. If you're protecting an oil refinery, one set of skills is required. If it's a presidential palace, quite another face must be displayed. Alas, in a world with so much instability, we find our services in ever greater demand.'

'They say that eternal vigilance is the price of freedom.'

'That's almost exactly what we told the Cuprex Mining Company when they woke up and found that their African copper mines were being threatened by a murderous insurrection led by the Lord's Resistance Army. Eternal vigilance, and twelve million dollars plus direct expenses: *That's* the price of freedom, on an annualized basis.'

'And a bargain, I'm sure.' The deputy minister grabbed a small canapé from a silver tray that seemed to float through the crowd.

'It's why I wished to speak to you, to be candid. I speak to you informally, this is understood, yes? I do not come as a registered agent of any company.'

'We are standing together at a reception, eating small triangles of cured meat on toast. What could be more informal?'

'I knew we should get along,' Belknap said conspiratorially. 'What we seek to fulfill is a *substantial* order for small arms.'

'Surely Grinnell has its regular supplier.' Pärt was scrutinizing the bait.

'Regular suppliers do not always suffice for irregular demands. There are some who say I am given to understatement. I like to think I am only precise. When I say 'substantial,' I mean . . . enough to equip five thousand men, and fully.'

The deputy minister blinked. 'Our entire army consists of fifteen thousand men.'

'Then you see the problem.'

'And this is to protect, what – installations, mines?' Black brows knitted in frank disbelief.

Belknap returned his curious, penetrative gaze with a bland one. 'Minister Pärt, if you ever entrust me with a secret, you should feel confident that I will never divulge it. I speak institutionally as well as personally. One cannot prosper in the security business without earning a reputation for trustworthiness and discretion. I understand that you have questions. I hope you will not think ill of me if I decline to answer them.'

The deputy minister gave him a hard stare, which softened after a few seconds into something like approval. 'I wish I could train my fellow nationals in the virtue of discretion. Greatly to my regret, they are not all so tight-lipped as you, Roger.' His eyes darted around, making sure that no one could overhear, and then he prompted, 'But you somehow supposed I could be of help.'

'I was given to understand that you might be able to facilitate the kind of arrangement we require. I need hardly say that it would surely be profitable for all concerned.'

Belknap recognized the quickness of greed in the deputy minister's face; it seeped through his veins like a drug and hurried his speech. 'You said it was a substantial order you required.'

'Substantial,' Belknap repeated. Andrus Pärt was seeking reassurance about his kickback. 'Which translates to substantial benefits and finder's fees for the . . . matchmaker.'

'We are a small country, of course.' The man was testing him, tugging at the line.

'Small, yet rich in its customs, I had thought. If I am mistaken, if you do not have a vendor such as we seek, say so at once. We will look elsewhere. I should hate to waste your time.' Translation: Don't waste mine.

The deputy minister waved to a tall, cadaverous dignitary across the room. He had spent too much time with the Grinnell director; it might become conspicuous, which would not do. 'Roger, I do want to be of help. I do. Let me brood for a few minutes. We will talk again shortly.'

With that, the Estonian plunged into a crowd of chorus directors and music enthusiasts. Presently Belknap was able to hear Pärt's voice exclaim, 'A boxed set of highlights from the festival – what a marvelous idea!'

There was a rustling followed by admonitory hushing. On a raised, stepped platform on the far side of the room, the Empire State Chorus had assembled. Grinning from ear to ear, the baritones began snapping their fingers, and then singing. After a few bars, the room quieted enough to make them audible:

For nowhere in the world around
Can ever such a place be found
So well belov'd, from sense profound,
My native country dear!

Belknap felt a shoulder tap, and turned to find the deputy minister at his elbow.

'Our national anthem,' Pärt whispered with a fixed smile.

'You must be very proud,' Belknap replied.

Through gritted teeth, the minister reproved, 'Don't be unkind.'

'Not unkind, I hope. Merely impatient. Can we do business?' Belknap spoke in murmured tones.

The deputy minister nodded, then gestured with a head tilt to the room off the main hall. They would speak there, out of view.

'Forgive me,' the Estonian said in a low, confiding voice. 'It's all very sudden. And irregular.'

'As it has been for us,' Belknap said. The deputy minister was still being coy; it was time to ratchet up the pressure. 'I seem to have caused you more inconvenience than I had intended. There are other avenues for us to explore, and perhaps we should do so. Thank you for your time.' A curt bow.

'You misunderstand,' Pärt said, with a shade of insistence but not panic. He understood that the Grinnell director was doing what all businessmen do: threatening to walk out in

324

order to hasten matters to a conclusion. 'I do wish to help. Indeed, I may be able to.'

'Your mastery of the subjunctive is admirable,' Belknap said in hushed reprimand. 'I still fear that we waste each other's time.' *Now it is for you to win me back* was the unspoken subtext.

'Earlier, Roger, you made a point about confidences and discretion. You observed that they are a mainstay of your business. Just so, caution is a mainstay of mine. You must indulge me in this respect. There may be occasions on which you are grateful of it.'

Drifting in from the banquet hall, in three-part harmony, came the words *Forever may He bless and wield / O graciously all deeds of thine . . .*

'Perhaps we will both need to compromise in our adherence to our cherished principles. You asked about our regular suppliers. I am sure a man of the world such as yourself understands that there can be upheavals in this business as in all others. No doubt you have heard reports of Khalil Ansari's death.' He studied the Estonian's expression as he pronounced the name. 'No doubt you understand that established distribution networks can fall into disarray, while new ones establish themselves.'

Andrus Pärt looked uncomfortable; he knew enough about what Belknap was speaking about to realize that it was not an affair to be casually discussed – certainly not by a career politician like him. He needed to dig enough to be sure of his hunches; he did not wish to dig so far that his hands were soiled. Those would have been his calculations.

Belknap was weighing every word. 'I know you are a man of taste. I am told that your country house in Paslepa is a thing of beauty.'

'It is a humble place, but my wife enjoys it.'

'Then perhaps she will enjoy it twice as much when you buy her a place that's twice the size.'

A long, lingering look: This was a man pulled in different directions by avarice and uncertainty.

'Or perhaps not.' Another jerk on the fishing line, to set

the hook: 'I enjoyed my conversation with you immensely. But, again, perhaps it is time for me to look elsewhere. As you . . . cautioned me, Estonia is a very small country. I believe your message was that large fish seldom appear in small ponds.' Another curt bow, and this time Belknap really did walk toward the exit, where he heard the mass voices belt out *This native country of mine!*

A warm round of applause broke the silence, though it was muffled somewhat by the one-handed clapping from those holding glasses, napkins, canapés.

A hand on Belknap's shoulder, a word whispered in his ear. 'Estotek,' said the deputy minister. 'On Ravala Puiestee.'

'I could have gotten that from directory assistance.'

'I assure you, the real nature of this entity is closely guarded indeed. I have your word that you will divulge it to no one.'

'But of course,' Belknap replied.

'The principal goes by the name Lanham.'

'An odd name for an Estonian.'

'But not so odd for an American.'

An American. Belknap's eyes narrowed.

'I think you will find that your needs can be met,' Pärt went on. 'We are a small pond. But some of our fish are sizable indeed.'

'Impressive,' Belknap said frostily. 'This native country of yours. Shall I send Lanham your regards?'

The deputy minister looked suddenly uneasy. 'The most intimate relationships are sometimes conducted at more than arm's length,' he said. 'Let me be clear. This isn't someone I've ever met face-to-face.' He held himself stiffly, as if suppressing a shudder. 'Nor do I care to.'

CHAPTER EIGHTEEN

Tallinn's business district was scarcely featured in the tourist brochures, yet many considered it to be the authentic heart of the city. The heart of the business district, in turn, was where the building where Estotek had its offices, a twenty-story erection sheathed in mirrored glass, was. A full mile outside the Old Town, it was just a block away from such contemporary landmarks as the Reval Olümpia and the Stockmann Shopping Center, not to mention the Coca-Cola Plaza Cinema and the neon-lit Hollywood Nightclub. The district was, in short, a city that looked like every other city, which was precisely what made businessmen feel at home. WiFi Internet access was beamed from eateries, hotel lobbies, and bars. *We are modern, just like you* was the message that was being transmitted, though with an edge of desperation that lessened its credibility. At this hour of night, the Bonnie and Clyde Nightclub – another peculiarity of Tallinn, Belknap noticed, was that the nightclubs actually, and doggedly, called themselves 'nightclubs' – was still well lighted. Immediately adjoining the tallest hotel was an Audi and Volkswagen dealership: The locals were no doubt proud to have assembled the equivalent of a strip mall in the middle of their financial district.

The building was blocky and dark, each facade set in a white enameled facet of steel. It could have been airlifted into any one of five hundred cities and looked equally at home. Belknap got out of the taxi and wandered around on foot. In case anyone was watching, he made his gait slightly unsteady; he would look like a drunken businessman trying to remember which building his hotel was.

It was Gennady Chakvetadze who had found the address for him. Even in retirement, he retained his tendrils of influence, and made a few discreet phone calls to the municipal record keepers.

The real nature of this entity is closely guarded indeed, Arvo Pärt had said, and he had not exaggerated. Estotek, it emerged, was an Estonian corporation with an offshore charter; its registration records listed only its domestic assets, which were negligible. It was a firm that had no active operations and no significant holdings; it rented space on the tenth floor of an office tower in the business district, paid its registration fees in a timely manner, and was otherwise a phantom. A shell corporation, in short, configured in such a way that it was not required to disclose its subsidiary offshore business entities.

Belknap had been puzzled. 'Don't they at least have to list officers, principals?' he had asked Gennady.

The Russian sounded amused by the question. 'In the civilized world, certainly. But in Estonia, the securities regulations and the financial codes were drafted by the oligarchs. This will amuse you: The listed principal is the name not of a person but of another company. Who's the listed principal of that company? You may well ask. It's Estotek. It's like something out of M. C. Escher, yes? And in Estonia, it's perfectly within the law.' The retired KGB man chortled. The crooked timber of humanity was, for him, a source of solace.

Now Belknap hunched up his jacket as a wind gusted through the glass and steel canyon that was downtown Tallinn. It was helpful that it was dark outside; mirrored glass became transparent at night. But an assessment of the building's security was still difficult. Hooded closed-circuit video cameras were mounted at the corners of the lower part of the building, providing security guards with a view of the sidewalk and the mollusk-shaped parking garage that it shared with another office building. Yet what sort of measures had been implemented inside? One thing was certain: This night was his best chance to enter unobserved. By tomorrow, the deputy minister might well have communicated with his contacts at Estotek, have told them about the Grinnell director; if so, the chances were good that they would see through the ruse and be alerted. But the deputy minister would not do so now; he would be listening to tedious goodwill performances from the world's finest choral groups. He would be squeezing hands and smiling. He would be fantasizing about his new country estate, and thinking about how he would explain it to his friends and associates.

Belknap crossed the street, withdrew a small flat pair of field glasses, and squinted, trying to make out the security guard on duty in the lobby. He saw nothing. He saw . . . a curling wisp of smoke drifted from an interior pillar. There was a guard in that lobby all right. He was smoking. And he looked tired.

Briskly, the American checked himself in a reflective window. His dark suit fitted the part he was playing; the black leather Gladstone bag – it and its contents came courtesy of Gennady – was somewhat bulkier than the usual corporate briefcase but otherwise nothing very noticeable. Now he took a deep breath, approached the entrance, flashed his ID, and prepared to sign himself in.

The guard gazed at him sleepily, pressed a buzzer that released the front door. He had the widening girth that most Estonian men had acquired by their early middle age, the product of a diet of pork, fat, pancakes, and potatoes. He took a last drag on his cigarette and resumed his place behind a granite counter.

'CeMines,' Belknap said. 'CeMines Estonia. Floor eleven.'

The guard nodded stolidly, and Belknap could guess what he was thinking. A foreigner, but then Tallinn was overrun with them. It was doubtless unusual for CeMines, a medical-science company, to have visitors at this hour, but Gennady had placed a call to the guard bank, letting him know, in his Russian-inflected Estonian, that a visitor was en route. Some sort of system failure requiring the attentions of some sort of technician.

'You come to make fix?' asked the guard in halting English.

'Sensors indicate a refrigeration-coil malfunction in the

biostorage unit. No rest for the wicked, right?' Belknap spoke with a confident smile.

The guard had the perplexed look of someone whose English had been overtasked. But the import of his thoughts was plain enough: Making trouble for a rich foreigner might be more than his job was worth. After a long moment, he had the visitor sign in, jerked a thumb toward the elevator bank, and lighted up another cigarette.

Belknap, for his part, felt his apprehension level rise with the elevator. The hard part was ahead of him.

Research Triangle Park, North Carolina

Gina Tracy fingered a curl of black hair next to her ear as she spoke to the others. 'There's been a screwup. Really regrettable. Apparently the guys we sent to South America removed the wrong Javier Solanas. Can you believe it?' South America seemed so far away from the lacquered slate floors and frosted glass of the Theta facility, and yet this was where the critical decisions originated. Sometimes Tracy felt as if she was at an aerospace mission-control center, guiding probes on other planets. 'They were supposed to take out the Ecuadorian trade representative.' She glanced at the instant message that had flashed on her computer screen. 'Instead they got some harmless rancher with the same name. I mean, shit.'

There was a moment of hushed silence; only the white-noise purr of the climate-control system was audible.

'Oy, gevalt,' said Herman Liebman, the loose folds of his neck quivering with frustration.

'And these are supposed to be our top guys,' Tracy went on. 'Total A-listers. Maybe we should've used people in-country. Something to be said for local talent, you know?'

'These things happen,' fluted George Collingwood, spreading his fingers across his beard, his short curly hairs neatly trimmed. Someone had once remarked that his beard looked almost vaginal, and Gina sometimes smiled when she looked at him, thinking about it. She did so now.

He tilted his head. 'You think it's funny?'

'In a dark and bitter and blackly comic sort of way,' Gina assured him.

John Burgess's watery, pale eyes caught hers. 'You have a recommendation?' Filtered daylight picked out comb tracks in his white-blond hair.

'We need to think hard about how to prevent this kind of thing from happening again,' she said. 'I really hate when this happens.'

'We all do,' Collingwood said.

'I've got to learn to be philosophical about it,' Tracy said. Some might consider them bloodless technocrats, she knew, but the truth was, they really cared about their work, and it was a struggle not to take it personally when things went wrong. 'George is right. We're going to slip up from time to time. Get too caught up in it and you lose the bigger vision. That's what Paul would say.' She turned to the savant. 'Isn't it?'

'I regret this,' Paul Bancroft said. 'Very much. We've made errors in the past, and there will, inevitably, be errors in the future. Still, there's solace in knowing that our error rate continues to be well within the parameters that we've established as acceptable – and our error rates have been improving over time. That's a heartening trend-line.'

'Even so,' Liebman persisted grumpily.

'What's important is to situate these lapses in the larger context of success,' Bancroft went on, 'and to look forward, not backward. As you say, Gina, we need to learn from our mistakes and determine what additional safeguards can protect against such errors in the future. The calculus of risk produces an asymptotic curve. Which means that there's always room for improvement.'

'Think we should send our boys back to get the right one?' Burgess asked.

'Forget about it,' Collingwood said. 'That would be too much of a coincidence. I mean, in the unlikely event that someone were keeping track of the deaths of people named Javier Solanas. But still. A risk-assessment analysis will tell

331

you it's not worth pursuing. Any developments elsewhere?'

'I'm sure you've heard the news story about a woman in northern Nigeria who's about to be stoned to death,' said Tracy. 'Apparently a village court found her guilty of adultery. I mean, how medieval is that?'

Paul Bancroft furrowed his brow. 'I hope you're not forgetting the larger view here,' he said. 'We can have the boffins confirm this, but I'd project that this intensely publicized event has a highly beneficial effect on HIV transmission rates. It's the baby-in-the-well syndrome all over again. The world media focuses on one woman with mournful eyes and an infant in her arms. The plangent iconography of the madonna and child. Yet the medieval law of these unlettered mullahs is probably going to prevent thousands of AIDS cases. Which is to say, thousands of painful, lingering, ravaging, costly deaths.'

Collingwood blinked. 'It's a no-brainer,' he chimed in, turning to Tracy. 'Why do you think HIV seropositivity rates are so low in Muslim countries? When you penalize and stigmatize sexual promiscuity, transmission rates plunge. Look at the map. Senegal has one of the lowest rates of HIV in sub-Saharan Africa. It's ninety-two percent Muslim. Now look at its neighbor, Guinea-Bissau, which has half the percentage of Muslims that Senegal has – and an HIV rate that's *five* times higher. Stone away, I say.'

'Anything else in that continental sector?' Bancroft asked.

Burgess scanned his console for an electronic list of items. 'Well, what about the minister of mines and energy in Niger? Isn't he blocking important aid projects?'

'That got nixed, remember?' Gina Tracy looked annoyed. 'Too many knock-on effects. We already went over this.'

'Remind me of the play here,' said Collingwood. 'I've been meeting with the systems people all morning.'

'Executive summary? I'll break it down into broad strokes.' Burgess paused, collecting his thoughts. 'First, Minister Okwendo is too high-profile. Second, he's likely to be replaced by Mahamadou, the finance minister. Which is fine, but then the question is, Who's in place to succeed

Mahamadou? If he's replaced by Sannu, that's fine. But it's even money that he'll be replaced by Seyni. And ultimately that could make things even worse. Instead of removing the minister of mines and energy, it would be better to remove Diori, the assistant minister involved. Diori's number two is a relatively benign character, all our intelligence suggests: His father was a kleptocrat, but the result is that the son has enough money that he's not in government to make more.'

'Interesting,' Dr. Bancroft said pensively. 'Diori would appear to be the strategically sound choice. But let's be sure to take it to the second-team boffins to see whether their calculations accord. An independent assessment is always valuable, as we've learned the hard way.' The look he gave Liebman spoke of their shared history.

'Running a fresh set of models could take a few days,' Burgess warned.

'A country like Niger, with a relatively tiny ruling elite, is extremely susceptible to wide output variances given minuscule input variances. We'll want to be safe, not sorry.'

'No argument here,' said Liebman, tenting his liver-spotted hands beneath his chin.

'All right, then.' Bancroft gave Burgess a grave look.

'Meanwhile, how's the absorption of the Ansari network coming along?' Liebman asked. 'After all the effort we spent in taking it over, I certainly hope it proves its worth.'

'Are you kidding? It's turning out to be another one of Paul's masterstrokes,' said Collingwood. 'Proper integration will take a while, the same as with a corporate acquisition. But there's every reason to expect that it's going to enable us to gather really valuable intelligence on its clients. And knowledge is –'

'The power to do good,' Bancroft put it. 'Everything we learn goes to support the larger cause.'

'Absolutely,' Collingwood said, nodding vigorously. 'The world is awash in munitions. Right now, they flow toward the highest bidder. Even worse is when the bidding is split, and you've got both sides of a civil war armed to the hilt. There were thirty years of that in Angola. Totally irrational.

Now we're going to be able to guide the firepower to the states and factions that *ought* to get it. We'll be able to pacify provinces that had been making themselves miserable for decades, because they've been given just enough arms to wage war and not enough to win. That's always the worst state of affairs.'

'Our geopolitical analysts are quite clear about this. In situations of non-eliminationist civil war,' Bancroft said, 'a swift and decisive victory by one side is nearly always preferable, from a humanitarian point of view, to protracted conflict.'

'It hardly matters which side. Getting bogged down in the supposed grievances and aggressions – the you-started-it crap – is a huge mistake. Now we'll be able to run the numbers, pick a winner, and guarantee the optimal outcome. Think how crazy it is that the Ansari network was able to prop up these mountain tribes in Burma. Small arms, second-rate artillery, paid for by drug money. For years, it kept them at war with the Myanmar government. Like they ever really had a chance. That's wrong. Wrong for the tribe. Wrong for the country. Nobody likes a repressive authoritarian regime, but longstanding conflict is even worse. Then, once the military has stabilized the social order, we can get to work on engineering the regime so that it's less repressive and takes better care of its citizenry.'

'You're saying that the rebels' Ansari contacts are going to switch sides?' Liebman asked.

'Who knows more about the weaponry caches of the Wa people or the Karenni than their former suppliers? Who knows more about how the guerilla militias are organized? We're giving the Myanmar generals a trove of intelligence – and a shipment of NATO-grade weaponry. Overwhelming force is key. And before you know it, you get peace through pacification. From a global perspective, the age of rebellion is about to be over.'

'Unless it's a rebellion *we* sanction,' Liebman prodded.

'Toppling a regime by open warfare is always going to be a last resort,' Collingwood said, nodding vigorously. 'But if it comes to it, sure. It's an option. And our roll-up of the major networks isn't by any means finished. Of course, the Ansari acquisition gives Theta more *direct* benefits as well. At the end of the day, do-gooders also have to do what it takes to protect themselves.' He turned to Bancroft. 'You'd agree with that, wouldn't you?'

'The quills of the porcupine,' Bancroft said.

'When threats to our own security arise, abroad or at home, we deal with them.'

'As best we can,' the aging savant agreed.

Collingwood traded glances with Burgess and then Tracy. He took a deep breath. 'Then, Paul, we need to talk about Andrea.'

'I see.'

'Paul, you're too close to the situation. Forgive me for speaking bluntly. But there are decisions to be made here. You need to leave them to the professionals on the ground. She's become a problem. When she went to Rosendale, she crossed a line. You thought she'd listen to reason. Now we know that you overestimated her.'

'Or, from another point of view, underestimated her.' There was something veiled in Bancroft's tone.

'Your judgment was colored.'

'You always like to think the best of people,' Tracy said. 'Which is a great starting assumption. But you've also taught us that we shouldn't resist changing our beliefs in the face of new evidence.'

Through the filtered light, Bancroft suddenly looked years older than he usually did. 'You want me to delegate a case involving my own cousin?'

'Precisely because she *is* your own cousin,' Tracy said.

Bancroft stared into the middle distance. 'I don't know what to say.' Had she imagined it, or was there a tremble in the philosopher's voice? When he turned back to face the others, he looked ashen.

'Then don't say anything,' Burgess said, in a gingerly tone of both respect and solicitude. 'You've trained us well. Allow us to shoulder some of the responsibility here. Leave this case in our hands.'

'Like you always say,' Collingwood put in, 'doing the right thing isn't always easy.'

'Weathering the goddamn Kirk Commission isn't going to be a cakewalk, either,' Tracy put in.

'You're too young to remember the Church Committee hearings,' an older man at the table, Herman Liebman, told her. 'Paul and I do. These things run in cycles.'

'So do monsoons,' Collingwood said heavily. 'A historical perspective's not much use if you're in the path of the storm.'

'A fair point,' Bancroft agreed. His eyes narrowed. 'Knowledge is power. Goodness knows we've turned over enough rocks from the senator's past. What squirmy things have we found?'

Collingwood turned to John Burgess and gave him a you-tell-him look.

'Not enough,' Burgess, the former Kroll Associates investigator, said with a twitch of a smile. 'For our purposes, we'd need something big, and we're not coming up with it. Frankly, what we have wouldn't make the front page of the *South Bend Tribune*. Favors for major donors? Sure. But it's pretty much what politicians call constituency service. Illegal donations? Not really – he's stood for office four times, against some decently funded opponents. One made that accusation more than a dozen years ago, but the details were so complicated that the legal experts couldn't agree whether it was outside the lines or not. Separate donations from companies where CALPERS, the California public employees retirement fund, held a plurality of shares. If the two companies are really units of a single company, then the donation is in excess of the legal limit.' A wan smile. 'A reporter asked Bennett Kirk about the charge at a press conference. Kirk said, 'Sorry, could you explain it to me one more time?' and everybody cracked up. That was the end of that scandal. Otherwise? He may have had a sexual encounter with a waitress in Reno twenty years ago, but the woman in question has denied it up and down, and even if she didn't, I don't know that it would get media pickup. The journalists have put a halo on this guy. At this point, you'd have to prove that he molested every last kid in the Harlem Boys' Choir to get any traction.'

'Can't be brought, either,' Collingwood said in his fluting voice. 'I mean, you already know about the medical condition. He's kept it secret, but if it got out, it would only bring a wave of public sympathy. Meanwhile, he's got his eyes on posterity. He knows he's not going to be alive to run again, but he'll be around and functioning long enough to make a heap of trouble for us.'

'It's like the Samson effect,' Burgess added. 'The illness doesn't help us. He's in good enough shape that he just might collapse the pillars and bring down the goddamn temple.'

'You say knowledge is power.' Collingwood gave Bancroft a meaningful look. 'The trouble, of course, is what the Kirk Commission knows. Somehow the senator has gained information that he just shouldn't have. That's what makes him a real threat to our entire enterprise.'

'And we still have no clue how?' Bancroft's gaze was attentive but not anxious.

Collingwood shrugged.

Gina Tracy looked impatient. 'I still don't get why we can't just remove Senator Kirk. Accelerate the inevitable. Take the thorn out of our paw.'

Bancroft shook his head gravely. 'You plainly haven't thought it through.'

'Can you imagine the storm of controversy and attention?' Collingwood shot her a reproving look. 'Might prove more dangerous than the committee itself.'

'But we're the goddamn Theta Group,' the black-haired woman persisted. 'Theta as in *thanatos*.' She glanced at Burgess. 'Greek for death, right?'

'I'm aware of this, Gina,' said Burgess. 'But the same risk-assessment procedures that apply elsewhere in the world apply here, too.'

Tracy gave Bancroft a petitioning look. 'There's got to be *something* we can do.'

'Rest assured that I shall not have the work of the Theta Group derailed by a cornhusking pol from Indiana,' Bancroft told her. 'You can be certain of this. The Theta Group must continue to be the arrowhead of benevolence.'

'Extreme philanthropy,' Burgess half-chuckled. 'Like extreme sports.'

'Please don't make a joke of my life's work.' Bancroft spoke softly, but with a chastening look.

A long moment of silence was broken by the sound of apprehensive voices from the communications center on the level below. Then a pasty-faced man mounted the spiral staircase and greeted the senior managers with a grim expression. 'There's been another message from Genesis.'

'Another one?' Tracy asked, crestfallen.

The man from the communications center handed a sheet to Paul Bancroft. To the others, he said, 'The guys downstairs take this seriously.'

Bancroft looked at the sheet briefly, his eyes widening. Wordlessly, he passed the sheet to Collingwood.

'I don't like this,' Collingwood said softly, his anxiety undisguised. 'What do you think, Paul?'

The philosopher had a look of intense focus. A stranger would take him to be reflective rather than fearful; the others knew that was his way in the face of crisis.

'Well, my friends, it would appear that we have larger worries to contend with,' Bancroft said at last. 'Genesis is escalating the threat level.'

'We'll follow the relocation protocol,' said Collingwood, studying the communication. 'Suspend the operation here for the moment, shift over to one of the other facilities. Maybe the one near Butler, Pennsylvania. We can do it seamlessly, overnight.'

'I hate the idea that we're running scared, though,' said Liebman.

'We're in this for the long haul, Herm,' said Bancroft. 'Short-term inconveniences for the sake of long-term security are of no great moment.'

'Yet why is this happening now?' Liebman asked.

'With the Ansari network under our belts,' Burgess told the elderly analyst, 'there will be absolutely no stopping us. We're just at a time of transition. Which means a time of vulnerability. We ride this out, and we'll be unconquerable.'

'The world will be our terrarium,' Collingwood put in.

Liebman still sounded fretful. 'But to let Genesis . . .'

'Inver Brass perished the first time because of overreaching.' Bancroft's voice was mesmerizing in its intensity. He had regained his air of mastery and command. 'Genesis will do it again. We just need to make it through the next few days. Genesis *will* be destroyed.'

Liebman looked less sanguine. 'Or we will be.'

'Have you become a doubter, like Thomas in the Garden of Gethsemane? Have I lost your confidence?' Bancroft's face was unreadable.

'You've never been wrong about the big things,' said Liebman, stung.

'You're kind to say so,' Bancroft replied icily.

Though Liebman hesitated to speak again, his decades of loyalty and friendship compelled him to address the great man with candor. He cleared his throat. 'But, Paul,' he said, 'there's always a first time.'

When the elevator pinged at the eleventh floor, Belknap stepped out, maintaining the slightly blasé look of the over-tired air traveler for whatever cameras might have been installed in the car. Estotek was on the floor below; the eleventh was given over to CeMine. As Gennady had explained, CeMine was a pharmaceutical startup specializing in 'biomarker' research; the aim was to develop bioassays – simple blood tests – that could replace surgical biopsies for certain kinds of cancers. The company boasted that it was based on 'strategic cooperation among industry, academia, and government.' Many partners, many pockets.

It was one of three small offices on the floor; Belknap chose it because its work was least sensitive, from the point of view of confidentiality, and therefore would have the lowest level of security. All that stood between him and the

CeMine offices was a steel-clad door with a narrow slate of steel-mesh reinforced glass.

After making sure that there was no security camera in the hallway, Belknap moved a narrow tension wrench into the keyway of the latch knob, pushing from the far end in order to maximize sensitivity. Then he thrust the rake pick into the keyway and worked back, dragging the pick so that it pushed against all the tumblers. No go. As he feared, it was a double-sided lock. After he raked the top tumblers, he reversed the pick and raked those on the bottom. Only after another several minutes of intense, agonizing concentration did the latch retract and the door swing open.

No alarms. As he anticipated, the offices, which housed the company's finance and legal department, relied upon the building's security. Break-ins were rare in such settings. Ordinary precautions would suffice.

Belknap closed the door behind him. The office suite was dimly lit from fluorescent strips inset along the inner walls, the emergency lighting that building codes around the world required. He let his eyes adjust and walked through the space carefully, flashing a penlight around. The workplaces were mainly open-plan, save for a few enclosed offices at the windows. The carpeting was gray with a large diamond pattern. After a few minutes of inspection, he chose an area where a computer and telephone console was plugged into the floor. As with most office buildings constructed in the past decade or so, the subflooring held a weave of optical and coaxial cables. What were called carpet tiles, usually about two feet by two, were now commonplace, and he was not surprised to find them here; the floor panels could be lifted up for easy access to the wiring below. He lay on the floor and lifted up the carpet tile adjacent to the plug cluster. Flanging the tiles from below was a steel grid, and beneath the steel grid was the wiring. But how many feet of space was there between floors? Removing a crowbar from his Gladstone bag, he began prying up tiles, swiftly, quietly.

Then he pushed down a small fiber-optic camera. On the other end, it plugged into a digital camera, and displayed a flickering image on the flat-screen viewfinder. The snake camera, which produced a standard RCA output, was a mere quarter-inch in diameter and had a sixty-degree field of vision. It was four yards of black-clad cable attached to a small black case of electronics, where a small endocoupler converted the light from thousands of tiny fibers into a unified image. A small xenon light in the terminal cuff provided illumination as the snake cam made its way beneath the 'floating' floor. He pushed the wire further and further, snaking around obstacles, until it ran into a white irregular surface. The acoustic tiles of the ceiling below.

Now he pressed a trigger on the side of the terminal knob; a hollow trocar of hardened steel extended out from the same cuff that bore the miniature fiber-optic viewer and began to spin. It was like drilling with a pin. Eventually he maneuvered the head of the remote camera until it protruded through the just-bored hole.

At first, an irritating moiré pattern obscured the image; Belknap adjusted the controls until the Estotek floor came into sharper focus. The image was of a generic-looking office: rectangular desks, black chairs with oval seats and backs, the usual collection of printers, desktop computers, telephone consoles, in/out boxes. He adjusted the snake cam again, moving the head one way and then another until he brought into focus what he was looking for.

Recessed contact switches, unobtrusive and visible only to a trained eye, mounted in the top of the main door frames. Infrared motion detectors: small plastic boxes placed in high-traffic areas – walkways between cubicle clusters, along a long row of windows. The motion detectors would have been activated once the office closed for the evening, and they presented his most immediate challenge.

Belknap recognized the model. They were passive devices, designed to detect changes in temperature. When an infrared-emitting body entered the protected space, the devices would sense it and a flow of electricity within the device would be interrupted, activating the alarm.

He peered again at them. Again, they looked almost like

light switches; nothing that would detain a casual glance. A fresnel lens focused infrared radiation through a special filter. The sensor had had two reception elements, which enabled it to correct for signals caused by sunlight, vibration, or ambient temperature changes. Those conditions would affect the two pyroelectric elements simultaneously; a moving body would activate one sensor and then the other in rapid succession.

There was virtually no way that Belknap could descend without triggering the alarm. He would not attempt to.

Belknap busied himself removing the sixteen screws holding together the steel flanges that formed a section of the sturdy floor-supporting grid. Finally, he was able to lift up a two-meter L of steel, exposing a reticulated lay of fine wiring, like a beaded curtain. The requirements of versatility also made for porosity. Soon a jumble of carpet tiles, flanged bars, and steel pedestal assemblies formed a small heap.

With a few crude nips of a wirecutter, Belknap made a space, then lowered his Gladstone bag down it until it caught a few feet below the floor. Next, Belknap himself wriggled through the wiring, then scuttled around the airflow ductwork and the rigid piping that fed the sprinkler system. In the crawlspace beneath the subflooring he groped around, with just his small penlight to light the way, until he was inches above the ceiling tiles of the floor below, holding on to electrical cables to support his weight. Gently, he lowered himself onto the reverse side of the ceiling panels, spreading his body out on the thin metal frames – an array of T-beams, cross-tees, and suspension wires – in order to diffuse the downward pressure. The ceiling was designed to support a man's weight, since repairmen occasionally had to do work here. By contrast, the drop-in panels were of mineral fiber designed to absorb sound, not force. If he tried to stand up, he would fall through.

Now he reached down and partially unseated a meter-square panel from its frame – one of Estotek's ceiling panels – and opened his leather case. The next phase of the infiltration would be performed by rodents. He withdrew a squirming canvas bag from his leather case, high-pitched squeaks and grunts growing audible as he opened the drawstring top. Now he tipped the bag over. Its contents – four white rats – slipped through the opening left by the unseated drop panel and fell to the floor nine feet below. Then he reseated the panel and maintained a vigil through the tiny snake cam.

On the small camera screen, he watched the vermin racing around the floor, bewildered and disoriented. Then he directed the camera lens toward the nearest motion detector. The soft green light beneath the square fresnel lens had turned red.

The alarm had been triggered.

Belknap's eyes darted between his watch dial and the small digital viewfinder. Forty-five seconds elapsed before anything happened. Then a man in a brown Estotek uniform appeared with a small pistol in one hand, a large flashlight in the other. He peered around, and a long moment passed before a squeak and a flash of fur caught his attention. Cause and effect. First, the motion detector goes off; then a rat appears – and now a second rat flashing into view. The guard issued what was obviously a curse, though not in a language Belknap could understand. He recalled having heard that Estonian was unusually well supplied with expletives. The rats had been fed nothing in the past few hours save chocolate-coated coffee beans: They were caffeinated, even more energetic than usual. As lab specimens, they lacked the skills and instinct at concealment that their feral cousins would have mastered.

Another rat skittered into view; fecklessly, the guard leaped toward it with his thick-soled boots, trying to stomp on it. Belknap was reminded of children who tried to kick the pigeons on a city sidewalk: so close and yet so elusive.

The next part would require exquisite timing. Withdrawing the remaining rat from the tightly cinched canvas sack, Belknap lifted a corner of a ceiling panel and stuck its head through. Obligingly, it squeaked madly. Snipping off a piece of fiber-optic filament, Belknap knotted a length of it to one of the rat's hind legs. He then pushed a few inches of the squirming creature through the small crevice. It clawed the air wildly. Belknap pinched its tail hard to make it squeak.

Now the guard whirled around, saw the creature's small darting head protruding from a loose ceiling tile. A false dawn of comprehension showed on the Estonian's gray, fleshy face: Vermin – perhaps specimens being held by the medical science company on the floor above – had escaped through the ceiling.

'*Kurat! Ema keppija! Kuradi munn!*' A flurry of unintelligible imprecations: What couldn't be missed was the frustration and annoyance in the guard's voice. But not, however, alarm or anxiety. It was a pest-control problem, not a security breach, the Estonian had decided. He disappeared for a couple of minutes and then returned. Belknap knew the standard security protocols well, and if they were being followed, the guard had gone to cancel any central notification. It was a customary two-stage arrangement when live guards were deployed in combination with electronic sensors. The alarm first notified just the guard, who had perhaps four minutes to investigate its cause. If he deemed it an unwarranted alarm – and 90 percent of all such alarms were unwarranted – he would stop the notification from advancing any further. If he failed to do so, the alarm would then be relayed to a remote location. The guard had responded as a well-trained professional should have. He had identified the cause of the false alarm, had temporarily disabled the sensors in the sector, would maintain his own vigil. The appearance of vermin did not constitute a security concern. Exterminators could be called in the morning.

Belknap also knew, now, that only one guard had been stationed there. Had there been a second, the man would assuredly have summoned him, if only to gawk at the spectacle, a reprieve from the tedium of the posting.

The guard was now directly beneath him. He looked like another victim of the Estonian national cuisine. Yet he moved with surprising agility. For a few seconds he stared at the wildly scrabbling rodent. He started leaping up at it, batting at it – inches away from Belknap, who now pushed up the ceiling panel and, clenching a heavy wrench in his right hand, prepared himself for a sudden strike. It happened as if in slow motion. There was a long second in which the guard, having propelled himself into the air, saw the entire panel above his head lift up, saw a man in the shadows. There was a split-second of eye contact between the two men: The guard's face flashed dismay and astonishment and then a fearful sense of the inevitable as the heavy steel in Belknap's hand struck his forehead, concussing him with a dull *thunk*. The guard, knocked senseless, fell limply to the carpeted floor.

Belknap threw down the Gladstone bag and clambered down from the ceiling, swinging from a cross-tee to a desk a couple of horizontal yards away, and then onto the floor. Now he scrutinized the model number of the nearest motion detector. If he remembered its default settings correctly, it would have phased into a five-minute suspension cycle. Two of those minutes had already elapsed.

With almost automatic movements, he pulled on the sensor's white plastic casing, which popped off easily. If it were an old-style system, he would have been able simply to block the lens while it was off – perhaps with a piece of cardboard – and thereby prevent its activation when it was powered up. But the newer models came with blockage detectors and went into alarm mode if they sensed a visual obstruction of that sort. So Belknap set to work with a very small screwdriver. He removed the tiny corner screws that held in place the amplifier and comparator units. Just beneath them he saw four wires running into the device. Two were the alarm-circuit wires, the code 12vdc appearing in tiny print on the coated wire – voltage direct current. The two other wires were the ones he needed to manipulate. He stripped back the insulation and twisted them together. Then he reassembled the sensor. He proceeded to the other two sensors in the area and went through the same procedure. When the master control resumed, it would sense normal power, but the sensors would no longer be functional.

The files! Gennady had told him roughly what he should

be looking for. But first he had to find them. Assuming they were here in the first place.

The small power diode pulsed on; the system would indicate that the office was alarmed once more. Nervously, he moved an arm in front of the wall-mounted sensor. The green light remained steady. Deactivation had been successful.

The files he was looking for were probably locked in the large windowless space placed at the building core. He approached the door carefully, scrutinizing it carefully. If he had any doubts about it, they were dispelled by the battery of discreet alarm systems that protected it, beginning with a rubber mat, like a double-length welcome mat, in front of the door. At first he took it as a something to protect the carpet when heavy wheeled carts came in. A closer inspection revealed that it was a pressure mat. A series of metal strips were embedded between two layers of plastic, separated only by an intermittently applied spongy material. Step on the mat and the metal strips would touch, activating an alarm. Belknap pried up the carpet tile next to where the mat ended, and with the help of his penlight identified the pair of wires that led to it. He snipped one of them, rendering the pressure mat useless.

Trickier would be the recessed contact switch, similar to the one on the door leading to the outer corridor. A magnet in the top of the door held a switch in the adjacent frame in closed position. Once the magnet was moved away, the switch opened and the protection loop was broken. Belknap pulled up a chair and stood on it. He ran his fingertips along the smooth painted surface of the metal door frame until he felt a slight change in texture. Tapping with his nails, he confirmed that the hollow metal had given way to a thicker, more solid-sounding steel plate. He retrieved a bottle of acetone from his kit bag and wetted the area with the solvent, scraping away at the paint with a screwdriver until he uncovered the flat screw-heads that kept the door-frame unit in place. The unit had been masterfully concealed beneath putty, sealant, and paint. It was concealed no more.

Now he carefully removed the steel plate that protected

the alarm unit and revealed the tiny reed switch, two spring metal strips that were encapsulated in a glass tube, which was kept closed by the presence of the door magnet. With a pair of pliers he swiftly crunched the glass vial and clamped together the two metal reeds physically. Now he wrapped a piece of tape around the tiny metal strips, binding them together. He was just about to start working on the door lock when he had a sudden thought. He had stopped at the first contact switch he found. But might there be others? Now he continued to feel along the steel frame, tapping with his fingernail. There was indeed a second one.

Dammit! He cursed the gods and himself, grateful only for the reprieve granted by his second thought. How could he have been so careless? With movements that were more practiced and less tentative on the second go-round, he disabled the second contact switch, and then did a final inspection of the complete door frame before he set to work on the keyway with the tension wrench and rake pick.

Five minutes later the door swung open, revealing an airless space of about fifteen feet square, dominated by a bank of filing cabinets. There was another door frame on one of the inner walls, suggesting a room within a room. But perhaps it only led to a stairwell.

Belknap looked at his watch. So far, the after-hours infiltration had come off almost without a hitch, but the thought made him feel edgier, not more relaxed. Overconfidence could prove fatal; and no real operation ever went entirely smoothly. When things went smoothly, he wondered when the anvil was going to fall.

The cam locks on the steel cabinets connected to a hook-and-latch mechanism and succumbed to Belknap's focused attentions before long. He pulled open the drawers, removed a thatch of papers, began reading through them. Before long, frustration welled up: He was no expert, didn't know what to look for. He wished that Andrea were there to help him decipher the material. Yanking open one drawer after another, he finally found a file labeled R. S. LANHAM.

The file was empty. A meaningless name, an empty file –

it seemed a parable of futility, mocking his very hopes. The hound was chasing its tail.

After twenty minutes in the files, Belknap found himself fighting off waves of tedium. Yes, Andrea Bancroft should have been there: corporate documents – just her speed. But he forced himself to stay at it, speed-reading through business boilerplate. Only when he reached a tranche of papers stamped copy did he begin to find what he was looking for. These were offshore documents of incorporation, and his eyes raced across them so swiftly that at first he did not recognize the name *as* a name. As a name of a recognizable person, rather than an arbitrarily named business entity. But there it was: Nikos Stavros.

Softly, he pronounced the name out loud. It was a name he knew – that of a Greek Cypriot magnate. Nikos Stavros was a reclusive man whose list of holdings worldwide was legendary.

They included, Belknap saw, a 49 percent interest in Estotek.

Was Stavros in fact Genesis? Was 'Lanham' his alias? But Andrus Pärt had said he was an American. For that matter, then who owned the other half of the company – and what, precisely, did Estotek control? Belknap peered at an onion-skin page headed partnerships and struggled to make sense of it. He lurched to his feet and tried the knob to the interior door – which was, blessedly, unlocked. He switched on an overhead light and, as the fluorescents blinked on, he saw further banks of black filing cabinets. Ten minutes later, he was beginning to perceive the complexity of the enterprise, the largely submerged iceberg that was Estotek.

Eleven minutes later, he heard the arrival of guards in the hallway.

He bolted from the annex like a rabbit from its hutch and he noticed – heart-stoppingly – the familiar alarm tab inset in the flange of the interior door. The knob had turned; the annex door had swung open. But what he hadn't realized was that it was armed, that there was a separate alarm system in place. A silent one. There were not enough expletives even in the Estonian language to express Belknap's self-disgust.

And now he found himself face-to-face with four well-armed security guards. They did not look like the pudgy man in the lobby or the feckless night watchman in the brown uniform. These ones were professionals. Each carried a drawn gun.

Instructions were yelled at him in several languages. He understood 'Freeze!' He understood the directive about stretching his arms over his head.

He understood that the game was over.

The guard who spoke English came closer to him. He had leathery skin and a hatchet face. His gaze took in the files that spilled from the cabinets.

A triumphant grin stretched across his face. 'There was a report of rats,' he said in lightly accented English. 'And now we have caught the rat even as he nibbles at our cheese.'

Then he turned and said something to the youngest of his three colleagues, a twentyish man with yellow hair in a buzz cut, and the ropy, veined arms of a weightlifting enthusiast. The words were in a Slavic tongue; Belknap only made out the common Serbian surname Drakulovic – obviously the man's name.

'Corporate history – kind of a hobby of mine,' Belknap said in a hollow voice. He noticed that the English-speaking guard was holding a Gyurza Vector SR-1, a Russian-made pistol designed to punch through body armor. It could, in fact, penetrate sixty layers of Kevlar, and its chambered steel-core bullets would not ricochet, because they would penetrate. They would travel through his body like a pebble through the air.

'See, it's not the way it looks,' Belknap added.

With a sudden movement, the guard belted him across the face with the hand that held his pistol.

The blow landed like a mule's kick. Belknap decided to exaggerate its effect, which took little effort. He wheeled backward, windmilling his arms, and then he caught a glimpse of the guard's contemptuous look. The man was not taken in for a moment. A second, punishing blow landed – on the same cheek, the way a professional would do it. Belknap forced himself to stand erect, although he wobbled on his legs. It was not the time to resist, his instincts told him. The guard was trying to demonstrate his mastery, not to knock him unconscious. They would have questions for him after all.

'No movements,' the man said in a voice like gravel. 'Be still like a mannequin.'

Belknap nodded mutely.

One of the other guards spoke to the one with the yellow buzz cut in a snigger. Belknap understood little, save the name Pavel – the young man's first name. The young man approached, patted Belknap down, ensuring that he was disarmed. He fished out a small metal tape measure from Belknap's rear pocket and tossed it aside.

'Now, what are you doing here?' The rugged man, obviously their leader, spoke in the tone of a man hoping for a display of insubordination so as to have an excuse to deal out punishment.

Belknap remained silent. His mind raced.

The hatchet-faced guard stepped closer. Belknap could smell his sour, beefy breath. 'Are you deaf?' he demanded. The taunting of a playground bully, prelude to the violence on which he thrived.

Suddenly, impulsive, Belknap whipped his head around and caught the youngest guard's eyes. 'Pavel!' he said, his voice imploring and yet berating as well. 'Tell them!'

The senior guard narrowed his eyes. Confusion and suspicion played across his face. Pavel looked baffled, stunned. But Belknap did not avert his eyes.

'You promised me, Pavel! You promised me there would be none of this!'

The heavyset guard gave the yellow-haired bodybuilder a suspicious side glance. A facial tic twitched the young man's left eye. Evidence of tension. It was inevitable – but, to those so minded, suspicious as well.

Pavel murmured something that, to Belknap, hardly needed translation: some version of 'I don't know what he's talking about.'

'Oh, *please*,' Belknap burst out, indignant. He recalled Jared Rinehart's advice: *Suspicion, dear Castor, is like a river; the only way to avoid its flow is to divert it elsewhere.* The memory gave Belknap strength. He jutted his jaw, squared his shoulder, looked less guilty than aggrieved.

The senior guard's voice was menacing – though it was difficult to say toward whom, exactly. 'You know this man?' he asked Belknap.

'Drakulovic?' Belknap spat. 'I thought I did. Evidently not.' Belknap directed a furious gaze at the young man. 'You piece of shit!' he stormed. 'What kind of game are you playing? Do you think my boss is going to take this lying down?' Belknap was madly extemporizing at this point, sketching out a scenario that would intrigue but remain mysterious to the guards. He simply needed to buy time.

Belknap rolled his eyes theatrically as Pavel Drakulovic burst into a flurry of denials, protests. The outrage was genuine, but it came off as defensive, possibly spurious. Belknap noticed that the two other guards had subtly positioned themselves a few steps away from him, closer to the leader. Drakulovic was now an uncertain quantity; nobody wanted to be closely associated with him, at least not until the matter was resolved and clarity restored.

He continued to protest until their leader directed some brief, harsh word of remonstration at him, and shut him up. Again, Belknap could guess at the message: 'Not another word out of you. We'll sort this out later.'

Now Belknap lifted his chin. Time to drop another name, to sow more confusion. 'I'm just telling you that Lanham isn't going to be happy with you guys. Last time I do *him* a favor.'

The black-eyed guard suddenly looked wary. 'Who did you say?'

Belknap took a deep breath and let it out slowly, his mind working furiously.

R. S. Lanham. An American, according to Andrus Pärt. The 'R' could stand for Ronald, Richard, Rory, Ralph. But Robert was the likeliest; it was among the most common first names in the United States. A Robert could go by Rob, or Bert, or eschew a diminutive altogether, but if one had to stake a wager on the outcome, Bob was safest.

'Trust me,' Belknap said, 'If you knew Bob Lanham as well as I do, you'd know he's the last person you want to piss off.'

The black-eyed guard gave him a curious look. Then he flicked on a small communicator, spoke into it briefly. Then he turned to Belknap. 'The boss comes soon.'

The boss. Not Nikos Stavros. The other owner, then. The principal owner. The man who used the name Lanham.

Andrus Pärt: *This isn't someone I've ever met face-to-face. Nor do I care to.*

The leader now spoke in a low, reassuring voice to his young companion. A quick side glance at Belknap. They did not trust him. But the black-eyed man took and pocketed Drakulovic's sidearm all the same. He was on probation for the time being. It was the only prudent thing to do. Drakulovic sat down on a small stool in a corner of the room, winded, wanting to protest further but resigned to the sidelines.

Belknap looked around him, at the remaining guards, saw their pistols held steady, nothing in their gaze but indifferent professionalism. His mind raced, his eyes darted. *You must get out of here.* There must be something he could do.

The sounds of arrival. *The boss.* Rapid Estonian but spoken, unless Belknap were mistaken, with an American accent.

Then the outer door swung open again and, accompanied by two young blond gunmen, the man who ran Estotek walked in.

His hair was black, dyed, gleaming in the overhead lights. The face was deeply pockmarked, each facial indentation a dimple of shadow. Jet-black eyes sparkled like jewels of malevolence. The mouth was as thin and as cruel as a well-healed knife wound.

Belknap found himself fixated on the two-inch-long scar that curved across his forehead like a second left eyebrow, and the ground beneath him seemed to swell and buckle like a sudden wave. Vertigo swept through him. He had to be hallucinating.

Belknap squeezed his eyes shut and opened them again. *It couldn't be.*

Yet it was. The shadowy Estonia-based mogul, the man who had taken over the quondam Ansari network, was no stranger to him. They had met, years before, in an apartment on East Berlin's Karl-Marx-Allee.

The images returned to Belknap, sickeningly. The Turkish flatweave on the floor. The ebony-framed mirror, the large Biedermeier desk. The twin boreholes of the man's shotgun, his eyes.

Richard Lugner.

The man had been killed that day. Belknap had seen him die with his own eyes. Yet here he was before him.

'It's impossible!' Belknap blurted the words, his thoughts given speech.

The slight widening of the man's vulpine stare only confirmed the identification. 'Would you stake your life on that?' he asked in a horribly familiar nasal rasp. In his left hand he held a large pistol.

'But I saw you die!'

CHAPTER NINETEEN

'You saw me die, did you?' Lugner's lizard-like tongue flickered across his lips, as if searching for a fly. 'Then it's only fair that I get to see *you* die. Only, there will be no stagecraft this time. You see, I've become quite an aficionado of reality as I've grown older. Older but wiser. As opposed to you, Mr. Belknap. When last we met, you were a stripling lad. Too old to be fuckable, but not too old to be fucked with.' He laughed dryly, horribly.

Belknap forced air into his lungs. He recognized the pistol that Lugner was holding. Matte-black, with a grooved, slab-like unit containing the bolt and barrel: a nine-millimeter Steyr SPP. Effectively a foot-long assault rifle.

'All these years later,' Lugner went on, 'I'm afraid you've lost your dewy deliquescent youth and only grown coarser. Thicker and coarser.' He took a step closer. 'The pores on your face, the veining under your skin, the shape of your features – it all grows steadily coarser. Every year, you've grown less like spirit and more like meat. Less soul and more body.'

'I don't . . . I don't understand.'

'Not much to show for four billion years of evolution, are you?' Richard Lugner glanced at his armed guards. 'Gentlemen, behold the resignation in his eyes.' He turned to Belknap. 'You're like an animal in a trap. At first, the animal – mink or fox, weasel or stoat – struggles wildly. It claws at the steel cage, lashes out this way and that, twists and howls and thrashes. A day passes, and the hunter who has set the trap does not appear. The animal thrashes, then sulks. Thrashes, then sulks. Another day passes, and another. The animal grows weak from lack of water. It slinks to the bottom of the cage. It waits only for death. The hunter arrives. But the animal has given up hope. It opens its eyes. And it does not thrash. Because it has accepted death. Even if the hunter sets it free, the animal has sentenced itself to death. It has accepted defeat. There is no reversing course.'

'Have you come to set me free?'

A sadistic grin twisted Lugner's face. 'I've come to set your *spirit* free. Death is man's destiny. I am the one who will help you achieve that destiny on an accelerated schedule. There's nobody who can help you. Your own employers, I happen to know, have effectively disowned you. Your former colleagues know you're damaged goods. Who do you think you can turn to – some grandstanding Midwestern senator? Some vaporous bugbear nobody's ever seen? God, perhaps? Satan, more likely.' A harsh laugh. 'It's time to put away childish things and face your extinction with dignity.' He turned to the English-speaking guard. 'This gentleman will be allowed to leave this building.'

The guard raised his eyebrows.

'In a body bag.' Lugner's slitlike mouth stretched wide.

'Actually, you might want to bring more than one.' Belknap kept his voice level.

'We'd be happy to double-bag you, if you like.'

Belknap forced himself to laugh, a loud, carefree laugh.

'I'm pleased my wit isn't lost on you.'

'If you think you're a wit, you're half right,' Belknap snorted. 'Naw, the joke's on all of us. I wouldn't have chosen you all as companions for my final voyage. But I guess it's not the sort of thing you usually get to choose. I won't be leaving this place alive. That's true. But, one small detail I forgot to mention: Nobody here leaves the building alive. Yes, triacetone triperoxide is a wonderful thing. A real mind-blower.' A grin so wide that Calvin Garth's choristers would have been envious.

'How boring, these lies of yours,' Lugner said, a moue settling on his slashlike mouth. 'How uninventive.'

'You'll see. I've wired up the place with triacetone explosives. On a timer. I'd hoped that I'd be long gone by now. But of course I've been detained. And now destiny is about to play its final card.' He lowered a hand, glanced at his watch. 'So there's some comfort in that. I know I'll be killed. But so will you. Which means that I can die with a certain satisfaction. A life that claims yours hasn't been lived in vain.'

'What offends me isn't that you're lying, but that you're lying so badly. Put some effort into it, man.'

'You'd like to think I'm lying because it wounds your pride to acknowledge that you walked into a trap.' Belknap's voice was exultant, almost madly so. 'Ha! Do you imagine for one moment that I didn't know exactly which alarm I was triggering? What kind of an amateur do you take me for, you pockmarked piece of shit?'

'You're fooling nobody,' Lugner repeated stolidly.

'What you don't seem to understand is this: *I don't care.*' Belknap spoke with the gaiety of the scaffold. 'I'm not trying to persuade you of anything. Just letting you know. For old times' sakes. So you understand the deal. When you die, I want you to know why.'

'And if I left now? Just to play out this absurd scenario.'

Belknap spoke slowly, crisply, enunciating his consonants with care. 'The elevator would have returned to the lobby by now. Sixty seconds to get out there, another thirty seconds at least for the elevator to appear – sorry. It doesn't give you enough time, especially with your limp. The guards here – well, they're extra. Deal-sweeteners. Because, really, this is just between you and me. But I don't think their English is very good. So you don't need to worry about them fending for themselves. And if they're truly loyal, they'll *want* to be vaporized with their boss. Like Hindu brides throwing themselves on the funeral pyres of their husbands. Estonian *sati*. Only this time we're talking about triacetone triperoxide: nectar for the god of thunder. Can you smell it? A little like nail-polish remover. But then you knew that. You *can* smell it, can't you?' He took a few steps closer to Lugner.

'Shall we count out our remaining seconds out loud?'

Lugner's gaze grew only more piercing as Belknap spoke, yet he noticed that the blond guard to his left had grown pale. Belknap made a small bye-bye hand gesture at him, and, suddenly, the man bolted. The second began to follow, spooked. In a lightning-fast movement, Lugner shot him in the face. The Steyr's report was loud yet strangely echoless in the enclosed office space. The others looked at Lugner, stunned.

Now! While the second guard stared at the blood-sprayed face of the slain man, Belknap swung his arm out and snatched this pistol from him. He discharged two rapid volleys, taking out the heavyset man and the remaining blond bodyguard. As Lugner whirled toward him with his hand-gun, Belknap threw himself behind one of the heavy steel filing cabinets. A round punched through the steel plate and, slowed by the dense paperwork, left a bulge on the opposite side. He noticed his small tape measure on the floor nearby. *So you can measure yourself for a coffin.*

Think! The brush-cut man with the veined, ropy arms would be scrambling to retrieve his weapon – would have fallen on the heavyset guard to retrieve it from his jacket. *Visualize!* Belknap blindly snaked an arm around the cabinet and squeezed the trigger twice, rapidly. The shots seemed unaimed, but they were guided by his memory of the body, of where he anticipated the brush-cut man would be. A stricken cry of agony told him that at least one round had struck its target. The man was panting now like a wounded animal, and a noisy stridor told him that air was filling the pleural cavity through the bullet hole, causing his lungs to collapse.

Lugner remained. He would be cannier than any of them. Belknap forced clarity into his racing mind. *What would I do?* He would not risk being overaggressive; instead, he would adopt a defensive posture, perhaps crouching down, making himself a difficult target. His objective would be to get out of the room and lock the door, so that – assuming the talk of explosives proved a hoax – he could dispose of his adversary on his own terms, and at his leisure. He would quietly begin creeping toward the door, would have done so already. He would perhaps seek to distract his adversary from his actual course of action.

Seconds passed like hours. Belknap heard a sound from his left, felt an impulse to whirl in that direction and shoot. But no, it was not the sound of a man; in all likelihood, Lugner had balled up a piece of paper and tossed it across the room, hoping to distract him while he . . .

Belknap stood up abruptly and without looking, let alone aiming, shot toward the doorway – directing his fire low, as if at a fleeing cat. He dived behind the steel cabinets again, replaying what he had seen. He had been right: Lugner had been just where he thought! But had he connected? There was no cry of pain, no gasp.

After a few seconds of silence, Lugner spoke in a steady, well-controlled voice. 'You're a foolish gambler. Nobody beats the house.'

It was the voice of someone who was in complete command of the situation. Yet why would he give himself away? Lugner was a liar through and through. A glimmering realization fluttered its wings in Belknap's breast. Lugner's voice was *too* controlled, too masterful. He had been wounded, perhaps mortally. His game was simply to tempt Belknap into exposing himself. He heard Lugner take a step, and then another. The steps were slow, and heavy, the steps of a dying man. A dying man with a carefully aimed pistol.

He placed his black knit cap on a length of tape from his metal tape measure, pushed it up just above the file cabinet. It was an old trick, the hat or helmet held on a stick, meant to draw out a sniper's fire.

Lugner was too smart to fall for it – a fact that Belknap was counting on. He would be aiming the sights of his pistol to the left, expecting a fast roll. Belknap leaped up like a jumping jack, appeared just a foot or two away from the crude decoy. Lugner, as he had anticipated, had trained his pistol low and to the left. As Belknap squeezed the trigger of the Vector SR-1, he saw an expression flicker across Lugner's sadistic, scowling countenance. The expression conveyed something that the rogue agent had often inspired but seldom experienced: horror.

'I *am* the house,' Belknap said.

'Damn you – '

The first round struck Lugner in the throat, exploding his larynx and cutting off his final words. The projectile easily punched through flesh, through the steel-reinforced door behind him, while its shock waves destroyed the flesh in the region. A splatter zone of arterial blood outlined his upper body against its white-painted surface. The second round, aimed just slightly higher, struck him in the face, hitting just below the nose, blasting a third nostril through flesh and bone and, invisibly, sending hydraulic pressure waves through the region, liquefying the tissue of the medulla and cerebellum. 'Hydrostatic shock' was the technical term, and its effect on the central nervous system was instantaneous and irreversible.

Ten minutes later, Belknap was race-walking down the sidewalk in the Estonian night. He had arrived in Tallinn hoping to reduce the uncertainties, the unknown. Instead, the unknowns, the uncertainties, had only multiplied.

Nikos Stavros. What role did he play in all this?

Richard Lugner, alias Lanham. Was he – had he been – Genesis after all? Or just another pawn of his? What really happened on that fateful day in 1987, when Belknap and Rinehart converged on Lugner's apartment on Karl-Marx-Allee?

Only one thing was certain: Nothing about that sequence in East Berlin was as it had appeared. Had the stagecraft been managed by Lugner alone?

Belknap swallowed hard. Had Jared Rinehart been deceived, as he'd been? Or had Jared – the thought scalded him like acid – been part of the deception? It had all seemed so effortless on Jared's part, the way he suddenly appeared right at the critical moment. To save Belknap's life? Or to help Lugner escape with a piece of theater that would ensure that the hunt was called off for good?

The sidewalk seemed to buckle now as another wave of vertigo swept over him.

His best friend. His most trusted ally.

Jared Rinehart.

Belknap tried to tell himself that it was the stinging wind that was making his eyes moist. He wanted to think about anything other than what he needed to think about.

Had there been other operations in which Jared Rinehart had deceived him? How much fakery had Belknap been subjected to, and *why*?

Or had the two of them been jointly victimized?

Jared Rinehart. Pollux to his Castor. The rock. The one person he could always count on. The one person who had never failed him. He could almost see Jared now, as a wraith-like vision. His reticent warmth, his keen intelligence, his irresistible combination of wry detachment, resolute commitment, unflappable equipoise. A partner through good times and bad. A brother in arms. A protector.

Images came to Belknap like a flipbook animation. The shootout in the room on the Karl-Marx-Allee, the gun battle in the outskirts of Calí – they were among a dozen such events, in which Jared's timely intervention proved crucial. *Be reasonable*, he exhorted himself.

Rinehart was a hero, a savior, a friend.

Or he was a liar, a manipulator, a conspirator in some scheme so far reaching and nefarious as to stagger the imagination.

Which was more likely? *Be reasonable*.

Then he remembered what he had counseled Andrea Bancroft. *The truth isn't always reasonable*.

He wanted to collapse to his knees, wanted to retch, wanted to clamp his hands to his ears, wanted to roar at the heavens. Those were luxuries he denied himself. Instead, as he returned to the Georgian's lakeside house, he forced himself to face the evidence of his senses, to ask the questions that confronted him. It felt like swallowing glass.

Who was Jared Rinehart really?

PART THREE

CHAPTER TWENTY

The flight from Tallinn to Larnaca International Airport, in Cyprus, was uneventful; the storms preceded it. Calvin Garth had not been pleased when Belknap told him that he needed to make use of the chartered jet – there were flight plans to be filed, logistics to be accounted for – but finally relented. A version of old-school ties. Gennady Chakvetadze, after no little grousing of his own, had taken care of the paperwork. He retained his contacts within the Estonian ministry of transport; the impossible was made possible.

The darker storm clouds accompanied the conversation with Andrea Bancroft.

'I don't want to talk about it right now,' she told him when he asked about her visit to the Rosendale facility. 'There's stuff I'm still processing.' There was something in her voice that disturbed him, some sense of a trauma undisclosed.

He debated telling her about Jared, about his fears, but held back. That was his problem; he would not make it hers. He did tell her about Nikos Stavros; here, he knew, her experience with corporate due diligence would be helpful. She rang off and called him back ten minutes later, with a swift précis of the man's holdings and recent activities, at least according to the available business records.

Once more, though, the brittleness of her tone alarmed him. 'About the archives in Rosendale,' he began again, 'at least tell me this. Does the foundation have any Estonian holdings?'

'Some infant-morality, prenatal-care programs in the early nineties. That's about it.'

'Suspiciously little?'

'Non-suspiciously little. On par with Latvia and Lithuania. Sorry.'

'Anything else raise a flag?'

'I told you, I'm still processing . . .' This time there was a quaver in her voice, he was certain of it.

'Andrea, what happened?'

'I just . . . I need to see you.'

'I'll be back before too long.'

'Tomorrow.'

'You said you're flying to Cyprus, right? Larnaca? Kennedy has direct flights there.'

'You don't know what risks you'd be running.'

'I'll be careful. I've *been* careful. I used my credit card to book a flight out of Newark to San Francisco, assuming the account's being monitored. Then I got a friend to book two seats on a flight to Paris, JFK to Orly, using his card, with me as the fellow passenger. My name will show up on the flight manifest but not in the financials. And it gets me into the same international terminal as my flight to Larnaca – a flight that's not going to be fully booked. Forty minutes before the jet to Larnaca departs, I'll just show up at the counter with my passport and cash and buy a ticket. People make last-minute trips all the time – death in the family, urgent business meetings, whatever.' She paused. 'I'm just saying, I've thought this through. I can do this. And I'm going to.'

'Dammit, Andrea. It's not *safe*.' If his worries about Jared Rinehart were borne out, he brooded, no place was safe for him. 'Larnaca especially. You're barging into a realm where you don't belong.'

'Tell me where I *do* belong. Tell me where it *is* safe. Because I'd like to know.' She sounded on the verge of tears. 'I am flying to meet you whether you like it or not.'

'Please, Andrea,' he protested, 'be reasonable.' The wrong words to use, for her and for him.

'I'll see you tomorrow afternoon,' she told him, and he could hear the finality in her voice.

The prospect of seeing her gladdened him and frightened him. She was an amateur; and Larnaca – *his* Larnaca – could easily turn into a killing field, especially if he was going to be confronting Genesis. The thought of harm coming to her chilled him. *If I didn't know better, Castor, I'd say you were bad luck.*

Reclining in his seat, Belknap let the eddies and whirlwinds swirl through the landscape of his mind.

Nikos Stavros. In the rare interviews he had given, he spoke of having enlisted in the Cypriot merchant marines out of high school, and described his father as a hardworking fisherman. He spoke vividly about fishing on a moonless night, shining a five-hundred-watt lamp at the water and attracting a school of mackerels that he would throw a net around. What he tended not to mention was that his father owned the largest fleet of fishing vessels in Cyprus. Nor did he dwell on the fact that his company, Stavros Maritime, made much of its income by ferrying crude for the major oil companies. What distinguished him from competitors with larger fleets was a gift for anticipating the spot market in oil. His tankers could ferry twenty-five million barrels of crude at any time, the value of the cargo varying wildly depending on the fluctuations of the commodities market and the vagaries of OPEC. Stavros was generally credited with a remarkable acuity in predicting those chaotic fluctuations; his fortunes had risen through an acumen usually associated with the canniest Wall Street traders. His own net worth was unknown; he was believed to have extensive holdings, but hidden within a battery of private and unreported partnerships. It was all very suggestive: but of what?

If you were wrong about Jared Rinehart, what else were you wrong about? The question seared him. Maybe his life's journey had been no journey at all, but a manipulated march through a labyrinth of deception. His sense of resolve, his sense of himself, had been compromised beyond retrieval, so it seemed to him. Rage at what had befallen Jared had been his soul's own sustenance: He had put himself in harm's way for Jared; would, indeed, have given his life for his.

And now?

For all he knew, Jared Rinehart was himself Genesis. Hadn't he been in all the right places? The guile, the stealth, the mastery of machination – all these traits equipped him for the role. He had declined promotions that would have taken him out of the field, reduced his mobility, compromised his ability to travel freely. And all the while he was constructing a shadowy realm of terror.

A shadowland that encompasses the globe. Yet its creator would remain anonymous, never glimpsed, never sighted, never recognized. *Like the dark side of the moon.*

Was Rinehart capable of such enormities? Belknap's very soul rebelled at the possibility. Yet he could not rule it out.

As Belknap reclined in a fuguelike state, images and information and uncertainties swirled through his mind in a dust storm of data, until he heard the hydraulic whine of the plane's landing gear. He had arrived.

The Republic of Cyprus, a third the size of Massachusetts, held an outsized fascination for the contending powers that had divided the island back in 1974. Cyprus was much nearer to Beirut than to Athens, and in more than geographical terms. While the breakaway Turkish polity of Northern Cyprus languished, the Cypriots of the south had created a haven of relative prosperity, nourished by tourism, financial services, and shipping. The Republic of Cyprus, a Greek client state, had six excellent ports and a merchant marine with almost a thousand large container ships, not to mention another thousand that sailed under the flags of foreign nations. Given that the island had twenty airports as well, it was inevitably a transshipment point for heroin between Turkey and Europe, a region where the associated activity of money laundering took place all too freely. It was frequented by American tourists, and, with equal diligence, American DEA agents.

Larnaca was named for a Greek word meaning 'sarcophagus' – named after death. It was among the most charmless cities in all of Cyprus. Its streets were laid out in a maze that only a longtime resident could make sense of – and even they could not keep track of the frequent name changes – while Lebanese immigrants huddled in urban squalor in the north of the city. The surrounding land was parched, barren, the local restaurants crowded out by franchises of international chains: KFC, McDonald's, Pizza Hut. It had all the charm of a Bridgeport strip mall set down in a desert. Sand flies made the beaches unappealing for sunbathers. But, past the scrubby salt pines and the long, pencil-like wharfs, its marinas were crowded with yachts and with freighters, and not a few of each were the property of the legendary shipping mogul Nikos Stavros.

After a long delay, aluminum stairs were motored over to the plane, the door opened, and he stepped out into blue-skied morning. Passport control was cursory. He did not dare reuse the Tyler Cooper papers; he had to trust that the papers that Gennady had furnished him were, as the retired spy had assured him, truly uncompromised. So far as he could tell, they were. The taxi ride into town took fifteen minutes. It would take him longer to content himself that he had picked up no unsought companions.

Belknap found himself struggling not to wilt under the strong Cyprus sun, which made everything seem preternaturally bright, and almost disguised the seediness of the city and much of its surrounds. He had seven hours before Andrea's flight would arrive. Much of this time would be spent scouting out Stavros's residence.

Was he being followed? Almost certainly not, he decided. But he would spare no precautions. He spent a full hour darting in and out of the shops and stalls in the old Turkish quarter, changing his wardrobe twice – he put on a couple of cheap kaftans before changing back to a Western tourist's ensemble of guayabera shirt and khaki trousers.

The address he had, 500 Lefkara Avenue, was at once accurate and curiously uninformative. He finally determined that Nikos Stavros essentially owned a hillside and adjoining beach on the very outskirts of Larnaca. The residence overlooked the sea, and was little less than a citadel. The walls were vast, unscalable, and wire-topped, with security cameras mounted every ten yards; even from the sea, a series of buoys hinted at precautions like flat-nets and perimeter cable. A bomb dropped from the air could shake the place. Other than that, however, it would be difficult indeed to penetrate.

From the nearest hillside, a sandy, scrubby elevation, he could make out the dazzling emerald turf, obviously the product of intensive irrigation. The house was a vast three-story Levantine mansion of white stucco with elaborate balconies and gables, the whole structure extending outward into several points, like a vast starfish or a work of sharply folded origami, whose symmetries took a while to detect. Surrounding it was perhaps forty acres of land. Close to the house, he made out elaborate flower gardens, sculpted bushes, a sheltering topiary of cypresses. Through binoculars, Belknap took in the various outbuildings: stables, swimming pool, tennis court. He saw several low hutlike structures, positioned over a berm line, that would have been invisible from the main house: kennels for guard dogs, without a doubt. They would help patrol the place at night, their powerful jaws as deadly as any bullet. Uniformed figures patrolled the perimeter; focusing on them closely, he could see that they carried assault rifles.

He lowered his binoculars, feeling overwhelmed. He recalled what Gennady had said about trail dogs and catch dogs. Was he playing out of position? Had he exceeded the limits of his competence? Even if the technology of surveillance was surmounted, the shipping magnate was protected by an armed brigade. Exhaustion coursed through him.

The situation is hopeless but not serious: something Jared Rinehart liked to say. Remembering Jared's voice caused something close to physical pain, like regurgitating lye. It could not be true. It had to be true. It could not be true. It had to be true. A spinning solenoid of doubt and conviction – an alternating current of recognition and denial – was consuming his ebbing powers of concentration.

Why was he even here? For the past nine days he had been consumed with the mission of rescuing Jared Rinehart – or avenging him. He had been propelled by a certainty that had perished the previous evening. Now the Hound was chasing after something else, something hard, inviolable, essential. He was chasing after the truth.

Andrea's voice: *Tell me where it is safe.*

A shadowland that encompasses the globe.

Nowhere was safe. Nowhere would be safe. Not until Belknap had made it so. Or was killed in the attempt.

The sun was brilliant – noon in the Mediterranean, the sky that inimitable Mediterranean azure – and yet it could all have been inky blackness. Belknap prided himself on seeing through deceptions, yet he had spent much of his life as a victim of one. His belly clutched and cramped. Maybe it was time to admit the futility of his efforts. *And let Genesis have his way?*

Out of the pain came a renewed sense of determination. Stavros's estate was ultra-secure. But it surely had at least one weakness. Swirling mists gave way to crystalline clarity, and another line of Jared's: *When there's no way in, try the front door.*

Half an hour later, Belknap drove up to the estate in a rented Land Rover; to a pebbly-faced man at the outermost gate he passed on a message that was relayed to another, and another. He and his vehicle were searched, and then waved on through. He parked as directed, on a shaded graveled lot, as tidy and carefully raked as a Japanese sand garden. At the front door, he repeated his message to a manservant in formal attire. It was simple, and it was powerful: 'Tell Mr. Stavros that Genesis sent me.'

Once again it proved its efficacy. The manservant, a gaunt man in his sixties with a slightly jaundiced complexion and hollows beneath his brown eyes, did not offer Belknap a drink or issue any other pleasantries. He spoke English with a vaguely Levantine accent, but his movements were stiff and proper, almost prissy – another residue, perhaps, of the island's colonial past. The foyer had elaborate coffered ceilings of mahogany; intricate wainscoting adorned the coral-hued walls.

'He will see you in the library,' the manservant told him.

As the man turned, Belknap caught a fleeting glimpse of a small blued-steel Luger inside his black jacket. He knew he had been meant to see it.

The library had more oak paneling than bookshelves; overhead, an intricate crystal chandelier looked as if it were taken from a Venetian palazzo, and probably had been. So far, the place was very much as Belknap had envisaged it, from the Regency period furniture to the minor Old Master paintings.

Nikos Stavros, however, was not. Belknap had expected a barrel-chested man, a strong jaw, and piercing gaze, and beefy grip – the familiar type of the Greek shipping magnate, the sort who had grown to appreciate the finer things while not shying from the rough-and-tumble of the shipyard when necessary.

The man who scrambled to his feet and took his hand in a clammy, limp handshake was, on the contrary, an unimpressive specimen. His gaze was watery and distracted. He was slight of build: sunken-chested, with narrow wrists and the spindly calves of a boy. His thinning, almost colorless hair was gathered in stringy clumps that lay flat against his scalp, sweat-pasted in place.

'Nikos Stavros?' Belknap scrutinized him closely.

Stavros dug into one ear with a long-nailed small finger. 'You can leave us, Caius,' he called to the gaunt man. 'We'll be talking in private here. Everything's fine.' His tone belied his words. The man was obviously frightened.

'So, how can I help you?' Stavros asked Belknap. 'I sound like a shopgirl, don't I?' The man emitted a short dry laugh and licked his lips nervously. 'But seriously. My whole career has been based on cooperation.' He clasped his hands together in an effort to stop them from trembling.

Belknap turned around and saw that the manservant remained standing on the threshold to the library.

The door closed quietly; the interior surface was upholstered with stud-tufted leather in the Jacobean style.

Belknap took a long step toward Stavros, who seemed to cower in his presence.

Yet he had let him in. Why? Because he felt he had had no choice, obviously. He did not dare incur the wrath of Genesis.

'Cooperation is one thing,' Belknap said gruffly. 'Collaboration is another.'

'I quite see,' said Stavros, who obviously did not. Here was an immensely wealthy man, yet he was practically quivering with fear. Belknap was amazed. 'I'm always game for collaboration.'

'Collaboration.' The operative's eyes narrowed. 'With our adversaries.'

'No!' Stavros yelped. 'Not that. *Never* that.'

'Decisions have been made on the strategic level. As to which operations to *acquire*. Which subsidiaries to *spin off*. Which partnerships to *shut down*.' Belknap's references were veiled, vague, threatening; his aim was both to confuse and to connect.

Stavros nodded vigorously. 'Tough calls, I bet.'

Belknap ignored him. 'Let's talk about Estotek,' he said. Though he was feeling his way through the part, he could betray no hint of uncertainty or hesitancy. He would bear down, ask what he needed to ask, and improvise if necessary.

'Estotek,' Stavros repeated, swallowing hard. 'Sounds like a birth control pill.' A strangled chortle. Once more, the magnate licked his lips nervously. They look chapped. Spittle had gathered in the left corner of his mouth. This was someone under stress.

Belknap took another menacing step closer to the Cypriot shipper. 'Do you think you're funny? Do you think I'm here for an ice-cream social?' Belknap reached out and grabbed the magnate's white silk shirt, jerking him closer to him in a gesture that hinted of bottomless reserves of violent fury.

'I'm sorry,' Stavros said. 'Now, what was the question again?'

'Would you like to live out the remainder of your existence in a wholly immobilized state of unbearable pain and nauseating disfigurement?'

'Let me think – no?' Stavros started coughing wildly. His face was flushed when he turned to face Belknap again. 'Estotek. It's a shell company, isn't it? A storefront, basically. It's how we do business. But you know that.'

'What's at issue isn't my knowledge. It's your *conduct*.'

'Quite. I quite understand.' Stavros turned to a small cluster of liquor bottles and, with shaking hands, poured a drink for himself. 'Where are my manners?' he said. 'I should have offered you one. Here, take this.' He handed the heavy-bottomed tumbler to Belknap.

Belknap took it and immediately threw its contents in Stavros's face. The alcohol stung the Cypriot's eyes, and he blinked tears away. The behavior was outrageous; but Belknap intuitively knew that it was crucial for him to test the limits of such outrage. Only someone backed by extraordinary power would dare abuse the magnate like this.

'What did you do that for?' the Cypriot mewled.

'Shut the hell up, you goddamn shit sausage,' Belknap growled. 'You're becoming a greater liability than an asset.'

Stavros blinked. 'You're from . . .'

'Just came from Lanham.'

'I don't understand.'

'An alliance was formed. An acquisition was made. You're part of us now.'

Stavros opened his mouth, but nothing came out.

'Don't lie to me,' Belknap rumbled. 'You did wrong. You sailed too close to the wind.'

'Please, I didn't tell them a goddamn thing! You've got to believe me!'

Now he was getting somewhere. 'Who?'

'Those investigators got zip. I gave them nothing.'

'Tell me more.'

'Nothing to tell.'

'What are you hiding, goddammit?'

'I'm telling you. They got nowhere, those Washington bastards in those brown suits. The lawyer that Lugner recommended was with me. John McTaggart, right? You guys can ask him. Those Kirk Commission drones made all kinds of noises, like you'd think. But we stonewalled all the way.'

'Except that wasn't your only meeting with them, was it?'

'It certainly was!' A squawk of fear and indignation. 'You've got to believe me.'

'Now you're telling us what *we* have to do?'

'No! I didn't mean it that way! Don't misunderstand me.'

'Again with the orders.' *Keep him off-balance.*

'Please. I don't know how the Kirk Commission learned what it learned but I do know I wasn't the source. Why the hell would I have leaked? What sense does that make? It's my ass that's in a sling. They were talking about deregistering my fleet if I were found in contempt of the U.S. Congress. Like that. I reminded them I'm a Cypriot national! They kept going on about one of my American subsidiaries. They were way out of line. And I told them so.'

'Your ass was in a sling, all right,' Belknap said. 'That's how those Washington aliens gave you an anal probe. Come clean. It'll be better this way. We just need to hear it from you.'

'You got the wrong idea. I squeezed my cheeks hard. Hey, I'm a Cypriot, we know what you gotta do. Nothing got through, nothing came out. I was like a drum. Please – McTaggart will vouch for me. You have to . . . please trust me on this.'

Belknap was quiet for a long moment. 'At the end of the day, it doesn't matter whether I trust you.' He dropped his voice to a hushed tone. 'What matters is whether Genesis trusts you.'

As he said the word, the shipping magnate blanched visibly.

Belknap was proceeding on instinct, taking advantage of a basic mechanism of paranoia. As the corpulent princeling in Oman had made clear, much of Genesis's power stemmed from the fact that nobody knew precisely who he was or who might secretly be in his employ.

'Please,' the Cypriot whimpered. His eyes darted restlessly. 'I need to go to the bathroom,' he stammered. 'I'll be right back.' He darted to an adjoining room, and then through a small door.

What was he up to? Not summoning backup; he could have alerted his armed manservant with the press of a button. Something else, then.

Suddenly Belknap knew. *He's calling his partner in Tallinn.*

When Stavros returned a minute later, he looked at Belknap strangely; a host of small doubts had sprouted, it seemed, like plant life in a desert after a rain. 'Richard Lugner is – '

'Dead,' Belknap said. 'That's right. See, he tried to renegotiate terms with Genesis. Let that be a lesson to you.'

Stavros's veal-white face paled even further. He stood there stiffly, his silk shirt stained with Scotch, but also darkened by sweat around his underarms and shoulders. He shuddered as Belknap held his gaze. 'He – he . . .'

'Was lucky. It was quick for him. It won't be for you. Y'all have a good day now.' Belknap gave him a look of smoldering contempt as he left, shutting the heavy door behind him. The sense of triumph was fleeting, dissolved by a maelstrom of uncertainties – and, as well, by the recognition of a certain truth: Wounded animals were always the most dangerous.

As Belknap drove his Land Rover down the sandy escarpment and along the coastal road, he found his mind spinning. The meeting with Stavros had proved informative in ways that Stavros would not have been able to appreciate – but Belknap himself hadn't yet fully parsed its content. One fact was surely significant: To Stavros, Genesis was a feared enemy – an enemy that needed to be placated and appeased, but an enemy all the same. Lugner had not been an agent of Genesis, but an adversary. That was a surprise. Would there be a way to play one entity against the other?

He admitted to himself, if reluctantly, that he welcomed Andrea's help, her expertise . . . maybe even needed it. But not just her help. Her – what? Her keen intellect. Her perspective. Her capacity to consider and explore contradictory ideas. But there was still more to it, wasn't there? As strenuously as he had sought to discourage her from coming, he had been secretly grateful when she had persisted. He had planned to join her at the Livadhiotis Hotel Apartments, on

Nikolaou Rossou. She would be arriving there within the hour if her plane were on schedule.

In his rearview mirror he saw another car leaving the narrow hilly road that led only to Stavros's estate. Was it Stavros himself? The car veered off into the large marina, and, maintaining a careful distance, Belknap now followed. Through a line of scrubby pines, he saw someone – not Stavros – get out of the car and walk toward the waterfront with powerful, confident steps. Belknap moved closer.

The man was tall and slim but moved with coiled strength, like a mountain cat. He was talking to the man in a booth by the parking lot, and when he turned and gestured toward his sedan, Belknap felt his stomach plunge.

No, it couldn't be!

Short brown hair, elegantly elongated limbs, eyes concealed behind sunglasses – but Belknap knew those eyes, knew their soulful gray-green gaze, because he knew this man.

Jared Rinehart.

His friend. His enemy. Which was it? He had to know.

Belknap had leaped from his car, was on his feet and running – racing, *sprinting* – before he realized what he was doing.

'Jared!' he called out. *'Jar-ed!'*

The tall man turned to look at him, and what Belknap saw in his eyes was plain and undisguised: fear.

Jared broke into a run, fleeing as if afraid for his life.

'Please, stop!' Belknap called out. 'We need to talk!'

It was a nearly comical understatement. But so much emotion surged into Belknap's chest – not least the hope against hope that Rinehart could explain everything to him, could help his life make sense again, anneal the hairline cracks by the clarity and logic and sanity that seemed his natural element. *Please, stop.* Yet Rinehart was charging across the marina as if Belknap posed a mortal danger. He swept down the long wharf with remarkable speed, his feet ghosting along the planked surface. Belknap was gulping air as he gave chase. He let himself slow down a little. A pier, projecting into the water. *Where could Pollux go, for God's sakes?*

A stupid question that was answered moments later, when Jared leaped onto a motorboat that was docked nearby. The key was in the ignition, in compliance with marina rules, and, seconds later, Rinehart had sped off into the green waters of Larnaca Bay.

No! He had spent the past two hundred hours searching for this man. Now that he was in his sight, he would not give up.

Acting on unthinking impulse, he leaped onto a small runabout – a Riva Aquarama, elegant as a high-end sports car, with a helm of polished dark wood and chrome, a hull of fiberglass. Belknap released the ropes that trussed it to the wharf-side posts, pushed up the hatch over the engine, and twisted the key. The motor turned over and then rumbled.

The helm console, too, looked like the dashboard of a vintage sports car: large round dials, light-blue lettering against black, set in glossy dark wood; a ridged steering wheel of white and powder blue, with chrome spokes. Now he pushed the throttle. The rumble became a roar, matched by a splashing sound as the propellers churned away. The orange needle in the oil-pressure gauge moved up in jerky increments; the amperes gauge swung all the way forward. As the motor surged, the boat lurched higher in the waves. But where was Rinehart?

He peered through spume and spray and the glare of sun against the ocean; it was like peering through a heat scope at someone lighting a cigarette. Too much flare. The waters had looked deceptively placid from the shore; in fact, the waves were powerful, heaving like a leviathan struggling for breath, rising higher the further out he got. Ahead of him and to his right, above a bermlike swelling of the waters, he caught a glimpse of Pollux, his lithe frame protruding above the helm. Spume from bow and stern thrusters told Belknap that he was turning, preparing for some maneuver. Belknap kept the throttle at full speed. It was physics at this point. Rinehart was on a larger boat, a Galia, with oversize propellers that left a wide foamy wake. It was a bigger boat and a more powerful one: but not a faster one. It was the difference between a sedan and an eighteen-wheeler. Another upheaval of water occluded Belknap's view. He was now perhaps a mile and a half from the shore, and Rinehart was turning his Galia in an arc that actually was helping Belknap to gain on him.

Belknap's hands cramped around the boat's controls; his heart pummeled his chest. He was getting closer, closer.

He could see Rinehart in partial profile now, see his high cheekbones and the shadows beneath them.

Don't run from me!

'Jared!' he bellowed.

The other man did not reply or even turn around. Had he heard him over the drone of the motor, the churning water?

'Jared! Please!'

Yet Rinehart remained erect and immobile, his gaze fixed on some unseen destination.

'Why, Jared? Why?' The words spilled from Belknap in a roar like that of the ocean itself.

The drone of the Galia grew louder, and then disappeared into another, enveloping sound: the bass blare of a freighter's horn.

At the same time, Jared did something with Galia's controls and the boat thrust upward, and then surged forward, swiftly widening the distance between them.

The large ship had been coming in along the sea lane from Akrotiri Bay, to the west. A vast black-hulled vessel flying a Liberian flag, it was one of those behemoths that seem impossible to miss, but at any distance are easily overlooked on the full-horizon vista of the open seas. Now Pollux maneuvered his Galia over to the bow end of the freighter. *Madness!* He was coming suicidally close to its bow. As a high wave blocked Belknap's view, he wondered whether suicide was, indeed, Jared's intention. After the wave crested, Belknap realized Rinehart's game.

No splinters. No wreckage. Nothing at all. Jared had

succeeded in his aim: to conceal himself behind the freighter.

Belknap knew the limits of his own nautical experience well enough not to try to pull up close to the freighter or approach its hazardous wake. Instead, he moved at an angle past it, in order to gain a sight line on the waters behind. Standing at the cockpit, Belknap swung the car-style steering wheel hard to the right while peering over the spray-fouled windshield.

At last Belknap had the angle he had sought. The Liberian behemoth was a bulk carrier, he noticed; its cargo could be ore or orange juice, fertilizer or fuel. Once containerized, they all looked the same. The vessel itself was perhaps forty thousand deadweight tons and at least five hundred feet long. Now he could see to either side of it. He scanned the seas, glimmering and glinting in the overhead sun like desert sands, and felt something cold wash over him.

Jared Rinehart – his friend, his foe – had disappeared.

As Belknap returned to the marina, the roiling in his mind matched that of the ocean. Had Rinehart ever really been kidnapped in the first place? Had that, too, been an elaborate ruse?

The anguishing suspicions returned. The idea that his best friend and soulmate – yes, Pollux to his Castor – was a *traitor*, a traitor, not least to him, was like a knife to the heart. For the thousandth time, he cast about for another explanation. He flashed back on Jared's stricken face: the face of someone to whom Belknap was a threat. Why? Because Belknap could now see through the subterfuge – or was there some other reason? The questions surged and swelled and filled him with a nausea that battered at him like seasickness.

Amid the turbulence was a single point of solace: the knowledge that Andrea was here. His watch told him that. His career had been short on companionship and long on isolation. It was one reason that Pollux had come to matter so much to him. Field agents were discouraged from putting down roots, and those who could not accustom themselves to loneliness never stayed the course. But one could tolerate a condition without welcoming it, and now, more than ever, he yearned for a reprieve, a respite. He glanced at his watch again.

She would be in the room, waiting for him. He would be alone no longer.

As he drove to the Livadhiotis Hotel Apartments, on Nikolaou Rossou, he had to force himself to pay attention to the road, the traffic, the other vehicles. His speed was determined not by the posted signs, but by what other drivers had established as normal, which was considerably faster. The hotel had been chosen not for its comfort, but for its proximity to the major roadways, and Belknap took in the various trucks and trailers that were headed either to the harbor or to the airport. There was a yellow-and-red DHL van, its driver with his hirsute arm out of the open window, as if propping up the roof. A green-and-white tanker with its long cylindrical cargo of liquid propane. A cement truck with its slowly rotating drum. A white, windowless Sky Café van.

He felt his scalp prickle, and he glanced yet again at his watch. It was wrong to have let her come; he should have tried harder to dissuade her. He didn't, because her mind was made up. Yet was it also because, on some level, he wanted her to come?

The Livadhiotis Hotel Apartments had a large brown marquee with its name in mock stone-and-chisel–style lettering. The flags of nine nations, chosen apparently at random, projected out from the marquee in a failed attempt to signal some sort of international stature. Above the ground level were three floors with arched, almost semicircular windows. The rooms came with kitchenettes – that was what made them 'apartments' – and the place had the familiar old-sponge smell of cheap housing in hot climates. A man in a motorized wheelchair barked a greeting when Todd Belknap entered. His vein-webbed face had a sheen that made Belknap think of the leaves of certain tropical plants. His hands were gnarled and powerful-looking. Something in his gaze seemed veiled, at once aggressive and furtive.

But Belknap was in too great of a rush to dwell on the curled lip of the crippled hotel clerk. He collected his key – it was the old European system, the room key attached to a rubberized weight, and returned to the front desk when the guest left the building – and made his way to the room he had checked into that morning, one floor up. The elevator was slow and small; when he got out, the hall was dim. The hall lights were on a timer, he remembered: another cost-saving measure. Inside the room, the old-sponge smell grew stronger. He closed the door behind him. He saw Andrea's bags on the floor near the veneer-on-fiberboard dresser and felt something like relief fluttering in his chest. She had been in his thoughts far more often than could be explained by the nature of his pursuits. Her fragrance, her hair, her soft, glowing skin: He had not been able to leave these things behind when he flew across the Atlantic.

'Andrea,' he called out. The bathroom door was open, the room dark. Where was she? Having a coffee at one of the nearby cafés, perhaps – adjusting to the time zone. The bedspread looked rumpled, as if she had stretched out on it to have a nap. Then his heart started to trip-hammer, swifter at comprehension than his head. The folded white paper on the small bedside table: It was a note.

He picked it up, read it quickly, and was struck by a bolt of fear and fury. He forced himself to reread it more slowly. His stomach was a small, hard ball.

Everything about it heightened his sense of dread. The paper was hotel stationery; the writing was in pencil. Both features would stymie any attempt at forensic scrutiny. Nor was the message worded as a kidnapping note. *We have taken possession of the package*, the note said. *Enjoy your stay*. Yet what truly made his blood freeze was its sign-off: GENESIS.

CHAPTER TWENTY-ONE

Dear God! Had Jared Rinehart's appearance been a ploy to distract him while the abduction had been orchestrated? Belknap's horror turned into fury – fury, first, at himself. *He* had allowed this to happen to her. Yet his own anguish, his own gut-clutching guilt, was a luxury that he could not afford – that *she* could not afford.

Think, dammit! He had to think.

The abduction had to have been recent – which meant that every moment would count. It was an elementary calculation: The more time that was allowed to elapse after an abduction, the smaller the odds of recovery.

The island of Cyprus had been cursed for decades, torn by strife and enmity and conflict, corruption, and intrigue. Yet it was, after all, an island. That circumstance, he dimly sensed, was the crucial one. The foremost priority of Andrea's kidnappers would be to get her off the island. Larnaca was not the busiest harbor in Cyprus, but it was the site of the island's busiest airport. *What would you do?* Belknap placed steel-rigid fingers on his scalp, forcing his mind to operate as theirs must have. Speed was the imperative. A conviction grew within him: They would have bundled her into an airplane. He breathed deeply, inhaling through his nostrils. Through the stale smells of mildew and cigarette smoke, the citrus and bergamot notes of her cologne were was still detectable. She had been here very recently. She was on the island still. He had to go with his best guess and pursue it as hard, as fast, as he could.

He blinked, and suddenly he knew. The windowless Sky

Café van: It was out of place. Airline foodstuffs and provisions were always trucked in early in the morning, before the regular schedule of departures began. Yet the van was on the highway bound toward the airport in the middle of the afternoon. It was wrong, as wrong as a FedEx man making deliveries then. He remembered how his scalp had prickled, his subconscious mind picking up on the anomaly. Now needles of apprehension jabbed at him.

Andrea had been in that van.

Larnaca International Airport was only a few miles away, to the west. He had to get there as soon as he could. A few seconds could make all the difference. There was not a moment to lose.

He bounded down the stairs, taking them three or four at a time, and ran through the deserted entrance hall. The man in the motorized wheelchair had vanished, as he expected. He climbed into his Land Rover and started up the engine even before he slammed the door. Now, tires squealing, he turned onto the road that led to the airport, heedless of the eighty-kilometer speed limit, veering around slower-moving vehicles. Larnaca's airport had the highest ratio of private jets to public carriers of any international airport in the world. It was this fact that told Belknap what he needed to know. Whizzing past a sprawling desalination facility, the blue tanks and white tubes of an industrial alembic, he veered into the exit ramp to the airport, where, a minute later, he swerved around the Queen's building and the flight-connection center, a tall rectangular structure of darkened glass and dun-colored stone, LARNAKA AIRPORT spelled out in blocky blue letters. Thirty international airlines and thirty chartered airlines were served, but Belknap was interested in neither. He needed to go past the main buildings and toward the fourth terminal. He pulled up to the smaller building, tires skidding, and raced inside. The floors were overpolished stone tile, a pattern of beige and coral, and his rubber-soled moccasins maintained their grip as he ran past the usual duty-free stores, the words 'duty' and 'free' separated by the airport's pyramidal seal, bottles of wine gleaming beneath icy-bright fluorescents. He darted around columns covered with small blue square tiles. The terminal was a blur of gates and check-in stations, and lackadaisical security guards who made unexcited noises of remonstration, for a man racing madly about was assumed to be a passenger afraid of missing his plane. He peered through the large plate-glass wall of a waiting area that faced the runway, and saw a Gulfstream G550 on the runway. A private plane, obviously, though capable of long-distance flight. On the tail, the small but unmistakable logo of Stavros Maritime – three intersecting circles around a star, turquoise against yellow. The engines were already fired up, the plane prepared for taxi and takeoff.

Andrea was inside. It hit him with the force of certainty.

He turned around, darted past one of the blue-tiled columns, and crashed into one of the uniformed security guards.

'I'm so sorry!' Belknap said, making vigorous apologetic gestures. The guard was angry, but he also knew it was hazardous to alienate the sort of VIPs who frequented the terminal. He took refuge in his native tongue, cursing the American in Greek. He did not notice that he had been relieved of his walkie-talkie, the small two-way radio that hooked onto his nylon belt.

Pretending to be winded, Belknap wandered to a pay-phone, in a row of them across from one of the check-in stations. He dialed the number of the airport, asked to be connected to the air-traffic controllers. In a low, guttural voice, he spoke to the man who finally answered. 'The air-craft on the runway at Terminal Four contains a bomb,' he said. 'High explosives. Altimeter charge. Expect a further communication.' He clicked off.

Now he made two more phone calls, to the U.S. Drug Enforcement Agency's offices in Nicosia, the country's capital, which was now the last divided capital in the world. Carefully employing certain codewords and professional abbreviations, he conveyed an unambiguous message. The Gulfstream about to depart from Larnaca contained a large shipment of Turkish heroin, a shipment that was ultimately on its way to the United States.

Belknap could not be sure which would respond the fastest, the ATC or the DEA, but either would immediately order the grounding of the aircraft. He glanced at his watch. Though the DEA had its offices in the capital, he knew that it employed a small detail that was stationed at the Larnaca airport. How long would it take to mobilize it? He took out a handkerchief and discreetly wiped down the telephone receiver.

He looked at the Gulfstream; the plume of hot air from the engines, visible only from the distortions it produced in the scene behind it, was diminishing. The pilot had been ordered to power down. Two minutes passed. Three minutes. A fast-moving van with a collapsible ramp on its roof pulled up to the jet, joined swiftly by another one. Next, a canvas-topped truck pulled up, filled with Cypriot military police-men. Others – their garb told Belknap they were American DEA agents – joined them. The Cyprus authorities had pledged full cooperation with the United States on matters of drug enforcement, and, as a beneficiary of American mili-tary, security, and financial assistance, Cyprus had to at least appear to honor the pledge.

Now Belknap raced down to a steel door that led onto the tarmac, flashed a plastic ID card at the guard. 'DEA,' he grunted. He jerked a thumb toward the activities outside, pushed at the steel gate bar, and made his way toward the scrum of officers that surrounded the Gulfstream. It should have been the last place that an interloper like himself should show his face, but he knew from experience that an interagency massing like this was easy to penetrate. It was like crashing a wedding; everyone would assume that you belonged to the other family. Besides, nobody ever suspec-ted the presence of a sheep at a gathering of wolves: The plethora of armed and uniformed law-enforcement people seemed to assure that no outsider would dare join them.

Belknap turned to one of the men he had identified as DEA. 'Bowers, State,' he said. Meaning: a member of the

U.S. State Department, or an American operative with a cover job supplied by that department. It hardly mattered which assumption was made. The man he spoke to wore a khaki-colored shirt with a round patch at the shoulder, U.S. JUSTICE DEPARTMENT lettered across the top, DRUG ENFORCEMENT AGENCY curving up the bottom. A stylized rendition of an eagle flying against a blue sky over a curved section of the green earth. The man wore a pin that identified him as a special agent.

'You know the bird belongs to Nikos Stavros?' Belknap asked.

The American just shrugged, head-pointed to another American, obviously his superior.

'Bowers,' Belknap repeated. 'State. We got the notification same time as you. A twenty-three-five.' That was the bureaucratic designation for an urgent-action summons. 'Just here to observe.'

'McGee. The Cyps stormed it a minute ago.' The American had cowlicked blond hair, small ears that jutted out, and a band of red across forehead, cheeks, and nose – the way a man who stands outside a lot gets sunburned. 'They got a message about explosives, some altimeter rig.' The sound of barking dogs emerged from the cabin. The door had been opened and a ramp had been extended and latched onto it.

'We were told it was a transshipment of heroin.' Belknap looked bored, unfriendly. He knew that nothing was more likely to excite suspicion than a display of friendliness, an ingratiating air. Internal-affairs officers always gave themselves away by their cordiality.

'It's probably a few kilos of bullshit,' the blond American said, with a border-state half-drawl. 'But we'll see, right?' A testing glance.

'You will,' Belknap replied. 'I'm not hanging around here all afternoon. You got registration info on the craft?'

The man paused a beat too long. 'Pending.'

'Pending?' Belknap gave him a look. 'If I wanted smoke blown up my ass, I'd get out my ass-bong.'

The DEA man laughed. 'Well, it's no big mystery, is it?'

'You've confirmed Stavros, is all I'm asking. How about the pilot?'

'Pilot's a full-time Stavros employee, too,' the DEA man said, nodding. 'And here he comes now.'

Frogmarched by two well-armed Cypriot agents, the pilot made his way down the aluminum stairs, protesting vociferously.

Belknap took out the walkie-talkie and spoke into dead air: 'Bowers here. Call it confirmed that pilot belongs to Stavros.' A bit of theater for the American, McGee.

The blond DEA man conferred briefly with one of the Cypriots, then turned back to Belknap. 'No drugs yet. But a drugged-up passenger.'

Belknap looked up to see the small dazed figure of a semiconscious woman, half-escorted and half-dragged by two powerful Cypriot policemen.

It was Andrea.

Thank God! She seemed intact, unmarked, though her eyes drooped, her limbs were slack. Opiate intoxication by all indications. A debilitating state but a rapidly reversible one.

On the tarmac near the green military vehicle, the pilot was professing bewilderment, ignorance. Yet Belknap had no doubt that he was acting on orders from Nikos Stavros.

Nikos Stavros – who must have been acting on orders from someone else.

'I wonder who that is,' McGee said, glancing at the stuporous Andrea.

'You don't know? We do. A Yank, from Connecticut. We get first dibs on her. Pilot's all yours.'

'You can't big-foot us,' McGee groused. It was as much as a concession.

Belknap did not reply to him, but he spoke into the walkie-talkie again: 'Taking the girl into custody. We'll pass her back to DEA-Nicosia in a few.' He paused, pretended to be listening through earbuds. 'No big,' he said. 'Let's show the DEA boys just how efficient we can be. May need a medic.'

Taking advantage of the confusion of the moment, he approached Andrea and took her from the Cypriot policemen, seizing her by both elbows, his movements brusque and professional-seeming. The other members of the DEA would look to McGee to complain if there was cause to, and the Cypriots had been instructed to defer, operationally, to the Americans.

'I'll call you when I fill out the F-83,' Belknap said to McGee. 'Any discrepancies and the computer spits it right now.' He spoke in a tone that disguised his exertion, the fact that he was bearing most of her weight. Moments later, he had walked her to one of the electric carts that had ferried some of the military policemen to the plane. The driver, a blunt-featured Cypriot, was obviously accustomed to taking orders; Belknap sat down on the rear bench beside Andrea, and gave the driver his instructions in curt, simple terms.

The driver turned and looked at Belknap, and if he were seeking authorization in his granite-faced countenance, he evidently found it. The electric cart rolled off.

Belknap felt her pulse, which was slow. Her breathing was shallow but regular. She had been drugged; she had not been poisoned.

He directed the driver to his black Land Rover and enlisted his help in transferring her to the backseat. Then he dismissed the man with a casual salute.

Alone with her at last, Belknap inspected her shrunken pupils. She made noises, soft, slurry noises, somewhere between murmurs and whimpers. More evidence of opiate intoxication. He set off quickly, and got a room at the first motel he saw – an ugly one-story structure of mustard-painted cinderblock, styled like an American roadside lodge. He carried her into it and felt her pulse again. No sign of recovery. No sign that she was emerging from the stupor.

He stretched her out on the narrow bed and moved his fingers over her knitted cotton shift. His suspicions were confirmed. Beneath her left breast was a Duragesic patch – an adhesive square impregnated with a transdermal fentanyl preparation. It was a powerful synthetic opioid, and the patch – designed for cancer patients and others suffering chronic pain – would steadily release it into her bloodstream, fifty micrograms per hour. Given her level of sedation, there had to have been at least one more patch, stealthily suppressing consciousness. He kept looking, vaguely uncomfortable at the liberties he had to take as his hands roamed her body. He found a second patch attached to her inner thigh and removed it as well. Were there more?

He could take no chances. He stripped her of all her clothing, including her undergarments, and inspected her nude body.

At the right side of her thigh, he saw a small dark bruise, an oval of bleeding below the skin. Examining it more closely, he saw a puncture wound, as if she had been messily jabbed by a large-bore needle. Was that how she had first been subdued at the room from which she'd been abducted – jabbed with a fast-acting sedative? If so, she must have struggled; it was not a normal injection site. *You didn't make it easy for them, did you?* Belknap thought admiringly.

He continued his inspection. Two more adhesive transdermal patches had been attached within the crease of her buttocks. The Duragesics, in combination, would steadily keep her sentience submerged while remaining just below lethal dosage.

Who had done this to her?

Some of the fentanyl residue would continue to diffuse from her epidermis even after the patches were removed. He ran a bath and helped her into it, vigorously soaping the areas where the patches had been. The activity was both intimate and clinical. The use of such patches to keep a captive subdued for long periods was hardly new. But it alarmed him to contemplate what they might have had in store for her. He remembered the story about the man whom Genesis had kept alive for two years on IV nutrition while he was completely immobilized within a steel box. A Poe-like imagination, Ruth Robbins had called it. Belknap shuddered.

Over the next hour, Andrea grew less groggy. Her vocalizations gradually became recognizable as English. Speaking in short sentences, she made it clear that she had little memory of what happened to her after she arrived. He was not surprised. The powerful drugs would have induced retrograde amnesia, removing memory of events immediately preceding as well as following the abduction. Just now, she wanted only to sleep. Her body craved it in order to rid itself of the drug.

The alert among various levels of officialdom would put his adversaries on the defensive, Belknap knew. For the moment, then, she would be safe.

But Nikos Stavros would not be. Leaving her sleeping peacefully in the narrow bed, he got into the Land Rover and raced back to Stavros's estate. The winding road was as he remembered it, but when he reached the gate, he was puzzled to find it open.

Near the grand house, its terra-cotta roof tiles glowing in the setting sun, he saw three police cars. The manservant he had met before, Caius, looked ashen. Conferring with the locals, once more, was the man he recognized from the airport, McGee.

He pulled up in his black Land Rover, and with a brusque nod at the DEA man, he strode into the house.

There, in the library, were the bullet-riddled remains of Nikos Stavros. His body looked even smaller than in life, the limbs even spindlier. Blood puddled around him. His eyes were open, holding a lifeless gaze.

Belknap looked around the room. Bullet holes flecked the ornate woodwork in the library. He picked up a misshapen piece of lead that had penetrated a wood chair, hefted it, got a sense of its weight, its diameter. They were not military-issue; they were U.S. special-ops hollowpoints with partial copper jackets – the very kind Belknap had himself always favored. It was as if someone was intent on implicating him.

Through an open window near the front hallway he heard the sound of McGee on a cell phone conferring with his higher-ups. Mostly it was an exchange of details, ballistic and location. Then Belknap heard him say in a quiet voice, 'He's here.' A pause. 'No, I saw the photo, and I'm telling you that he's here, now.'

As Belknap made his way back to his Land Rover, he saw McGee turn to him and wave, with a wide grin and a friendly look.

'Hey,' McGee said. 'Just the man I wanted to talk to.' The voice was cordial, ingratiating.

Belknap ran to the car and roared off at top speed.

In his rearview mirror he could see confusion among the officials he had left behind. They would be calling in for orders – should they pursue? But by the time authorization came, it would be too late.

He flashed on Stavros's frightened visage during his visit earlier that day. It was as if the magnate had thought that death itself had come to pay a call.

Had he been right?

CHAPTER TWENTY-TWO

Amarillo, Texas

'That thing still recording?' the large Texan asked with a grin. He had been expansive in defending himself from his critics, and seemed pleased that the reporter – was he from *Forbes* or *Fortune*? – didn't interrupt him in midflow. The wall behind him was filled with photographs of him hunting, fishing, and skiing. A framed cover of a trade magazine proclaimed him the buccaneer of beef.

'No worries,' said the smaller, bearded man in the visitor's chair drawn up before the Texan's mahogany desk. 'I always bring spare batteries.'

'Because I can be a big talker when I get worked up.'

'A man doesn't get to be the CEO of one of the country's largest beef producers without knowing how to explain where he's coming from, I'd guess.' The smaller man's eyes were bright beneath his thick-framed glasses, and he smiled easily. Not like most journalists, in the Texan's experience.

'Well, the truth is eloquent, like my pappy used to say. As for those rumors concerning the misuse of employee pension funds – rumors is all they are. The offer that I've proposed is in the best interests of the shareholders. What I'm saying is, Do the math. Aren't shareholders people, too? Maiden aunts and little old ladies, plenty of 'em. You ever hear those community groups worrying about the shareholders?'

The man with the tape recorder nodded vigorously. 'And our readers will want to hear more about that. But, while there's still that good light from the outdoors coming in, I'm thinking that our photographer's going to want to take a few shots of you. That okay?'

A toothy smile. 'Bring it on. The left profile's best, I'd say.'

The smaller man left the Texan's corner office and returned with another man, powerfully built, with a square head and short light-brown hair, not immediately identifiable as a wig. He carried a camera bag and what looked like a tripod in a case.

The CEO extended a hand. 'Avery Haskin,' he said. 'But you knew that. I was telling your colleague Jonesy there that my left profile's probably best.'

'I'm Smith,' said the photographer. 'And I'll make it as quick as I can. You mind sitting just the way you are, at your desk?'

'You're the boss,' Haskin said. 'No, wait – *I'm* the boss.'

'Funny guy,' Smith said. Standing behind the CEO of Haskell Beef, he opened what looked like a tripod case and removed a captive-bolt pneumatic gun.

The Texan turned around in his chair and saw what Smith had in his hands. Immediately his smile vanished.

'What the hell – '

'Oh, you recognize it. Well, you would, wouldn't you? It's what cattlemen use to slaughter cows, isn't it?'

'God*dam*mit – '

'Be a mistake to move,' Smith interrupted in a chilly voice. 'Course, it might be a mistake *not* to.'

'Listen to me. You fellers animal-rights activists? You gotta know something. Killing me won't change a goddamn thing.'

'It'll save the pensions of fifteen thousand workers,' Jones said airily, fingering his facial hair – wool-crepe fibers affixed with stipple wax. 'Fifteen thousand of them, one of you. Do the math, huh?'

'But I like that you assume we're animal-rights whackos,' Smith put in. 'Natural assumption, when you dispatch the chief of a beef-producing company with the very instrument of professional slaughter. Leastways we thought so. It'll definitely put the investigators on the wrong track.'

'Remember the pol we clocked in Kalmikiya last year?' Jones traded glances with Smith. 'How the government flew in a toxicologist from Austria? Nobody could figure it out. Decided it was a real bad case of seafood poisoning.'

'Bet our friend Avery here isn't much for seafood,' said Smith. 'You an organ donor, Avery?'

'What?' Sweat beaded on the Texan's forehead. 'What did you say?'

'He is now,' Jones reminded his colleague. 'I filled out the forms in his name more than a week ago.'

'So here we go,' Smith said, adjusting the lead-length of the captive-bolt stunner. 'A veritable bolt from the blue, huh? A pretty funny way to go for a cattleman.'

'You think it's funny? Oh, Jesus, please, sweet Jesus . . .'

'Fact is, one day we'll look back on this and laugh,' said the man with the captive-bolt gun. He caught Jones's eyes.

'And laugh? You're off your rocker!' Avery Haskin's voice rose in incredulity and rage.

'Oh, I didn't mean *you*,' said Smith, as he sent the bolt deep into Haskin's brain. Unconsciousness was instant, irrevocable, but the pons and the medulla at the base of the brain – responsible for respiration and heartbeat – would remain intact. At the hospital, an EKG would confirm that the CEO was brain-dead. Then the organ harvesting would begin.

Prime meat, Smith reflected. A fine destiny for the buccaneer of beef.

New York

All great cities, in Belknap's experience, were surrounded by an industrial wasteland, and New York was no exception. As he drove, he could see, to either side of him, vast tanks of liquid natural gas and redbrick factories, dominating but disused, like the mastodon skeletons of a bygone industrial era. Factories gave way to warehouses in various states of disrepair, and then the looming blocks of abandoned housing projects. Evidence of human habitation gradually became visible: culverts littered with fast-food detritus, pavement sparkling with fragments of green and brown glass, the shrapnel of alcoholism. *If you were homeless, you'd be home by now*, Belknap thought sourly. He changed lanes abruptly, swung the steering wheel too hard, keeping himself awake by the juddering and slewing of the rented car.

Andrea Bancroft, who had been half-slumbering beside him, yawned and blinked.

'How are you doing?' he asked. She did not respond at first. He placed a hand on hers, gently. 'You doing okay?'

'Still a little deafened from the trip over,' she said. They had traveled directly from Larnaca to Kennedy International Airport, but not in an aircraft made for passengers. Instead, they took a DHL jet, a windowless cargo hauler whose pilot Belknap had known for years. They had been, in effect, stowaways. The chartered DC-8 had returned to Tallinn, and he didn't know what names might have been added to the international watch lists that the commercial airlines were obliged to track. The freighter solved a number of immediate problems. Still, a cargo jet was not designed for passenger comfort. Outside the cockpit, hinged benches were attached to the bulkhead, for backup crews, but the soundproofing, like the heating, was fairly perfunctory.

'Sorry about the ride,' Belknap said. 'It seemed better than the alternatives, though.'

'I'm not complaining. At least I'm finished vomiting.'

'Your body was trying to get the fentanyl out of your system.'

'I'm just sorry you had to see it. Not very romantic.'

'The bastards could have killed you, or worse.'

'Right. I must remember to send you a thank-you note. Anyway, now you've heard all my secrets. I was running my mouth for a while, wasn't I?'

'It passed the time.' His eyes were smiling.

'I still feel kind of wiped.'

'Four Duragesic patches. That's going to pack a punch.'

'Four, huh.'

'I told you. Two on your ass, one on your shoulder, one on your inner thigh. All infusing a powerful narcotic into your bloodstream. Plus there's a nasty bruise on your thigh you should keep an eye on.'

'Say, how did you get all those patches off me anyway?' She was blushing.

'How do you think? No nurse matron at hand.'

'I get the picture.'

'Respiratory depression isn't a real healthy condition, okay? What was I supposed to do?'

'I'm not complaining. Christ. I'm grateful.'

'You're embarrassed. Which is crazy.'

'I know it is. I know it is. It's just a little . . . further than I usually go on a first date. The stripped-naked part.'

Belknap kept his eyes trained on the traffic ahead of him and said nothing. After a while he asked, 'Still no memory of your abduction?'

'I remember arriving at Larnaca, I remember checking into the place on Nikolaou Rossou. Then it's like a black fog. The drugs, I guess. There's a long period where I can't remember much at all. Just flashes and glimpses. Maybe I hallucinated this, but I had a memory of you holding me. For hours.'

He shrugged. 'I guess I was scared.'

'For me?'

'Which is why you're bad news, sister. A good agent should be unattached.' He spoke gruffly, but couldn't avoid a catch-in-the-throat moment of recollection. 'Jared always said that.'

'You think Stavros knew what he was in for?'

'Hard to say. Stavros was pulling strings, but he was in the grips of his own puppet masters, who were pulling *his* strings. Rashly, this time.'

'They feel threatened.'

'We've been trampling on a tripwire,' Belknap said. 'The piano was supposed to drop on our heads.'

'And I've been rummaging through the records of the piano factory.'

He eyes darted to the rearview mirror, keeping tabs on the vehicles around him. Instinct would tell him whether they were being followed. He glanced at a bent-over woman on the roadside with a shopping cart filled with bottles: a plant? No, the real thing, he concluded, with the kind of matted hair that required weeks of neglect. 'You told me about what happened at Rosendale. You can't let it prey on your mind.'

'Doing what I did – does it change a person?' Her voice was small.

'It does if you let it.'

She shuttered her eyes. 'When it happened, I felt like I was going to hell. Like I'd crossed a line, gone to a place I could never return from. And somehow, after what happened to me in Larnaca, I don't exactly feel that way anymore. Because there's a kind of evil here that doesn't play by any rules I know about.' She opened her eyes, and there was a glint of defiance in them. 'Now I feel I'm going to hell only if they drag me there. And I'll go kicking and screaming.'

He looked at her gravely. *You killed two people*, he thought. *Two people who wanted to kill you. Welcome to the club.* 'You did what you had to do. Nothing more, nothing less,' he said. 'They thought you were weak. They were wrong. And thank God for that.'

They were wounded, he knew, both of them, in ways both deep and invisible. Yet he also knew that to take the time to tend to an injury would slow them down, maybe with fatal consequences. There would be a time for healing, but that time was not now.

'So what now?' Andrea said tonelessly. 'What are we looking at?'

'A goddamn spiderweb.' At a concrete cloverleaf, Belknap off-ramped onto I-95 South. 'And you know what you find when you come across a great big spiderweb? Somewhere in the vicinity, a big fat spider.' He turned and looked at her closely. There were hollows beneath her eyes, like yellowish bruises. She was exhausted. But he did not see the staring look of fear that some people acquired after a traumatic episode. She had undergone a shattering experience, but had not been shattered by it.

'You still mad at me for going to Cyprus?' Her hazel eyes glinted in the morning light.

'Mad and glad. I was there, driving around Stavros's place, and it was the middle of the day there, and the sun was blazing. And you weren't there. And, to me, even though it was the middle of the day, it felt like night. There was a kind of darkness to it all.'

'Darkness at noon,' Andrea mused. Another look of wan amusement. 'That could make a good title for a novel, don't you think?'

'I'm sorry?'

'Never mind. A lame joke. So what's the plan?'

'Go back to something you just said. About them being threatened. Because we're not the real threat. Something else frightens them more. Something or someone. Stavros was scared – but not of me. He was scared of what he thought I represented: Genesis. But also of Senator Bennett Kirk, the Kirk Commission. They were linked in his mind.'

'Could Genesis be working through the Kirk Commission?' she asked. 'I'm just trying to connect the dots.' She shook her head. 'Christ. A United States senator in the pocket of a crazed maniac? Now there's a thought.'

'I don't know that Kirk's in anyone's pocket, exactly. Like you say, maybe the idea was that Genesis was using him. Working through him. Feeding him stuff, maybe.'

'Meaning the senator's a cat's-paw? But that's insanity!'

Belknap shifted lanes and increased speed, simply to see whether any other vehicle followed suit. 'Meaning the senator's a critical player in this. Probably without even realizing it. Because I've been thinking of something that Lugner said, too. Something about a grandstanding Midwestern senator. Made me wonder whether Genesis was using the Kirk Commission, that he – or she or it – had somehow enlisted it for his own purposes.'

'Or hers, or its.' She wriggled in her seat, shifting to face him again. 'Is that why we're driving to Washington?'

'Glad you're alert enough to read the traffic signs.'

'I'm getting a Daniel-in-the-lion's-den vibe. Are you sure

this is the safest course of action?'

'On the contrary. I'm sure it isn't. You want me to do the safest thing?'

'Hell, no,' she answered without hesitation. 'I want to make things right. I'm not built for living in fear, okay? I'm not built that way. Cowering in a cave somewhere isn't my style.'

'Mine neither. You know, you could have made a kick-ass government agent. The salaries aren't much, but you can't beat the parking spaces.' Belknap's eyes darted once again to the rearview mirror as he spoke. Still no sign that they had been followed. I-95 was the busiest corridor in the whole Northeast. There was protection in the sheer profusion of humanity.

'Join the world and see the army.' Andrea stretched. 'Do we have an operating hypothesis? Let's go over this one more time. Do we think Paul Bancroft is Genesis?'

'What do you think?'

'Paul Bancroft is a brilliant man, a visionary, an idealist – I truly believe that. But also a dangerous man.' She shook her head slowly. 'It's the extremity of his vision that makes it monstrous. But what motivates him isn't vanity. It's not a personal lust for power or money.'

'A man tries to impose his system of morality on the rest of the world, I'd say that – '

'But wouldn't we all do that, if we could? Remember what Winston Smith says in Orwell's *1984*: 'Freedom is the freedom to say that two plus two equals four. If that is granted, all else follows.''

'Two plus two equals four. That works.'

'Does it? Is freedom your freedom to assert what *I* believe to be true? Is it your freedom to do what *I* believe is right? I mean, just think what might follow from that. There are a lot of people who are just as convinced in their moral codes as they are in the fact that two plus two equals four. What if they're wrong?'

'You can't always doubt yourself. Sometimes, Andrea, you've got to be willing to take your own side of an argument.'

'No, Todd, you can't always doubt yourself. I'll give you that. But if someone else is going to define my freedom. I'd rather it be people who weren't completely sure they were always right. Uncertainty can be a discipline. Not in the sense of being rudderless or indecisive, but in the sense of knowing we're not infallible. Of being open to the possibility that our judgments aren't definitive and beyond revising.'

'You're the niece of a big thinker, and you sound like one, too. Maybe *you're* Genesis.'

She snorted. 'Please.'

'Assuming it isn't Jared Rinehart,' he added bleakly.

'You really think it could be him?' Andrea's gaze returned to the road, which spooled before them like an endless gray river.

'Maybe.'

'The way you described him running away from you, the way he looked – reminds me of something Paul Bancroft once told me. He said common sense isn't a matter of seeing what's in front of your eyes. It's a matter of seeing what's in front of the other fellow's eyes.'

'What are you getting at?'

'Genesis. You think maybe it's Jared Rinehart.' She turned to face him. 'Maybe Jared Rinehart thinks it's you.'

The Comfort Inn, near Washington's downtown convention center on Thirteenth Street, had the familiar green-and-yellow awning projecting from redbrick walls. Belknap requested a room in the rear of the building. Two beds. The room was small and dim: All the windows looked out on brick walls. It was just what he was after. Once again anonymity would provide security. They ate at a fast-food restaurant, and then Andrea stopped at a copy shop with Internet access before they turned in for the night. The decision to share a room was not discussed; it just happened. Neither wanted to be separated – not after all they had been through.

Belknap could tell that Andrea had something on her mind, and continued to study her, looking for the subtle fissures of delayed trauma.

'You want to talk about Rosendale?' he said, finally, after

they had both brushed their teeth. He wanted her to know that this door was open; he wasn't encouraging her to go through it.

'There's . . . what happened,' she said haltingly. 'And then there's what I learned.'

'Yes,' he said simply.

'I want to tell you about what I learned.'

'I'd like to hear it.'

She nodded quickly. He could see the effort with which she pulled herself together. 'You need to understand – in the world of securities research, there's what we call the raw-data stage. That's where I am.'

Even in the yellowish glow of the cheap lamp, she looked beautiful. 'Should I want to wait for the glossy cover page and the spiral binding?'

Andrea half-smiled, but her eyes were intent. 'I'm seeing patterns of payments. All around the world. Timing suggests the possibility of electoral manipulation.' She was focused now, speaking with growing confidence.

'Swinging elections? Getting favored candidates in office?'

'All circumstantial, but that's part of it, I think. Can't leave the fate of Partido por la Democracia in the hands of ordinary citizens, I guess.'

'Slow down, Andrea. Walk me through this.'

'I started to wonder when I found records of a series of exchange-rate hedges. The details don't matter. What's significant is that the Bancroft Foundation was slipping millions of dollars into foreign banks at various points. Greece, the Philippines, Nepal, even Ghana. Well, it turns out that the years and places aren't random. Each corresponds to a major change of government. In 1956, millions of dollars are converted into Finnish markkaa, and the next thing you know Finland has a new president. A close-run thing, too. The guy defeats his opponent by just two electoral votes, but he stays in power for the next quarter-century. From the pattern of yen conversions, it looks like Japan's Liberal Democratic Party might have been a big beneficiary of the foundation. There are all sorts of local elections that led to parliamentary-level consolidations, and to go by the timing, the outcomes were guided by Bancroft money. Chile, 1964, the election of Eduardo Frei Montalvo? A major Bancroft presence in the Chilean peso.'

'And you know this how?'

'Basically, there's evidence of a lot of exchange-rate optimizing, probably because they were shifting tens of millions of dollars into the local currency and the foundation wasn't nearly as rich as it would later become. Likewise, in 1969 you see a major conversion into the Ghanaian cedi. I looked at the foundation's official reports, and there were no major initiatives in Ghana dating to that time. But it's the same time that the head of the Progress Party, Kofi A. Busia, is sworn into power as prime minister. I'm sure the guy was irresistible to Paul Bancroft.'

He glanced at Andrea. 'What did he do?'

'Start with who he was. This guy had a Ph.D. from Oxford University, had been a professor of sociology at the University of Leiden, in Holland. I bet the Bancroft people were convinced that he was just their kind of guy, a cosmopolitan committed to the common good. Looks like he disappointed his backers, though, because two years later he was ousted. Dead two years after that.'

'And you think the Bancroft Foundation – '

'Maybe because it was West Africa, and nobody was focused on it, they got a little sloppy. I was able to track a series of currency trades from March of that year. Looks to me like Bancroft bought Busia the country of Ghana for twenty million dollars. Now it seems like they're trying the same thing in Venezuela. The foundation's like an iceberg. Partly visible. Mostly submerged. Turns out they basically control the National Endowment for Democracy. Meanwhile, its official report acknowledges all these grants to various Venezuelan political groups.' She pulled out a piece of paper, showed him.

Fundación Momento de la Gentei
  $64,000

Instituto de Prensa y Sociedad - Venezuela
    $44,500
Grupo Social Centro al Servicio de la Acción Popular
    $65,000
Acción Campesina
    $58,000
Asociación Civil Consorcio Justicia
    $14,412
Asociación Civil Justicia Alternativa
    $14,107

Belknap looked it over. She must have uploaded the document online before she left and printed it out at the copy shop. 'Pin money,' he grunted. 'Chump change.'

'These are just the official subventions. They buy you the names of the relevant principals, that's all. Based on currency-conversion data, I'd guess that the real transfers are actually a hundred times greater.'

'Christ. They're buying themselves another government.'

'Because the people aren't smart enough to decide for themselves. That's how they figure it.' She shook her head. 'And so much of the stuff is done through computer networks. There's a guy I know, Walter Sachs, who's a real whiz at the tech stuff. Works at the hedge fund I was at. A strange cat in some ways, but brilliant.'

'You're talking about an I.T. guy at a hedge fund?'

'Strange, I know. Graduated near the top of his class at M.I.T. Working at the hedge fund is his way of not working. It's tiddlywinks for him. Means he can spend most of the day vegging out. He's a whiz with an ambition deficit.'

'Andrea, you need to be very careful who you talk to, who you trust,' Belknap said sharply. 'For their sake as well as your own.'

'I know.' She sighed. 'It's just so goddamn frustrating. All this information, so little knowledge. Theta. Genesis. Paul Bancroft. Jared Rinehart. Rome. Tallinn. Arms dealing. Political manipulation. It's like we're looking at all these tentacles and we're still not sure who the octopus is.'

They thrashed through what they knew for a few minutes longer, but made no real progress. Exhaustion, a bone-deep enervation they both shared, befogged their concentration like dark fumes, and, by mutual assent, they turned in. He chose the bed closest to the window. A shared room with separate beds: There was intimacy, and there was distance. It seemed right.

Sleep should have come easily, but it came with difficulty. He awoke several times in the night, staring at the hateful visage of Richard Lugner. At other moments Jared Rinehart appeared to him, shimmering with an unearthly glow, walking through the corridors and recesses of Belknap's mind.

I'll always be here for you. Rinehart at the funeral of Belknap's wife.

Know this, my friend. You will always have me. Rinehart, on the phone just hours after Belknap heard about Louisa's death during an operation in Belfast.

In a life of inconstancy, Jared Rinehart had proved the one constant thing. His cool intelligence, his steadfast loyalty, his quick, mischievous wit. He was a friend, an ally, even a polestar. Whenever he was needed he would suddenly appear, as if guided by a sixth sense.

What was the truth? If Belknap had been wrong to trust Jared, what else could he trust? If he had been so wrong about this man, could Belknap trust himself? The questions pierced him like cold steel. He turned and tossed and gathered clammy sheets around him, and stared at the ceiling for what seemed like an hour.

He heard distant traffic sounds, and nearby breathing, Andrea's. At first her breaths were deep, metronomic. Then they began to grow ragged. He heard her cry out in her sleep, muted sounds of distress, and when he turned toward her, her arms were flailing out as if to protect her from unseen assailants.

He came to her, touched her face. 'Andrea,' he whispered.

She thrashed again in her sleep, convulsed by nightmares, and he held her flailing arms.

'Andrea,' he repeated.

Her eyes blinked open, staring, terrified. She was breathing hard now, as if she had been running.

'It's okay,' he said. 'You were having a nightmare.'

'A nightmare,' she repeated, her voice thick with sleep.

'You're awake now. You're here with me. Everything's okay.' The dim light – street illumination leaking from the edges of the window blinds – modeled her cheekbones, her soft skin, her lips.

Her eyes focused now, registered the comforting lie. 'Please,' she said. 'Please hold me.' A whispered command.

He pushed the damp hair from her brow, put his arms around her. She was slender and firm in his arms. She was warm and made him feel warm.

'Andrea,' he said. He breathed in deeply, somehow intoxicated by her fragrance, her warmth, her presence. Her face glowed like porcelain.

'It's not over, is it?' she asked. 'The nightmare.'

He drew her nearer to him, and she clutched at him, at first with fear, and then with something else, something like tenderness.

His moved his head closer to hers. 'Andrea,' he murmured, and she pressed her lips to his, and clasped him in her own arms, and soon their two bodies felt as if they were one, flexing and shuddering and flushing. It was a way of denying the violence and death they had seen, an affirmation in the face of negation, a way of saying *yes* in a world of *no*.

CHAPTER TWENTY-THREE

Nobody was more avid for publicity than a senator without seniority. That was why Senator Kenneth Cahill, a freshman from Nebraska, fit the bill perfectly. During the campaign he doubtless received plenty of ink in the local papers; once he was elected, he and his staffers would have been maddened by the ensuing dome of silence. People who run for public office seldom relish silence.

The gambit was childishly easy. When 'John Miles' from the Associated Press phoned his office, requesting an interview on the subject of a 'key provision' Cahill had supported in an Interior Appropriations bill – half a million dollars for upgrades to the Littleton Wastewater Treatment Plant, and county-wide improvements to the storm-water collection system in Jefferson County – the senator had responded just as Belknap had predicted. Cahill's staffers had practically offered to send a car for him.

Nor did Belknap choose his affiliation randomly. Associated Press reporters, he knew, were generally anonymous, and, as an additional precaution, he had made it clear that he wasn't a Washington reporter, so none of the staffers would have expected to know him. The AP had almost four thousand employees in two hundred fifty bureaus; saying you were from the AP was like saying you were from New York. Even a fellow reporter wouldn't expect to recognize a colleague. Not that anybody at Cahill's office would be scrutinizing his bona fides. To a junior senator, publicity was oxygen, and Cahill, who ranked second to last in seniority in the august body to which he had just ascended, was starved for it. 'Miles' made an appointment to visit at three o'clock.

Belknap appeared in the lobby of the Hart Building at five before the hour. He had a yellow lanyard around his neck holding a thick plastic badge with a magnetized strip. The word 'press' appeared in bold capital letters above the name John Miles, the assignment verification code, his institutional affiliation and nationality, and a passport-size photograph. It was good work. The guard had small, squashed features, heavy-lidded eyes, and, despite his squinty, suspicious gaze, was about as fierce as an unweaned puppy in Belknap's quick appraisal. He had the visitor write his name on a sign-in list and waved him through. Belknap was wearing a pair of tortoiseshell glasses along with a jacket and tie, and carried a briefcase that was rolled swiftly through a metal detector unopened.

Around him was a scattering of people who were obviously Hart Building regulars: K Street lobbyists, Senate aides and pages, reporters and messengers. He took the elevator to the seventh floor.

As he got off the elevator, he placed a quick call to the Nebraskan's press secretary. He had been delayed – another interview had run long, the story was more complicated than he had realized; he'd be there as soon as he could.

Then he made a left turn down a long, windowed hall and walked into the anteroom to the impressive duplex suite belonging to Senator Kirk, a man who had all the seniority that the Nebraskan lacked and was putting it to startling use. Belknap knew that Kirk would be in his office; he had a committee meeting an hour earlier, had another coming up in forty-five minutes.

'I'm here to see Senator Kirk,' he said to the weathered-looking blonde who sat at the reception desk. Primly dressed in a dark-green jacket and high-necked blouse, she looked less like a praetorian guard than a prep-school headmistress – the hair was colored to a deep-hued honey blond; nothing brassy, nothing frosted – but was no less intimidating for that. 'I'm afraid I don't have anything on the senator's schedule. What did you say your name was?'

He paused. Why was this so hard? *Follow the plan*, he exhorted himself. *Roll the dice or you're not in the game.*

'My name,' he said, swallowing hard, 'is Todd Belknap.'

'Todd Belknap,' she repeated. The name meant nothing to her. 'I'm afraid the senator is a very busy man, but if you'd like to try to schedule an appointment at some point, what I'd suggest is that – '

'What I need you to do is convey a message. Tell him my name. Tell him – I'm assuming that this is a privileged conversation – that I'm a senior officer at Consular Operations. And tell him that I've come to talk about Genesis.'

The woman looked confused. Was this man a religious zealot or a source within the intelligence services? 'I can certainly deliver the message,' she said uncertainly. She gestured toward a row of worn brown leather chairs on the wall adjoining the door and waited for him to take his seat before she picked up her handset and spoke in a low voice. She was not speaking to the senator, he was certain, but to a senior aide. It was as he expected. Then she glanced behind her, to the closed door that separated the reception area from the rooms where the work of the senator's office was done.

In less than a minute, a bald, squat man with nails bitten to the quick bustled out of the inner door. His fishbelly-white face wore a breezy, unconcerned smile; only a small facial tic betrayed the tension he was at pains to conceal.

'I'm Philip Sutton,' the man said. 'The senator's chief of staff. What can we do for you?' He spoke in a low voice.

'You know who I am?'

'Todd Beller, was it? Or Bellhorn – was that what you said to Jean?'

'I'll save us both some time.' The operative's voice was calmly disabused, not reproachful. 'You just ran a computer check from your office or you wouldn't be talking to me. I'm betting you pulled up records from the State Department database. What did you find?'

Another small tic rippled through his cheek. He did not answer immediately. 'You're aware, aren't you, that the senator is under the protection of the Secret Service?'

'I'm glad to hear of it.'

'Owing to the nature of the commission hearings, there have been various threats.' Sutton was no longer smiling.

'I passed through metal detectors on the way in. You can search me if you like.'

Confrontation glinted in Sutton's eyes. 'But there's no record of your having come into the building,' he said fiercely.

'Would you prefer that there were?'

Sutton's gaze met his for a long moment. 'I'm not sure.'

'Will the senator meet me?'

'I couldn't say.'

'You mean you haven't decided.'

'Yes,' the portly aide replied, his pale eyes alert. 'That's exactly what I mean.'

'If you're certain we have nothing to discuss, just say the word. You'll never see me again. But you'd be making a mistake.'

Another long moment elapsed. 'Look, why don't you follow me? We'll talk in my office.' In a louder voice he said, 'Fact is, lots of people misunderstand the senator's views on agricultural price supports. I welcome the opportunity to clarify them.'

The facial-recognition system had been installed at the Hart Senate Building without hoopla or, indeed, any official notice. The system was still considered experimental, although in tests it had so far proven to be 90 percent accurate. The security cameras were connected to both a local and a remote computer database, and fed into a multiscale algorithm. Each camera would, in low-resolution mode, swiftly identify the appearance of a headlike object, at which point the camera would switch into a high-resolution mode. As long as a face was turned at least 35 degrees toward a viewing lens, the image could be automatically manipulated – rotated and scaled, so that it could be compared to reference images. The transposed video image was then captured in an eighty-four-byte code – a numeric faceprint, based on sixteen facial landmarks – and compared to hundreds of thousands of stored data files. The system was capable of comparing ten million faces every ten seconds, with a numeric value assigned to each comparison. If the value was high enough, a provisional match was triggered and the tracking camera would switch into its highest-resolution mode. If the match was further confirmed, offsite operators would be notified. Only then did human beings peer at the two images, supplanting the mathematics of local-feature analysis with old-fashioned human judgment.

That was happening now; analysts were replaying the video feed and comparing it to the reference faceprint. There seemed little doubt. The computer could not be fooled by glasses or alterations of facial hair; the facial indices it analyzed were virtually unchangeable: cephalic, nasal, orbital. The angle of the chin, the distance between the eyes – such metrics could not be changed with hair dye or eyewear.

'It's a match,' said a slack-bellied operator, who spent much of the day in a darkened room munching on corn chips, with a rhythmic hand-to-mouth motion that sometimes went on, nearly uninterrupted, for hours. He wore an untucked Hawaiian-style shirt and cargo pants.

'Then you click on that red box, and that's it.'

'Then everyone's notified?'

'Then whoever needs to be notified is notified. Depends on the guy. Like, sometimes it's a matter for the lobby guards and the D.C. cops. Sometimes, though, it's someone the CIA or the FBI just wants to keep tabs on, like a foreign national, and they definitely don't want to alert the target. They play it how they play it. That's not our call.'

'Just click on the red box.' He returned a finger-clutch of Fritos to the bag and stared at the screen.

'Just click on the red box. Feels good, doesn't it? Click, and they'll take care of everything.'

The man in the Stratus coupe had a last sip of his coffee, then gripped the cup lightly in his fingers. It was an Anthora-style paper cup, the blue ersatz-Greek letters proclaiming it's our pleasure to serve you. He crushed it into something wrinkled and shapeless and tucked it between the cushions of the seat beside him. He always left his rental cars as dirty as possible; sometimes he would sprinkle sand and ash from a cigarette receptacle on the seats. That way the rental company would be sure to vacuum it carefully, to wipe it down, and leave less of *him*.

He watched the woman leave the motel, relishing the incongruity: an expensive-looking bird leaving a cheap-looking nest. The woman wore no makeup and seemed to have chosen clothing that disguised her figure rather than flattered it, but you could tell she was pretty. Justin Colbert found himself smiling. But that was out of line. One didn't mix business with pleasure. Not usually.

The order of business was different with this woman, anyway. A higher degree of difficulty was involved. There could not be another slipup. Not this time.

That was why they'd called in the best. That's why they had called in Justin Colbert.

Now he powered down the driver's-side window and fluttered a road map. 'Ma'am,' he called to her. 'I'm sorry to bother you, but I'm trying to get back onto Route 495, and . . .' A helpless shrug.

The woman looked around warily, but she was unable to resist Justin's helpless look. She walked over to the car.

'You just get onto 66,' she said. 'A couple blocks north.'

'And which way is north?' Justin asked. The timing was right: They were unobserved. His wrist brushed against her forearm.

'Ouch,' she said.

'My watchband – sorry about that.'

The woman gave him a strange look: a small flare of puzzlement, giving way to suspicion, giving way finally to stupor and incomprehension and the loss of consciousness.

It's my pleasure to serve you, he thought, chuckling to himself.

Colbert was already out of the car when she started to collapse; he caught her by her elbows. Four seconds later he had positioned her in the trunk of his coupe and closed it gently. The plastic tarp would keep any messy body fluids from wetting the carpet-lined trunk. Five minutes later he was on the Baltimore-Washington Parkway. He would check on her in an hour or so, but there would be enough oxygen to sustain life during the trip.

Andrea Bancroft was more valuable alive than dead. At least for the time being.

CHAPTER TWENTY-FOUR

On the seventh floor of the Hart Building, the two men sat at a desk across from each other, and tried to size each other up.

There was no alternative. Senator Kirk's chief of staff wanted to know whether Belknap could be trusted. What he could not know was how hard Belknap had been struggling with the question of whether *Kirk* could be trusted. The operative had scanned Nexis, read the standard profiles and biographical sketches, and tried to form an image in his mind. Without access to Cons Ops files, he was handicapped. The facts only went so far. Kirk had been born in South Bend, into a prosperous farming family. He attended public schools, was president of the student council, played hockey and football, attended Purdue, got a law degree from the University of Chicago, clerked for a Federal circuit judge, and returned to Indiana to take a job at a law school in South Bend. Four years later, he was elected Indiana's secretary of state, and then lieutenant governor, before making a Senate run. For Kirk, the first time was a charm. He served on the Banking, Housing, and Urban Affairs Committees, the Subcommittee on International Trade and Finance, the Armed Services Committee, and, by the beginning of his most recent term of office, had become the ranking member of the Select Committee on Intelligence.

Was there anything in his earlier career that presaged the explosive course he was now pursuing with the Senate probe? Belknap searched for patterns, but in vain. Like most senators from the Midwest, he championed bills providing incentives for the use of ethanol as a gasoline substitute – the ethanol being derived from corn, and so a product of the region's vast cornfields. He did nothing contrary to the interests of ConAgra and Cargill. But aside from the customary forms of constituency service and major-donor courtesies, his record was moderate, pragmatic. Perhaps he was a bit of a wheeler-dealer, a little too fast to make concessions in order to get his provisions enacted into law. But in a deliberative body that was increasingly polarized, he had emerged as something of a statesman. Nor was there evidence of untoward, unexplained wealth. Belknap decided to respect what his gut was telling him. The man was no knave, no villain. He was what he appeared to be. To assume as much was to gamble, but it was a gamble he was willing to take. Besides, if there were a violent solution – a backdoor approach to the Kirk Commission – someone would already have exploited it.

That was why Todd Belknap had decided to do the one thing that only he could do: tell the truth. Once again, he would sneak in through the front door.

Now Philip Sutton leaned forward across his cluttered desk. 'Everything you've said so far checks out. You said they're trying to shitcan you. The record says you're on administrative leave. Time of recruitment, duration of service – it's all on the money.'

'There's a reason for that,' Belknap said. 'It's kind of a manipulation, you could say. I figure if I tell you the truth, the honest, verifiable truth, you'll come to trust me a little.'

A half-grin spread across Sutton's jowly mouth. 'Honesty? I'm in politics. That's a filthy lowdown trick that we only rarely resort to.'

'Desperate times, desperate measures,' Belknap said. 'Does your record search include any reference to 'administrative retrieval'?'

Sutton's expression told him the answer to his question.

'You know what it means, don't you?'

'I can guess. This part of your total-candor strategy?'

'You got it. Including fessing up about the strategy.'

413

Sutton let his professional bonhomie evaporate; his eyes bore in. 'Talk to me about Genesis.'

'I'd be glad to, with the senator's permission,' Belknap said slyly.

Sutton got up and padded down the hall, surprisingly light on his feet for someone of his girth. He returned quickly, made a summoning gesture. 'The senator will see you now.'

At the end of a short hallway of narrow offices was Bennett Kirk's own office. It was large, filled with dark wooden furniture that had undoubtedly been floating around the Senate since the Gilded Age, and, unlike the rooms occupied by administrative assistants, double-height. Sunlight filtered gently through vast sheer curtains.

Senator Bennett Kirk – tall and loose-limbed, with the unmistakable mane of silver hair – was already standing when Belknap came in, and he took his measure with the speed and acuity of a seasoned pol. Belknap could feel Kirk's gray eyes roam over his face, probing, assessing, searching. There was a glint of something relenting – a glint of approval, even. His handclasp was firm but not showily so.

'Glad you could see me, Senator,' said Belknap. Up close, he thought he saw something almost haggard in the older man's distinguished countenance – not tiredness so much as the effort of concealing tiredness.

'What have you got to tell me, Mr. Belknap? I'm all ears. Well, quite a bit of mouth, too.'

Belknap smiled, charmed by the man's down-to-earth style despite himself, and despite the seriousness of his mission. 'Let's not bullshit each other. Genesis was my open sesame. That was the word that got me through the door.'

'I'm afraid I don't have the faintest idea of what you're talking about.'

'We don't have time for this,' Belknap snapped. 'I'm not here to play gin rummy.'

Kirk's eyes were wary. 'Then let's see what cards you got.'

'Fine. I've got reason to believe that someone code-named Genesis is a dangerous force in the world. Genesis – again, whatever it is that goes by the name – is a direct threat to you. And to others. You need to be careful of being used by this person.'

The senator and his chief of staff exchanged glances. There was a hint of *I told you so* in the exchange, but Belknap couldn't have said who told whom what. 'Go on,' said the politician, his voice taut. 'What do you know about him?'

Belknap sat up very straight and told him the stories that he had heard.

After a few minutes, Senator Kirk cut him off. 'Sounds like tinfoil-hat stuff, doesn't it?'

'If you thought so, you wouldn't have let me in.'

'Truth is, we've heard these stories, too – or some of them, anyway. Sourcing's poor across the board.'

'I grant you that.'

'But you say you've been directly threatened by Genesis. How?'

In for a penny, in for a pound. Belknap exhaled heavily and told him, in abbreviated form, about what had just happened in Cyprus. 'I am counting our conversation as privileged,' the operative emphasized.

'That goes without saying.'

'It goes better *with* saying.'

'I understand,' Bennett Kirk said with a genial smile that did not reach his eyes. 'Just what do you know about this Genesis?'

'I've done a lot of talking already,' Belknap said carefully. 'What do *you* know about him?'

Kirk turned away. 'What do you think, Phil? Think it's time to open our kimonos?' The words were bantering, but his tone was edged with apprehension.

Sutton shrugged.

'Would you like his name, address, and Social Security number?' the senator asked.

Belknap stared. 'Yes.'

'So would we.' Another long glance was exchanged between the regal-looking senator and his pudgy, disheveled chief of staff. 'Belknap, my gut tells me you're a straight shooter. But your record talks about administrative retrieval. Meaning, formally, that your clearances have all been revoked.'

'You knew this since before we started to talk.'

'You said it yourself: Our conversation is privileged. But you can appeal to me in my role as the head of the Senate Committee on Intelligence. I've got to appeal to you as a man, and as an American. Can I do that?' He broke off.

'Privilege goes both ways. Frankly, Senator, I have so many of this nation's secrets in my head that talk of clearance is a bureaucratic absurdity. Not to put too fine a point on it, I *am* one of those secrets. I've spent my career in and out of special-access programs.'

Sutton gave the senator a sidelong glance. 'You make a good point,' he said to Belknap.

'Fact of the matter is,' Kirk said, 'all our communications from Genesis have been via e-mail. Strictly untraceable, or so they assure me. There's the sign-off; there's information that's often fragmentary and sometimes less so. But he's never been more than a byline to me. You ask whether I'm being used. How can I answer that? Functionally, the role he's performing is that of a confidential informant – only with an extraordinary knowledge of an extraordinary range of activities. There's always the threat of disinformation, but we take nothing at face value. Either the info checks out or it doesn't. Other possibilities? Score-settling? Sure. Every investigation is propelled by people leaking dirt on their enemies for self-interested purposes. So what's new? That doesn't make the revelations any less valuable as far as the public interest is concerned.' The logic was dry, hard, and difficult to dispute.

'It doesn't bother you that you have no idea who your chief informant is?'

'Of course it does,' Sutton growled. 'That's not the point. You can't order what's not on the menu.'

'So you don't care that you're dealing with the devil.'

'The devil you don't know?' Sutton raised an eyebrow. 'You're being dramatic. Try being specific.'

'Fine,' Belknap said, tight-lipped. 'Has it occurred to you that Genesis might be an alias for Paul Bancroft?'

The senator and his chief of staff exchanged glances again. 'If that's what you think,' Kirk said, 'you're dead wrong.'

'You've mixed up the cat and the mouse,' Sutton added. 'Genesis is Bancroft's mortal enemy.'

Belknap paused. 'You've been informed about the Theta Group?' He was groping, disoriented.

'So you know about that, too,' said the senator after a pause. 'The picture we've got is still preliminary. But Genesis is collecting information. Within a few days, we should have enough to proceed with.'

'You don't mess with something as powerful and august as the Bancroft Foundation,' Sutton explained, 'unless you've got bandoliers draped over both shoulders.'

'I understand.'

'Glad one of us does,' said Senator Kirk.

Another moment of silence fell. Each sought to reveal as little as possible while learning as much as possible: It was a delicate balance.

'You say these e-mails are untraceable,' Belknap began.

Sutton stepped in: 'Untraceable is right. And please don't talk about a trap-and-trace – believe me, we've already looked into the situation. The thing goes through an anonymizer – one of those special routing services that strip off all the identifying codes, all the ISP digits and so on. Impossible to track back any further. That's a high-level assurance.'

'Show me,' Belknap said simply.

'Show you what? An e-mail from Genesis?' Sutton shrugged. 'Whatever your security clearance used to be, the proceedings of the commission are closely guarded. Air-gapped. I'll print you out a sample, sure. But you won't learn a goddamn thing.' He stood, went over to a terminal on the senator's desk, keyed in a series of passcodes; a minute later, a single sheet of paper purred its way through a nearby laser printer. He handed it to the operative.

Belknap looked at the nearly blank paper.

1.222.3.01.2.33.04
105.ATM2-0.XR2.NYC1.ALTER.NET (146.188.177.158) 164 ms
123 ms 142 ms
To: Bennett_Kirk@ussenate.gov
Fr: genesis
Financial data on the entity referenced prev. to follow by the end of the week.
– GENESIS

'Not a real chatty fellow,' Belknap grunted.

'You know about SMTP?' Sutton asked. 'I didn't, either, before this thing came up. But I've picked up a thing or two.'

'It's all Greek to me,' the senator said, with a smile. He walked over to the window as Sutton cleared his throat.

'It's like the e-mail postal service,' the pasty-faced aide explained. 'Or the software equivalent. Usually it gives you the return address. But here, it's like it's been remailed, by some anonymizer in the Caribbean, and that's the end of the story. As to how it got to this anonymous remailer? Anybody's guess. You can put all these number under a goddamn electron microscope. Doesn't matter. This is the most uninformative piece of paper you'll ever come across.'

Belknap folded the sheet of paper and inserted it in his pocket. 'In that case, you won't mind if I take it with me.'

'It's a gesture of good faith,' Sutton said. 'We're moved by your candor. Your desperation. Call it that.' That wasn't quite it; Belknap knew that Sutton was as almost as eager to identify their informant as he was.

Belknap turned to Senator Kirk. 'Can I ask you something? How did you get started, anyway? I mean, the whole Kirk Commission thing – the whole ball of wax. It's a shitload of work, for one thing. What do you get out of it?'

'It's not the usual valedictory endeavor of an aging politician, is that what you're saying?' A smile played across his age-etched face. 'Yep, I'm a regular South Bend Cincinnatus, aren't I? Politicians always talk about serving their country. That's the rhetoric: public service. But we're not all lying, at least not all of the time. Most people in Congress are highly competitive people. They're here because they like to win, and they like to win in public, and they're out of high school and you've got to figure out another way to get this aside from being student-body president or making a long pass on the gridiron. They're temperamentally impatient, disinclined to put their head down for ten or fifteen years, which is what it takes to really make it to the top in banking or law. So they end up here. But the place changes you, Belknap. It does, or it can.'

'For the worse, in a lot of cases.'

'In a lot of cases, sure.' The senator shifted in his seat, and Belknap thought he saw a fleeting grimace. 'But what we do, and ultimately who we are, is determined less by character than by circumstances. I didn't always think that. But it's what I think now. Winston Churchill was a great man. He would always have been an immensely talented one, whatever the course of history. But he was great because circumstances called him to be, and because they called upon something he richly possessed. He got Germany right. But he got India wrong, never got that Britain's colonial subjects wanted to be citizens, and of their own country. The same sort of single-mindedness that protected him from appeasement and temporizing in one case stopped him from rightful and just compromise and concession in another. But forgive me. I'm speechifying, aren't I?'

'You're good at it.'

'An occupational hazard, is what it is. Look, you can argue whether intelligence reform is my Germany or my India – and I'm not pretending to be even a bush-league Winston. But you can't dispute that there's a problem here. Some people who do intelligence oversight, they hunker down and they go native, they stop seeing the problems. That didn't happen with me. The more I learned, the more worried I got. Because beneath the lumber, there's termite holes and a lot of rot. And we can paint and repaint this house, but unless we're willing to lift up the floorboards and peer behind the drywall and check it out from pillar to post, we're just part of the problem.'

'Still, why you?' Belknap persisted.

Sutton himself looked at the senator expectantly, seemingly wondering how he would answer.

Bennett Kirk was smiling; his eyes were not. 'If not me, who?'

Belknap had left the senator's suite and was halfway down the hallway toward the elevators when he realized that something was amiss. How? Belknap could not have said: The awareness was beneath the level of conscious knowledge.

The Hart Building was constructed around a central atrium, a sort of internal courtyard, with elevator banks to either side; and when he walked out of the duplex suite, he caught a quick glimpse of the Calder mobile. But that was not what caught his attention. Fingertips will pick up the slightest irregularity in an otherwise smooth surface, and the focus of a trained and field-seasoned operative had precisely that kind of sensitivity. The presence of four uniformed National Guardsmen in the lobby where there had been two. The men who were stationed on several floors at the railing that faced the atrium – civilians only at first glance; plainclothes operatives at a second. The slightly oversized jacket, the too-vigilant gaze, the casual act – a passerby admiring the vast Calder mobile – prolonged beyond the casual.

A cold fear washed over Belknap. He saw a pair of men, also dressed as civilians, push through the revolving door of the main entrance. They did not have the gait of civilians: They fell into step with each other. Neither checked in with the guard at the station; neither moved to the elevator banks. They were not visiting; they were taking up an agreed-on position.

A dragnet, then. One that was still in formation.

Had Senator Kirk or his chief of staff sounded the alert, after all? That wasn't credible to him. Neither had betrayed the slightest vibration of excitement or apprehension; nobody in the suite of connected offices had. There had to be another explanation. The operating assumption had to be that a visual identification had taken place; yet his specific destination was plainly not known to those who would apprehend him. Therefore he had been detected while in the lobby. They knew he was in the building. They did not know exactly where. If he had any chance of escaping the dragnet, he would have to take that into account and make use of it.

And soon – the odds were already against him, and they got worse with every passing minute. He visualized his position as if in an aerial photograph. The seventh floor of the Hart Senate Office Building. A vast parking lot across the street, to the north on C Street. A wedgelike block carved out by Maryland Avenue to the south. To the west, the landscape was one of parks and hulking capital buildings; to the east, buildings and blocks grew smaller and less grand, becoming interspersed with apartments and stores. *Now, if you could just strap on a rocket pack and fly . . .*

He reviewed other options: Could he prompt an evacuation of the building by pulling a fire alarm, phoning in a bomb threat, or starting a trash-can fire, and then try to vanish into the panicked crowds? But that was exactly the sort of countermaneuver they would be prepared for. The fire exits would be guarded from outside; a high-level security protocol would circumvent efforts to activate a building-wide alarm. Security officers would do their own investigation first before any evacuation proceeded.

He was not completely unprepared, though. He turned and headed back to where he had seen a sign for men's and women's restrooms, the genders pictographed, in the usual way, with isosceles triangles. He locked himself in a stall, opened his briefcase, and swiftly changed into the neatly folded uniform he had brought with him. The glasses and shoes went back in the briefcase. When he emerged, he was attired in the standard-issue camouflage uniform of the Army National Guard, which was a familiar presence in all such federal buildings. The tunic and trousers rippled with green-gray-tan fractals were authentic; one would have to look closely to realize that his high black lace-ups were not government-issue combat boots but cheaper, lighter knock-offs. His hair was just a little long for the role, but, again, it was an irregularity few would notice.

Which left the briefcase itself to be disposed of. When he was in business drag, the briefcase complemented his disguise. Now it was utterly incongruous. He emerged from the stall quickly, keeping his face turned away from the row of mirrors in front of the washbasins, and reached a wide circular trash receptacle near the door to the hallway. Glancing around to make sure nobody was looking, he dropped the case inside and then covered it with a wadding of brown paper towels. It would not be found anytime soon.

Now he strode down the hallway, taking care to put on a bit of a strut: the stride of a man on duty, on display, not someone in a rush. He took the staircase at the far west, the wall adjoining the Dirksen Senate Office Building. The staircase had none of the modernist grandeur of the semi-circular stairs that rose from the atrium, but they were wide, as required by the fire code. At the landing of the fourth floor he saw another guardsman, standing post. A light-skinned black man with a smooth-shaven head that did not conceal an advanced case of male pattern baldness. The man had a bulky combat pistol holstered to his belt; attached to a shoulder sling, he held a semiautomatic rifle, an M16A2 with a plastic buttstock. Belknap noticed that he had activated the burst-control device: three rounds per trigger pull. At close quarters, three rounds would be plenty.

Belknap gave the man a brusque nod, taking care to meet his eyes forthrightly without inviting conversation, which could be disastrous. On impulse, he took out a radio communicator in hardened plastic, which resembled the standard military model, and started speaking into dead air.

'Did a quick walk-through of six, no sign of our guy,' Belknap said, his voice bored but professional. He noted the other man's unit number, then spoke into the handset again. 'Are we coordinated with the 171-Bs? I feel like we're slathering on too many units here. It's a goddamn crush.'

Make of that what you will, Belknap thought as he made his way down the next flight of stairs. The last flight of stairs, the one that led to the ground stairs, was easily accessible behind a broad steel push-bar-equipped door.

A fire door, in fact. Unlocked. But armed. A rectangular red-and-white sign warned FIRE DOOR. KEEP CLOSED. DO NOT BLOCK. A second sign further warned: EMERGENCY EXIT ONLY. ALARM WILL SOUND.

Dammit! Frustration hammered his chest from within. He turned back and made his way to the adjoining public hallway. As he strode down the hall, he counted three and perhaps four plain-clothed operatives. None gave him a second look; he was seen but not noticed; the camouflage uniform indeed conferred a kind of camouflage, albeit that of a spurious familiarity rather than invisibility.

A handful of people were stepping into one of the elevators, on their way to the ground floor. It was an opportunity: Again, acting on impulse, Belknap stepped into it seconds before the door closed.

A young woman standing next to him was talking quietly to another young woman: 'And so I go, 'If that's how you feel, like, why are we having this conversation?''

'You didn't!' her friend replied.

An older man talked to a younger associate, both of them lawyers by all appearances, about some line item that needed to be 'stopped before reconciliation.'

Belknap felt the gaze of some of the civilians on him. He also sensed that at least one person in the elevator was no civilian at all. He was a large man with arms that dangled away from his sides, suggesting the bulked-up musculature of a bodybuilder. He had short red hair and an almost matching reddish complexion, so that from a distance he had appeared bald. It seemed that he seldom wore the shirt he had on: The collar did not fit his thick neck, and despite the tie, he had to keep it unbuttoned at the top. The man – a fellow operative, it seemed clear – stared steadily, stonily, ahead of him. His jaws moved in a slow rhythm; he was chewing gum. Belknap saw the man's face blurrily reflected on the stainless steel of the elevator door. Belknap was behind him. He did not look up; he knew that the elevators were connected to the building's video surveillance system, that each had a wide-angle lens embedded in the center of its ceiling. It was important not to turn his face toward it.

In his mind he scrolled back to the lobby, trying to visualize its geometry. How far was the main entrance from the elevator? Thirty paces, give or take. He might just make it.

Belknap's attention flitted among the few quiet conversations taking place as he counted the remaining seconds and willed himself to feel calm. An electronic *bing*. A small LED by the floor indicator changed from the red that signaled descent to the green that signaled ascent.

The doors rolled back, and everyone stepped onto the polished slate of the Hart Building lobby. The ride had taken perhaps fifteen seconds; he had known days that went faster.

Belknap held back for a lingering moment. It would be better not to have the muscled operative's gaze settle on him again. All it would take was a passing thought, a moment of doubt – the hair, the shoes, the subtle irregularities of the uniform, his very presence on this elevator – and the game would be over. But the red-haired man was taking up a position by a phone booth across the hall; there was no alternative but to push past him.

Belknap continued walking, his heavy-soled boots quietly thunking against the polished floor, looking straight ahead, as if he meant to cross to the opposite wing of the building. All those leaving the building would be scrutinized. He would not betray his intentions until the very last moment.

He took fifteen paces. Eighteen paces. He had walked past another layer of plainclothesmen, shielded by the effrontery of his uniform, when a man in a brown suit suddenly gave a shout.

'That's him!'

He pointed at Belknap, his eyes narrowed with certainty.

'Where?' Belknap heard another man call out.

'Which one?' a guardsman shouted, cradling his rifle in his arms.

Belknap joined the chorus: 'Where?' he called out, craning his head behind him, as if the suited man had pointed not at him but at someone further away.

'Where?' Belknap repeated.

It was an uncomplicated, unsubtle ruse that would buy him only seconds. But if seconds were all he could get, seconds were what he would take. The lobby guard's station was only a few yards away. Agency arrogance made it almost certain that the guard would not have been informed of the operation. Belknap could exploit that. Now he approached the man with the squashed features and heavy-lidded eyes, still seated by his clipboard, his lists, and the small video-display panels.

'We've got an emergency situation,' Belknap said. He whirled around and pointed out the brown-suited man. 'How did that man get in here?' he demanded.

The lobby guard looked stern, pretending to be in control of the situation. Seven seconds had elapsed since Belknap had been burned. He had no weapon – he could not get one through the metal detector – and so his only option was to sow as much confusion as he could. The techniques for doing so came under the rubric of 'social engineering' in the training manuals. The difficulty was that many of his adversaries had undergone the same training. The man in the brown suit was fast and agile; Belknap's dodges had not wrongfooted him in the slightest. When Belknap stole a glance, he saw that the man had drawn a handgun, doubtless one that had been strapped under his jacket. A delicate game of intentions: If Belknap acknowledged the man's weapon and refused his orders, the man would effectively be authorized to shoot. But not if Belknap were unaware of the weapon. Belknap turned his head around, maintaining eye contact with the lobby guard at his booth even as he walked toward the man in the brown suit – toward a man who had a gun trained on him. Right now, Belknap's chief weapon was precisely that he had no weapon: an unjustified use of force in front of one or more witnesses would create career complications, even for someone in the 'special' services.

Now Belknap turned to face the suited operative. 'What is your problem, man?' he protested.

'Hands where I can see them,' the man said. He gestured

toward another man, someone behind Belknap. When Belknap craned around, he saw the red-haired man from the elevator. He was closing in, race-walking with a fast stride. By now, three uniformed guardsmen had their rifles out, though their faces betrayed confusion. It was all taking place so fast, and with so much misdirection, that they were less than confident about their target. To raise his hands would straighten that out in an instant; Belknap decided against doing so.

He replayed the geometry. Two operatives. Three guardsmen. One uniformed, unarmed lobby guard. A dozen other people, mainly visitors, most of whom had come to realize that there was a disturbance under way, though the state of their knowledge did not go much beyond that.

Belknap threw back his shoulders and put his hands on his hips. It was a stance of belligerence, yet there was nothing threatening about it: The hands were empty, unarmed, unclenched. His feet were planted at shoulder's width apart. It was a stance that meant: I'm in charge. Policemen were taught to use it in order to assert control.

It was a lie, of course. Belknap was not in charge. As a result, it bewildered without menacing. Observers – including the three guardsmen – would not see a fugitive taken into custody. They would see a uniformed man claiming to be the brown-suited operative's superior. The very illogic of the tableau would impede their ability to respond confidently to a rapidly changing situation – and that was precisely what Belknap required.

Now Belknap took another step closer to the man in the brown suit, looking into his eyes, ignoring the gun. He heard the footfalls of the muscled operative, who was closing the distance between them in the fastest way, walking straight toward him. *A mistake*, Belknap thought. It meant that all three men were aligned, and, more to the point, it meant that the operative's .357 pistol – doubtless already drawn – was useless, at least for the moment. The caliber only ensured that a shot aimed at Belknap would travel on and hit the operative in the brown suit. For a few seconds, at least, Belknap knew he had nothing to fear from the red-haired man. Now Belknap took another step toward the man in the brown suit, who, just as Belknap anticipated, stood his ground: The gunman did not dare appear weak by retreating. He was perhaps two feet away from him now, maybe even a little less.

'I *said*, What is your problem?' Belknap repeated the meaningless taunt as he tilted his upper body back, his hips slightly forward, a pantomime of haughty indignation. The other man's combat pistol – a full-sized Beretta Cougar – now pressed against Belknap's taut stomach. It had an eight-round magazine, Belknap knew, because it stuck out half an inch from the bottom of the grip. The suited man could shoot him at any time. But Belknap had given him no cause – and the nine-millimeter round, aimed at center mass, would probably hit his red-haired comrade.

A rapidly closing window of relative safety. Now – Belknap swivel-cocked his hip and slammed his forehead down on the other man's face, smashing the bridge of his nose. Only a thin, spongy layer of cranial bone separated the brain from the nasal cavities, Belknap knew; the hammer-blow force would have been communicated through the ethmoid bone to the dura mater.

'Oh, no you don't!' roared the red-haired man as the suited man sagged to the floor. Belknap heard the *snick-click* of a round being chambered.

The next three or four seconds would be as crucial as those preceding them. Belknap saw a clear fluid glistening on the fallen man's upper lip and realized that it was cerebrospinal fluid. Nobody would assume that Belknap was harmless from this point; it was no longer a weapon to seem weaponless. He dropped forward, sprawling across the man at his feet, as if felled by an invisible blow, and grabbed at the Beretta that hung limply from the man's fingers. As he rolled over, he released the 8045 Cougar magazine from the grip and hid it in his pocket. When he looked up at the red-haired bodybuilder, it was with a Beretta in his hand.

An impasse: two men with drawn handguns. Belknap rose smoothly to his feet. 'A Mexican standoff,' he said.

A terrified hush had come over the civilians in the lobby; the last six seconds had made it clear that this was no longer a mere disturbance. Men and women began to cower, or freeze in place, obedient to some obscure animal instinct.

'Do the math and think again,' the snarling operative said.

Twelve seconds, thirteen seconds, fourteen seconds.

Belknap glanced at one of the guardsmen who was in his line of vision. 'Arrest this man!' he yelled. The operatives were on hand to identify the target; the guardsmen were expected to apprehend. But whom? So long as they were not completely certain, their automatic weapons were useless.

'You have a point,' Belknap said to the operative. 'You got fast reflexes? Here, catch.' He tossed the Cougar at the musclebound operative – who reacted, reflexively, precisely as Belknap anticipated. He lowered his gun hand in order to reach out with his other hand and grab hold of the Beretta. A second-and-a-half window of opportunity. Like a striking cobra, Belknap grabbed the long barrel of the other man's pistol and wrenched it from his grasp. The pistol – a Glock .357 – was now in Belknap's hand. In the blink of an eye, he tucked his gun inside his combat vest so that it was aimable but concealed.

The red-haired man blinked. He leveled the Cougar at Belknap with an unsettled look. Belknap had given him his gun, then grabbed his own: It made no sense. The man was smart enough to worry.

Belknap spoke to him in a low, confiding voice. 'Listen to me *very* carefully. Follow my instructions precisely and you won't get hurt.'

'You need glasses?' the operative demanded, waving his gun hand. 'You got a death wish, asshole?'

'That Cougar feel a little light?' Belknap flashed a quick smile.

The operative's florid countenance paled a little.

'You caught up now, or are you waiting for the Monarch

Notes? I squeeze my trigger finger right now and a piece of lead goes whizzing through your torso. You can see the muzzle press against the tunic, you can see where it's aimed. Now, I figure you've spent a real long time working on that body of yours. All it takes is a split-second of disappointment on my side and you're going to be in physical rehabilitation for two, three years. What did you load this morning? Federal Hydra-Shoks – those nasty expanding hollowpoints? Whatever it was, you need to imagine the slug traveling through your body, crushing organs and chewing up nerves.' He kept his voice soft, almost reassuring in tone. 'I'm guessing you'd like to protect that physique of yours. You can, too.' He bore in, asserting mastery through his eyes. 'Take me in. As far as anybody can see, you've got a gun trained at my head, and they'll guess that you've cuffed my hands beneath the tunic, POW-style. Now you're going to call out, in a loud voice that everyone can hear, that you've got me, that you're in charge of the prisoner. Then you escort me out of the building, side by side.'

'You're crazy,' the operative snarled. Yet, tellingly, he did not raise his voice.

'My advice? If this Glock contains full-jacketed round-points, take the hit. You'll get a nice pension, and with any luck it won't hit the spinal column or any of the major nerve branches. But if you've loaded the pistol with expanding slugs, the kind with high stopping power?' Belknap knew that the man had. 'Then you're going to spend the rest of your life asking yourself why you didn't do the sensible thing. Decide *now*. Or I decide for you.'

The red-haired operative inhaled deeply, shakily. 'I've got him!' he bellowed to the guardsmen. 'The prisoner's in my custody. Make way!' Another deep breath. From any distance, the fear and nausea on the man's face would read as impatience. 'Goddammit, I said *make way!*'

Belknap's role, in turn, required him to look surrendered and dispirited. It came surprisingly easily.

The gantlet in front of the building was a blur of shouted commands. Belknap kept his eyes mainly downcast, occasionally glancing around to see the rope strung from sawhorses, the tight-faced guardsmen with rifles raised and aimed at him.

The red-haired man performed his part well, because all he had to do was to be the professional that he was. The fact that it was over in such a short period of time was what Belknap mainly had going for him. Less than sixty seconds in all. By the time the red-haired operative – Diller was the name someone had called him – had marched him down to the car, the hard part was over.

Following Belknap's barked command from the backseat, he simply gunned the motor and drove off before the other armed men could join them. Near Maryland Avenue, as the vehicle stopped at a light, Belknap reached around the driver's seat and smashed the flat side of the pistol into the other man's temple, rendering him unconscious. Then he scrambled out at the Metro stop a hundred feet away. Soon others would arrive in pursuit, but the head start he had would suffice. He knew how to disappear. Once he had boarded the Metro, he stepped into the area between cars. Jolted by the movement of the train, taking care to keep his footing, he discarded his tunic, tossing it to the side of the track. Then, using a sharp pocket knife, he sliced off his camouflage trousers as well, taking care to avoid the fabric beneath them and to retain the contains of his pockets.

The man who had stepped onto the Metro looked like a member of the National Guard, a common sight in mass-transit venues. The man who stepped into the next car was wearing a green T-shirt and nylon track pants, like a jogger – an even commoner sight.

As the train hurtled down its subterranean tracks, Belknap felt the folded sheet of paper he'd secreted in his right pocket.

Genesis. *You can run*, he thought. *Let's see if you can hide.*

CHAPTER TWENTY-FIVE

Answer the phone, Belknap silently implored, not for the first time. *Please answer the phone.* The cord between them was a delicate one. She had his cell number; he had hers. But he was most of the way to Philadelphia already. They would have to choose a safe place for a rendezvous. Consular Operations would not rest until he was apprehended.

Answer the phone!

He had so much to tell her. As he drove north on Route 95, his mind kept returning to his harrowing escape from the Hart Senate Office Building. He was not surprised to hear a report on the local radio news that the government had conducted 'security exercises' at some federal buildings and was currently analyzing vulnerabilities. 'Some tourists and visitors to the Senate offices were taken aback when they were caught up in a surprise rehearsal conducted by a joint unit of the Army National Guard and the Secret Service,' the newscaster noted sunnily, adding, with a chuckle, 'You might say they were "caught off-guard."' *Just one of thousands of official lies*, Belknap mused, cheerfully accepted and regurgitated by an increasingly supine Fourth Estate.

He pulled the car over to a rest stop and speed-dialed her phone again. Finally, the rhythmic electronic purring ceased; there was a click, and he detected the sound of an open line. 'Andrea!' he said, the words rushing from him. 'I've been so worried!'

'No need to worry.' A strange voice – a man's – was on the other end.

Belknap felt as if he had swallowed ice. 'Who is this?'

'We're Andrea's caretakers.' The accent was strangely

431

indeterminate; not American or English, but not identifiably foreign, either.

'What have you done to her, goddammit?'

'Nothing. Yet.'

Not again! His nerve endings were shrieking at him.

How had they found her? Nobody had followed them: He was certain of it. Nobody had even tried . . .

Because they didn't need to.

He flashed back to the puzzling bruise on Andrea's thigh, the hard red hematoma, the puncture wound, and he cursed his failure to think it through. Her captors would have been too skillful to have injected her there, however much she struggled; nor would they have needed a large-bore needle to inject a liquid.

The explanation should have been obvious. They had implanted something inside the deep fascia of the thigh. A transponder, probably capsule-sized. In effect, a miniaturized homing device.

'Talk to me!' Belknap implored. 'Why are you doing this?'

'You've been careless. Genesis has decided that it was time to assume custody. You've been in the way, you see. As she has been.'

'Tell me she's alive!'

'She is alive. She'll soon wish she weren't. We'll need a few days to be sure we've learned everything we need from her.'

Another voice in the background. *'Todd! Todd!'* A woman's voice, high-pitched with terror.

Andrea's.

Suddenly the screams were cut off.

'If you lay a hand on her, so help me God,' Belknap rumbled, 'I will – '

'Enough with your empty threats. You'll never find Genesis. So you'll never find her. I suggest you go to some quiet place and meditate upon your own arrogance. A gravesite on the banks of the Anacostia River, perhaps. No doubt you're feeling unlucky in love. But remember, Mr. Belknap, a man creates his own luck.'

'Who *are* you people?' Belknap felt as if a balloon had been inflated in his chest. He struggled for breath. 'What do you want?'

A dry, toneless laugh. 'To teach the Hound to heel.'

'*What?*'

'We may be in touch with further instructions.'

'Listen to me,' Belknap said, breathing heavily. 'I *will* find you. I *will* hunt you down. You will be accountable for everything you do. Know this.'

'More empty threats from a three-legged mutt. You still don't understand. It's Genesis's world. You just live in it.' A beat. 'For the moment, anyway.'

With that, Andrea's captor clicked off.

Andrea opened her eyes and stared out at whiteness. Her head pounded. Her mouth was dry. Her eyes were sticky.

Where was she?

Whiteness was all she could see. After a few long moments, the whiteness came to seem less ethereal and cloud-like, more like the surfaces of something real and hard and unyielding. Where was she?

She had been in Washington, had been walking down the block to a local newspaper-and-coffee place when . . . and now? She tried to inventory her surroundings.

A ceiling of white, with recessed fluorescent lights that shed a uniform penumbra of a cold-white glow. The floor: four feet beneath the bed – a hospital-style cot, it seemed – where she had slept a drugged sleep. She wanted to get out of bed, but how? Laboriously, she mentally rehearsed and then performed the complex series of movements that the maneuver required: the shifting, the rotating, the extension of the legs. An act performed every day without thinking now felt like a delicate and demanding operation. She remembered getting riding lessons as a little girl, learning how to dismount a horse, the easy fluid motion starting out as half a dozen commands. Brain damage? More likely evidence that the sedation had not fully dissipated. She felt exhausted. She wanted to give up.

She would not give up.

Once she had gotten out of bed, she knelt down and inspected the floor. She was wearing a hospital johnny, was barefoot, could feel the floorboards beneath her toes. The floor was constructed of wooden planks, but immensely thick, like a ship's hull, and layered with a hard white coating. She banged the floor with her heel and made almost no sound: Concrete probably lay beneath the lumber. The walls, when she examined them, seemed constructed of similar material and were covered with a similar white substance. It resembled the sort of epoxy paint that was used for ships and factory floors, and formed a dense, unchippable surface. She would have had a hard time gouging it with a screwdriver. All she had were her fingernails.

Get ahold of yourself, Andrea. There was a locked door, hinged on the outside, with a small shuttered window at the top. Near it was another ceiling-mounted lighting fixture – a simple fluorescent circle, ensuring that the entire room was drenched in light. A security measure, or a method of psychological intimidation as well?

Where had they taken her?

The room was about twenty feet by twenty, with a small adjoining alcove that contained an old-style bathtub of enameled cast iron and a stainless-steel commode of a kind she had seen in movies set in prisons. She scrutinized the cot. A simple frame, fashioned of tubular steel. Braked casters. Several holes designed, it was clear, for IV poles. It was hospital-issue, then.

Then she heard a noise at the door: the sliding of its narrow window hatch. A man's eyes at the slatlike opening. She watched as the door opened, saw how the guard held the key turned in the keyhole as he pushed up on the stainless-steel lever knob, saw the simple redbrick wall of the hallway outside her cell. Every little detail could be valuable, she told herself.

Once he had stepped inside and released them, the level knob returned to the horizontal position with a spring-loaded *thunk*. She didn't know much about locks, but she could tell it was a high-security device: Even if a prisoner had somehow smuggled a lockpick inside, the door would not open without simultaneous pressure on the lever knob. Both had to be pushed away from their default positions with active pressure against the vector of the springs.

The guard had pale skin, a pug nose, a weak, dimpled, chin, and wide-spaced pale-green eyes that seemed never to blink and made Andrea think of a pike. He was dressed in olive-drab khaki with a thick military-style belt.

'Stand at the rear wall,' he commanded, with a hand on a black plastic device – some sort of stun gun, it seemed. He sounded like a Southerner who had spent much of his life in the North.

Andrea did as she was instructed, standing at the wall opposite the door. The guard quickly glanced beneath the cot, then entered the bathroom and gave it a thorough inspection.

'All right,' he said, finally. 'There's not a chance in hell you can break out of here, so do us both a favor and don't trash the place.'

'Where am I? And who are you?' Andrea spoke for the first time. Her voice was stronger, steadier, than she had thought it would be.

The guard just shook his head, scorn and amusement in his eyes.

'Do I get a change of clothing?'

'That's probably okay,' he said. He was not in command, then; there were others whose orders he was following. 'Though, really, what's the point?'

'Because you're going to let me go in a day or so?' She tried to catch a glimpse of his wristwatch.

'Sure. One way or the other.' The guard looked amused. 'I suggest you make peace with your God all the same, ma'am.'

'Please,' she said, 'tell me your name.' If she could establish some human contact with the guard, she might be able to learn more from him, to get him to see her as more than just a parcel.

'Ma'am, this ain't no church social,' the man said, his pike eyes staring. 'I'll give you that for nothing.'

Andrea now sat on the bed, clenching the blanket with one hand.

'Sorry about the quality of the bedding,' the guard volunteered. 'Ballistic nylon, heavy canvas on the outer seams – it's called a suicide blanket. All we had around.'

'Where you from? Originally, I mean?' Another foray. She could not let herself be discouraged.

A slow smile appeared on the guard's face. 'I know what you're trying to do. I may be a Southerner, but it don't mean I'm stupid. One of us will be back with chow in a couple of hours.'

'Please – '

'Shut your pie hole.' A slow polite smile as he removed his cap. 'Ma'am, it's only the sheerest professionalism that stops me from raping you within an inch of your life and maybe an inch or so beyond.' He put his cap back on. 'Have a nice day, ma'am.'

As the man made his way out, Andrea asked, 'What time do you have?'

'You really want to know how much time *you* have, isn't that right?' the man replied. 'Not a whole hell of a lot.'

Belknap had struggled to keep his tone light when he telephoned Andrea's friend Walter Sachs at the hedge fund for which she used to work. It was crucial not to scare him off. Andrea had trusted him. Belknap would have to as well.

Belknap had agreed to meet him in the place he suggested, which turned out to be some sort of natural-foods eatery in Greenwich, Connecticut. To judge from the sparse number of customers, its offerings left something to be desired. Taking a seat toward the back, Belknap kept an eye out for a man in a green linen jacket.

Finally he saw a tall man with a long, rectangular face arrive. His brown-and-gray hair was buzzed short on the sides, almost whitewall-style. He had a cleft chin and a torso that seemed a little undersized for the rest of his body. Belknap gave him a little wave, and he sat down at the chair opposite him. His eyes were slightly reddened and glassy, as if he had been smoking pot, though he didn't smell that way.

'I'm Walt,' the man said.

'Todd,' said Belknap.

'So,' said Walt Sachs. He wriggled his fingers in the air. 'Lot of cloak-and-dagger shit. Sudden meetings with strangers. What's up with Andrea, anyway?'

'She's fine. We're talking because I know she confided in you a certain amount.' A waitress appeared and set down a plate.

'Complimentary,' the waitress said. 'Specialty of the house. Carob cookies.'

'What exactly *is* carob?' Walt asked Belknap. Maybe he was trying to break the ice.

'Couldn't tell you,' Belknap said, suppressing his impatience.

Walt looked up at the waitress. 'You know, there's something I've always wondered. What exactly *is* carob?'

The waitress, dressed in a T-shirt of unbleached cotton and coarse linen balloon trousers, smiled brightly. 'Carob comes from the pod of the carob tree. It's fat-free, fiber-rich, nonallergenic, high in protein, and oxalic-acid free. And it tastes just like chocolate.'

'No, it doesn't.' Walt gave her look of piercing incredulity.

'Similar. Many people prefer it to chocolate.'

'Name one.'

'They say it's nature's healthiest confection.'

'Who's 'they'?'

'They just do, okay?' The waitress's smile remained fixed.

Sachs tapped on one of the slogans printed in fake cursive on the menu. 'Says here, 'To question is to grow.''

'Give him a cup of the calming Kava Kava,' Belknap said. His own sense of desperation and panic was welling up, but he could not afford to frighten or alienate the man. He had to appear calm and in control.

'Actually, I'll have the Tisane of Tranquility.' Sachs fidgeted an earlobe that had once had a stud and now merely a small puncture scar.

'Me too,' Belknap told the waitress.

'So where's Andrea?' Walt asked again. 'I'm guessing I'm not here because your hard disk crashed.'

'Did you tell anyone where you were going – that you were seeing me?' Belknap asked.

'The instructions were real clear on that, Todd-man.'

'That's a no?'

'That's a no. Logic gate: open.'

Belknap removed the page he'd received from Senator Kirk from his breast pocket, handed it to Sachs without a word.

The computer tech unfolded the page, waving it in the air. 'Clammy!' he said. 'Smuggle this out in your ass, did you?'

Belknap's murderous gaze bounced off him. 'We're wasting time,' he snapped. 'I'm sorry,' he added. 'It's just that there's . . . some pressure to this.'

The computer guy unfolded the page, glanced at it, and said solemnly, 'Have a carob cookie.'

'The source code on the e-mail. Does this tell you anything?'

'I have a theory that nobody likes carob cookies,' Sachs went on. 'Though maybe I'm being a little rash. There are generations yet unborn.'

'Walt, please focus. Is this a dead end or not?'

The technicians snorted. 'How can I put it? It's like a blind alley along a dead end in a cul de sac just off another dead end.' He took out a mechanical pencil and circled a string of digits. 'Ends don't come any deader. You know what an anonymous remailer is?'

'I've got the general idea. Broad strokes. Maybe you should tell me more.'

Walt stared at him for a moment. 'E-mail's a lot like regular mail. You go from one post office to another, maybe stop at a vast mail-sorting complex, then you're off to your local post office. A typical e-mail probably has about fifteen to twenty rest stops along the way. Everywhere it goes, it leaves a piece of itself, like a crumb, and it picks up a code, like a visa stamp, that says where it's been. Say you're in Copenhagen and you're using your AT&T account to send a message to Stockholm. That e-mail's going to hop here and hop there, and at some point it's probably going to pass through Schaumburg, Illinois, before hopping through a bunch of other networks and arriving at your friend's computer in Sweden. Which could take a few seconds.'

'Sounds complicated,' said Belknap.

'But I'm *way* simplifying. Because that one e-mail isn't sent as one e-mail. The system tears it into pieces – a bunch of little packets, because to keep things zipping around, everything needs to be the right size for the pipes, the system of routers. Remember, the system has to carry billions of e-mails every day. All of the little packets are assigned a special identification number so they can be sewn back together at the other end. Now, most people aren't interested in seeing all that header info, so e-mail programs typically don't display them. But they arrive with the e-mail. You go into source-code view to see them. Then you can run a simple program like traceroute, and it's like having an itinerary for that message.'

'How secure is the system?'

'Using a standard Internet service provider? Hackers like to say that ISP stands for 'Internet surveillance project.' This is the least secure form of communication ever: Without encryption, every e-mail is a postcard. You feeling me?' As he spoke, he started to crumble one of the carob cookies into pieces, then crumbled the pieces into smaller pieces. 'Then there's the fact that every computer has a unique digital signature, a unique BIOS identification number, same as every automobile has a one-of-a-kind VIN, a vehicle identification number. So IP address tracing is just the start. There are lots of sniffer programs that automatically scan traffic for certain strings. A lot of trap-and-trace technology that the government doesn't even make public, and private-sector versions that are even stronger. I mean, say you're a hotshot coder. Who you gonna work for – the National Security Agency, for a salary in the high five digits? Pu-leeze.

Not when recruiters from Cisco or Oracle or Microsoft come around in their Porsches, dangling big bucks, stock options, and free cappuccino.'

'But what you were saying about system security – '

'Sniffers, yeah. See, under the hood, e-mail systems all work the same way. SMTP is the messaging algorithm, and POP – post office protocol – is what runs the servers. But with the best anonymous remailers, well, it's like an invisibility shield.'

'An invisibility shield,' Belknap repeated. 'But all you're really talking about is a firm that automatically strips out the header data from messages and resends them, right?'

'Naw, that's only part of it.' A decisive shake of the head. 'A simple dip-and-strip isn't going to take care of the problem. Because then Big Brother could just monitor your incoming traffic. If it's just an encryption game, well, that's the one thing the NSA's halfway decent at, see? So an effective remailer has to have a whole network in place. If you're a user, you send with a local program like Mixmaster, something that will scramble your message so that it arrives with a series of time delays. It's as if you were sending all your vowels seven seconds after you send your consonants, so they arrived as separate clusters. Then another message has the reassembly instructions. That way, you can't rap-and-trace the incoming. Second thing is, how do you allow for a 'reply' function? Anybody can rip the header off a message, like blacking out the return address. Figuring out a return route while keeping it untraceable – that's the art.'

'And remailers can do that?'

'This one can,' Sachs said. Professional admiration had crept into his voice. He tapped on the last string of digits. 'This was remailed by Privex, which is one of the very best in the business. A Russian computer scientist set it up a few years back in Dominica. That's in the eastern Caribbean.'

'I know where Dominica is,' Belknap said tightly. 'It's a big tax haven.'

'And served by a big fat fiber-optic undersea cable. The place is *wired*. Not like here, but you'll almost never find a remailer based in the United States. Nobody wants to hassle with U.S. crypto regs.'

'So how do we trace it?' Belknap asked.

'I just explained,' Sachs said, slightly peeved. 'You don't. You can't. There's a giant roadblock called Privex. Privex masks your IP address with its IP address. Beyond that, it's impossible to see. Strictly no entry.'

'Oh, come on, Andrea's told me about the things you can do,' he said in a coaxing voice. 'I'm sure you could make headway.'

'You never told me where she is.' A note of unease entered Sachs's voice.

Belknap leaned forward. 'You were about to explain to me how you're going to beat the Privex system.'

'You want me to say that the tooth fairy is real and Santa Claus wriggles down your fireplace on Christmas Eve? I'd be happy to. It just might be true. I mean, I very much doubt it, but I'm not absolutely and totally and galactically positive. There aren't a lot of things I'm absolutely and totally and galactically sure about. This, however, is one. Privex has handled millions and millions of communications. And nobody has ever breached its security. Never. Not once. We'd know if they had. And people have tried. They've run sophisticated statistical techniques to do traffic monitoring, real fancy algorithmic shit. Forget about it. Privex makes sure that your message is spliced and blended so it's statistically indistinguishable from all the others. It's got programmed IP rotation, tunneling services, and major-league dedicated servers. I mean, *governments* make use of its services, for Chrissakes. They don't play around.'

Belknap was silent for a long moment. He wasn't able to follow the details of Sachs's explanation. And yet somewhere in his mind was the glimmer of an idea, like a tiny luminescent fish in an underwater cave. 'You said Privex was based in Dominica.'

'The servers are, yeah.'

'Can't be hacked.'

'Nope.'

'Fine,' Belknap said, after another long pause. 'So we break in.'

'You don't listen. I just explained to you that there's no hacking, no cracking, no end runs here. Nobody's ever hacked a Privex traceroute. It's a virtual fortress.'

'Which is why we need to sneak in.'

'Like I said – '

'I'm talking about the physical plant. The actual facility.'

'The physical . . .' Sachs trailed off, bemused. 'I'm not following.'

Belknap was hardly surprised. The two men inhabited radically different worlds. Belknap lived in a world of real things, real people, real objects; Sachs dwelled in a vortex of flowing electronics, of cascading zeros and ones: It was a world of virtual agents, virtual objects. To find Andrea Bancroft, they would have to join forces. 'Privex might be a *virtual* fortress,' the operative said. 'And carob is virtual chocolate. But somewhere in Dominica, there's a bunker with a lot of whirling magnetized disks, right?'

'Well, sure.'

'All right, then.'

'But it's not like they're going to leave the door unlocked, you know, and let you waltz right in.'

'You never heard of breaking and entering?'

'Well, sure. That's what hackers do. They bust through firewalls and pick the virtual locks and siphon off pass codes and install digital-surveillance systems. Happens at every cybercafé.'

'Don't play dumb.' It was all Belknap could do not to slap the wobbly little laminate-topped table.

'Given that I graduated summa cum laude from M.I.T. and I'm still working as a goddamn techie at a Coventry hedge fund, a lot of people would say I'm not just playing,' Sachs snorted.

'Suppose someone beamed you over to this rugged island nation and into the Privex building itself. Would there be a copy of this e-mail, unstripped, somewhere on the servers or storage facilities?'

'Depends when it was sent,' Sachs said. 'Files older than seventy-two hours would be automatically deleted. That's the 'reply' window. For that set interval, it has to retain a copy of the original in order to process responses. Probably has a multiterabyte storage system.'

Belknap leaned back in his chair. 'You know something, Walt? You're looking a little pale. You could use a little sun. Maybe you're spending too much time playing video games. The kind where you get extra lives for every enemy you shoot.'

'You can't get any good if you don't practice,' Walt admitted.

'The sunny Caribbean is calling to you,' Belknap said.

'You're crazy,' Walt said, 'if you think for one minute that I'd allow myself to get caught up in something like this. How many national and international laws would you be violating, do you think? Can you *count* that high, G.I. Joe?'

'Don't you want something special to tell the grandkids?' Belknap shot him a sly look. He knew men like Walt Sachs, knew that his protests were partly directed at himself. 'I bet there are spreadsheets with corrupted sectors to be attended to back at the office. Keep your head down, Walt, and soon you'll qualify for the company's dental policy. Why help save the world when you can get dental?'

'I bet there aren't even any direct flights to Dominica.' Walt broke off. 'Why am I even talking about this? This is *crazy*. This I do not need in my life.' He stared at the one surviving gray-brown cookie, neglected on the earthenware plate, dipped a finger in the sandy remains of the other. 'Would this be . . . dangerous?'

'Be honest with me, Walt,' said the operative. 'Are you hoping I say no or are you hoping I say yes?'

'Doesn't matter what you say,' the technician sulked, 'because I'm not doing it. I'm not even thinking about doing it.'

'I wish you would. Because I need to find the person who sent that e-mail.'

'And why's that?'

'A lot of reasons.' Belknap stared at the technician hard, and made a decision. 'Here's one,' he went on, struggling to keep his voice level. 'I lied when I said Andrea was okay.'

'What do you mean?'

'She's not okay. She's been kidnapped. And this is probably the only way we'll ever get her back.' The information would either scare the technician off for good or ensure his cooperation. *Roll the dice or you're not in the game.*

'Oh, Christ.' Genuine concern fought with fear and the instinct for self-protection. His already reddened eyes grew redder. 'So this is, like, for real.'

'Walt,' he said. 'You have a choice to make. All I can say is that she needs you.'

'So what's the story here? You figure this out, you get Andrea back, everything ends up fine?' He picked up the carob cookie with trembling fingers and then returned it to the plate.

'It all depends,' Belknap said. 'Are you in or are you out?'

Roland McGruder's fifth-floor walkup on West Forty-fourth Street in New York – a neighborhood that used to be called 'Hell's Kitchen' before the realtors decided that 'Clinton' had certain advantages when it came to sales – was crowded and untidy, as if in homage to the cramped rooms offstage where he plied his theatrical craft. As he often apologized to friends, it wasn't as if he were a set designer.

Given pride of place was his mounted Tony award medallion, Best Makeup for a Theatrical Production. Near it, on a desktop stand, was the signed photograph of Nora 'Knock 'Em Dead' Norwood, the finest belter – in his opinion – since Ethel Merman. *To my darling Roland*, she had penned in her loopy, round handwriting, *who makes me look the way I feel. Eternal gratitude!* Another was from Elaine Stritch, with an equally effusive message. It was one of the dicta that the old-timers held with: Make friends with the makeup artist, and they'll always make you look good. A lot of the younger divas, though, could be impossible: imperious, cold, even rude, treating Roland like some guy with a broom. That kind of attitude was why he stopped doing film work.

There's no people like show people, as the old song had it. But Roland had worked with other people who were not show people at all. They didn't leave signed photographs. In fact, they made him sign all sorts of scary-sounding nondisclosure agreements. But they had other ways to indicate their gratitude, not least with payments that were quite lucrative for the little time they asked of him. It had started, years back, when he was asked to give training sessions to a few government spooks, explaining the basic techniques of disguise. Though Roland was discreet, his name had obviously spread in the intelligence community by word of mouth. Every once in a while he'd have an unexpected visitor with peculiar requests and an envelope fat with cash. A few of them were even semiregulars.

Like the fellow he was helping now. Six feet, regular features, gray eyes. Basically a blank slate as far as Roland was concerned.

'I can use wax and make a dental appliance that will wrap around the upper gums,' Roland explained. 'Good-looking guy like you, it's such a shame. But it'll change the contours of the face pretty dramatically. How about blue eyes?'

The man showed him the passport: HENRY GILES was the name, and it stipulated that the passport bearer had brown eyes. 'Stick to that script,' he said.

'Brown eyes, then, no problem. There's a subtle latex wash I can do around the eyes that crinkles a bit – looks natural, but it definitely adds age. We can work on the corners of your mouth, too. Maybe add just a bit to the nose. But we keep the balance, we keep it subtle. You don't want people to be admiring your makeup artist, am I right?'

'I don't want people to take a second glance,' his visitor said.

'Easier if you can stay out of direct sunlight,' Roland cautioned. 'It's hard to get dermal appliqués that work equally well in all kinds of lighting.' He studied the man's face a little more. 'I'm going to give you a mandible appliance, too. Orthodontic wax is easy to mold, but don't expect to be getting a lot of use out of it. Be careful when you talk.'

'Always am.'

'In your line of work, I guess you have to.'

His visitor winked. 'You're a good man, McGruder. I'm grateful to you, and not for the first time.'

'You're sweet. But please. I just do what I get paid to do.' He smiled happily. 'Don't they say that happiness is having to do what you want to do? Or is it wanting to do what you have to do? I can never keep that straight. Or anything else, much.' He inserted two wedges of orthodontic wax into a microwave. 'We'll have you out of here in no time,' he said.

'Appreciate it. Really.'

'Like I say, I do what I get paid to do.'

An hour later, after his visitor had left, McGruder made himself a cranberry and vodka, and did something else he was paid to do. He dialed a phone number that rang somewhere in Washington, D.C. He recognized the voice of the man who answered.

'You told me to let you know if Mister Man showed up, right?' Roland took a long sip of his cocktail. 'Well, guess what. I just got done with him. So what do you need to know?'

CHAPTER TWENTY-SIX

A sliding sound. The same guard as before, one hand on the lever knob and the other at the keyhole, easing the heavy door open on its hinges. Andrea Bancroft stood at the far wall even before she was told to. But the guard was not alone this time. Another man – taller, lankier, older – stepped in after him. A few murmured words were exchanged, and the guard left, apparently stationing himself behind the door.

The tall man took a few steps toward Andrea and regarded her appraisingly. Despite his size, there was something cat-like about his movements, she decided. He was elegant, somehow too elegant, and his gray-green eyes settled upon her with almost penetrative force.

'Two men were killed at a storage facility at Rosendale,' he barked. 'You were there. What happened?'

'I think you know,' she said.

'What did you do to them?' His voice was loud yet tone-less, and he was no longer looking at her. 'We need answers.'

'Tell me where I am,' Andrea demanded. 'Goddammit – '

The tall man's eyes roved across the walls of the cell as if searching for something. 'Why did you travel to Cyprus?' he demanded. Yet it somehow seemed that the question wasn't even directed at her. 'There's no point in keeping secrets anymore.' Suddenly he turned over the nylon-and-canvas blanket on her bed, his fingers probing the heavy fringe of canvas along the outer seams.

'What the hell are you – '

The man turned to her with a worried look, placed his fingers to lips in a brief, frantic signal. 'If you don't cooper-ate with them,' he intoned, not meeting her eyes, 'they'll have no reason to keep you alive. They're not big on second chances. I suggest you start talking if you know what's good for you.'

He wasn't speaking to her at all, then. He was speaking for the benefit of unseen listeners.

His long fingers suddenly yanked at a wire that had been cunningly concealed beneath the canvas. With a series of forceful jerks, he removed almost a yard of a thin, silver-colored wire. At its end was a small globular device that had been concealed in one corner of the suicide-blanket seam.

'Fine,' he blared, 'sit down and start talking to me. I'll know if you're lying. You see, there's very little about you I don't know.'

Then he twisted the black plastic globule until a snapping sound could be heard.

The man turned toward Andrea and spoke quietly, urgently. 'We don't have much time. When the recording cuts out, they'll assume a malfunction. But there's a chance someone will notice the problem sooner rather than later.'

'Who are you?'

The man looked at her, his face taut with fear. 'A prisoner, just like you.'

'I don't understand.'

'I told them I'd be able to get to you. That I'd know how to interrogate you, that I'd know your weakness. It's the only reason they've put us together.'

'But why – '

'Probably because of who you are, and who I am. There's something we have in common.' His expression was harrowed. 'You see, I'm a friend of Todd's.'

Andrea's eyes widened. 'My God. You're Jared Rinehart.'

Washington, D.C.

In his office, Will Garrison glowered silently for a few moments. The alert had flashed on his desktop monitor, an interagency message that was instantaneously relayed by the Consular Operation Intranet. Confirmation was swiftly secured. The name provided by the informant in New York had been added to the FAA watch list, and now it had been triggered. One 'Henry Giles' was on the move. *Bet you didn't think we'd be on to this one, Todd-o.*

Yet Gareth Drucker was frustratingly hesitant when Garrison arrived with the news. Behind those rectangular rimless glasses, his eyes seemed veiled, shifty. He stood against the Venetian blinds, his slim form silhouetted against the afternoon light, and seemed reluctant to meet Garrison's gaze.

'There's a shitstorm coming, Will,' Drucker said, exhaling noisily, 'and I don't even know whose shit it is.'

'Goddammit, we can't screw around at a time like this,' Garrison exploded. 'We need to strike, and we need to strike now.'

'It's this goddamn Kirk Commission,' Drucker said. 'I'm already getting my balls fricasseed over the Hart Building debacle. There's a time for stepping up and there's a time to duck and cover. My political instincts tell me that if there's one more operation goes awry, we could all be answering questions about it for the next twelve months.'

'You're not going to dispatch another retrieval?'

'I have to think about it. Oakeshott tells me that Kirk's guys have developed protective feelings toward our rogue. That's the word he's received, and Oakeshott's pretty wired with the boys on the Hill. Go talk to him.'

'Fucking Oakeshott,' Garrison fumed. 'So what's the deal with Kirk? This because Castor's got something on them? Or he's masquerading as a goddamn whistleblower?'

The director of operations pursed his lips. 'We don't know. But say he's convinced these godforsaken investigators that he's a whistleblower, and then we come down and clobber the guy. How's that going to look?'

'How's it going to *look*? How's it gonna look if you let a goddamn unhinged rogue go wreak havoc yet again? He's a menace, and you know it as well as I do. You read the internal report from Larnaca. The bastard murdered a prominent businessman, a guy we used as a confidential informant more than once. Belknap is out of control; he's deranged with rage and paranoia – a menace to everyone he encounters. I mean, Ruthie Robbins was killed just four goddamn days ago!'

'I got investigators telling me Castor wasn't the doer. She was sniped, and he's no sniper. Larnaca is looking more complicated than we thought. Meanwhile, I got people raising a lot of questions about Pollux. There may be some surprises there. There are some dark holes in that vita, and we don't know what's in 'em. But I'm guessing it's more than a bunch of golf balls.'

'Shit. The ankle-biters are throwing up a bunch of distractions. Chasing after rocking-horse dung. I'm so sick and tired of the goddamn cult of Castor. Young shit-for-brains who refuse to see what's in front of their faces, always trying to come up with some other explanation. Like that Gomez kid. Ought to be given walking papers, or posted to fucking Moldova.'

'Junior analyst Gomes, you mean? He's raised questions, that's true. But he's not the only one. Trust me on this. Something isn't trig, okay? Something isn't right.'

'No argument there. Something isn't right.' *And it won't be until I set it right.*

Garrison had calmed down some by the time he made his way down the hall and poked his head in the office of a junior member of the operations directorate.

A heavyset man with brown hair, blunt features, and a puffy face swiveled to face him. His name was O'Brien, and he had been a protégé of Garrison's at the beginning of his career. His desk was cluttered with family photographs and a nonregulation PDA on a cradle. He wasn't trig, he wasn't tidy, but Garrison knew he would come through.

'What's up, Will?'

'How are the kids, Danny?' He paused to remember their names. 'Beth, Lane? They doing good?'

'They're doing good, Will. What's up?'

'Need to requisition a jet.'

'So do it.'

'Need you to do it. Got to keep things special-access.'

'You don't want your signature on the authorization paperwork.'

'You got it.'

O'Brien swallowed hard. 'This going to get me in trouble?'

'You worry too much.'

'As the lawyers say, that's nonresponsive.'

'We really don't have time to play pattycakes. Operational time has already commenced.'

'This part of the Castor recoup?'

O'Brien was slow but he wasn't stupid. 'You see, Danny,' Garrison said levelly, 'we've tried teams before, haven't we? This time we're going to play it different. A single top-drawer operative, like a single well-aimed arrow.'

'Who?' O'Brien asked. 'Who's the passenger?'

Garrison's quilted cheeks spread in a tight smile. 'Me.'

He wasn't just making a virtue of necessity. On reflection, Garrison had realized that he'd actually have a better chance of catching Belknap on his own. A multiperson team was too easy for a skilled operative to detect, and could be slowed by coordination problems. In fact, Garrison recalled a time when Belknap had apprehended a rogue single-handed because he knew that the arrival of a team would, as it said, 'spook the hare.' Drucker's reluctance would serve him well.

'You?' O'Brien's eyes widened. 'Can I ask you something, Will? You were a legendary field op in your day – everybody knows that. But you're all grown up, at the top of the goddamn tree, just about. Whatever you need done, can't you send someone to take care of it? I mean, what good is seniority if it doesn't keep you safe in the office?'

Garrison made a harrumphing noise. 'You know what they say. You want a job done right, you better do it yourself.'

'They sure don't make 'em like you anymore,' O'Brien said, shaking his head. 'Which, all told, might be a good thing. So, you going . . . equipped?'

Garrison nodded.

'Need a requisition there, too? Or are you taking care of that part?'

'A soldier always does his own packing, Danny.'

'You sound like you're going off to war.'

'I'm going off to *win*, Danny.'

They had come close, so close, in Washington the other day, and if Garrison had been on the scene personally, it wouldn't have merely been close. Castor was a wily son of a bitch, but he'd never been able to outplay Garrison. Garrison had been around long enough to learn every damn trick, dodge, and subterfuge that had ever been invented. You didn't retrieve somebody like Belknap. That was just asking for trouble. With a customer like that, the only way to make sure he could do no more mischief was with a bullet in the brain. You wrote the end, not to be continued. When the story was over, it was over. No sequels. No jaw-jaw. Just war-war.

'Where to?'

'Dominica. Fifty clicks south of Guadeloupe. You need to get my ass in the air within the hour. Chop-chop, baby.'

'What's in Dominica?' O'Brien was already reaching for the telephone.

'I don't know,' Garrison murmured, half to himself. 'But I can guess.'

Jared Rinehart sat close to her. 'There's so much I wish I could explain.'

'Where are we?'

'My guess? Somewhere in upstate New York. Someplace rural, remote. But also in striking distance of Montreal and New York.'

'I keep thinking this is all a nightmare, and I'm going to wake up from it.'

'You're half-right,' Rinehart said. 'It's a nightmare, all right. Listen, there's no time. We need to talk about Genesis. Todd was on the trail, wasn't he?'

Andrea nodded.

'I need to know exactly what he's found out. Where does he think Genesis might be located?'

She swallowed hard, trying to think. 'Last thing I know, he was meeting with Senator Kirk.'

'Yes, we know that. But he must have had ideas, suspicions,

instincts. Please, Andrea, this is vital. He must have said something to you.'

'He was turning over rocks. Going through the possibilities. He even wondered whether you were Genesis.'

Rinehart looked startled, even wounded.

'Or Paul Bancroft, or – but I think he knew it wasn't anybody we'd thought of. I think he'd decided it was someone else altogether.'

'This isn't helpful. You've got to rack your brains. He trusted you, didn't he?'

'We trusted each other.'

'Then he must have let something drop.'

'You mean like he knew and was trying to keep it a secret? That's not how it was.' Andrea looked at the other man hard, feeling a tickling in the pit of her stomach. 'Otherwise he wouldn't have gone to see the senator.'

Yes, we know that.

Yet who was 'we,' and how did they know? 'Jared,' she said, 'forgive my confusion. But there's something I don't understand.'

'They could come for us at any moment,' he reproved. 'Please focus.'

'Have we been taken hostage by Genesis?'

'What are you asking?'

She knew. 'It's the others who want to know about Genesis, isn't it? And you're helping them.'

'You're mad!'

Yes, we know that.

'Or are you trying to find out who's on your heels? A threat assessment – isn't that what you call it?'

Suddenly she lashed out at him, but Rinehart caught her wrist in a grip of steel and abruptly threw her onto the floor. She fell hard, returned to her feet slowly.

Now he was standing before her, regarding her with a baleful gaze. The pretended fear had abruptly vanished from his countenance. It was replaced by contempt.

'You're a beautiful woman,' he said at last. 'Apologies for the unflattering lighting.'

'I suspect that's the least of my worries.'

The smile of a lynx. 'You have a point.' He reminded her of a figure from a painting by Pontormo or some such sixteenth-century Florentine. A little stretched, but with a coiled strength. 'Then again, we all have our roles to play. And yours is a crucial one.' She felt as if he were drawing her soul from her through the magnetism of his gaze.

'Please, have a seat.' He gestured toward the cot. 'And, just to head off any reckless lines of thought, do bear in mind, at all times, that I *am* a professional.' He produced a small metal stylus in his hand, like a conjurer. 'If I had a mind to, I could insert this into the back of your neck, between the second and third cervical vertebrae. In a flash. It's a matter of *Fingerspitzgefühl*, as the Germans would say. Don't be misled by the fact that I don't carry a lot of hardware on my belt. I don't need to.' For a moment his eyes were twin beams of absolute malevolence. Then he blinked and once again his countenance assumed a deceptive civility.

'I have to admit, you really had me there for a while.'

'It was worth a shot. Clearly, Todd has taken you as his helpmate.' He smiled his feline smile, all teeth and no warmth. 'He always did have a weakness for clever women. But it's clear you have no actionable intelligence for us. No great surprise there.'

'Is Todd such a threat to you? Am I?'

'On the whole, I'd say we don't respond to threats. We make them. And then we carry them out. More so now than ever. The Ansari network is among the world's largest, and now it's ours. Nikos Stavros himself has been a formidable presence in the transshipment of arms, and Stavros Maritime is in our control as well. As are a dozen other wholesalers in armaments and munitions. I'm aware that you know something about business. In the corporate world, it's called a rollup.'

'A rollup. As in the strategy of acquiring many small firms in the same product category in order to create a market-dominant player. I know about rollups, all right. Coventry Equity backed a few.'

'Nobody imagined it could be done in the parallel economy, the so-called black market. I think we've proven otherwise. Which means, of course, that we're poised to become even more powerful than ever before.'

'Who's "we," kimosabe?'

'I think you know.'

'Theta.'

'You've named the seed crystal.' Another mirthless smile. 'Do you understand what we're on the verge of becoming?'

'I understand that you people have been manipulating elections around the world.'

'That's merely a sideline. So few countries have meaningful elections anyway. In most of the world, the gun is ascendant over the ballot box. It's why we have proceeded as we have. We now effectively control the availability of revolutionary violence. The only way for nonstate forces to gain weaponry is through us. We can ensure the stability of regimes that would otherwise be overturned. We can destabilize regimes that would otherwise have clung to power. Which means we're moving into a whole new phase of operations, you see. We're operating beyond the level of the nation-state. Soon it will be clear what we've built – in effect, our own league of nations.'

Andrea looked in the tall man's clear resolute eyes. 'Why? What's your goal?'

'Don't affect ignorance, Andrea. I think you understand perfectly well.'

'I understand that you're Genesis. That much I understand. That's why you wanted to know whether Todd was going to be able to track you down.'

Jared Rinehart's green-gray eyes widened. 'You really think I'm Genesis? Hardly. Hardly, Andrea.' He spoke louder, becoming agitated. 'Genesis is a purely negative force in the world. Genesis is an agent of destruction.'

Her mind reeled as she strove to absorb his response. *Genesis. Enemy thine.* After a long moment she spoke softly, almost intimately. 'You fear him.'

'I fear the allure of chaos and destruction. What rational

man doesn't? Genesis has foot soldiers everywhere, has been constantly recruiting mercenaries and confederates – '

'You fear him.'

'I assure you that Genesis is the coward. That's why nobody has been allowed to see Genesis.'

'Then how does he recruit? How can he operate?'

'In the information age, that's child's play. Genesis trawls so-called secure chat rooms on the Internet, identifies soldiers of fortune who communicate via Internet-relay chat systems. Genesis is able to wire payments remotely, even as he hires other informants to file electronic reports on them. And because nobody knows who is and isn't working for Genesis, a generalized paranoia sets in. It's all been quite craftily done.' There was both resentment and admiration in Rinehart's voice. 'Genesis is a spider in the center of a web. Occasionally a filament will catch the rays of the sun and we'll see it. Genesis has kept its own face hidden. Yet Genesis has no positive program for the world. He, she, it, is dedicated only to our destruction.'

'Because Genesis wants to replace you?'

'Perhaps. We'll know more soon. Because we've got the very best on the case.' He allowed himself a small smile. 'When it's all over, Genesis will be remembered as nothing more than a bump in the road.'

'What is it that you really want, anyway?'

'As if you don't know. Your cousin said you were an apt pupil. He had even imagined that you might assume an important role in the organization.'

'Paul Bancroft.'

'But of course. It was he who devised the Theta Group in the first place.'

Andrea felt her stomach flip over. 'And now you're about to give it an army of its own. Do you know how monstrous that sounds?'

'Monstrous? It astonishes me that you could have learned so little from your own cousin. Everything we do is calculated exquisitely to serve the general welfare of humanity. In a corrupted world, the Theta Group is a force for the truest idealism.'

The line Paul Bancroft had quoted from Manilius returned to her with a shudder: *To pass beyond your understanding and make yourself master of the universe.*

'What I really don't understand,' she said, 'is why we're even having this conversation. Why are you still here?'

'Call me a sentimental fool. But I want to get to know you, before . . .' He looked away. 'It's obvious that Todd Belknap adores you. I'm curious to learn what sort of person you were. To talk freely and candidly with you, so that you'd know that you could talk freely and candidly with me.' He paused. 'You won't believe me, but Todd is someone I truly care about, in my fashion. I love him like a brother.'

'You're right,' Andrea said. 'I don't believe you.'

'Like a brother. Which, I grant, is a complicated tribute in my case, given the awkward fact that I killed my own brother. My fraternal twin, no less. The really awkward fact is, I can't even remember why. Of course, I was hardly more than a child at the time. But I digress.'

'You're a sick man,' Andrea said in a trembling voice.

'In the pink of health, actually. But I know what you're trying to say. I am . . . different from most.'

'If Todd had ever known who you really were . . .'

'He knew *a version* of me. People are complicated, Andrea. My friendship with Belknap was something I worked very, very hard to cultivate and sustain, and if that meant that distractions had to be eliminated, I saw to that.'

Distractions had to be eliminated.

'You kept him isolated,' Andrea said in a low voice. 'Off-balance. And when anyone came too close, when he formed a real relationship with someone, you . . . made it go away. And when he was grieving, you were always there to comfort him, weren't you?' Her voice grew louder, fiercer. 'He thought you were his only true friend. And all the while you were the one manipulating him, murdering those he loved, keeping him off-balance. Those times when you rescued him – those were all staged, too, weren't they? This man would have done anything for you. And all you ever did was to betray him.'

'And yet I did care for him, Andrea,' the tall man replied softly. 'Certainly I admired him. He had – has – extraordinary skills. There's really nobody he can't track down when he has a mind to.'

'Which is why you latched on to him in the first place, isn't it? He told me about East Berlin all those years ago. What was that – a twofer?'

'You *are* a clever thing. As it happens, I'd recently re-cruited Lugner at that point. I knew he was someone we'd be able to make use of, and I was right. At the same time, it was also becoming apparent that this young Mr. Belknap was even better at finding people than Lugner was at disap-pearing. Lugner's only chance was to get the Hound to think the hunt had been successful. He needed an authoritative post-action report on his death, and after our elaborate stagecraft, that's what he got.'

'But you got something even better. The Hound's loyalty and devotion. Strengths of character that you set out to turn into weaknesses.'

He nodded, with a hint of a smile. 'I'm a sensible man. A rare talent like Todd's is one you want to have on your side.'

'And you made sure of that when he was still a junior officer. You recognized right off the bat that he had skills you envied. Skills you wanted to exploit.'

'My dear, you read me like a book.'

'Yeah, *Helter Skelter*.' Repugnance filled her like a scald-ing fluid. 'How can you even live with yourself?'

'Don't judge me, Andrea.' Rinehart was silent for a long moment. 'It's odd – I'm having the conversation with you that I always wished I could one day have with Belknap. I don't imagine he'd be able to understand me any better that you have. But try, Andrea. Try. Not every difference is a dis-ability. Years ago, I sought out the services of a shrink. A very well respected one. I essentially booked an afternoon with him.'

'You don't seem the type.'

'I was a young man then. Still, as they say, finding myself. So there I was, in a cozy office on West End Avenue,

Manhattan, spilling my guts out. Talked about absolutely everything. There was an aspect to my nature that troubled me – or, rather, what troubled me was precisely that it didn't trouble me, and I knew it ought to. I guess the way to put it, Andrea, is this: I was born without a moral compass. Even as child I was aware of this. Not at first, of course. I found out about this deficit the way you find out that you're color-blind. You find that others see a distinction that you can't quite make out.'

'You're a monster.'

Rinehart ignored her. 'I remember when our pet Labrador had puppies, more than it could take care of, it seemed to me, and I borrowed one of those puppies to experiment on. I was fascinated by what was revealed when one slit open its abdomen with an X-Acto knife, and I remember fetching my brother to show him what I'd found, the way the small intestines looked like earthworms, the way the liver looked just like chicken livers did. I got no sadistic thrill from this – it was just a matter of disinterested curiosity. Yet when my brother saw what I'd done, he looked at me as if I were horribly disfigured, a monster. Such fear and disgust. I simply didn't understand.' Rinehart's voice was haunted. 'I came to understand, as I grew older. But never to *feel*. Other people had a set of moral intuitions that guided them unthinkingly. I never had that. I had to learn the rules, as one learns the rules of etiquette, and to conceal those instances when I violated those rules. As with my brother's death in a presumed hit-and-run accident. I suppose it was because I learned to conceal this aspect of myself that I ended up in the covert ops business: Concealment, subterfuge became second nature to me.'

Andrea was roiled with nausea. 'And you told everything to a shrink?'

Rinehart nodded. 'He was quite insightful. Finally he said, 'Well, I'm afraid our time is up.' Whereupon, simply as a precautionary measure, I strangled him at his desk with my necktie. Now, I ask myself, did I know that I was going to kill him when we started the session? I think that I did, on some level, because I was careful to leave no fingerprints in his office. Made the appointment under an alias, and so forth. And knowing this, even on an unconscious level, is surely what enabled me to speak so freely to him.'

'As with me.' Andrea breathed the words.

'I think we understand each other.' Rinehart's tone was not unkind.

'And yet you tell me that you're a force for good. That the Theta Group is a force for good. Do you really expect anyone to take the judgment of a sociopath seriously?'

'Is it such a paradox?' Rinehart was leaning against the wall opposite her cot. His expression was both attentive and remote. 'You see, this is how Dr. Bancroft changed my life. Because, intellectually, I very much wanted to devote my life to the good. I wanted to do the right thing. Yet I had a hard time *seeing* it, and ordinary people seemed to operate by such a complicated clutter of different considerations that I found it was sometimes impossible to anticipate these very strongly held judgments they had. I desperately needed some clear guide to right action. And that's when I encountered the work of Dr. Paul Bancroft.'

Andrea just stared.

'Here was a man with a brilliantly simple algorithm – a clear, clean yardstick, an objective metric,' Rinehart went on. 'He showed that morality wasn't some subjective faculty of perception after all. That it was a straightforward matter of maximizing utility. And that people's intuitions were quite likely to lead them astray.' Rinehart's voice grew animated, his gaze intent. 'I can't tell you how captivated I was – even more so after I met the man himself. I'll always remember something he said to me once. He said, 'Compare yourself to the man who refrains from flaying alive random strangers because the very thought of doing so is repugnant to him. His is merely the morality of disgust. If you refrain from doing so, by contrast, it's because you've reflected upon the axioms and principles involved. Ethically speaking, whose is the greater achievement?' It was a gift, his saying that. But the greatest gift was the rigorous system of morality he set forth. The calculus of felicity.'

'You don't say.'

'The runaway trolley car. You know this one, don't you? Activate the switch, and it detours to kill a single person instead of five.'

'I remember,' Andrea replied testily.

'And that would be the right thing to do. Obviously. But now, Dr. Bancroft said, imagine that you're a transplant surgeon. By taking the life of one stranger and using his organs, you could save the lives of five of your patients. What's the difference between the two situations, logically speaking? Why, none at all. *None at all*, Andrea.'

'None that you can see, anyway.'

'The logic is crystal-clear. And once you take it to heart, it changes everything. The old prejudices fall by the wayside. Dr. Bancroft was the greatest, noblest savant I'd ever come across. His philosophy has meant that I really could devote my life to the greater good. It gave me an algorithm that could replace this missing thing – but it was better than what it replaced, like some kind of bionic eye. He showed that ethical choices were to be settled by intellect, not by emotion. Doing the right thing, he told me, isn't always easy – for anybody. It takes work. And Todd should have told you that I'm a *fiend* for work.'

'Paul told me – ' Andrea broke off. 'He told me that every life matters. What about mine? What about *mine*, goddammit?'

'Oh, Andrea. Obviously, given all that you know about our operations, appropriate measures must be taken. But your life will matter in *so* many ways, as will your death.' Rinehart sounded almost tender.

'My death,' she echoed dully.

'Everyone on this green Earth is on death row,' Rinehart said. 'You know this. People talk about killing as if it's some mystical abomination rather than what it is – essentially a scheduling matter.'

'A scheduling matter.'

'Speaking of which, you're blood type O, correct?'

She nodded numbly.

'Excellent,' said Rinehart. 'The universal donor. Any exposure to hepatitis, HIV, syphilis, malaria, papilloma, or other blood-borne diseases?' His basilisk eyes drilled into her.

'No,' she whispered.

'I hope you've been eating. Important to keep your organs healthy, maintain your iron levels, all that. I think you know why you're not being sedated – we don't want your organs suffused with CNS depressants. That's not good for the recipients. I mean, I'm looking at a young woman in excellent condition. You've got resources that could save half a dozen lives. In addition to the blood, I'm looking at a liver, a heart, two kidneys, two corneas, a pancreas, two fine lungs, and no doubt a great array of vascular grafts as well. *So* glad you're not a smoker.'

It was all Andrea could do to keep from doubling over and retching.

'Take care of yourself,' Rinehart said as he turned to leave.

'*You* take care yourself, you twisted bastard,' Andrea croaked. It was rage and rage alone that stopped her from falling apart. 'Didn't you say that Todd Belknap could find anyone if he had a mind to?'

'Well, exactly.' Rinehart smiled as he rapped on the steel-plated door. 'That's what I'm counting on.'

CHAPTER TWENTY-SEVEN

The Commonwealth of Dominica, a wrinkled oval of land located between Martinique and Guadeloupe, was a former British colony, and had a cuisine that suffered for it. There were, however, other compensations. A relative newcomer to the tax-haven industry – it passed the International Business Companies Act No. 10 only in 1996 – it had swiftly earned a reputation for efficiency and discretion. As a sovereign nation, it was unaffected by American and European regulations, and the Act made it a criminal offense to reveal personal information, expressly including information about criminality. There were no exchange controls on fund movements, no statutory oversight of businesses operating in its bailiwick. Thirty miles long, half as wide, the island boasted dense forests, valleys, and waterfalls, along with a rugged shoreline. Though it had only seventy thousand inhabitants, many of whom lived in the capital city of Roseau, its electrical and communications infrastructure was of an unusually high standard. Ecologists regularly complained about the various antennae placed on top of mountains in the major forest preserves. Elsewhere, indicator lights annoyed scuba divers. For them, such signs of modernity violated a cherished illusion of Edenic isolation.

Belknap had no such illusions. Nor was he in any mood to admire the tropical luxuriance of the place. Immediately upon arriving, he and Walt Sachs made their way to a shack-like structure that was about three hundred yards from Melville Hall, the main airport. A bright yellow logo identified the outfit as Island Rent-a-Car.

'My name is Henry Giles,' said Belknap. 'I reserved a

four-wheel-drive.' He had removed the dental appliances, but his mouth still ached.

'The four-by-four got wrecked, mon,' the man behind the counter said in a melodious lilt. 'Got wrecked in Carnaval last January. Never quite worked since then.'

'Do you often let people reserve cars that don't work?' Sachs spoke up. The long trip had not put him in a good mood.

'Musta been a mix-up. Sometime my wife answer the phone, you know. And she ain't been right herself since the 1976 hurricane.' Belknap gave the man a closer look and realized he was considerably older than he seemed at first glance. His head was smooth-shaven and gleamed in the tropical heat, his skin tarry black, almost viscous-looking.

'What can you give me, my friend?'

'I got a Mazda. Two-wheel-drive, I'd guess you'd say, though I'm not sure it's always so many as two.'

'What do you drive?'

'Me, mon? I drive that old Jeep over there.' He pronounced 'over there' as 'ober der.'

'How much to rent?'

The man made a whistling sound of disapproval and deliberation, sucking air through his gapped front teeth. 'But those are my wheels.'

'How much to make them mine?'

The rent-a-car man made him part with two hundred dollars, U.S., before handing over the keys to his Jeep.

'So where you going, mon?' the man asked as he pocketed the cash. 'What you come to see in dis island paradise?'

Belknap shrugged. 'I've always wanted to see the Boiling Lake.' The Boiling Lake – a geothermal oddity, the result of a flooded fumarole – was one of the island's better-known attractions.

'You in luck, then. It don't always boil, see. Most of last year, it just steamed, mon. But this year it's mighty hot. You best watch yourself around it.'

'I'll bear that in mind.'

Once they were on the road, headed south toward Roseau,

Walt's already sour mood grew worse. 'You're gonna get me killed with this goddamn G.I. Joe business,' he whined. 'At least you can defend yourself.'

Belknap gave him a look but didn't respond.

Fruited branches – limes, bananas, guava fruit peeping through thick waxy leaves – brushed by them as they drove, the suspensionless Jeep amplifying every bump in the road. The landscape was as verdant as any Belknap had ever seen.

'Know what?' Walt pouted. 'I'm beginning to think your boot ROM has a bad checksum.'

'I'm guessing that, where you come from, them's fightin' words,' Belknap replied heavily.

'Where are we headed, exactly?'

'The Valley of Desolation,' replied Belknap.

'You're kidding,' Walt said.

'Look at a map.'

'You're *not* kidding,' Sachs said, and sighed. The ten-hour trip – they had changed at San Juan to a small prop plane – left them both feeling soiled and weary.

'Privex is in Roseau,' Walt said primly.

'Wrong. That's just a P.O. box. The actual facility is just above the village of Morne Prosper.'

'How do you even know that?'

'Walt, my friend. This is what I do. I'm a finder. Privex is on the lee side of that mountain, because it's not just dependent on the island's generous fiber-optic supply. It also has a cluster of satellite dishes sucking up Internet transmissions from the sky.'

'But how –'

'Because deliveries must be made. These routers and servers and hubs and switches – all the bits and pieces of the whole information architecture – need to be replaced on some schedule. They don't last forever.'

'Got it. So when EMC delivers parts for the Connectrix, someone has to get those parts to the facility. What telecom folks call the last-mile problem.'

'Cisco, actually. They're using something called the Catalyst 6500 Series Supervisor Engine.'

'But how – '

'Did I know they'd order one? I didn't. So I ordered one for them. Phoned the top network hardware companies, said I was calling from Dominica, gave them the P.O. box, and tried to place an order for half a million dollars' worth of application servers and such. Got a hit at Cisco. Long story short, I found out that they'd hired a helicopter company to do the delivery to Dominica. So I called the copter company.'

'And that's how you got location.'

'Long story short,' Belknap repeated.

'Incredible.'

'Like I said, this is what I do.'

'So where's this place again?'

'Perched up high above the Roseau Valley.'

'Hence the Jeep,' Walt said. 'To drive up that mountain.'

'We're hiking. It's safer. A Jeep in the village is likely to attract scrutiny. Make it harder to arrive at the facility unnoticed.'

'I guess that means going by helicopter is out of the question. Jeepers creepers. This trip is *not* as advertised.'

'No cruise, either,' Belknap snapped. 'Sorry. You can apply for a refund afterward.'

'Oh, crap. Look, I'll be in a better mood after I've eaten and showered.'

'Not on,' Belknap said. 'No time to stop.'

'You're kidding,' Walt said, running a hand through his brown-and-gray hair. His eyes looked even more irritated than usual as he shot Belknap a look. 'You're . . . not kidding.'

Twenty minutes later, Belknap hid the Jeep in a copse of soursop trees, their dense evergreen leaves effectively camouflaging the vehicle. 'We hike now.' They got out onto spongy ground, and the warm humidity seemed to wash over them like bathwater.

Belknap glanced at his watch again. Time was indeed running short: Andrea's life was in the balance. Genesis could have her killed at any moment.

If she hadn't been killed already.

Belknap's stomach clenched; he could not allow himself even to consider the possibility. He had to hold himself together.

Why had Genesis grabbed her? Perhaps there was something she knew, some detail that she didn't even know was significant – but that he might. Or perhaps – possibly a more hopeful thought – it was evidence of desperation on the part of Belknap's shadowy adversary. Yet where was she now? What had Genesis planned for her? He refused to think about the nightmarish scenarios for which Genesis was notorious. He had to force himself to remain in the present. Simply getting through the next few hours would be difficult enough.

One foot in front of the other.

The ground was boggy in places, slick and mucky in others, and the ascent grew only steeper the farther they traveled. A sulfurous smell seeped from volcanic fissures. Ropelike vines dangled across the paths. Hundred-foot-tall gommier trees towered overhead, their intertwined branches forming a canopy that filtered out most of the sunlight. The two hiked with their heads down. At one point, Walt yelped. Belknap whirled around to see a gigantic frog, perched on a stump with a pelt of fluorescent green moss.

'They call that "mountain chicken,"' Belknap explained. 'It's a delicacy.'

'If I ever see that in a bucket of Popeye's, I'm suing.' They were only a third of the way up and Walt was already gasping for breath. 'I still don't see why we're not driving up this way,' he grumbled.

'Want to have a trumpeteer announce our arrival while you're at it? I told you, the idea is to get there unnoticed. We drive a Jeep up the road, there'll be a dozen electronic sentries marking our progress.'

Ten minutes later, Sachs begged for a rest. Belknap agreed to a three-minute break, but for a reason of his own. For the past several hundred yards, he had a nagging sense that they were being followed. In all likelihood it was simply the sound of forest fauna disturbed by their presence. Yet if there were human footfalls in the distance, he would be able to hear better if they kept still for a few minutes.

He heard nothing – yet that was not entirely reassuring. If someone were following them, a skilled pursuer would try to match footfalls with them and remain motionless while they were motionless. *No, dammit, you're imagining things.*

'Keep an eye out for snakes,' Belknap warned Sachs as they resumed their hike.

'All I see are lizards and mayflies,' Sachs said, panting. 'And not enough lizards to deal with the mayflies.'

'A good deal for both the lizards and the mayflies, when you think about it.'

'So it's just people who get the short end of the stick,' the tech huffed. After a while, he said. 'I've been thinking more about what you've told me about Genesis.'

'I should hope so.'

'Nah, I mean, just the way that nobody's ever seen the fellow, the way he-she-it communicates only electronically. It's like we're dealing with an avatar.'

'An avatar? That's something Indian, right?'

'Well, originally, yeah. Like, Krishnu is an avatar of Vishnu, an advanced soul who takes on a physical incarnation to teach less-advanced souls. But nowadays, people who play computer games use it to talk about their online alter egos.'

'Their *what*?'

'There are these multiuser computer games people play, and some of them are incredibly complex. All kinds of people around the world can log in to the system and play with, or against, one another. So they develop an online character that they're in charge of. It's kind of their virtual self.'

'Like a screen name?'

'Well, that's just the start. Because these characters can be very textured, very complicated, with a whole history and reputation that affects the strategies that other players are going to use with them. You'd be surprised how sophisticated online computer games can be these days.'

'I'll bear that in mind,' Belknap said, 'if I ever become a quadriplegic shut-in. Otherwise, I gotta say I find the real world pretty damn challenging enough.'

'Reality's overrated,' Sachs said, still trying to catch his breath.

'Maybe. But it'll burn you if you don't watch out for it.'

'You trying to tell me that the Boiling Lake is on the way?'

'Not far, actually,' Belknap said. 'But it's no joke. People have gotten severely scalded there, even died. The temperature can really soar. It's no goddamn hot tub.'

'And I was so looking forward to taking a cooling dip there,' Sachs replied sourly.

It was past midnight by the time they heard wind chimes and realized that they had reached the village. From a distance, they saw a chute of white water, a narrow, nearly three-hundred-foot-high waterfall. A breeze cooled them a little. Then they sat together on a flat mesa-like rise. Glinting in the moonlight, a cluster of large satellite dishes looked like a floral bouquet from another planet.

'So they've set up a satellite-based counter-net,' Sachs said, marvelingly. 'A virtual private network. That's top-of-the-line equipment from Hughes Network Systems.'

The building itself was a low-slung structure of cinder-block and concrete, painted a dull green that made it blend into the forest when viewed from a distance. Up close, though, it was like a gas station perched on a mountain. A paved parking area, edged with nursery-planted shrubs that looked spindly compared to the vegetation that grew wild. Power and telephone lines that snaked up the mountain converged on a utility annex that must have housed a transformer. There was clearly a backup diesel generator in the ground beneath it.

'What kind of security, do you know?' Sachs couldn't quite keep a tremble from his voice.

'I've got a pretty good idea, from my researches,' said Belknap.

'An electric fence?'

'Not in a jungle like this. Too much wildlife. Everything

from manicou to iguanas to feral dogs – you wouldn't get a security barrier, you'd get a goddamn barbecue. Same reason a perimeter alarm's no good. It would be triggered three times an hour.'

'So there's, what, a gunman inside?'

'Nope. The guys who run this place believe in technology. They're going to have a state-of-the-art motion detector, that sort of thing – which you can't have if you've got some night watchman in the place. Trouble is, the night watchman might get drunk, or fall asleep, or take a bribe – all problems that don't afflict the technological solution. That's how they think.'

'That's how *I'd* think,' Sachs said. 'I'd wire up a detect-and-delete heuristic. How do we deal with that?'

'There's a lot of heat in that place, a lot of sensitive equipment. Ergo, there's got to be a powerful cooling system, too.' Belknap pointed toward some aluminum ductwork on the roof, a wide hood with a vertical grill. 'The place is practically windowless. Take a look. There's a condenser unit just outside the rear door, and a fan, so cool air is forced in.' He pointed. 'That's the other end of the ventilation system – it's where the warm air is pushed out. Wide ductwork to minimize resistance. So we get on the roof, we unscrew the grill, and we wriggle down.'

'And then the alarm goes off.'

'You got it.'

'Which, if standard security protocols are followed,' warned Sachs, 'will kick the machinery into autodelete mode in about fifteen seconds. All files totally erased. A place like Privex would rather risk losing data than leak it.'

'Which means we need to work fast. Unplug the brain before it can activate the erase procedure. That's the key. The guys who run this place live in town. It'll take them half an hour to get up here. It's the machines we need to outsmart.'

'Now what? Because I'm not up for any derring-do, okay?'

'All you need to do is wait for me to open the back door, and then scoot right on in.'

'And how you're going to do that?'

'Watch and learn,' Belknap grunted.

Belknap removed a rope ladder from his backpack and a two-foot piece of metal tubing. He extended the tubing – it telescoped to several times its original length – and twisted it several times until two hooks protruded from it. He scanned the facility's roofline until he found a place where a white pipe extended along the top of the building's nearly flat roof, and he flung the hooked tube toward it. It caught with a *clank*; the nylon ladder now dangled from it like a long black shawl. He tested its grip with a few tugs, then scaled it rapidly.

Now, on the roof, he knelt before the ventilation grate and, with a wide screwdriver from his kit, removed the flat heads from all four corners. Belknap laid the grate gently on the roof. A stale smell emanated from the wide aluminum duct. The flow rate was high enough to produce a very faint breeze.

Headfirst, he clambered in, pulling himself over the bend, using his hand and legs like a lizard. A few yards into the duct, he became aware of the dead silence, the complete absence of light. All he could hear was his own breathing, eerily magnified by the metal tube. He kept moving down the pitch-black tunnel, wriggling and pulling himself forward with his hands, foot by foot, and, painfully, around a bend. The sounds of his own breathing were eerily amplified. Then he found himself upside-down, the blood pooling in his head as abruptly he slid a few yards deeper into the duct.

Which narrowed unexpectedly. His hands reached forward, seeking purchase, but slid back on what had become a slippery, almost greasy surface. Too late, he realized that the jointed section had connected ducting of two different standards, two different widths. He breathed in, and found that the dimensions of the duct prevented his chest from expanding fully. Only shallow breaths were possible. A primal sense of claustrophobia began to creep up on him. He moved a few feet further, straight down now. He had thought he would have to strain to control his rate of descent. Instead, he found the walls of the duct pressing against his chest. He had to struggle simply to move. His cell phone, in a breast pocket of his tunic, now gouged painfully into his ribs. He worked it free, and then it slipped from his grip, falling and smashing on some hard unseen surface below him.

Would it trigger the motion detector? Evidently not; it was too small. His own problem was that he was too big. He was effectively trapped.

Trapped.

Panic was the one thing he could not afford. Yet now trivial thoughts were starting to loom large in his mind – such as the sense that he could not know whether his eyes were closed or not in the pitch darkness. He reminded himself that he couldn't be any more than twelve feet from the end. Then his mind began to race. Sachs was a civilian, had no expertise relevant to the physical world. If Belknap were stuck here, Sachs would have no idea how to get him out. He would remain here all night. And who knew what fate would befall him if he was found by whatever security goons Privex employed?

It was his own damn fault – the operation had been foolhardy, desperation ascendant over prudence. He had improvised a plan of action without taking his usual precautions. He'd settled on a plan without a backup plan. Christ on a raft!

His fear had triggered sweating, and the sweating, he dimly sensed, would help smooth his passage. A cheap irony. He exhaled fully, reducing the diameter of his chest, and wriggled further, like a snake or worm, propelled by small movements from all his limbs, even his fingers. He gulped for air – and once more felt the sheet metal pressing against his rib cage. If he got stuck, could he back up somehow? He felt entombed, buried alive.

A hundred alternate entrance routes filled his head amid clouds of regret. He was wheezing now, his breath reduced to a whistling stridor, his very alveoli constricted by stress hormones. When he was a young child he had experienced episodes of asthma, and he never forgot what it was like. It was as if you had been sprinting and then were forced to breathe through a straw. There was air, but not enough, and somehow the insufficiency seemed worse than none at all. He had not felt like that for decades, but it was how he felt now.

Goddammit!

He wriggled another yard, slick with perspiration, blood pounding in his ears, pressure mounting in his chest. *Snug as a bug in a rug.* And then his stretched-out hand touched something irregular. A grate. At the other end. He pressed at it and felt it yield slightly. Just slightly, yet enough to give him heart. Now he banged at it with the heel of his hand – and he heard it fall clanging onto the floor.

A second later, he heard a loud, piercing beeping noise.

Oh, Jesus – the motion detector had already been triggered while he was still trapped in this infernal metal tube, his hips bruised further with every snaking move. The alarm noise, rhythmic, mindless, ceaseless, grew subtly louder with each beep. Soon, no doubt, the beeping would give way to a steady whine, and the security system would be activated. A million or so e-mails erased. The journey here had been in vain. Their last lead was about to be destroyed.

He would have screamed if he had only been able to get enough air into his lungs.

Andrea Bancroft shuddered as she remembered Jared Rinehart's lynxlike gaze, the abrupt way he slipped from persona to persona, multiple personalities that were each under his tight control. His gifts for deception were frightening. Yet the glimpse she'd had into his true self was even more frightening. To him, Belknap was an instrument, but something more as well; he had an unwholesome fixation on the man he had so cunningly manipulated. At the same time, it was clear, he feared Genesis as much as she and Todd did.

What was the real reason for that? Why was she here?

Andrea Bancroft found herself pacing, a caged animal, struggling to keep hope flickering in her breast. *Pessimism of the intellect, optimism of the will* – it was the mantra of a Spanish literature teacher she'd once had, an old campaigner who revered the prewar communists and Republicans. She recalled a bit of verse from the Spanish poet Rafael Garcia Adeva, whose works she had been required to translate:

El corazón es un prisionero en el pecho,
encerrado en una jaula de costillas.
La mente es una prisionera en el cráneo,
encerrada detrás de placas de hueso . . .

The heart is a prisoner in the chest,
Locked inside a cage of ribs.
The mind is a prisoner in the skull,
Locked behind those bony plates . . .

The lines came to her, but they carried no solace. At least a real prisoner knew where his or her prison was located. She had no idea where she was. Was it indeed in upstate New York? Quite possibly. She did know that it was not an actual prison; Rinehart had called the place a 'monastery,' and she suspected the reference was not merely a joke. An abandoned monastery would have plenty of cells like this one, which could easily be retrofitted to make escape a physical impossibility. Maybe not for Todd. But she wasn't Todd. For her it was impossible.

A physical impossibility. Yet a prison was not made up of walls and doors alone. There were people, and where there were people, surely, there was the possibility of the unexpected. She recalled the pike-eyed stare of the guard: *It's only the sheerest professionalism that stops me from raping you within an inch of your life and maybe an inch or so beyond.* Her eyes returned to the fluorescent light by the door, its hateful sterile glare calling to mind an interrogator's lamp.

A prison that was not a prison. There *was* a slightly makeshift air about some of the facilities. Though the commode was prison standard, the ancient bathtub was not. The ceiling light fixture near the door was within reach; in a standard prison, it would have been behind a cage. She could probably kill herself if she wanted to – again, not standard prison outfitting. The guard who had brought her 'chow' – a man with hairy forearms, a scrubbed bronzed forehead, a dense, close-cropped black beard tight on his jaw – had carried not the washable tray of a large institution but a foil tray from the kind of frozen dinner sold at supermarkets. She had washed it out simply to give herself something to do; they would retrieve it, no doubt, whenever the next scheduled visit was.

She decided to fill the tub; she inserted the rubber stopper and twisted both taps all the way. The water that poured from the faucet was flecked with rust, evidence of disuse. As the tub filled, she sat on the cot, her fingers starting to tear at the heavy-gauge foil of the dinner tray in idle agitation, and her eyes once more settled on the glaring fluorescent fixture by the door.

She walked over to it. A circular fluorescent tube, powered by an AC circuit. All that electricity, racing around and going nowhere. *It's trapped here, too.* That was Andrea's first thought.

Then she looked down at the foil strip in her hand, and she had another.

Sixty-three goddamn years old, Will Garrison thought, and his field skills had never been sharper. He had parked the Toyota Land Cruiser in the village, behind a liquor store fronted with sun-clouded Plexiglas. He had stopped drinking ten years before – hell, he was probably in better shape now than then. Then he had started the climb.

On the trip over, he had studied the NSA satellite imagery of Dominica, magnified to the point where you could see the individual fronds of the palm trees, the indicator lights on the AT&T antennae. From this bird's-eye view, it was easy to see the Privex facility. Thick black-clad cables converged on the small bunker-like structure; round silvery dishes clustered overhead.

Dammit if Castor didn't have balls. Garrison had to give

the bastard that much credit as he watched him clamber up to the facility's roof. Castor was going to unlock a Fabergé egg with a goddamn crowbar. Amazing. *Now, why didn't we think of that?*

Garrison concealed himself behind a profusion of Caribbean elephant ears, the giant leaves bejeweled with glimmering drops of evening dew. It was just a matter of waiting. He had taken some Motrin as insurance, but so far his knees weren't even aching. Belknap was in the building. Before long, he would be leaving it. But he wouldn't get far. Just when Todd Belknap thought that he had succeeded, he was safe, no one knew he was there, his defenses were relaxed . . . *that* was when the Hound would be put down.

Now he stretched out, with the stock of the Barrett M98 sniper rifle against his cheek. The rifle, dappled with a green-and-black camouflage paint job, had been fitted with an integral silencer and loaded with subsonic ammunition; the combination of the two factors meant that it would be inaudible at distances beyond a hundred meters or so. As a young trainee, Garrison had won prizes in target competitions. But true skill lay in finding a position that required no skill, and he had done so. A ten-year-old could make this shot.

Once Belknap was taken care of, Garrison might even take an extra day or so to enjoy the island. They said the Boiling Lake was something to see.

He glanced at his watch, peered through the scope, and settled into a zone of watchful waiting.

It would not be long now.

Fighting to suppress his panic response, Belknap expelled the last ounce of breath from his body, curled his fingers around the rim where the grate had been, and pulled himself through. His head and then his torso slid out at a painfully awkward angle, and he collapsed on a hard floor gasping for breath.

He was in.

As the infernal *beep beep beep* continued to grow louder

and louder, he forced himself to his feet and looked around in the dim silvery light, the space brightened by hundreds of small illuminated LED displays. *Fifteen seconds before autodelete.* He raced over to a large metal structure that looked like a giant Sub-Zero refrigerator – the beeping was coming from it – and found a thick power cord behind it. It was as thick as a snake, and required a surprising amount of force to pull it out of the wall plug.

After a brief pause, the beeping resumed.

Oh, Christ – a battery backup, no doubt, with enough power to run the autodelete program.

How many seconds remained? Six? Five?

He followed the other end of the power cord to a flat box, the size of a steel ingot, by the base of the mammoth network server. As the beeping grew deafening, he grabbed it, yanked it hard, and another plug came loose – the plug connecting the battery to the system.

The beeping stopped.

Blessed silence. Belknap's legs were wobbly for a moment as he made his way to the door. He retracted the four-point dead-bolt system that secured the steel-clad door to the cinderblock framing, opened it, and whistled softly.

Sachs darted inside the door. 'Mother of God,' he said. 'They've got enough power to run the entire U.S. defense network. God, I'd love to take this for a spin.'

'We're not joyriding, Walt. We're searching for a goddamn electronic pin in an electronic haystack. So get your magnifying glass out. I need a digital fingerprint. I'll take a partial. But I'm not going home empty-handed.'

Walt wandered around, poking among tall racks of servers and routers, boxes that looked like DVD players but that sprouted hundreds of tiny, brightly colored wires.

Finally, he stood stock-still, contemplating what looked like a large black cooler. 'Change of plans,' said the computer maven.

'Speak.' Belknap shot him a questioning glance.

'How much room you got in that duffel bag of yours?'

'Are you improvising, Walt?'

'Is that a problem?'

'No,' Belknap said. 'It's the one damn sign of hope so far.'

Sachs ran a hand along his close-cropped temple. 'I'm staring at a five-terabyte storage system. Give me a minute and I'll give you a backup tape of the whole goddamn thing.'

'Walt, you're a genius,' Belknap said.

'Tell me something I don't know,' Sachs replied.

Will Garrison idly swatted at a mosquito. He had dry-swallowed a Malarone on the way down, but couldn't remember how long it took before the antimalarial became effective. He stared through the low-light scope of his rifle, adjusted it on its bipod until the red-dot reticle was precisely centered on the doorway where Todd Belknap would soon be appearing.

If you want a job done right, he thought to himself again, *you've got to do it yourself.* Wasn't it the truth.

Sweet dreams, 'Henry Giles.' Farewell, Castor. Bye-bye, Belknap. From behind him he thought he heard the noise of a broken twig or branch, as if from a footfall. But that made no sense, did it?

It couldn't be Belknap – he was still inside, and so was the amateur he'd dragged in with him. Who else knew he was here? Belknap had no backup, no team or support personnel.

He stole a quick glance behind him. Nothing. There was nothing at all.

He was moving his finger back behind the trigger guard when he heard another sound and craned his head again.

Suddenly he felt the most god-awful terrific pressure around his neck – a searing band biting into his flesh, and then a sense that his head was going to explode from too much blood.

Finally he caught a glimpse of his assailant. 'You!' he gasped, but the word died in his mouth. And then the darkness of the night was replaced with a deeper, truer blackness, which was the extinction of consciousness itself.

*

'Silly rabbit,' Jared Rinehart murmured to himself as he re-wrapped the catgut cord of his garrote around one of its wooden handles. An old-fashioned device, and one of the few that had not been improved upon by modern technology.

The cord was not even wet with blood. Amateurs often went for steel wire of an excessively thin gauge: A properly constructed garrote did not cut into the flesh; it compressed the carotid arteries and the internal and external jugular veins, preventing blood from entering and leaving the brain. Done properly, it should be wetwork without wetness. As here: The only fluid released was the urine that now spotted the aging spymaster's trousers.

Rinehart dragged the body downhill, the sound inaudible above the noise of the million buzzing midges and stone flies and the piping of little tree frogs, until he reached a trail of reddish volcanic soil. He removed and folded Garrison's clothes, placed them in a plastic trash bag, and stowed the bag in his rucksack. He could simply dispose of the corpse in the underbrush, but there were better options.

Soon a sulfurous miasma become pungently evident, and the vegetation thinned, gradually giving way to slippery mats of lichens, moss, and grasses. Scattered vents and mud pots released wisps of steam that shone silver in the filtered moonlight.

Ten minutes later, walking by the intermittent light of a half-moon in a partly cloudy sky, Rinehart looked past a boulder and saw a milky-looking circle of water mostly obscured by steam. It was the lake. He heaved the body – even in the available light it was obviously an unpleasant specimen, with its withered dugs, varicosities, and dorsal pelt of coarse graying hair – over a ridge of crumbling pumice. It bounced down the steep declivity and plunged into the churning, bubbling waters,

After a few hours of simmering amid the harsh sulfur fumes, its flesh would peel away from the skeleton. Teeth and bones would drift to the bottom of a two-hundred-foot-deep lake. One could not send divers into water of its temperature, even if the authorities had reason to do so, and

Rinehart very much doubted that they would. He was pleased with himself. It was quite a creative way to keep the Cons Ops boys guessing.

He flipped open his cell phone and phoned a number in the continental United States. Reception was crystal-clear.

'Everything's on schedule,' he said. He paused, listening, before he spoke again. 'Will Garrison? No worries. Let's just say he found himself in hot water.'

CHAPTER TWENTY-EIGHT

A puddle of water had formed outside the prisoner's cell, the guard noticed angrily, and he hastened to open the door, inserting the key, pushing down on the lever handle, and stepping inside the cell.

The bitch had let the bathtub overflow. That was not the guard's last thought, but it was among his last thoughts. He also had time for puzzlement at the way his hand was no longer just grasping the lever handle but was spastically clamped onto it. He wondered at what looked like a strip of twisted foil attached to the inside lever knob, connected to something high up, something he could not see. He knew that the puddle of water at his feet had indeed come from the bathtub faucet, and he even noticed the little blue logo on a paper packet of salt floating on the puddle he had stepped into. The perceptions arrived in a cluster, a panicked mob swarming a gateway; he could not have said what came first and which came after.

There were also many thoughts he did not have. He did not reflect on the fact that a tenth of an amp of current could cause a beating heart to defibrillate. He did not notice the fact that the doorway was darker than before, because the lighting fixture overhead had been smashed open. The searing, vibratory pain that swept through him, through his arm, his chest, his legs, swiftly cleansed him of consciousness. He could not see, therefore, that his limp body now kept the door from shutting, could not sense the woman leap over his body, could not hear her light footfalls as she raced down the monastery hall.

*

Andrea's feet ghosted along the tiled flooring in great soft strides. The element of surprise was in her favor now; soon it would not be. She scarcely allowed herself to register the oddity of her surroundings, the round columns and the archways overhead like those of an old chapel. Stone, heavy beams, tiles. A faded gilt engraving on a wall, what looked like Cyrillic lettering beneath a bearded icon. It was an Eastern Orthodox monastery, then, but the guards were American, so what did that really tell her?

A man in drab khaki at the end of the long hallway: He had looked up, taken stock of the situation, was reaching for something on his combat belt, a weapon of some kind. Andrea darted into one of the side niches, some sort of sacristy. A dead end.

Or was it? She closed the door behind her, but the room did not darken much. There was a jumble of heavy wooden chairs, and she climbed on top of a stacked set of them until she could see a crawl space that led onto another tiled expanse. She sprang forward, her feet toppling the stack of heavy chairs even as her hands made contact with the stone ledge. Now she pulled herself up and clambered through the narrow space and onto a sort of breezeway.

Overhead, perhaps twenty feet above her, was a spandreled ceiling; to her right was a tall bricked half-wall – too tall to climb over – and yet she could feel the air move against her face, could hear the call of birds in the distance, the sound of rustling leaves. She darted toward where the outdoor light was most visible, and, as she rounded a corner, her lungs filled with air, her body seemingly weightless, fueled by adrenaline and hope, a lunging body, appearing from nowhere, crashed into her. She was slammed onto the hard floor.

The man was winded as he stood over her. 'Like mother like daughter,' the man said, breathing heavily.

She recognized him at once: The motorist with the map in Washington. The man who had abducted her. The Brillo-like curls of graying hair, the eyes that glittered like the plastic bead eyes of a stuffed toy, the oddly small mouth and weak, dimpled chin.

'Don't touch me,' Andrea said, coughing.

'See, your mom was never with the program, either. She didn't want to die, didn't care that it was for a good cause. In the end, we had to inject the ethanol straight into the inguinal artery. A tiny puncture mark.'

'You killed my mother.'

'You say it like it's a bad thing,' the man snorted.

Without warning, Andrea lashed her left leg out, trying to spring off the tiled flooring. The man reacted swiftly, and she caught his left foot in her abdomen. She collapsed again, winded, as he hammerlocked her neck from behind, his left knee jammed into the small of her back, his right leg wrapped around her ankles, clamping them. 'One jerk and the spine snaps. A painful way to go.'

The veins in her neck felt distended to the point of bursting. 'Please,' she gasped. 'I'm sorry. Whatever you say.'

He lifted her to her feet and spun her around. He had a gun in his hand. Andrea took a fast look. The gun was black. The muzzle was blacker.

'Navasky,' the man barked into a miniature walkie-talkie. 'On deck.' With contained brutality, he frogmarched Andrea along the breezeway. The guard with the waxy skin and pale pike's eye – Navasky, it must have been – appeared at the other end of the tiled breezeway.

'Son of a bitch,' he drawled, and grabbed at his stun gun.

'Daughter of, to be precise,' said the first man.

'J-man ain't gonna want to hear about this.'

'Maybe J-man won't need to. We can jump the schedule, put her in a permanent coma now. She ain't likely to run her mouth any.'

Each man grabbed one of her elbows. She thrashed mightily but their iron grip was unshaken.

'She got spirit,' said the Southerner. 'So tell me, Justin, you being the expert and all, can she still get wet if she's a vegetable?' His breath was dank.

'Sex is pretty much a hindbrain thing,' the other man said. 'Don't need a functioning cerebral cortex for that. So the answer's yes, if we do the job right.'

Andrea thrashed again with all her strength. Nothing. It did nothing.

'What are *you* doing here?' the man at her left, the man named Justin, called out to another man who had now appeared at the end of the walkway. 'Thought you were a foundation boy.'

'Got your distress signal,' the man called back. He held up a miniature walkie-talkie like theirs, returned it to his trouser pocket. 'New protocol.'

'Good timing,' said the Southerner, sounding relieved.

Andrea stared, her sense of horror escalating. Twenty yards away was a powerfully built man in a well-tailored gray suit. The nameless man who had visited her in Carlyle, and who had seemingly dogged her steps since then. The thug who had warned her to keep silent with his blandly cryptic threats.

She felt the grip of the two others relax slightly in the presence of another armed man, and – a sudden erratic impulse – she once again lunged forward, this time twisting from their grip, and raced forward, because she could move in no other direction. As if in slow motion, she saw the gray-suited man pull out a heavy revolver from beneath his jacket and hold it perfectly level. *Better a quick death*, she thought.

She stared at its borehole, now just fifteen feet away, stared like a prey animal mesmerized by a cobra, and saw the tongue of blue-white fire pulse from it as the man squeezed the trigger, twice, in rapid succession.

At the same instant, she saw, in his eyes, the serene confidence of a marksman who seldom missed.

Yale University, the third oldest university in the United States, had been founded in 1701, but most of its physical structure – including the collegiate Gothic buildings that it was invariably associated with in the mind of the public – was less than a century old. The newer buildings typically housed science departments and research laboratories, and tended to be further from the oldest parts of the so-called 'Old Campus,' like the ring pattern of a classic European city. So it was a point of pride among the university's computer scientists there that they were housed in a building that dated back to the nineteenth century, however extensive the interior renovations may have been. The Arthur K. Watson Building was a redbrick structure with arched facades that honored Victorian ambition and a Victorian sense of grandeur. It stood opposite the Grove Street Cemetery, and there were some who claimed to find the Arthur K. Watson Building itself somewhat sepulchral.

Belknap himself felt a sense of foreboding as he and Walter Sachs stood on the sidewalk opposite it. Once again, he had a faint sense of being observed. But by whom? His field instincts and his field skills contradicted themselves: If he really were being shadowed, his own maneuvers should have confirmed it. Professional wariness was surely pushing at the boundaries of paranoia.

'Tell me your friend's name again,' Belknap said tensely.

Sachs sighed. 'Stuart Purvis.'

'And remind me how you know him.'

'We were classmates, and now he's an assistant professor in the computer science department.'

'You really trust this guy? He's fifteen minutes late. You sure he's not on the phone with the campus police?'

Sachs blinked. 'He stole my girlfriend in freshman year. I stole his when we were sophomores. We called it even. He's a good guy. His mom was, like, big in the installation-art scene during the sixties. Stuff with girders and beams, but with curves and shell forms. Amazing stuff. Like, imagine if Georgia O'Keeffe were redoing *Tilted Arc*.'

'I have no idea what you're talking about.'

Sachs hefted the nylon knapsack in his arms. 'Dude, bottom line is that we're dealing with a gargantuan storage tape. An ocean of data, okay? Your pissant little desktop from Dell isn't gonna help. Stu, on the other hand, helped set up the Beowulf clusters at Yale. That's, like, two hundred and sixty central processors seamlessly linked in a massively parallel architecture. That's power. We need to hitch a piggyback ride on it.' He perked up. 'Ah, there he is.' He waved. 'Yo,

Stu!' he shouted to a man in a white guayabera shirt, black pants, and leather sandals.

The man, in his late thirties, turned and waved back. The thick black frames of his glasses were fashionable or the opposite of fashionable, depending on the degree of irony with which they were worn. He smiled at his old friend, revealing a fleck of green lettuce between two incisors. The opposite of fashionable, then.

Stuart Purvis led them around the front of Watson Hall to a green enameled custodial entrance at the rear of the building. It led directly to the basement, where the main computer laboratories were situated. Belknap noticed that the junior professor's neck was spotted with reddish bumps of ingrown hairs, his jaw and upper lip smooth-shaven but shadowed with the greenish-gray of what would have been a heavy beard.

'So, my man, when you called for a favor, I thought you meant a job recommendation,' the junior academic said. 'But I guess you want a ride on Big Bertha here. Totally out of bounds, you know. If the supervisor were to find out – wait, I *am* the supervisor. We've got ourselves an infinite loop here. Or maybe it's just a self-nested operation, like a distributed autoregression function. Hey, you hear the joke about Bill Gates and the screensaver?'

Sachs rolled his eyes. 'As a matter of fact I did, Stu, and you just gave away the punch line, numb nuts.'

'Shit,' said Purvis. He walked along the concrete floor with an odd sort of stutter step, and it was only then that Belknap realized he had an artificial leg. 'So, Walt the Whiz, how many terabytes you talking about?' He turned to Belknap. 'We used to call him Walt the Whiz when we were undergrads.'

Sachs grinned. 'Because I was so good at getting digits from the honeys.'

Purvis gave him a look. 'The honeys? *Please.* You were lucky if you got Fembots.' He turned to Belknap, sniggering through his nose. 'And all he got was their serial numbers.'

The basement of the Watson building was vast and

cavernous, evenly illuminated with diffuse fluorescent lights that had been positioned to minimize screen glare. They could have been in a morgue, Belknap decided, with all those banks of stainless-steel drawers. A thousand small fans cooled powerful chips, creating a wash of white noise.

Purvis knew exactly where he was going: halfway down a central walkway, then a quick right. 'I'm assuming that's four-millimeter digital linear tape,' he said to Sachs, suddenly businesslike.

'Well, SDLT.'

'We can do super digital. Ultrium 960's what we prefer, but the Quantum SDLT is totally reliable.' Sachs lifted the heavy spools from the nylon bag and Purvis mounted them on an autoloader that looked like an old-fashioned videocassette player. He pressed a button and the tape started spinning with a high-pitched squeal.

'Step one,' Purvis said, 'is reconstruction. We copy the data onto a rapid-access memory format. A hard drive, basically.' He was speaking for Belknap's benefit. 'We use a data-correction algorithm I wrote myself.'

'Which means it probably has more bugs than features,' Walt gibed.

'Walt, you still don't get it. Those bugs *are* features.' An allusion to a years-old argument, obviously. 'Whoa, Nelly!' he exclaimed abruptly. 'What are we dealing with here, the entire U.S. Census databank? I guess now I see why they had to use SDLT.'

'Contents may have settled during shipping,' Sachs said wryly. 'In other words, expect some data expansion because of encryption.'

'Never gets any easier, does it, Walt?' Purvis pulled out a keyboard from a rolling drawer at midriff level and started typing. The screen filled with numbers, and then the numbers gave way to what looked like the jagged graphics of an oscilloscope. 'Jeepers creepers! See, we run basically a statistical probe, which classifies the code according to certain frequencies that are characteristic of different cryptosystems.' He shot Belknap a look. 'It's just a statistical analysis.

It can't read it, but it can tell you what language you're look-ing at.' Under his breath he murmured, 'Come to papa. Okay. I'm feeling you now.' Now he turned to Sachs. 'The tape starts with the sixty-four-bit key. The actual data is there underneath block encryption. It's just a parameterized algorithm. Put your right foot in and your left foot out, you do the hokey-pokey and you turn yourself about. Or, more precisely, you do a little bitwise XOR and variable rotation. And Bob's your uncle. Well, more like your second cousin's wife's uncle on his mother's side twice removed. But that's where the Beowulf cluster comes in. I gotta say, I'm impressed by what I'm seeing. It's great security, actually. Phenomenal. So long as somebody doesn't, like, steal your backup tape.'

'Can I key in the search parameters?' Walt asked.

'We script in Prolog. But we can switch to Python if you like. You still a Python partisan?'

'You know it.'

Purvis shrugged, stood up. 'Knock yourself out.'

Walt sat at the keyboard and began to type.

'See, it's kinda like ice fishing,' Purvis explained to Belknap with the air of an inveterate teacher. 'You don't exactly see what you're doing, no more than you can see into the water. But you carve out a hole, and you drop in your bait, and then, in a manner of speaking, the fish come to you.'

'Nobody's interested in your cockamamie analogies, Stu,' Walt grumbled. 'We just want answers.'

'That's life, isn't it? We all arrive on Earth wanting answers. And we have to content ourselves with inane analo-gies.' He peered over Sachs's shoulder. 'And . . . we've got a bite! Or a few thousand bites, if you're thinking of actual binary digits.'

'Any way to speed this up?' Belknap asked.

'Are you kidding? This system's like a cheetah on Dexe-drine. Feel the G-forces, man.'

'Can we print out the file?' Sachs asked.

Purvis snorted. 'Like, on paper? You are *so* old school, Walt. Haven't you heard of the paperless office?'

'I think I crumpled up that memo before I read it.'

'Fine, Mr. Eaton Twenty Pound. I'm sure we've got some monks in the scriptorium.'

'You probably wipe your ass with virtual paper,' Sachs growled.

'Okay, okay. We'll laser it out, you Gutenberg geek.' Purvis rubbed his irritated neck, then moved to another console, tapping out some instructions. At the adjacent alcove, a large office-sized copier hummed and ejected a single page.

'That's it?' Belknap asked.

It was identical to the page given to him by Senator Kirk's chief of staff, except for a longer header.

'Looks like it's hashed out,' Purvis said.

'Gonna run a traceroute on this,' Walt said urgently. 'Then print that out, too.'

'That's kind of like a digital *ping*,' Purvis told Belknap. 'You know, like in the old submarine movies. Or, like, sending a carrier pigeon down a long tunnel. It flies out to the end, and it comes back, and it tells you what it saw along the way, because, really, it's not so much a carrier pigeon as a parrot!'

'Stu,' Sachs balked, 'my friend here isn't going to be submitting a teacher-evaluation form. We just need the numbers.'

Soon three more pages slid from the laser printer.

'Yowza,' said Purvis, looking at the top sheet. 'So we've got thirty-eight-byte packages, each making thirty hops. Oh, the places you'll go.' He circled several of the strings of numbers. 'We've been to the Perth Academic Regional Network, at AS7571. We've swung around Canberra RNO and Queensland, stopped off at the Rede Rio de Computadores at Brazil, Multicom in Bulgaria, EntreNet in Canada, Universidad Tecnica Federico Santa Maria in Chile, Ropácek and SilesNet in the Czech Republic, Azero in Denmark, Transpac in France, SHE Informationstechnologie AG in Germany, Snerpa ISP in Iceland – brother, I am dizzy! Somebody's playing catch-me-if-you-can.'

'The more hops, the more middlemen, the harder to follow,' Sachs said.

'Don't recognize this one.' Purvis keyed in another number. 'Ah, so! MugotogoNet in Japan! ElCat in Kyrgyzstan! It's a wonder this lil' packet didn't pick up traveler's diarrhea.'

Sachs turned to the last page of the traceroute printout, his eyes bright. To Belknap, it just looked like another list of cryptic alphanumeric strings

```
> hurroute (8.20.4.7) 2 ms * *
> mersey (8.20.62.10) 3 ms 3 ms 2 ms
> efw (184.196.110.1) 11 ms 4 ms 4 ms
> ign-gw (15.212.14.225) 6 ms 5 ms 6 ms
> port1br1-8-5-1.pt.uk.ibm.net (152.158.23.250) 34 ms 62 ms
> port1br3-80-1-0.pt.uk.ibm.net (152.158.23.27) 267 ms 171
> nyor1sr2-10-8-0.ny.us.ibm.net (165.87.28.117) 144 ms 117
> nyor1ar1-8-7.ny.us.ibm.net (165.87.140.6) 146 ms 124 ms
> nyc-uunet.ny.us.ibm.net (165.87.220.13) 161 ms 134 ms 143
> 10 105.ATM2-0.XR2.NYC1.ALTER.NET (126.188.177.158) 164 ms
```

'So what does this tell us, Walt?' Belknap said. His voice was hard with impatience. 'Where in the world is this Genesis?'

Sachs blinked several times. 'Point of origin should be here, but . . . I mean, I can tell you it's New York State,' he said. 'Stu? Check the terminal ISP code.'

'They say it's better to travel hopefully than to arrive,' Purvis said. 'You remember that ex-girlfriend of mine who used to read the last pages of a novel first, so she knew how it ended? She found that comforting somehow.'

'Stu, goddammit!'

'Ah,' said Purvis as the UNIX machine flashed a response. 'Just a few hours away. Bedford County.'

'That's where Katonah is,' Belknap said softly. 'That doesn't make any sense.' Yet even as he spoke he remembered something he had been told at Senator Kirk's office, something about Genesis burrowing into the Bancroft Foundation. Had Genesis burrowed in so far that it was actually inside it?

'Does not compute?' Purvis snorted. 'Well, shit, we've

got a BIOS serial number, too. Basically the license plate of the machine. Can't do any better than that.'

'He's right, Todd,' said Sachs. 'That's degree-zero as far as the trace goes.'

'Can I put the Beowulf back online, now?' Purvis yawned. They're gonna be pissed off at Yale–New Haven Medical Center. They're trying to get it to read MRI scans, you know.'

'Katonah,' Belknap said to Sachs. He felt suffused with a bewildering mixture of hope, desperation, urgency. 'Anything more we can do with that license plate? I need the physical location of that unit.'

'Listen,' Sachs said. 'I'll stay here and try to scan the commercial databases, see if I can get a lead on that. Meanwhile, maybe you'd better make your way over there.' He turned to Purvis. 'Give him a wireless laptop, omega-compatible.'

'This isn't the goddamn Salvation Army, Walt.'

'Just do it. You'll get it back.'

Purvis sighed resignedly and unplugged one from a nearby workstation. 'Don't do Internet porn on it,' he told Belknap with a sullen glare. 'We'll know if you do.'

'Hope I'll see you again one day,' Sachs told Belknap. 'I'll call you as soon as I have anything useful to report.'

'You're a good man, Walter Sachs,' the operative said with genuine warmth. Then he winced at his own carelessness. 'Dammit. Almost forgot. My cell phone was destroyed in Dominica.'

Sachs nodded. 'Take mine,' he said, handing him a small Nokia. 'And take care.' A half-smile. 'You don't get bonus lives in the game you people play.'

'Maybe that's because it's not a game,' Belknap said grimly.

Andrea stared at the blue-white flame that pulsed from the gun muzzle, and screamed in terror. The shots were loud, deafening, as they echoed in the stone breezeway. Impassively, the man reholstered his revolver; despite its bulk, it disappeared beneath his perfectly tailored jacket, leaving no visible bulge.

Andrea Bancroft was bewildered. She was still alive. Unharmed. It made no sense. She whirled around, saw the limp, lifeless bodies of the two men who had taken her captive. A small dark hole, like a third eye, appeared on the forehead of each.

'I don't understand,' she breathed.

'That's not my problem,' said the man, his expression formal, almost studious. 'My instructions are to take you away from here.'

'Where?'

Powerful shoulders moved upward in a shrug. 'Anywhere you want to go.' He had already turned and was walking away. She followed him to a low swinging gate, and then a series of wide brick steps leading to a large, closely mown field. A few hundred yards away, she saw what could have been a playing field, but was, she realized, a helipad. Four rotorcraft – aging military models by the look of them – were stationed there. Andrea struggled to keep up with the nameless man.

'Where are we?'

'About ten miles north of Richfield Springs. Maybe five miles south of Mohawk.'

'Where?'

'Upstate New York. Town's called Jericho. Theta bought it from the Eastern Orthodox Church about a decade ago. Too few brothers for the space. The usual story.' He helped her onto a small helicopter, belted her in, and handed her a set of ear protectors. Stenciled on the helicopter, white on royal-blue, was the logo ROBINSON and the model number, R44: trivial details that caught in her mind like burrs.

'Listen,' Andrea started. 'I'm kind of at a loss here . . .' Her whole body stated to quake. 'My mother – '

'Was a very special person.' The man reached over to her, put his hand on her forearm, gripping it firmly. 'I once promised your mother I'd look out for you. The two of you. Only, I let her down. I wasn't there when she needed me.' There was a faint catch in his voice. 'I can't let that happen twice.'

Andrea blinked hard, trying to take in the meaning of his words. 'You said you had instructions,' she said abruptly. 'Whose? Who gave you these instructions.'

He met her eyes. 'Genesis,' he said. 'Who else?'

'But at the Bancroft Foundation – '

'Let's just say I got a better offer.'

'I don't understand,' she repeated.

'Hold on to that thought,' he grunted as he started the engine and the rotors began their *whomp whomp whomp*. 'Now,' he yelled, 'where to?'

There were only two options. She could try to hide from Paul Bancroft or she could try to confront him. She could go to Katonah or as far away from Katonah as was possible. She did not know which was more prudent. She did know that she was tired of running, tired of being chased. In an instant, she made up her mind.

'You got enough gas to reach Bedford County?' she asked.

'And back,' he assured her.

'I'm not coming back,' Andrea said.

A small smile broke into his solemn expression, a crack in the ice. 'Hold on to that thought, too.'

Another rented car. Another paved roadway. Framed by the windshield, the highway was an endless current of concrete, ornamented only by small tar-daubed fissures and battered, rusting guardrails. To either side, blast-carved shale sloping upward like the banks of a river. The road before him was taking him where he needed to go. The road before him was the distance he still had to traverse. It was foe and it was friend. Like Genesis?

He had passed the exits to Norwalk, Connecticut, before his cell phone rang. It was Sachs with an update.

'I did what you said,' Sachs told him, his voice tight with excitement. 'I just got off the phone with Hewlett-Packard customer service. Pretended to be a computer-repair guy. Called in the BIOS number, they ran it through the sales records. Purchaser was the Bancroft Foundation. But that's not a surprise, is it?'

Acid splashed at the back of Belknap's throat. 'I guess not,' he said. Yet what did it mean? That Paul Bancroft was Genesis after all? Or simply that Genesis had infiltrated the foundation? 'Good work, Walt. Look, you've got Senator Kirk's private e-mail address, right?'

'It's the destination point on the traceroute, sure.'

'First, I want Senator Kirk to send a message from his private e-mail address.'

'You mean, you want me to send a message *as* Senator Kirk.'

'That's it. Say you'll be using a masking system to preserve confidentiality on your end.'

'I can use an opaquing VPM system.'

'Fine. Say it's urgent that they set up a chatroom in ninety minutes. Ask why someone named Todd Belknap came to ask questions about Genesis.'

'I get it,' Walt said over the phone. 'You're trying to keep Genesis online, so to speak. You want him at the actual machine, right? In meat space.'

'Meat space, did you say?'

'Yeah,' Sachs grunted. 'It's what they used to call the real world.' He paused. 'You think this will actually work?'

'I don't know if it will work. All I know is that it *has* to work.'

'You know what they say, buddy. Hope is not a plan.'

'That's true,' Belknap returned in a hollow voice. 'But it's the only plan we've got.'

Midtown Manhattan

Mr. Smith was puzzled and, though he prided himself on keeping an even keel, even a little irritated. The instructions had arrived on his PDA in unusually bare-bones form. Normally he got a complete profile of the target. This time, the directive contained merely a location and a handful of visual specs.

Did they no longer trust him to use his best judgment on assignments? Had his controller changed, the result of some personnel shakeup he hadn't heard about yet? Was there to be a permanent change in procedures?

No matter. He sat at the outdoor café in Bryant Park and took another sip of his cappuccino. He would complete the assignment first and voice his misgivings later. He was a professional, after all.

Sit at the table closest to the corner of Sixth Avenue and Forty-second Street, he had been instructed. The target would appear at the low stone ridge that ran across the park, separating the concession area from the back lot of the New York Public Library. He was to use the pen.

The man appeared at the appointed time, six feet tall, lean, sandy-haired – just as described.

Mr. Smith decided to get a closer look at his target, and he ambled toward the stone ridge with a genially distracted air. The target looked up at him.

Mr. Smith blinked. The man was no stranger.

On the contrary.

'Why, Mr. Jones,' he said. 'Fancy meeting you here.'

'My dear Mr. Smith,' said his sandy-haired colleague. 'Does this mean we've been given overlapping assignments?'

Mr. Smith hesitated for a moment. 'It's the damnedest thing. The truth is, *you're* my assignment.'

'I am?' Mr. Jones seemed surprised. But not very surprised.

'I must assume so. I wasn't given a name. But yes, you match all the assignment indices.' His target, he knew, was someone whose identity had been revealed to the Kirk Commission. How the slipup had happened was unclear. Some error on Mr. Jones's part? In any event, security dictated the elimination of an asset who had been 'burned,' exposed.

'You know what's just as strange,' said Mr. Jones. 'You match all *my* assignment indices. Simply a matter of a compromised identity, I'm told, but you know the security protocol.'

'It's quite possibly a mix-up, don't you think?' Mr. Smith shook his head amiably.

'Some desk jockey accidentally types the name of the

operative in the blank meant for the name of the target,' said the man with sandy hair. 'And there you go. Quite possibly nothing more than a simple clerical error.'

Mr. Smith had to agree, it was a possibility. But given the high level of operational security and oversight, surely not a probability. And he *was* a professional.

'Well, my friend,' said Mr. Smith. 'We'll get to the bottom of this together. Let me show you the message I got on my Treo.' He placed a hand in his breast pocket, but what he pulled out was an object that resembled a steel-barreled pen. He clicked on one end and a tiny dart shot out.

Mr. Jones looked down. 'I wish you hadn't done that,' he said, pulling out the spent dart from his chest and handing it to Mr. Smith. 'That's chironex venom, I assume.'

'Afraid so,' said Mr. Smith. 'I *am* sorry. You shouldn't experience any symptoms for another few minutes, I'd say. But as you know, it's irreversible. Nothing to be done once it's in your bloodstream.'

'Darn,' Mr. Jones said in the tone of mild annoyance usually provoked by hangnails.

'You're being awfully dignified about this,' said Mr. Smith. He was feeling almost sentimental. 'I can't tell you how sorry I am. Please believe me.'

'I do believe you,' said Mr. Jones. 'Because I'm sorry, too.'

'You're . . . sorry.' Mr. Smith was suddenly aware that he had been sweating profusely for a few minutes, and he was not given to perspiration. The outdoor light was beginning to hurt his eyes, as if his pupils were dilated. And then there was a growing sense of vertigo. All were symptoms of an anticholinergic reaction, characteristic of many poisons. 'The cappuccino?' He choked out the words.

Mr. Jones nodded. 'Do you think me a rule stickler? I *am* sorry.'

'I don't suppose . . .'

'No antidote, either. It's a methylated derivative of ciguatera toxin.'

'The one we used in Kalmikiya last year?'

'That's the one.'

'Oh, dear.'

'Believe me, if they somehow kept you alive, you'd wish they hadn't. It ravages the nervous system permanently. You'd be a twitching, spasmodic imbecile on a ventilator. No kind of life, really.'

'Well, then.' Mr. Smith was experiencing flashes of hot and cold, as if alternately blasted with fire and encased in ice. As for Mr. Jones, he noticed that his face was turning gray, the first sign of a diffused accelerated necrosis.

'It's weirdly intimate, isn't it?' Mr. Jones said, reaching over to the railing in order to steady himself.

'Being each other's murderers?'

'Well, yes. Not the word I would have chosen, of course.'

'We need a thesaurus,' said Mr. Smith. 'Or . . . what's another word for 'thesaurus'?'

'Perhaps we're both the victims of a practical joke,' said Mr. Jones. 'Though I don't quite see the humor in it. Truth is . . . I don't feel so good.' Mr. Jones slid to the ground. His eyelids started to flutter and twitch uncontrollably. His extremities were beginning to jump and jerk in cascades of convulsions.

Mr. Smith joined him on the paving stone. 'That makes two of us,' he wheezed. The light no longer bothered him, and for a moment he wondered whether he was starting to recover. But that wasn't it. The light wasn't bothering him because he was shrouded in darkness. He could smell nothing, could feel nothing, could hear nothing. Nothing at all.

There was only a sense of absence. And then there was no sense of anything at all.

CHAPTER TWENTY-NINE

Katonah, New York

Belknap pulled over at a distance from the drive to the Bancroft Foundation, climbed over a stone wall, and made his way toward the headquarters in the dim light of early evening. It was like encountering a camouflaged jumbo jet in the forest: At first he saw nothing, and then he saw something so large he wondered how he could ever have missed it. It was after hours on a Sunday. Officially the place was no doubt uninhabited. But he couldn't assume that. And where was Andrea? Was she somehow being held captive on these very grounds?

On the side of the drive, by an ancient linden tree about thirty yards from the office building, he crouched down, checked his watch, and then opened the wireless notebook-sized PC that the computer scientist had given him. Following Sachs's instructions, he keyed his way into the chatroom, a virtual space for real-time communication. Sachs had done what he'd asked him to do; and Genesis, prodded by what appeared to be a senatorial request, had agreed to communicate in the chatroom, albeit via an opaquing system. Now it was the appointed time. The wireless computer seemed sluggish, but it did its job.

'Questions have arisen about your relation with Bancroft,' Belknap typed.

A quiet *ping*, and a string of words appeared in a box underneath.

Your job, Senator, is to 'identify the rot and remove it,' in your words. I can only point you in the right direction.

Belknap typed 'I must know whether your information is tainted by the method by which you acquired it.'

A rejoinder appeared seconds later.

The 'fruit of the poisoned tree' is a legal doctrine. The evidence I have supplied you is for you to use to guide your investigations. You must prepare your own evidentiary exhibitions.

'But what is your interest in this?' Belknap typed, and then scrambled further down the drive.

My interest is in bringing a monstrous conspiracy to an end. Only you have the ability to stop it.

Another sprint, and then he typed: 'Yet your name inspires terror across the world.'

My name, yes. But then my renown resides in the fact that I do not exist.

Belknap's heart began to thud as he approached the main door of the foundation's headquarters, still carrying the wireless notebook. He peered through the door's leaded glass. It was unlocked, and as he entered the darkened, empty entrance hall he smelled lemon oil and old wood. He also grew aware of music, playing softly. String instruments, an organ, voices – something baroque. He typed and transmitted another question, and then crept silently in the direction of the music. The perfectly mitered floorboards did not squeak or groan beneath the Persian runners. The door was ajar to the small office from where the music was emanating. He saw the back of a high chair, silhouetted by the glow of a larger computer screen.

Belknap could almost imagine that his pounding heart was audible throughout the mansion.

A soft *tap-tap-tap* of keys, and, on Belknap's own computer a few seconds later, another line of script appeared.

The commonweal can only be served one at a time. For each is as precious as all.

The hairs on Belknap's nape stood up. *He was in this room with Genesis.*

The mastermind – the puppet master – was seated just twenty feet away from him.

From a CD player on a bookshelf, recorders piped, then a rich mezzo sang sad liturgical music. Bach, Belknap decided. One of the masses? Dimly he associated it with an Easter service he had attended, and the name came to him. 'St. Matthew's Passion.' He put the computer aside and pulled a handgun soundlessly from his jacket.

Finally Belknap spoke. 'They say that everyone who sees you dies.' He trained a gun at the back of the tall office chair. 'I'd like to test that hypothesis.'

'That's kids' stuff,' replied Genesis. The voice was – not that of a man. 'Fairy tales. You're too old for that.' The person in the chair slowly revolved to face him.

It was a boy. Straw-colored hair that formed a heap of curls, apple cheeks. He was slender in his T-shirt and shorts, his legs and arms almost hairless.

A boy. Twelve, thirteen?

'You're Genesis?' Belknap's voice was hushed in astonishment.

The boy smiled. 'Don't tell my dad. I mean it.'

'You're Genesis.' A statement this time. The room seemed to spin slowly, like a platform at an amusement park.

'Genesis is my avatar, yeah.' His voice was not a child's soprano, but it wasn't an adult's baritone, either. 'I'm guessing you're Todd Belknap.'

Belknap nodded, speechless. He grew aware of his slack jaw, struggled to remember to breathe.

'Call me Brandon.'

Brandon Bancroft. Not the father. The son.

'Want some Sprite?' the boy asked. 'No? I was gonna have some.'

CHAPTER THIRTY

'Where do you want to touch down?' Andrea heard the man's voice in her headphones; the chopper noise made it hard to communicate otherwise. 'You got several helipads to pick from. House? Office?'

'House,' Andrea said. She was going to confront her cousin face-to-face, and confront him where he lived.

The wash of the helicopter's downdraft flattened the grass below and puffed at the leafy trees that encircled the landing site. As soon as she felt the bump of the steel skids against the earth, she clambered out of the craft and, as the nameless man flew off, broke into a trot, bounding down a bosky path, treating a stone wall like a vaulting horse, hurtling through a grove of trees, and then racing up to Paul Bancroft's house. The smell of old wood and old rugs was as she remembered it. The door was open, and she raced up the stairs. A room that was obviously his study was empty. In his bedroom she saw an unmade bed. As if he had turned in for the evening and then been summoned. All she knew was that he wasn't home.

'Where's Andrea?' Force returned to Belknap's voice as he fought to regain his focus.

'I thought *you* were going to be Andrea. She should be here in a moment. She's great, isn't she?'

'Yes,' Belknap said. Once more, the room seemed to spin slowly.

'You look kinda pale. Sure you don't want that Sprite?'

'I'm good.'

Brandon nodded. 'That's what I hear.' He looked down

shyly. 'They were gonna do bad stuff to Andrea. But one of my guys on the inside figured out where she was. Got her on a copter. She wanted to come here.'

Andrea – safe? Yet could he trust the message or, indeed, the messenger? Apprehension and elation cycled through him.

'You like Bach?' the boy asked.

'I like this,' Belknap said.

'I like a lot of music. But this one always gets me.' The boy turned back to the keyboard, started typing a series of instructions. Belknap could see the boy's shoulder blades moving against the thin cotton of his shirt. 'Chapters twenty-six and twenty-seven of the Book of Matthew.' He touched a button on a remote controller, and the music was muted. The boy recited, 'And about the ninth hour Jesus cried with a loud voice, saying, *Eli, Eli, lama sabachthani? My God, my God, why hast thou forsaken me?*'

Belknap gave him an uncertain look.

'Don't worry, it's not like I've got a messiah complex,' Brandon said. 'When Jesus grew up, he learned that his father was God. I learned that my father *plays* God. There's a difference, huh?'

'God or the devil. Hard to say.'

'Is it?' Brandon met his gaze. 'They say the most diabolical thing the devil ever did was to persuade people that he doesn't exist,' he said. 'If you're facing off with the devil, you gotta turn that principle upside-down.'

'Persuade people that a fictional creation is real,' Belknap said, clarity starting to arrive. 'And those stories – they were just a way to magnify your authority as Genesis, weren't they?'

'Well, sure. Have you ever played multiuser computer games? You can create an avatar, a fictional alter ego, give him a path through the world. You know something about it now, don't you? I mean, that was you spoofing Senator K., right? Thought so.'

So Genesis was an electronic legend, nothing more, nothing less. With comprehension came awe. A legend dressed up with stories, rumors, tales that spread over the

Internet and then from person to person. 'But there was more to it than that, wasn't there?' Belknap prodded, thinking aloud. 'As Genesis, you could transfer money from one account to another. You could hire people who never saw you, could send instructions, monitor, reward. You could do a great deal. But to what end?'

Brandon was quiet for a few moments. 'I love my dad. I mean, he's my dad, right?'

'But he's not only your dad.'

Branded nodded miserably. 'He created something that's bigger than just him. Something . . . evil.' He whispered the last word.

'You father believes that the greatest good for the greatest number justifies any act at all,' Belknap said.

'Yes.'

'And what do you believe?'

'That every life is sacred. Not like I'm some pacifist or whatever. It's one thing to kill in self-defense. But you don't take lives on spec. You don't justify murder with a calculator.'

'So you spent months orchestrating events through underlings who had never seen your face, transferring funds, sending orders, monitoring the results – all remotely, digitally, untraceably. All in order to dismantle the Theta Group?'

'A multibillion-dollar operation.'

'Inver Brass squared,' Belknap said. ''Genesis' was a name you knew would inspire fear in your old man. And the Kirk Commission was your opportunity. It was going to help you enlist the authority of the United States government to uproot Theta. You've been collecting data files on its operations and parceling them out to the Senate investigators.'

'I couldn't think of any other way,' the boy said. He had, Belknap thought, a curious combination of self-assurance and fragility. 'Oh, don't take this personally, but could you ditch the gun? I have a thing about having those doodads pointed at me. Kooky, huh?'

Belknap had forgotten the gun was in his hand. 'Sorry,' he said. 'Bad manners.' He set the weapon down on the semicircular table by the door and took a few steps further into the room. 'Does your father know how you feel about Theta?'

'He doesn't like me reading Kant, let alone the Bible. He knows we disagree, but, like, he isn't moved by arguments. It's tough to explain. I told you, I love my dad, Mr. Belknap. But . . .' Brandon faltered.

'You felt you had to stop him.' Belknap's voice softened. 'Nobody else was in a position to. So it's as if you've been playing online chess with your father.'

'It's not chess when the pawns are human lives.'

'No, it's not.'

'Thing is, at first, I thought threats would be enough.'

'Threats to expose the Theta Group to the Kirk Commission.'

'Right. But they weren't. So I started to compile a detailed record – a digital dossier, like – of the group's operations. It hasn't been easy. But I've completed it. The file exposes every last root and branch.'

'You've completed the dossier, you say.'

The boy nodded.

'Meaning that with a few keystrokes and clicks, you can send it to every member of the Kirk Commission. And a thing of darkness will come to light.'

Brandon nodded. 'It's time to do it, isn't it?'

Genesis: a thirteen-year-old boy. Belknap fought to reel in his mind, to concentrate. 'Then Jared Rinehart was working with your father. He never had anything to do with Genesis.'

'Rinehart? *Gosh*, no. From what I hear, that's one scary dude. Glad we've never crossed paths.'

A voice from the doorway, silky, cold, and commanding. 'Until now.'

CHAPTER THIRTY-ONE

Belknap whirled around and saw the tall, lanky figure of the man who had been his best friend. Pollux to his Castor. Silhouetted in the doorway, his limbs looked especially slim, and the .45 pistol in his hand especially enormous.

'Times like this, I wish I wore a hat,' the lanky operative told Belknap. 'So I could take it off to you.'

'Jared . . .' Belknap husked.

'You have truly outdone yourself,' said Rinehart 'You've been amazing. Stupendous. Just as I knew you would. And so your labors are over. I'll take over now.' He glanced at the boy. 'Your father will be here momentarily,' he said with an icy grin.

'What have I done?' said Belknap, his heart pummeling. 'Christ almighty – what have I done?'

'What nobody else could have. Bravo – I mean that, Todd. The hard work was all yours. As for me, well, I'm just the old gent in the jodhpurs again. It's what all hunters learn. To catch the fox, follow the hound. I must say, we'd never have guessed where the fox was hidden. Not in a million years. But it makes sense of everything.'

'You used me. All this time, you – '

'Knew you'd never let me down, old friend. I've always had an eye for talent. And right from the start, I knew you were something extraordinary. The bureaucrats in Foggy Bottom were jealous of you. A lot of them didn't know what to make of you. But I did. I always admired you.'

Cultivated from the beginning. East Berlin, 1987.

Again, Belknap tried to choke out the words. 'All along, you – '

'Knew what you were made of. Knew what you were capable of. Better than anybody else. Together, we were always undefeatable. Nothing we couldn't do when I set my mind to it. I'd like to think of this as our greatest triumph, not simply our final one.'

'You *loosed* me. Set the bait, and sent me after it.' The sickening realization ravaged Belknap like a cyclone in his soul. 'You sent me off in pursuit of Genesis because it was the only way you could ever find him.'

The bait. The air itself has turned to a viscous, smothering substance, so it seemed to Belknap, as that realization was followed by others, each blasting at his very identity. The Italian girl. The Omani princeling. How many others? Each, unknowingly, had been enlisted in the service of Rinehart's gambit. The illusion could be maintained only if vouchsafed by reality – the participants had to be oblivious to the game master's strategy. None more so than Castor himself.

Comprehension seemed to vise Belknap's skull. When, in Tallinn, Belknap discovered the truth about Lugner, traitor turned arms dealer, the Pollux illusion was compromised. So a simple adjustment was made to keep the Hound on the trail of Genesis: The bait became Andrea instead. *Oh, Christ!*

Rinehart's plan had made use of everything that had kept Belknap human – his affection, loyalty, devotion.

If thine eye offends thee, pluck it out.

As rage and hatred pulsed through Belknap's being, Rinehart's betrayal made him wish he could root out his very capacity to care. But *no*! He would not become a monster: To turn into a man like Rinehart would cede his nemesis a kind of victory.

'When I look at you now,' Belknap said quietly, 'it's as if I'm seeing you for the first time.'

'And with such disapproval in your eyes. Are you mad at me?' Rinehart sounded almost hurt. The heavy pistol gleamed in the operative's hand. 'Don't you see that the Theta Group had no choice in the matter? Our very existence was in jeopardy, and, needless to say, our own efforts to track down the identity of the threat had proved futile.'

'You were Theta's inside ace,' Belknap said. He could almost hear the fluttering of dominos, a vast, twisty row collapsing in order. 'An American intel agent with top-level security clearance, able to feed them all the information the United States government possessed. Meanwhile, if Theta needed someone found, you'd – what, manufacture some plausible rationale that turned it into a Cons Ops mission? All this time I thought you had my back.' Fury pushed at his voice, like a substance held under enormous pressure. 'What you had was a knife in my back. You'd crossed over to the other side, you goddamn traitor.'

'It's naïve to speak of sides. My hope was really to bring the new establishments together. To merge them, in a manner of speaking. Why work at cross-purposes? Theta, Consular Operations – Paul and I agreed that in a rational world they should work together like two arms of the same body.' His eyes flickered toward the boy. 'Speaking of which, I won't lie to you. I couldn't be more shocked to learn the true identity of Genesis. Not just a child prodigy, but a prodigal son. The traitor at the breakfast table. The stranger beside you. Who could possibly have imagined?'

The stranger beside you. Belknap stared at Rinehart. A master of deception. A virtuoso of manipulation. How much of Belknap's own life had been orchestrated by Rinehart? Yet he could not allow himself to be distracted by personal drama. The stakes were too immense. He glanced back toward the pistol he left at the demilune table, and cursed himself. It was out of his reach, closer to Rinehart than to him. He could not move toward it without arousing suspicion.

'Over here,' Rinehart called out to an unseen figure in the hall, and Paul Bancroft appeared. He looked as if he had been roused from bed, as he must have been, and thrown on a sweatshirt hastily over a pair of khakis. He held a small gun in his own right hand. His knuckles were white.

'Meet your nemesis,' said Rinehart. 'And ours.'

The aging philosopher stared, slack-jawed. 'My son,' he breathed.

'I'm sorry,' Rinehart said almost tenderly. 'The scriptures begin with Genesis, but they end in Revelations. This is ours.'

Wild-eyed, the old man turned to Rinehart. 'There must be some mistake. It can't be!'

'And yet,' Rinehart pressed, 'it makes sense of everything, don't you see? It explains how he got access to so many files of yours. It explains why – '

'Is this true, Brandon?' Bancroft burst out. 'Brandon, tell me, is this *true*?'

The boy nodded.

'How could you do this to me?' The words came from his father in a howl of outrage. 'How could you try to destroy my life's work? After all the toil we've put in to make the world a better place – the organization, the planning, the *care* – you would sit here and undo it? In order to set the world back? Do you hate humanity that much? Do you hate *me* that much?'

'Dad, I love you,' Brandon said softly. 'It's not like that.'

Jared Rinehart cleared his throat. 'This isn't the time for the mushy stuff. What must be done is very clear.'

'Please, Jared!' The words exploded from the silver-haired savant. 'Please give us a moment.'

'No,' said the operative implacably. 'In just a few key-strokes, your son could send the Kirk Commission enough information to destroy us, permanently and irrevocably. To destroy everything you spent your life creating. Your own precepts must guide your actions now.'

'But – '

A chill entered Rinehart's voice. 'If your own precepts don't guide your actions now, your life has been a fraud. The greatest good for the greatest number – that's an objective that can't be compromised, as you've always said. Remember what you taught us? 'What is the magic of this pronoun "my"?" Genesis is your son, yes, but this is just one life. For the sake of your life's project – for the sake of the entire world – you must take it.'

Paul Bancroft raised the small revolver in his hand. It was visibly trembling.

'Or, if you prefer, I will,' Rinehart said.

Brandon, still seated, turned and looked into his father's eyes. There was love in Brandon's gaze, and resolve, and disappointment.

'Thy way, not mine, oh Lord, however dark it be.' The boy began to sing in a reedy, faltering alto. A tear rolled down his cheek. Yet Belknap somehow knew that he was crying for his father, not for himself.

Belknap spoke. 'He means that nobody has the right to play God.' He stared at the philosopher. Arrogance and self-regard had perverted his idealism, had made it monstrous. He was, ultimately, no god but a man – and a man who, it was obvious, loved his son more than anything in the world.

Visibly wracked, stricken, almost paralyzed with grief, Paul Bancroft turned to Rinehart. 'Listen to me. He'll see reason. At long last, he *will* see reason.' To his son he began to speak with ardor and panicked eloquence. 'My child, you say that every life is sacred. But that's the language of religion, not of reason. What we can say, instead, is that every life has value. Each life *counts*. And to make sense of that, we cannot be afraid to engage in counting. Counting the lives that we can save. The positive consequences of painful actions. You can see this, can't you?' He spoke fluently, frantically, defending a worldview against the powerful skepticism of the child's clear gaze. 'I've devoted my life to the service of mankind. To make the world a better place. To make your world a better place. Because *you*, my son, are the future.'

Brandon just shook his head slowly.

'Sometimes people say they don't want to bring a child into a world that's so troubled. In my own lifetime, there's been global warfare, genocide, gulags, man-made famines, massacres, terrorism – the destruction of tens of millions of lives because of human irrationality. The twentieth century should have been the greatest ever, and yet it was the century of the worst atrocities in our history. That's not a world I wanted to bequeath to you, my dear, dear child. Is that wrong of me?'

'Please, Father,' the boy began.

'Surely you can understand that,' Bancroft went on, his eyes starting to mist. 'My son, my beautiful son. Everything we've done has been logically, morally, justified. Our aim has never been power or aggrandizement. Our aim has only been the benefit of everyone. Don't look at the Theta Group's acts in isolation. Look at them as part of a larger program. Once you do, you'll come to understand the altruism that fuels it. The Theta Group is altruism in action.' Bancroft took a breath. 'Yes, sometimes there must be blood, and pain. Just as in surgery. Would you forbid surgeons from practicing their trade simply to avoid the short-term damage they must inflict? Then why – '

'This is a waste of time,' Rinehart snapped. 'With all due respect, we're not conducting a seminar here tonight.'

'Father,' Brandon said softly. 'Would you really justify one person's pain by another's pleasure?'

'Listen to me – '

'The truth matters. You manipulate people and lie to them because you decide it's in their interest. Only it shouldn't be up to you. When you lie to people, you take something away from them. You treat them as means to some other end. Nobody gave you that right, Dad. Unless you're God, you need to consider that you could be mistaken. That your theories could be wrong. "Not what I will, but what Thou wilt."' Christ's words on the cross.

Rinehart cleared his throat.

'Every life is sacred,' Brandon repeated.

'Please, my child,' Paul Bancroft tried to begin again.

'I do love you, Dad,' Brandon said. His apple cheeks and bright eyes conveyed an odd sort of serenity. 'But there are choices no human being has the right to make. Actions no human being has the right to take.'

The aging philosopher spoke in a rush. 'Brandon, you're not listening to me – '

'All I'm saying is, What if you're wrong?'

Paul Bancroft's eyes were glistening. 'Brandon, *please*.'

But the boy's voice was clear and calm. 'What if you've always been wrong?'

'My darling son, please – '

'Do it,' Rinehart broke in, turning a steely gaze toward Bancroft and gesturing with his own gun. He was dry-eyed, resolute, practical. His own survival depended upon the removal of Genesis. 'It's what your own logic demands, Paul. Shoot the boy. Or I will. Do you understand me?'

'I understand you,' Dr. Bancroft said in a small, ragged voice. He blinked away his tears, leveled his small revolver, swiveled his gun arm twenty degrees to his right, and fired.

A splotch of red blossomed on Rinehart's white shirt, a few inches below his sternum.

Rinehart's eyes widened, and, in one fluid motion, he raised his own gun and returned fire. Rinehart was a professional; the round entered Paul Bancroft's forehead, killing him instantly. The elderly sage slumped to the carpet.

A strangled cry came from the boy. He was white as a sheet, his features drawn in anguish. Rinehart now turned toward him, as a small wisp of smoke seeped from the chamber of his .45.

'I hated doing that,' the tall man said. 'And I don't often feel that way.' There was something wet in his voice, a faint gargling sound, and Belknap realized that fluid was slowly filling Rinehart's lungs. Perhaps fifteen or twenty seconds remained before asphyxiation overcame him. 'I took his life to honor his thought. He would have understood. And now I must do what he could not.'

Even as Rinehart spoke, Belknap leaped over to Brandon and placed his own body between him and Rinehart. 'It's *over*, dammit!' Belknap shouted. He heard footsteps in the hall outside.

Rinehart shook his head. 'You think I wouldn't kill you, Todd? You got to roll the dice or you're not in the game.' His eyes glassy and unfocused, his movements stiff and automaton-like, Rinehart fired in Belknap's direction. Belknap felt a searing kick in his own upper torso, just below the clavicle. The sheer Kevlar vest he wore beneath his shirt prevented puncture, but did little to defuse the impact of the round. A few inches higher and the bullet could have been

511

fatal. Every instinct told him to duck or run. Yet he could not do so without exposing the boy to harm.

'Good, Todd. Be Prepared. My Boy Scout.'

Belknap reached behind him, keeping the boy in place and shielded by his body. 'You're dying, Jared. You know this. It's over.' He stared into the other man's eyes, trying to reach him on some unspoken level, one mind to another, maintaining the gaze like a grappler's hold.

'They say everyone who sees Genesis's face dies,' Jared said unevenly, his pistol still leveled at Belknap. 'So I guess I've been warned. You and me both.'

'You're a dead man, Jared,' said Belknap.

'Yeah? Well, keep 'em guessing, I always say.'

Belknap sensed that Brandon had darted away somewhere, that Rinehart had to decide which target to take out first.

A woman's voice. Andrea's. 'Rinehart!' she shouted hoarsely.

She was standing in the doorway, had snatched Belknap's pistol from the table and aimed it at the tall operative. The safety was off; she had only to depress the trigger.

Jared craned his head. '*You*,' he said. The word came out like a groan, the sound of a nail pried from a board.

'What's your blood type, Rinehart?' Andrea's question was punctuated by a loud retort as the gun jerked in her hand. A round struck the tall man high in the chest, where a crimson freshet appeared moments later.

Now Belknap's eyes darted around the room wildly. *Would you just die?* he silently implored Jared Rinehart. *Would you please just die?*

He noticed that Brandon had retreated to a corner of the room, where he sat on the floor, his arms around his knees, his face cast down and hidden in the shadows. Only the rocking of his shoulders revealed that he was silently weeping.

Rinehart, incredibly, remained standing. 'You shoot like a *girl*.' He sneered, and turned back to Belknap. 'She's all wrong for you,' he told him confidingly, breath forced through fluid, half growl, half gurgle. 'They all were.'

Andrea squeezed the trigger again, and then again. A spray of blood and viscera spattered onto the computer screen.

Rinehart, his eyes still intently on Belknap's, began to raise his gun yet again, but it slipped from his hand. A rivulet of blood wept from the corner of his mouth. He coughed twice, and gulped at the air, swaying on his feet as he progressively lost control of his muscles. Belknap recognized the look: It was that of a man slowly drowning in his own blood.

'Castor,' Rinehart wheezed. Then, moments before he collapsed, he managed to reach out sightlessly with his hands and take a stumbling step forward, as if to strangle the other man or to embrace him.

EPILOGUE

It was a year later, and, Andrea had to admit, a great deal had changed. Maybe the world wasn't different, but her world certainly was. She made decisions that surprised her – decisions that surprised them both – but in retrospect they seemed both right and inevitable. Not that she had as much time to ponder these things as she would have preferred. Being the director of the Bancroft Foundation, she found, wasn't something you could do on the side. It was an all-consuming endeavor, at least if you wanted to do it the way it should be done.

The enormities committed by the Theta Group could never be set right. But, as she and her husband had agreed, the foundation proper had played a genuinely valuable role in the world, and, once the malignity had been cut out, it could be of even greater service. Another decision had emerged from a series of meetings that she and Todd had had with Senator Kirk before his death. It was to keep the existence of this terrible aberration a closely guarded secret. The revelations would otherwise have tarred every NGO and philanthropic institution in the world; in geopolitical terms, they would have been destabilizing in thousands of unforeseeable ways. The result could have been years, perhaps decades, of bitterness, enmity, and recrimination. The remaining Theta principals – those who had not managed to disappear – had been turned over to clandestine judicial proceedings organized by the Department of Justice's Office of Intelligence Policy and Review, all of which were classified and sealed as a matter of national security.

Her eyes drifted to the photographs on her desk. The

two men in her life. She had last seen them that morning, when she was leaving for work and they were playing basketball. Brandon was growing quickly – all elbows and angles, it seemed, skinny arms and gawky swagger. A fourteen-year-old.

'Now watch, people,' the boy had said in a sports announcer's voice as he galloped toward the basket, his black Pumas looking oversized below his slender calves. 'Witness the inimitable moves of Brandon Bancroft! He shoots! He scores!' The ball banged off the rim. 'And he speaks too soon!' His T-shirt was lightly spotted with perspiration, Todd's more heavily.

'If I didn't have these shin splints,' Todd said, hobbling slightly as he retrieved the ball. He dribbled twice, leaned back, and sank the ball through the net. The soft swooshing sound of the nylon weave against the pebbled rubber of the ball: Brandon dubbed it 'the music of the sphere.'

Andrea, standing by the privet hedge, shook her head. 'You're supposed to save your excuses for when you miss, Todd.' She could feel the morning sun on her face, and for a moment she thought it was only the sun that was warming her as she watched the two play.

'Hey, feel free to show your stuff,' said Brandon. 'Just for a minute or two, yeah?'

'Only, no Manolos on the court, lady,' said Todd, his expression both tender and playful.

'Step into lace-ups, though, and you might get a nice bidding war started between Team Brandon and Team Todd.' Brandon's voice was deeper, weightier than before. Even his eyebrows were a little darker, a little heavier than they were a year ago. Then he grinned – and that grin, anyway, hadn't changed at all. As far as Andrea was concerned, it was one of the wonders of the natural world.

Don't ever let them take that away from you. A silent prayer. Watching the two, she thought it had a good chance of coming true.

'It's always nice to be recruited, but I'll have to take a raincheck.' She turned away, almost embarrassed by her happiness. 'It's just that I've got people waiting in the office. You boys going to be all right?'

Her husband slung a sweaty arm around Brandon's narrow shoulders. 'Hey,' he told her, still slightly out of breath. 'Don't worry about us. You take care of the world.'

Brandon nodded. 'We'll take care of each other.'

Now it was early afternoon, and Andrea had already made it through three executive strategy meetings and two conference calls with regional administrators. At the moment, the senior program director was giving her an update of the foundation's health campaigns in South America, and, as she sat at her office desk, she nodded encouragingly as he summarized the developments.

Her eyes drifted again to the photographs on her desk, and then caught a glimpse of herself reflected in a chrome frame. She was a different person than she was a year ago; she didn't have to look in a mirror to recognize that. She could tell it from the way people responded to her. She had the authority and self-assurance of someone who had truly come into her own. And it was genuinely gratifying to be able to use the foundation's resources to make the world a better place – and do so the right way. The only way, as far as she was concerned. She took pride in the transparency of the foundation's operations. She hid nothing, because there was nothing to hide.

'The Uruguay project has been a model,' the director of the South American regional program was saying. 'We expect many other foundations and NGOs will study what we've done and emulate it.' The man – gray-haired, slightly stooped, and with a round, bespectacled face – had the careworn expression of someone who had seen much suffering and misery during his twenty years with the foundation. Yet he had also seen how suffering and misery could be alleviated.

'I hope they do,' Andrea said. 'In this line of work, copy-cats are what you hope for, because that's how you multiply the benefits. It's crucial that these regions aren't written off.

They can change. They can change for the better.' As she herself had changed.

Her husband and their adopted son had changed as well. As unlike as Todd and Brandon were, they had forged a relationship that she could not have anticipated. Brandon had, in some sense, lost his childhood, Todd his adulthood, and that made them fellow mourners for a while, and yet there was more to it than that. Nobody could keep up with Brandon intellectually, of course, but his emotional maturity – his basic kindness, his perceptiveness – was also remarkable, and enabled him to recognize something in Todd that was hidden from most people. The boy recognized Todd's vulnerability and ardor and desire to nurture, and he responded to it with his own vulnerability and ardor and need to be nurtured. A boy had found a father; a man had found a son.

And Andrea had found a family.

'The news from Guyana is not so heartening,' said the program director carefully. He was referring to a major vaccination plan they were trying to implement in its rural regions. It was of particular interest to her. She had made a visit to the Guyanese countryside just last month. The images of the Amerindian villages near the Moruca River were still fresh in her mind, their lives and travails heart-wrenchingly vivid. To see a village being decimated by a preventable epidemic in this day and age – it filled her with sorrow and anger.

'I don't understand,' Andrea said. 'Every detail was painstakingly worked out.' It was going to be a textbook example of how to ramp up public health even in regions with poor infrastructure.

'The campaign's potential is extraordinary, Ms. Bancroft,' he told her. 'Your leadership during your visit gave everyone hope.'

'What I saw during my visit last month,' she said, 'isn't something I'll ever forget.' Her words were heartfelt, fierce.

'Unfortunately, the minister of the interior has just withdrawn permission for us to continue. He says he'll have all the health workers we've hired deported. He's actually forbidding the inoculations.'

'You can't be serious,' Andrea said. 'There's no possible justification – '

'You're right,' the gray-haired man said gravely. 'No justification. Only an explanation. You see, the Amerindians whose lives would be saved tend to be supporters of a rival political party.'

'You're sure that's what's going on?' she asked, repulsed.

'We've heard directly from our allies in the administration.' The man's basset-hound eyes were sorrowful. 'It's appalling. Thousands will die because of this man's fear of democracy. And he's as corrupt as the day is long. This isn't just rumor. We know people who have obtained actual bank records of payoffs made to his offshore accounts.'

'Really.'

'Might I suggest that we could at least consider the option of, well, getting tough with the bastard? Let him know what we can prove – because that could cause quite a bit of trouble for him politically. Of course, we'd never do that without your permission.' The program director paused. 'Ms. Bancroft?'

Andrea was silent. Her mind filled with an image from her trip last month. It was of an Arawak mother – long, lustrous black hair, haunted, luminous eyes – cradling her baby in her arms. The nurse who had accompanied Andrea as she toured the clinic in Santa Rosa told her quietly that the baby had died only minutes earlier of diphtheria; they hadn't had the heart to tell the mother yet.

Andrea's eyes had filled with tears. Then the mother looked up at her and caught her expression, and realized what Andrea had been told. Her baby was no more. A soft wail emerged from the mother's throat, the sound of purest grief.

'Such a shame, too,' the program director went on in a soft, somber voice. 'I know what your feelings are about this kind of thing. I share them. But, Christ, the difference it could make to the whole region . . .'

'No other way?'

'If only,' he said, shaking his head firmly. Something in her face gave him encouragement, though, and his eyes seemed to brighten. 'You know how it is. Doing the right thing isn't always easy.' He gave her an expectant look.

'True enough,' she said quietly, struggling with herself. 'All right. Go ahead. Just this once, but – let's do it.'